T0294199

DEAL MASTER

Also by Adam Gittlin

The Jonah Gray Series

The Deal

The Deal: About Face

Nonseries

The Men Downstairs

DEAL MASTER

A NOVEL

ADAM GITTLIN

Oceanview Publishing
Longboat Key, Florida

ISBN 978-1-60809-180-5

Published in the United States of America by Oceanview Publishing
Longboat Key, Florida

www.oceanviewpub.com

10 9 8 7 6 5 4 3 2 1

PRINTED IN THE UNITED STATES OF AMERICA

For Hunter and Theo

For Mom and Dad

ACKNOWLEDGMENTS

I WANT TO thank Pat and Bob Gussin, Lee Randall, David Ivester, Emily Baar, and everyone else at Oceanview Publishing. I'm fortunate to be with a house that believes in, and backs, its authors to the fullest, and I'm excited about releasing our third book together. Pat—your prowess as an editor continues to amaze me. Not only do you possess a superior ability to thoughtfully dissect, and improve, a manuscript, you do so conscientiously until the novel is right no matter where around the globe your responsibilities take you. I appreciate your dedication.

Thanks as always to Mom and Dad for being constant champions of my writing career. Dad, it is with a heavy heart I experience the release of *Deal Master*, as while this is my fourth novel it is the first to come into the world without you as excited as if it's my first. You are missed every day. You've both taught me over the years the value of hard work and remaining true to one's vision. These lessons have fostered a desire in me to improve as a writer with each book I create. A challenge I accept because it will mean I, too, can show fortitude at the level each of you have shown me.

A special thank you to my agent, Susan Gleason, a terrific person to have in your corner to navigate the publishing world. Not only have you become a vital voice in the direction of my career, I tremendously value our discussions about my writing as well as where to take this series as a whole. I look forward to our next lunch at our usual table (and to discussing which TV series we're each binge watching).

Thanks to Gary Rosen, Howard Tenenbaum, and Andrea Soloway. My days working with you three, as well as so many others in the New York City commercial real estate industry, remain a driving force behind Jonah Gray and this series.

Thanks to Gail Rosen, Ivan and Robin Baron, "The Plotkin Clan," the Honorable Mickey Ravin, George Foster, Gary Green, Mike Rodriguez, and Amanda Colyer. Your contributions to *Deal Master* are both significant and appreciated.

Thank you, as always, to my tight-knit reading group. Your input, and more importantly, honest criticism, is a vital component in the overall quality of this work. You are all truly the unsung heroes in this process.

Saving the best for last, thank you to my incredible son Hunter. Watching you grow up is the truest, purest, joy in my life. Everything each day—from the moment my eyes open until they close—is for you.

DEAL MASTER

CHAPTER ONE

I'M FAMOUS.

I don't mean fifteen-minutes famous, I mean famous-famous.

I mean real-deal famous. Can't walk anywhere without eyes boring into me famous.

Kimmel, Colbert, Conan, Fallon—I've done them all. I've been on *60 Minutes*. I've been on *The Today Show* and *Good Morning America. Ellen.* A book about all I've gone through is in the works, as is a feature film Spielberg is apparently interested in directing. It's hard to say which has been more of a whirlwind—these last two years since I've been back in New York City, or the nine years before that I'd been on the run. One thing is for sure.

Jonah Gray is home. I brought Ivan Janse with me.

And our story, like the new one we're writing starring Manhattan's commercial real estate market, is apparently an extremely big deal.

Carolyn, my old executive assistant from my days at PCBL, peeks her head into my office.

"Jonah," she says, "it's time."

She waits for my approval. Standing head-to-toe in Assiagi—from the brown leather shoes to the "made-to-measure" navy, pinstriped suit to the white gold and black diamond cuff links—I nod my head "okay." In one swift motion she turns around, gives a signal, and a production team from *CNBC* swarms into my office like soldiers attacking an opposing front line. The space is contemporary. The carpeting is beige, the furniture—from the B&B Italia couches and accompanying lounge chairs to the coffee table to my desk—are all brown, sleek, knife-edged. The recessed lighting above is seamlessly incorporated into the beige ceiling. I stand up from the brown, leather chair behind my desk and turn around. The perpendicular walls of my oversized corner office on the top floor of One Hundred Five Park Avenue—a property my firm, Resurrection Real Estate Group, owns—are floor-to-ceiling glass. I look south over New York City from forty-nine stories up. I take a deep breath, and close my eyes.

All kinds of banging and clanging are happening behind me. A mishmash of voices throw around buzzwords like "producer" and "shot" and "position" as a temporary satellite "set" is constructed. I move my eyeballs around behind closed lids, standing in darkness, playing a game I've played for so many years. I let my eyes open. When they do I lock in on the first skyscraper to catch my vision.

Twelve Fifty Broadway, I think to myself. *Owned by a partnership of Murray Hill Properties and Jamestown. Built in 1968. Thirty-nine stories. Tenants include Visiting Nurse Service of New York, Newman Ferrara . . .*

Suddenly I hear someone speaking to me, but the words coming from their mouth are inaudible. I turn back around. Standing between the soldiers and me is Jake Donald, one of my closest friends and partners from my first New York City real estate life, chewing a hunk of the bagel and cream cheese he's holding. Once Perry and I returned to New York, Jake left PCBL. The three of us then formed Resurrection Real Estate Group, the hottest boutique commercial real estate firm in Manhattan.

Jake's wearing a black, custom-fit suit with a white button-down and silver necktie. Though it's still early, the knot of his tie is loosening, the top button behind it is already undone, and the suit's jacket is back in his office.

"Do you really think there was a shot of me understanding that?" I respond.

Jake chokes down the bagel and tries again.

"I've got Billy on the phone."

"And?"

"And he says they're prepared to take the full floor today. But because it's more space than they need, and they would be taking it predicated on the fact they won't be utilizing a few thousand square feet for at least eighteen months, they won't pay more than sixty-five bucks per foot."

"Too low," I say. "Look at the last few deals we've done in that building."

"I hear you. But Shales & Woodlock is looking like less and less of a competitor for the space by the minute. I had Jeremy run the numbers. We're still looking at a healthily positive deal. I'm thinking I tell him we can't start the lease any lower than sixty-eight bucks per foot, and we'll need to make up the loss on the back end."

Jake pauses. I don't respond.

"Jonah. Thoughts?"

"Didn't you already have a bagel this morning?" I ask.

Jake looks to his left, shifts his stance a bit, and looks back at me.

"What are you, my mother, now? You want to make money today or have a conversation about my caloric intake?"

"Jake . . ."

"Actually, this is helpful. Really. In fact, I'm going to head back to my office right now to look online for some good kale and bok-fucking-choy centric recipes," he says as he turns and begins walking away. "Let me know when you're ready to talk shop . . . asshole," he hurls back over his shoulder, setting off laughter from some of the soldiers.

As Jake storms out, he brushes past Perry blowing in.

"Jonah, I need you."

I know those eyes. She definitely needs me. But this isn't about real estate.

"Conference room. Now."

I follow Perry through the chaos in my office, towards the private adjoining conference room. My mind is racing. Between the three of us and our handpicked associates there are a ton of deals on the table at different stages, some for the purchase or sale of buildings, others for large blocks of space. In forty-five minutes I'll be on TV yet again commenting on the state of Manhattan's commercial real estate market for the entire financial world. Comments that will affect the stock market. Yet none of this is a match for the sight of Perry's flawless form from behind, walking in a tight-fitting, khaki-colored, Akris Punto waist wrap dress that stops a few inches above the knee and nude Jimmy Choo Cosmic patent leather pumps. Everything else, for the moment, falls away.

We step over the threshold, a glass wall dividing the space from my actual office, and I close and lock the glass door behind me. Perry heads straight for a button on the wall. When she presses it, the glass wall dividing the conference room from my office goes from clear to frosted in a blink.

She turns to me. Our eyes locked, she moves slowly towards me. She tugs at the tie around her waist. It unravels, and she starts unbuttoning the buttons lining the front of her dress from the top down.

"I wanted this, wanted you, in the middle of the night. But when I reached out, you weren't there."

"I was in my study working."

"I know exactly where you were, Superman," she says, continuing to unbutton her dress, "which means I was left to take care of myself. When it was you I was craving. And have been craving every second since."

Give her what she wants. What she needs. She's been through so much.

She'll get there. She'll open up.

I grab an iPad off the conference table. With one tap a sixty-inch flat screen on the wall comes to life. *CNBC* is on. David Faber is at the helm of *Squawk On The Street*, the show I'll be joining via satellite shortly. With another few taps on the iPad screen, I turn the volume all the way up.

"You'd better have taken your medication this morning," Perry says.

A couple years back, while not sleeping for four days and nights while clearing my name, I saturated my body with Life Fuel Energy Shots—code for insane amounts of caffeine and other stimulants. During a subsequent beat-down in Moscow, I had a heart attack because of it. Today, as will be the case every day for the rest of my life, I take four different types of medication.

"Ha, ha. Who knew pretty girls could be so funny."

Perry's dress slides down off her back and arms. Before it falls to the ground she catches it, and throws it over one of the conference table chairs. Wearing a satin bra and panty set the same nude color of her patent leather pumps, she steps to me. She grabs my tie, pulls my mouth into hers, and we kiss deeply. Our lips still together, I take off my suit jacket.

"There are fresh towels," she says quickly, motioning with her chin towards my adjoining, private bathroom. "With what I'm expecting out of you right now—we're both going to need a shower."

"I hope there's a fresh shirt in there, also," I respond, picking her up and laying her down on the conference table. "Because I'm not waiting to take this one off."

* * *

"So, then, Jonah, why aren't we seeing mergers like we saw a couple years back? With so many REITs performing so well, why aren't more joining forces?" asks Carl Quintanilla live from the floor of the New York Stock Exchange.

"Because firms are more comfortable today, Carl," I respond into the camera from behind my desk. "They are more confident in the market, and they are more confident in managing their place in the market to move forward. A couple years back many firms were skittish and looking to bolster themselves in an unstable environment. Today, the market is far from unstable. Quite the contrary, as we can see from the stock prices of many of the REITs we're discussing. Put another way, today firms are ready to see what they're made of on their own. They aren't afraid of the competition. They are welcoming it. Which is good for all of us."

"We all know your past, Jonah. I'll assume, if I may, you are comfortable with the kind of competition you're speaking of. These last few weeks, as I'm sure you know, there have been murmurs of some of the big boys looking to absorb you—successful as you have been, and as solid as your holdings are, your firm is still relatively new and would be a prime acquisition target. Is there any truth to the rumors? Or are you looking to turn Resurrection into a major player on your own?"

"Resurrection is very happy with our place in the market, Carl. We've recently acquired a couple of fantastic properties. We've been hired for the first time by some of the most well-known firms in the world to handle their Manhattan office space requirements. Being private and able to operate as we see fit, my two partners and I answering only to ourselves—"

I look slightly over the camera for a moment at Perry, who didn't think I saw her popping an Ativan while I was still in the shower and she was redressing, and Jake. Each is focused on my every word, understanding full well how each affects all of us. The proverbial double-edged sword. My ultra-high profile, as well as Perry's and my status as a power couple extraordinaire both professionally and personally, have been a coup for Resurrection's meteoric ascent. It also means I'd better know every word that comes out of my mouth long before it actually crosses my lips.

"—Is right where we want to be," I continue, my eyes again fixed on the camera. "That said, a smart businessman is always looking to improve his firm. When someone credible talks, I'll always listen. All those who have entrusted me deserve that."

"If Resurrection was a public firm, Jonah, a REIT, where would you be priced today?"

"Wait, I'm sorry, look at that," I say jokingly looking at my watch, the Girard Perregaux that makes me remember Amsterdam every time I look at it, "I believe we've run out of time."

Carl, as well as everyone in the room from Perry and Jake to Carolyn to the soldiers, chuckles.

"Thanks for your time today, Jonah."

"My pleasure, Carl."

* * *

I walk outside of One Hundred Five Park Avenue. The cool, fresh air swallows me. Even with my sunglasses the sun is bright. My black Maybach Landaulet is waiting out front.

Dante, my all-world chauffeur and errand boy, is dutifully standing next to the open rear door. Upon sight of me he comes scurrying, meeting me halfway between the building and car and taking my briefcase. A twenty-six-year-old from somewhere, Wisconsin, as always, he's dressed in a black suit with a white button-down underneath—both a size or two too small—and a wildly bright necktie. Today the tie is yellow-and-purple checkerboard.

"You know, I pay you enough to afford a man-sized suit. But yet you still seem to prefer to shop at GapKids."

"Don't even try it, boss-man. You know you love how my arms look in this tiny little jacket."

I laugh as I climb into the back of the car. I love this kid. He's an insanely hard worker, but it's more than that. A fledgling actor, he's never lost the light in his eye or the ability to make me smile no matter how intense my day is. Nor how much further from his professional dream he seems to be drifting. I'm not sure if it's his genuine love of himself, or life, or both. There's a spirit about Dante I can't help but root for. I hired him strictly as a driver as a favor to a friend. The errand-boy portion of his job came from his own accord. He felt I was paying him way too much to just drive.

"Confirming we're off to see Mr. Landis," he continues, leaning his head into the car and placing my briefcase down as I sink into the soft leather.

"That's right."

"Traffic is thick. I'm going to cut across town up here if that's all right and head down Eleventh Avenue."

The car pulls away and smoothly floats west across Forty-Second Street.

"Jonathan thanks you for dinner," I hear Dante say through the intercom system, as there is a partition between the front and rear cabins.

"It was my pleasure, Dante. Anniversaries are special."

"Jonah—it was our three-month anniversary."

Ah. Guess I'd missed the length-of-time part.

"And why shouldn't a blissful three months be celebrated?" I cover.

"Anyway, he texted me to thank you and say you can be his boss-man anytime. Then he texted me not to tell you that last part, but, well. Oh, I picked up your new suits from Assiagi this morning. They are hanging in your closet."

Great. I need more suits like I need a punch in the face.

Or like I need to be driven around in a one-point-three-million-dollar car.

Play the part.

"Get what you need," Pop would say.

Always.

At all costs.

Dante returns to captaining The Ship. Through my dark glasses, then through the darkly tinted glass of the Maybach, I watch a silhouette of Manhattan glide by. I think about Perry. She has always been an intense woman. But ever since returning to the city, after all she'd been through, there's been an even greater fire burning in her soul. In business, in the bedroom, in her need for fashion, she's taken power woman to a new level. I understand her need to shed the past like a reptile sheds a spent skin. I just wish she'd open up more.

We're destined to conquer this world together.

Aren't we?

My iPhone rings. It's Harvey West, my top property manager.

"What's up, Harvey?"

"Jonah, are you by chance near Three Twenty One?"

He's talking about Three Twenty One Park Avenue South, one of six Park Avenue South buildings in our portfolio.

"I'm not. I'm on my way to a meeting in the Meatpacking District."

"How soon do you think you can get over here?"

"Why?"

"Because we have a problem. In fact, we have two problems."

CHAPTER TWO

AFTER TURNING OFF the West Side Highway at Fourteenth Street and heading east, the Maybach turns right down Ninth Avenue, then makes a quick right on Gansevoort. I barely feel the nineteenth-century cobblestone underneath as The Ship's state-of-the-art shock system absorbs the uneven terrain. Luckman Meats, my best friend since birth, L's, century-old, family-owned meat distributorship, is a couple blocks away on Washington. After a couple hundred more feet, the target comes into view. Eleven Ninth Avenue. Most would, and do, see an old, rundown, two-story warehouse overrun by scaffolding with a coffee shop occupying a portion of the retail.

I see a pile of gold.

Standing out front is the owner of the gold bars, Jerry Landis. We pull up to the curb. Dante springs from The Ship, opens my door, and I jump out. Jerry is in his early seventies, and showing every day of it. Bald and overweight with knobby features, a simple man wearing a pair of Levis that could use another inch of length and a sky-blue button-down, he extends his hand upon seeing me.

"Jerry. It's nice to see you," I say, shaking his hand.

"Nice to see you too, Jonah."

Standing with Jerry is Norm Feller, Jerry's commercial real estate broker. Apparently the two have been friends forever, which is why an old-timer like Norm got the assignment of selling this property.

Tall, thin, pale, huge facial features, and overall generally Lurch-like, Norm is wearing a solid navy suit probably off the rack from a Big & Tall shop that's getting shiny from too many dry cleanings.

Norm has a reputation as a solid, middle-of-the-road broker who each year hits a lot of singles with the occasional double sprinkled in—which translates into he makes a decent living. This will undoubtedly be the biggest commission of his life. Something I feel good about—whether it comes from me or someone else—as Norm Feller has certainly paid his dues.

"Hey, Norm, been a while," I go on, taking my hand from Jerry's and moving it to him.

"It most definitely has," Norm responds, his eyes glued to the Maybach. "My God, Jonah, that is one hell of a car."

In the play of life, my role has been cast.

Props are, and will always be, a part of the game.

"Yeah, well, gets me from point A to point B, I guess."

Norm moves his eyes to me.

"Shall we head inside?" I continue. "It turns out I won't be able to stay very long. I have an unforeseen problem at one of our properties I need to tend to."

Jerry turns around and looks at the coffee shop.

"I thought we'd sit down in Jason and grab a cup of coffee."

We step into Jason, named after the famous restaurateur Jason Eder who opened the place over a decade ago. Jason is much more than meets the eye. It's a lounge-y, pseudo diner with distressed mirrors on the walls and a tin, patterned ceiling overhead that serves awesome American comfort food and is considered by many the linchpin of the Meatpacking District. The place is open twenty-four hours, with hardly ever a spot open at the pewter-topped bar. Into the wee hours it is a mad scene for celebrities, models, socialites, and celebrity/model/socialite wannabes.

We sit down at a brown Formica table in the center of the dining room, each of us in a different color, freestanding chair. Mine is red. A cute, perky, African American waitress with long black hair in a ponytail approaches the table.

"Good morning. May I start everyone off with some coffee perhaps? Or maybe some orange juice?"

"I'd love some coffee. Black," Jerry jumps in.

"Same," says Norm.

"Easy enough. And for you?" she asks, turning to me.

"Large iced coffee, please, with a little skim milk."

She scampers off.

"So, it must feel nice to be in the driver's seat," I start us off.

The two quickly glance at each other, showing their hand not even two seconds in. Sitting at the table with Jonah Gray means you're never in the driver's seat. You start as the passenger.

"Well, I don't know about that, Jonah. I'm just a guy who made bridal veils for a living. You know my father left me this building."

In fact, I do.

A building the city is going to condemn if you don't upgrade it.

A building you don't have the capital to overhaul.

"And? What does that have to do with the fact that, like any smart businessman, you're about to turn this passed-down property into a windfall that will fuel further financial growth for you and your loved ones? Anyway, I've been through the numbers. And while I know a bunch of firms have put very generous offers on the table, I truly believe mine will be better. And, more importantly, I'm the right buyer."

"Why is that?" asks Norm. "With all due respect, Jonah, a couple of the players involved have substantial holdings in this submarket of the city. Which puts them in a terrific position for handling the needs of this property."

"If I'm correct, the *couple* players you're referring to are Peddington and Wiler-Jenks."

Again, the two glance at each other.

In commercial real estate, like in any powerhouse industry, information is king.

Always has been, always will be.

"And while I agree they are certainly owners with substantial downtown holdings," I continue, "that doesn't mean they have the wherewithal to handle an undertaking like this."

I point outside, while keeping my eyes on Jerry and Norm.

"Let's be honest, gentlemen," I continue, "that scaffolding isn't there because you're doing a little window washing or façade touch-up. That scaffolding is there because this building is in danger of falling down."

I return my hand to my side.

"I have the connections a project like this needs. I have the relationships in Landmarks as well as in the building department that cuts through red tape. But even more than the ability to move mountains while my competitors are trying to still locate said mountains, I have the vision. The vision to make the Landis family proud, to turn what has been in your family for a century into an absolute gem of a piece of real estate. A property that will stand out in the tornado that continues to be the gentrification of the Meatpacking District."

The waitress reappears and sets our coffees down.

"What is the exact vision?" asks Jerry.

Glad you asked.

You get the abridged version.

Now let's start with a right jab.

"It starts with Jordan Hecht. For a project like this, I want a cutting-edge American architect—someone who knows how to fuse a contemporary tone with a historical neighborhood. I've already spoken with Jordan, a close friend, and should I obtain this building he's committed to me. He's in."

Throw in a left uppercut.

"Once the property, structurally, is not only sound but a beast, and the design course has been set, the air rights above the building I'll be obtaining in the purchase will allow me to add four twenty-five-thousand-square-foot floors of office space to the already existing one above the retail for a total of five floors—or one hundred and twenty-five thousand square feet of rentable office space. Space, for which I already have a tenant ready to take the entire block."

"The whole building?" Norm asks in disbelief.

"The whole building," I confirm.

"Who?" He goes on.

"I can't say. What I will tell you is that once my group is finished overhauling this property, it will be up-to-the-second technology wise. Because the tenant is one of the most important new-world tech firms still solely located in Silicon Valley. This will be their first office space on the East Coast. Something they feel it's time for since they just closed a two-hundred-million-dollar round of funding."

"Why are you so sure they'll commit?"

Pepper them with some body blows.

"Because not only am I an investor in their firm who sits on their advisory board, I've just been hired to handle their Manhattan office space requirement."

I lean in close, sending the message they should do the same.

"Moving on, I've seen a few of the Peddington and Wiler-Jenks preliminary renderings, in terms of what they plan on doing with the retail."

I have eyes everywhere.

Above, below, inside, and outside.

In this case, obviously, the eyes are inside.

Information.

Always.

"And let's just say," I go on, "it doesn't look like any of them have plans for keeping Jason around."

I lean back. They do the same.

"Are you sure?" asks Jerry.

"Again—I've just seen some drawings. You're talking about three hundred feet of retail frontage. I know big-box stores in drawings when I see them. The fact is Jason's lease is up in a year. They need to know where they are ending up—whether it's here or in another property—because if they do, in fact, need to relocate you're talking about negotiating, planning, construction; the works. Unfortunately for you, the longer you take to solidify a buyer, the clearer it becomes to them they need to move. Which is why I know for a fact they are now officially looking for a new location."

"How are you so sure?"

"Because Jason Eder hired me over lunch yesterday. I have no doubt I'll hit a home run for them in terms of finding a location that does nothing but strengthen their legacy—I already have some ideas. But would I rather see them have a reopening in the same space in the center of the neighborhood they helped pioneer? Hell, yes."

My phone vibrates. I have a text from Harvey West that reads: *I'm sorry to bother you, Jonah, but you are needed at Three Twenty One. SOON AS POSSIBLE. It's urgent.*

All this boxing has me thirsty. I suck down half my iced coffee through a straw and go for the crushing right overhand knockout blow.

"Gentlemen, like I said, I have an emergency and I need to leave. So here is my official offer. I know you have offers between sixty-five and eighty-five million on the table."

"We, um—" starts Norm.

"Please, Norm, no need to respond," I cut him off. "I know this to be the case. Now I'm going to have to dump a boatload of cash into this project—and that's just once I've paid you handsomely to get the right to do so. That said, this is a very valuable piece of property in the epicenter of an important submarket of the city. That's why I think the fair price is higher than what you've been offered."

My phone vibrates again. Another text, this time from Perry telling me Harvey is looking for me.

Fuck.

Something serious must be happening.

"I'll give you three thousand dollars per foot for the twenty-five thousand-square-foot plot of land, or seventy-five million dollars," I continue. "Plus I'll give you another twenty million for the building on top that's about to fall down—for a total of ninety-five million dollars."

I stand up. Jerry and Norm do the same.

"That's a hell of an offer to go with an interesting vision," Jerry says, extending his hand.

"What that is, Jerry, is ten million dollars more in your pocket than your highest offer," I respond as we shake. "I'll need you to act fast if you're interested, gentlemen. I have a number of exciting projects teed up. I need to know sooner rather than later which ones will have won my team's full attention."

On my way out of Jason, walking towards the open rear door of The Ship with Dante standing by, I can't ignore the unabridged version of my vision for Jerry Landis' property plastered on my mind's ten-story tall wall. The vision that also has me acquiring the small, adjacent auto body shop for a song enabling me to use the air rights and add yet another story or two of office space. The vision that has me putting the first Manhattan-based Absolut Vodka brand IceBar in the fifteen thousand square feet of basement space to mirror the IceBars in Stockholm, London, and Jukkasjarvi.

When I'm finished with this place, it'll be pulling down between thirty-five and forty million dollars annually in rent. Which means within two years the property will be worth half a billion dollars.

Though at this point it's no longer about the money.

Hasn't been for a long time.

It's always about winning.

Or, perhaps, never losing.

* * *

I step out of The Ship, hand Dante my sunglasses, and head into Three Twenty One Park Avenue South. Just as I pass the threshold into the sandblasted glass-and-steel barrel vault entrance vestibule, a bowed copper transom overhead, Harvey West is up on me. Harvey is average height, about five feet eight inches, but he carries himself much taller. He has a full head of salt-and-pepper hair on top of well-proportioned features, deep-blue eyes, and tanned skin. He's in terrific shape and always dressed impeccably—today he's wearing a charcoal-gray, three-piece Canali suit with a lilac button-down underneath—and looks about fifteen years younger than his actual sixty-five years. I've known Harvey a long time. He was my father's top property manager for years, overseeing the six Park Avenue South properties I inherited, buildings that are now part of the Resurrection portfolio. Harvey is like family. But he only got that close because he's so good at what he does—or he never would have lasted with my father. Today, Harvey doesn't just oversee the six Park South buildings. He oversees all property management for Resurrection. The managers of all the individual properties—which totals twelve different buildings around Manhattan—report to Harvey. Harvey reports to Perry, Jake, and me.

"What the hell is going on?" I ask.

"Not here. Let's go upstairs."

I start toward the passenger elevators, where I see tenants getting on a waiting car.

"No," Harvey says, moving in another direction, "let's take the service elevator."

"Why?"

"Trust me, Jonah. We want to be alone."

CHAPTER THREE

UNLIKE THE PRISTINE passenger elevators, the service elevators are dinged and nicked everywhere. The floors and walls are streaked with paint, grease. Harvey pushes the button for the twelfth floor. The elevator motor gently whirs as we ascend.

My mind riffles through the building's stacking plan.

Twelfth floor.

A full floor we're preparing for a new tenant.

"Construction issue?" I ask.

"I wish," Harvey responds.

The doors open on twelve. We step off. The second we do I see Shane Concord. Shane is an ex-Marine and ex-NYPD, a huge, barrel-chested man with no neck, legs like tree trunks, and lats so big he can barely put his arms down. He's dressed in a black suit, and I feel sorry for the button holding the jacket closed. A year back Shane decided to leave active duty for a more lucrative life in private security. At the time I was looking for a private security guard for Perry and me when it came to high-profile events and such, and a mutual friend introduced us. Today Shane, licensed to carry a weapon at all times, is on my payroll. And my top brass all have his direct cell number should they need him.

The service elevator doors close behind us, leaving a rolling echo. The fact Shane is here, and I didn't know he would be, is a bad sign. Past Shane the floor is wide-open, eighteen thousand raw square feet.

Recently leased to a mobile application marketing and public relations firm, this was the only vacant space in the property. In order to show it to prospective tenants over the last few months we power-washed the concrete slabs—the floor underneath, and the high ceiling over head—and painted the shell of the space white to catch the natural light coming in through the huge windows. Aside from this, the only other visible addition to the space is some new, aluminum, rectangular air-conditioning ductwork snaking around close to the ceiling.

"Good morning, Mr. Gray," Shane's deep voice says.

"Good morning, Shane. What the hell is going on?"

Shane turns to Harvey.

"This way," Harvey says to me.

"I assume I should do as I've been doing?" Shane says as Harvey and I walk away.

"Exactly," Harvey says.

"Which is?" I ask.

"To not let anyone on this floor, whether they work for us, are part of the construction crew—anyone."

I follow Harvey closely, our pace brisk. The soles of our shoes against the concrete make for a farrago of gritty, echoing steps. We move directly through the center of the space toward a small area where a couple of vanilla, interior offices have been constructed. We come upon the door for one. Harvey stops, and turns around to face me. He's about to speak, but instead, says nothing. He steps aside.

I cross the threshold. As I do, I feel myself miss a breath, my heart begins to race. My hands move to the top of my head.

"Fuck—me—" I push out in a loud whisper.

Lying on the ground I see the bluish-pale head of what appears to be a Latin man. He's bald. His eyes are closed. He's obviously dead, and has been for some time. I move forward, fully focused on the room. As I do, the rest of his body unfolds before my eyes. There is absolutely nothing else in the room. Stark, cloud-white walls, and a dead body in the center. I walk around him and stop at his feet, looking him over from the bottom up. My hands move from my head, and I cross my arms over my chest.

He is part of the cleaning crew—his uniform, matching gray pants and a shirt with the words "Spectrum Building Services" embroidered in gold above the heart, tells me so. He is fully dressed, with one exception. His black boots are off. They are placed carefully, neatly, next to his socked feet. His arms are perfectly at his sides, like he's been positioned in a coffin. I look at his face again and notice Harvey's shoes just past. I look up.

"Eduardo Esparanza," Harvey says, standing above him opposite me. "Sixty-two years old. He's part of the evening cleaning crew. I checked the cameras. He came in with the crew, but was the only one missing when they left."

I look down again at Eduardo. I notice a wedding band on his left ring finger. I look him over further. There don't seem to be any marks on his face or hands. There's no indication of any type of physical altercation, at least from what I can see of the parts of him uncovered.

"I didn't want to call the police without you seeing this first," Harvey continues.

I look up again at Harvey.

"Why not?"

"If this was an accident, whoever was with him would have reached out to the home office, police, someone. At least one other person knows this happened, but chose to remain silent."

Harvey points down at the body.

"Because you don't just die like this," he goes on.

I nod, in agreement of his assessment, as well as in appreciation for his keeping this low profile.

People need to feel safe in the buildings they spend most of their lives in.

Business is business.

And mine doesn't need a scandal.

"Who found him?" I ask.

"Luckily for us, the tenant has been bitching to Gary about the construction schedule seemingly falling behind."

Gary Winter. Chief Building Engineer for the property.

"I came here to walk the space," Harvey continues, "and then, upon finding Mr. Esparanza, called Shane to help me secure the floor. Only he and I—and now you—know."

"When you watched footage of the rest of the crew leave the property, how closely did you look at them?"

"How do you mean?"

"Was anyone acting in a manner that seemed odd? Unusual?"

"Nah—nothing I could see from the camera angles. The whole crew left over the course of a thirty-minute period. And as I said, everyone was accounted for."

"Any security irregularities yesterday?" I go on.

"None. Airtight as always. Everyone admitted had a tenant or guest pass for the prior twenty-four hours without incident."

I take my iPhone from my inside suit jacket pocket. Simultaneously a chime happens with a reminder box—"WSJ call in One Hour." I dismiss the reminder, continue to my contacts, find who I'm looking for, tap the screen, and hold the phone to my ear.

"I figured you'd want to call him," Harvey says.

By *him*, Harvey is referring to Detective Tim Morante of the NYPD. Morante was the cop on my ass when I fled the States eleven years ago, the man who had a simple choice two years ago when I returned unrecognizable to him as a plastic surgery poster child named Ivan Janse: keep chasing Jonah Gray, or finally chase the truth. Standing before him, giving him the fruits of my methodical preparation in words, I gave him all he needed to get to the bottom of what actually happened with the man *really* standing before him.

Morante chose to chase the truth.

Because he did, I was allowed to return home a free and innocent man.

Because he did, I—Jonah Gray—was able to reclaim my life.

Because he did, I was able to return Perry to her son.

Because he did, today, our bond is as strong as our mutual respect.

"Morante," a voice picks up on the other end.

"Detective, Jonah," I say.

"Ah—Jonah. Been a little bit. What's happening?"

"There's something I'd like you to have a look at. How soon can you be at Three Twenty One Park South? Alone?"

There's a brief pause.

"I need about forty-five minutes or so."

My eyes move from Harvey to Eduardo. Who's clearly not going anywhere.

"That's fine. I appreciate it. Go directly to the service elevator—please don't use the passenger elevators—and head up to the twelfth floor. When the doors open you'll see a big, burly fella named Shane. I'll let him know we're expecting you."

We hang up.

"You said there were two problems—right?"

"I did," Harvey responds. "Follow me."

* * *

The service elevator opens on the eighth floor. Harvey and I step out as a bike messenger, upright bike in tow, steps in. We walk past some small, rolling trash dumpsters and stacks of broken-down cardboard boxes in the immediate vestibule, then through a hustling and bustling Shipping and Receiving.

"So what exactly is going on?" I ask.

"Actually, I'm not sure," Harvey responds. "Madame Martine insists on telling you herself."

"Madame Martine? She's actually here, and not in Paris?"

"Oh—she's here, Jonah. She's here, she's pissed, and she said if you didn't come see her personally on the matter—whatever the matter may be—there would be a serious problem."

We come to a set of double doors that separates the space. Harvey turns the knob and one of the doors swings open. In an instant we step from back-office space into gorgeous, fashion-driven digs built out exclusively for one of the world's most well-known perfume houses in their U.S. headquarters.

We navigate the space effortlessly toward Madame Martine's corner office, as we built the space for her—at the direction of her architect and interior design team—therefore instinctively know every inch of it. A dazzling exhibition of how traditional and contemporary can tie together with the common thread of elegance, we traverse the thin layer of sea-grass carpeting underfoot. The furniture, like the eclectic art throughout, is a mixture of modern and classic. There is cutting-edge, minimalist track lighting overhead along with ornate, crystal-dripping chandeliers.

Tall, young, model-esque women drenched in up-to-the-second fashion crisscross in all directions. I feel all their eyes on me. Some because they recognize me from the media, others because they recognize the kind of guys who can help them go to those places they dream of going, and the rest because they only entertain the idea of sleeping with guys as tall as they are.

We come around the corner. Upon sight of us, Madame Martine's executive assistant Tiffany—who also looks like she just jumped off the runway—springs from her desk and into action.

"Jonah—thank you for coming right over," she says, her long, dark ponytail bouncing from side to side behind her with each Manolo Blahnik-spiked step. "Madame Martine has asked that you go right in."

Tiffany pulls open the door. We enter Madame Martine's office, which actually looks like a mixture of an office and an apartment. Yes, there's a huge, glass table serving as a desk, but there's also windowpane molding and sconces adorning the high walls and long, deep burgundy velvet couches around an oval, white marble-topped Provençal coffee table.

Madame Martine, in her sixties but looking closer to fifty with facial features carved from stone, high-cropped auburn hair, and a slim figure, slams the phone down upon sight of me. Wearing a classic, pink tweed Chanel skirt and jacket suit, her hands move to her hips.

"I am very upset, Joonah," she says, speaking perfect English lightly drizzled with a European accent most prominent when she says my name. "This is not why I moved into your building."

She starts towards me, fast, like a dart.

"Madame," Tiffany says, "May I bring you or the gentlemen—"

"Tiffany, leave us," Madame Martine cuts her off with a wave of her hand.

Tiffany immediately slinks out of the room, the door closing just as Madame Martine stops in front of me.

"You will excuse me if I don't feel like kissing you, Joonah—no?"

"Of course, Madame Martine. Whatever you like. But please— tell me what has you so upset."

Over the course of the last year or so—throughout the process of luring her from her previous, longtime address by doing everything in my power to make her new U.S. headquarters everything she had hoped and then some—we've become friends. Maybe I like looking after her a bit the way I wish I could my own mother at this stage in life. Maybe I'm drawn to her because she has the same unquenchable thirst I have for success.

For winning.

For never losing?

Whatever the reason, my concern is genuine. She knows this, which is why she pouts at the sound of my words, the little girl that still lurks deep inside coming through for a split second.

"Oh, Joonah, this is bad. Very bad."

"Tell me."

She turns around and heads back towards her desk.

"Please," she says, pointing at the couches while midstride.

Harvey and I accept the offer and move toward the Chianti-colored velvet couches. Just as we sit, Madame Martine joins us and sits down next to me holding a piece of paper.

"Look at this," she says.

I take the paper from her hand. On it is a picture of a sleek, pink glass perfume bottle. Written on the bottle in elegant purple script are the words "*Ton Amour.*"

"*Ton Amour,*" she says, the words rolling off her tongue, as she points at the picture. "In English, means 'Your Love.'"

"*Ton Amour,*" I say. "Sounds nice. New fragrance, I assume?"

"Ohh, Joonah—it's more than just a new fragrance. This is a *changeur de jeu.* Or, as you say, game-changer."

"Game-changer. Wow. How so?"

"Because, Joonah, in my world there are two things. On the one hand there is fragrance. Some good, some bad, some great, some eh—fragrance. But, on the other hand, is the one thing that comes along every once in a while that takes the art to a new level. Heaven in a bottle."

"Ah," I say. "And I'm guessing *Ton Amour* falls into the category of the latter."

"Correct, Joonah. *Ton Amour* is heaven in a bottle," she goes on, her eyes now closed as pure passion comes through her lips.

"It is a beautiful symphony of citrus, gardenia, and wild strawberries; a hypnotic mélange of nature's finest ingredients balanced with just the right undertones of galbanum and marine notes. It is as effortless as it is sophisticated, refined. It is a powerful woman running a billion-dollar company. Just as it is a gentle kiss on the neck."

Her eyes opened.

"It is a once-in-a-lifetime scent, Joonah. A true *changeur de jeu.* And the bottle—the bottle is the perfect complement to the scent. Smooth like silk in your hand, yet designed with a confidence, a boldness only fitting of the sweet juice it holds inside. I want you to hold that bottle, Joonah. I want you to take the slim glass stopper out of the bottle and just let the beautiful fragrance fill your nostrils. Would you like that? Would you like to hold the bottle in your hand and experience *Ton Amour,* Joonah? Perhaps be the first to see if it is a nice product for Perry?"

I don't answer. Confused, I look at Harvey—who is equally stumped by what's happening—then back at Madame Martine.

"Well, that is just not possible!" she screams, snatching the paper from my hand.

She shoots up, out of her seat.

"Because the prototype, the only bottle we have of *Ton Amour,*" she goes on, pointing at her desk, "was stolen last night right from my office—from my own desk!"

Ah.

Shit.

"You promised me, Joonah!" she goes on, stamping her high-heeled foot into the ground, her inner child coming through yet again. "I did not want to move from where I had been very happy for many years, but you—"

"Now, let's just relax, Madame Martine," I cut her off, standing up as well. "Until we are absolutely sure we have a problem, it would be a mistake for everyone if we get ahead of ourselves."

"This product, Joonah, is the basis of an upcoming *one-hundred-million*-dollar global rollout!"

"And you're sure it was removed from your office, not misplaced? And that this definitely happened last night?"

"The prototype arrived at 6:16 last evening from Paris. Tiffany waited here for it to arrive before she left. She put the package right on my desk, next to my computer, where I was to see it at 6:00 sharp this morning when I walked in. The package—unopened— as I, and only I, am to be first to see the bottle. After she placed the package in my office last night, she locked my door as I instructed her."

My mind drifts four floors higher.

"Do you often keep your office door locked when you are not here?"

"Not usually—no. But in special situations like this, I do. And if I am not here, I have Tiffany lock the door once it needs to be locked."

"How about the cleaning staff?" I go on.

"I'm sorry, Joonah?"

"The cleaning staff—the people who clean the office after hours. Throw out the trash from each office, things like that. Can they enter your office if it is locked? Do they have a key?"

"They do not. No."

"And you're sure Tiffany locked this door, and didn't forget— whether she told you so or not?"

"Yes. I am sure."

"How?" I counter.

"Because I do not think Tiffany wants a size seven high-heeled Christian Louboutin up her ass—if you'll pardon my Français. Plus, there are scratches around the door handle. Like someone tried to get in here—and success! They succeeded!"

I walk over to her office door. Using my iPhone, I take pictures of the lock system, which appears scratched and hacked like Madame said.

"Who else has a key?" I ask.

"Me, Tiffany, and in case of emergency, Laurent."

Laurent is her husband.

"Three keys. That is all," I say.

"Three keys. That is all," she repeats.

"What about the prototype?" Harvey chimes in. "Is there usually only one initial bottle made?"

"No. There are a few, but they are in the Paris headquarters. Because I am here—and need to be for the next few days before I return to Paris—one was sent for my inspection as we are so close to full-scale production."

"But there are others," Harvey goes on.

"Yes—which is not the point!" Madame Martine comes back, her voice elevating like someone's finger is on the volume button. "My competition is fierce, gentlemen. And these people, these animals, will stop at nothing to get their hands on a top-secret product like this. As far as I am concerned, Joonah, this is a security issue. And exactly the kind of thing you promised me could never happen in a property of yours."

She's thinking corporate espionage.

She's thinking her competition walked into my building—invisible—and stole the prototype.

No way.

No fucking shot.

"You double checked Laurent is in possession of his key?"

"I did. He has it. It is with him in Cape Town, where he is on business."

"I have no idea what happened here, Madame Martine, but I can promise you two things. First, our security is the best of the best—we take the issue of security extremely seriously, so I would be very surprised to find out there is a crack in our system. Second, you have my word, we will do everything we can to assist you in finding out exactly what happened here."

"I hope so, Joonah. Because the last thing I want to do is have to go public with something like this. It would mean war with my adversaries. And I think we both know the PR nightmare it would mean for you."

* * *

Eventually we make our way back up to the twelfth floor. We step off the service elevator, past Shane, and retrace our original steps towards Eduardo Esparanza. We come to the office and step inside. Standing at the dead man's feet with arms folded, just as I was earlier, is Detective Morante.

"Interesting," he says.

He steps towards me, unfolding his arms and extending his hand. We shake.

"Thanks for coming," I say. "This is Harvey West, who oversees all of our property management."

They shake as well.

"Harvey, nice to meet you," Morante says.

"Likewise."

Morante looks good. He's still looking fit. The dark hair topping off his dark eyes and skin remains thick, only today shows more salt than pepper. As usual, he's dressed in dark navy jeans and a crisp button-down, which, today, is charcoal.

"So," Morante jumps right in, "who is the deceased? And do we have any idea what went on here?"

We spend a few minutes going through all of what Harvey and I discussed earlier, all we know.

"As you might guess, Detective, I'd really like to keep this quiet for now." I add to the conversation, "The last thing I want to sound is callous, but until we really understand—"

"I get it, Jonah," he cuts me off, putting his hand up. "I'll be discreet. That said, in order to expedite this and begin the process, I'll need to get a crime scene team in here as soon as possible. Even though I used the service elevator, I got to it from the main lobby. Is there another entrance to the building—a service entrance that also leads to the service elevator?"

"There is. It's around the corner off Park, on Twenty-First Street."

"Good. I'll also need access to everything that has to do with the security system. The main access system, the cameras, the archived footage from the last few days, all of it."

"You got it," I respond. "And, since we're on the topic of security, there is another situation we have right now I'm hoping you can also look into for me."

"Here? Same building?"

"It's been an interesting morning."

CHAPTER FOUR

THE MAYBACH STOPS on Forty-Ninth Street, just west off the corner of Sixth Avenue. As it does, I see Perry crossing the street toward me on foot, as usual our lives inter-timed to the second.

Perfectly in sync.

"Enjoy lunch, Jonah," Dante says through the intercom. "I'm going to pick Neo up at the groomer and drop him at Silver Rock. Then I'll be back in a flash and waiting right here."

I get out and cross the street towards Del Frisco's, a monstrous, two-story, mahogany-lined power-steakhouse frequented—lunch and dinner—by both actual and aspiring masters of the universe. Perry, the sun bouncing off the brown lenses of her oversized sunglasses, has a chic, light, steppe-colored silk-blend parka on over the dress she'd removed hours earlier in the conference room. To my surprise, she's not alone.

"Stay safe and have fun—and make sure you get to class!" I hear Perry say as she ends a call with Max, her son who's currently studying at Syracuse University.

To the step, we merge right in front of the restaurant entrance. Even in the midst of our mad lives, intensity gives way to a sensuous second as our lips meet, her hand reaching up for the back of my neck, my arm reaching down around her waist, as we kiss.

"How's the boy?" I ask.

"He sounds great. How was the rest of your morning, babe?"

"Hectic. I'll fill you in back at the office after lunch."

"I probably won't make it back to the office this afternoon. I have Aisles, then Larry and Joan want me at their office to meet a new decorator they're thinking of using, then I'm meeting with the Reldon people downtown, all back-to-back-to-back."

"Then we'll catch up at home before we leave for the benefit tonight."

"Perfect," she says, then gives me another kiss.

I look at Nate Landgraff, one of our top-flight young superstar brokers, who's with her.

"I didn't realize you two would still be together for lunch."

Nate is an animal, with a nose like few for acquiring business. He's thirty years old, but already has an unbelievable book of business. He dresses the part to a tee, like he literally jumped off the pages of *GQ*. His tall, lean frame is always covered with perfectly shaped suits, beautifully paired bold dress shirts and ties, the latter always with a nice, thick knot my father would have been proud of, and the finest leather Italian shoes. He's got high cheek bones and strong facial features, his green eyes and tanned skin topped off by thick, dirty-blond, slicked-back hair. A year ago we chose ten brokers to join us out of a pool of close to four hundred applicants from the city's top firms. Nate was one of the chosen. We took him from Cromwell Rowe, a huge, well-known firm that back in the day was a benchmark. A company, unfortunately, that today offers little more than the names on the doors.

Nate is as bright as he is brash, as charming as he is cutthroat. He reminds me of myself ten years ago, which, as much as that scares me, is the reason I wanted him. Today, he's young, handsome, power-and-cash-drenched, all of which he's using to build a huge bank account and chase top-tier ass. Tomorrow, he'll be not only the type of asset that continues to add real wood to Resurrection's bottom line, but the kind of man Perry, Jake, and myself want representing what we all stand for. The kind of man who understands that if the things that matter in life are not in order, the last thing you want in the mix is money.

Because one day he'll learn.

We all learn.

"Neither did I, but young Natey-Boy here earned himself a nice steak at a table with the Big Dogs," Perry says, tussling Nate's hair like he's her younger brother.

"Is that right?" I respond. "How so?"

"The meeting he set up with Lennox was no fluke. They want us in for a full on presentation next week. And they made no secret of the fact we're one of three they are considering for the assignment—an assignment that will be a three-hundred-*thousand*-square-foot requirement."

I look at Nate.

"I snuck us in there at the last second, but it was all Perry who convinced them their decision should be between three firms as opposed to two."

"That—Nate—I have no doubt about," I say. "But Perry is definitely right. Steak worthy."

We step inside, immediately thrust into the din of hundreds of meshing voices. It's one p.m., but even the bar area is packed, cocktails being thrown around and down like it's happy hour. The maître d' is upon us in a blink, motioning to the coat check girl.

"Mr. Gray, it's nice to see you."

"You as well, Steve," I respond, discreetly handing him a Benjamin—U.S. hundred-dollar bill—with a magician's sleight of hand.

"As always, your table is ready. And your guest has already arrived."

I slide Perry's jacket off, and hand it to the waiting coat check girl who has left her post at Steve's urging.

"It turns out we're going to be four," I say.

"Not a problem, Mr. Gray. Your usual table has more than enough room for another setting. Right this way."

We're led through the bustling space. All three of us encounter acquaintances on the way and exchange the customary pleasantries, but all I can think about is Eduardo Esparanza's dead body. And how crazy it is this happened over the same night Madame Martine's prototype went missing.

Just as we reach the table, our guest, Pirro Melato, stands up. Pirro is the vice president of Assiagi—my hands-down favorite clothier's—U.S. operation. A simple man in his late forties of average height with thinning brown hair, horn-framed circular glasses, and rounded features to go with a rounded midsection; he, like myself, is wearing Assiagi fashion from head to toe.

"Jonah. Perry. So nice to see you both."

We go through the usual hellos and the introduction of Nate, and all sit back down. Immediately a waiter is upon us.

"May I bring everyone a drink? And perhaps some water?"

"Please bring us one bottle of still and another of sparkling," I say, starting where I always do since Perry likes the latter while I prefer the former.

Pirro also orders a Diet Coke, but the three of us are just doing water.

"I love this choice, Jonah, but we didn't need to do so fancy for a quick business lunch."

"Please, it's my pleasure, Pirro. I need to know those I'd even consider doing business with are keeping themselves in fighting shape. Besides—I have a confession to make."

"Which is?"

I'm using lunch with you to multitask.

In fifteen minutes, as he does this day each week, Lance Diskin will sit four tables from here.

When he does, I'll excuse myself to say hello to him.

He's the CEO of one of the fastest-growing banks in the country.

And I happen to know he's ready to make the jump from leasing corporate headquarter space to buying a building.

The proverbial two stones.

"I often find myself craving their chicken avocado club," I go on.

Chuckles all around.

"Actually, Jonah, I was just about to check in with you when you called. I have some news from our end."

"I'm happy to hear that, Pirro. As I've told you, we know full well the thought and care that go into the Assiagi retail boutiques— some of the finest retail boutiques of any brand in the world. And since—"

"Well, actually Jonah, it's not the handling of our real estate affairs I want to discuss," Pirro cuts me off.

I look at Perry, then Natey-Boy, and then back to Pirro.

"Then—what?" I ask.

"I don't mean to gloss over the real estate affairs. Obviously this is a major issue for us, and soon enough we'll be making final decisions in this regard. But we, Assiagi, have a proposition for you. In fact, we want to make you an offer we feel is the first of its kind in your industry."

"Ooohh—intriguing, Pirro," Perry coos. "Don't stop there."

Pirro inches forward in his seat, clearly excited about what he's about to put on the table.

"It's no secret that you—Jonah—are more than just a powerful man in your industry. Yours and Perry's story has proven to be one of massive interest. The late-night TV appearances, the magazines— while others at your level in your industry also grace the pages of *Forbes* and *Fortune*, you make frequent appearances in publications like *People* and *New York Magazine*. In the age of branding, Jonah, you—yourself—have become a major brand. And as a major brand, there are more eyes on you than most."

The waiter appears, placing the bottles of water on the table along with four glasses, each with lemon and lime wedges clipped to the lip.

"Where exactly are you going with this?" I ask.

Pirro waits for each of us to receive our desired water before continuing.

"We want to make you an offer to wear Assiagi clothing, and only Assiagi clothing. Nothing else."

Perry can't help covering her mouth as a bit of water sprays through her fingers. I start laughing with her.

"What—like a ball player?" Perry asks.

"Exactly! Like a ball player!" Pirro exclaims.

"Holy shit," says a dumbstruck Natey-Boy. "My fucking boys aren't going to believe—"

"Whoa!" Perry and I exclaim at the same time, our tones changing from fun to pissed on a dime as daggers shoot from our eyes at our young associate.

Apparently young Nate doesn't understand what it means to sit at the table with the Big Dogs.

"Why don't you and I have a little chat," I say as I begin standing, my eyes still on Natey-Boy.

"No," Perry says, grabbing my wrist, "let me handle this. You finish speaking with Pirro."

As I sit, Perry and Nate stand in unison, and she leads him away.

"Is everything okay?" asks Pirro.

"Everything is fine. Let me understand this. You would give me my clothes going forward, as opposed to me buying them?"

"Of course. We'd supply you with a wardrobe, and on top of that, pay you an annual sum for wearing said wardrobe."

"Why?" I ask.

"As I just told you, because—"

"No," I cut him off, "I mean, I already pretty much only wear Assiagi as it is. So why?"

"Because this means there are no other brands. Ever. I know you wear our clothes, Jonah, but I also know you enjoy Kiton and Canali as well. I've been watching."

"This is crazy. I mean, what if it's a weekend and I'm casual? I'm not always—"

"We would supply you with everything from overcoats in the winter to casual summer wear for when you're at your house in the Hamptons. You'll be covered with everything we offer in a given season for all settings. Obviously if you need outfitting for things we don't do—say if you're sporting or whatever—then, obviously, there would be no obligation."

Outfitting?

Sporting?

I turn to see where Perry took Nate. I see them in the bar area, only it doesn't look like the stern talking-to I expect. They're laughing, relaxed. I turn back to Pirro.

"Again, Jonah, we'd offer you annual compensation as well. One million dollars."

"A million bucks? To wear Assiagi?"

"Exactly."

"This is nuts. Pirro, I say this respectfully. I don't need the money." My phone rings. It is Morante.

"I'm sorry, but I have to take this call," I say, standing up. "I'll tell you what. I'll consider it—*consider it*—under one condition."

"Which is?"

"That I can give the million bucks to charity."

I step away, answering the phone as I do.

"Detective."

"Jonah. We're just about finished on the twelfth floor. While the team was working I went down to eight, but this Madame Martinique or—"

"Martine."

"Madame Martine had left the building. Her assistant said she'd be back towards the end of the day, so I'll stop back then."

"Great. Thanks. Find anything interesting on twelve?" I ask.

"We did. A few feet away from the body. According to one of the females on the CSI team, she's guessing it will turn out to be a very small piece of polymethyl methacrylate acrylic."

"Of what?"

"A fake fingernail. Painted a shade of light blue."

CHAPTER FIVE

THE MAYBACH PULLS up to the townhouse Perry and I share on Manhattan's Upper East Side, on Sixty-Seventh Street just off Fifth Avenue. The townhouse is called "Silver Rock," because the limestone façade is so shiny, so pearly white, that when the sun blasts it on a clear day it gives off a bright, eye-squinting reflection so silvery you'd swear you could see your reflection. Upon returning from Amsterdam two years ago, I learned my father's townhouse—the home I grew up in which is not far from here—as well as his six-building Park Avenue South commercial real estate portfolio and all of his other business holdings, had been held in trust for me the nine years I was gone. While I was a fugitive on the run, technically I was missing—so I couldn't be declared dead—and until I was found I couldn't officially be charged and tried. The state wanted to have all the assets in my father's estate—assets left to me—put up for auction. But the law said until I could be accounted for, the estate was to remain in trust. And unbeknownst to me I had a secret weapon on my side. Gaston Picard. He was my father's longtime friend and financial advisor and the man who helped me ultimately return home. Though Geneva-based, he was the trustee for my father's estate. He knew I was alive. He fought for my rights, and until such time as I could claw my way back to New York City, he made sure all the assets—from the commercial real estate holdings to the investments in other business and personal assets like Pop's townhouse—were maintained and run the same as they had always been.

In total, the business and personal holdings transferred to me were valued at just over nine hundred million dollars.

At first, I wanted to live in the home in which I grew up. But from the moment I saw the townhouse, all I could see when looking at it was my father lying on a gurney outside just after he'd been shot dead in the front doorway.

I sold the townhouse. And bought a new one.

This one.

"You and Perry will be leaving for the function at seven p.m. sharp, correct?" Dante asks through the intercom.

I look out the window, at Silver Rock's brilliant five-story façade.

"Yup. We'll be down at seven."

I walk through the doors, entering the huge entrance foyer. In the distance I hear Neo's short nails clicking on the marshmallow-white Italian marble underfoot as he trots towards me. Just as the day he first came into my life, an instant smile spreads across my face. Approaching fourteen years old now, my favorite white long-haired Chihuahua has lost a step—as well as a bit of his hearing—but he's as sweet and spunky as ever. Looking at him now, as is often the case, I can't help thinking about all we've been through together these last years.

He turns the corner, and when he sees me, picks up his pace to as close to a run as he gets these days. I bend over and reach down to catch him. When I do, and stand back up, I notice he has a tiny black bowtie around his neck as I hold him in the air.

"Well," I say as he licks my face, "looks like someone is ready for tonight's party."

I step off the elevator on the fifth floor, walk down the

battleship-gray walled hallway past a de Kooning, and enter our master bedroom. In complete contrast to the traditional bottom floor of the home, our floor is as contemporary as it gets, reflecting Perry's and my preferred décor. The hues of the suite are all grays—something Perry thought would be a cool take on my last name, as well as make for striking space. Slate-gray walls. Cool-gray bedding over the California king mattress on the Poltrona Frau frame. Cadet-gray wall sconces. A taupe-gray chaise lounge.

Fast Money's Guy Adami is on the huge flat screen discussing Apple's stock price from a value perspective. Perry is here, but I don't see her. I walk toward her closet.

Each of our walk-in closets separate into two sections. To the left, a room for our clothes. To the right, a changing area with mirrors, vanities, a sink, chairs, and a couch. I step into the latter, and I find Perry seated, naked, her back to me, in front of her vanity mirror. Her hair is up, her makeup freshly applied. Because of the TV's volume she doesn't hear me come in. She pops a pill. As she lifts water to her mouth to wash it down, her eyes catch mine in the mirror.

"Is that bow tie around his neck not the cutest damn thing ever?"

"What is that?" I counter, dismissing her remark. "Xanax? Oxy?"

She takes another swig of water. Then gets up and walks over to us. She kisses Neo, who kisses her back. I put my little man down. Perry wraps her arms around my neck.

"No big deal," she says, before kissing me. "My day was nuts."

"So was mine," I respond. "But I don't need to fucking—"

I stop myself. She takes her arms from me. Her eyes go sharp.

"You don't need to *fucking* what?"

"I worry about you, Per."

"Well, don't. I'm a big girl."

She turns around and retakes her seat at the vanity. She draws some lotion from a bottle and starts moisturizing her hands.

"I can handle my shit, Jonah. You more than anyone should know that."

"You can always talk to me, Perry. I want you to talk to me."

She sighs, drops her shoulders. I sense, hope, she's about to say something meaningful. Something that confirms she still trusts me, feels safe with me.

She moves her eyes to mine in the reflection.

"I know," she says.

Then moves her eyes back to her own, Perry and Perry staring each other down as she continues moisturizing.

Don't push her, I tell myself. *She just needs more time.*

I turn, Neo at my heels, loosen my tie, unbutton my top button, and head into the clothes room portion of my closet. In the center of the space is an island that holds slide-out trays, like drawers, for sterling silver collar stays, my watch collection, cuff links, and occasionally worn tie bars. I take my day's suit jacket off and toss it away, indifferent to where it falls. The tux I'll be wearing tonight hangs by the full-length mirror. I pull off my tie and shirt, toss them in the vicinity of the suit jacket, then unbutton my pants. I figure I'll pull out all the accessories I'll need before jumping in the shower, but after taking out a single sterling silver collar stay, I sit on the taupe-gray leather chaise lounge next to the island. Neo jumps up and lies down next to me. My eyes stare at the wall in front of me.

I think about part of the conversation Perry and I just had.

"I worry about you, Per."

"Well, don't. I'm a big girl."

A big girl who spent three years alone, imprisoned, not knowing if her son Max or I were alive or dead.

A big girl who suffered three years alone, imprisoned, tormented by something far worse than any physical punishment—her own fears, thoughts.

Perry's been through so much. Her past with her dick husband. Running with me in Europe. And, because of both, I can't help but think she's suffered every day since. Did I save Perry, I often ask myself. Or pull her deeper into the abyss of how dark this life, this world, can be?

Neo barks at me, shaking me from my thoughts. I look down at my boy. When my eyes meet his, he turns them away toward what I've come to learn over the years he wants me to look at. He's looking at my right leg. The pants covering my thigh have an inch-long, blood-soaked tear in them. The bottom half of the collar stay, and the tips of my thumb and index fingers holding it, wear a thick coat of my blood as well.

* * *

The sun sneaking away, the sky to the west transforms into a polished, glassy swirl of violet and cobalt. The rooftop terrace is mobbed. Women light up the evening in cocktail dresses from white to black, and the entire rainbow in between, while the men all sport different high-end takes on the tuxedo. The cause is a good one, and very close to my heart—an ASPCA fundraiser—so everyone from media to business to strictly socialite, philanthropic types is accounted for. Adorable dogs of all colors and sizes are led through the crowd in hopes of adoption.

Perry and I are at the sushi table, one of many different hors d'oeuvre and cocktail stations scattered throughout the veranda. Perry is dazzling in a deep berry colored one-shoulder gown; a tight, clingy Italian rayon dress that via a slit running from her upper thigh to the floor exposes her gorgeous left leg with each step she takes. Perry is holding Neo. I'm holding a plate out in front of me. The waitress behind the station, using chopsticks, supplies me with fresh pieces of sashimi and maki rolls. Nearby a Japanese chef in a high, circular hat continues to meet demand.

"Unreal!" a whiskey-drenched voice slices into our personal space. "I give twenty-five grand, I think I'm a hero. You give half a million bucks—you become this year's guest of honor!"

The tacky onslaught is from Mayan Beck, a fifty-something, usually drunk landlord with an inherited portfolio of about two thousand rental units in buildings scattered around the outer boroughs.

"Not quite, but nice try, Mayan," Perry says before I open my mouth.

"Oh no? Your beau didn't drop five hundred large this year?" he goes on.

"Oh—he absolutely did, Mr. Beck. But money alone isn't how an esteemed gentleman like Jonah Gray becomes an honoree. It's the fact that this—donation—you speak of is the tip of the iceberg."

"What the fuck does that mean," he presses, looking for a little conflict as he knocks back more rust-color booze from his lowball.

"It means don't slumlords read anymore? If they did, you might know a percentage of every dollar we earn goes to this cause. Or that Jonah—Mr. Gray to you—is in fact one of the most charitable men in all of Manhattan. Anyway," Perry goes on, casually, quickly, pointing from his face to his waist, "you should go for another look. You don't wear jealousy very well."

"What is it you want?" I finally interject.

Beck looks at me.

"Look at that. Now, how the fuck does a guy get a broad—"

Sly, fast, like a puma, I step to him, my free right hand grabbing his left triceps. I pull him close, like we might dance, Beck clearly as surprised as he is in pain from my grip.

"I will ask again," I whisper. "What is it you want?"

He looks from my face to my grip, then back.

"Ow! I—I—"

"Ms. York is owed an apology for your distasteful behavior. Wouldn't you agree?" I go on, still in a loud whisper.

He's wide-eyed. Surprised. He doesn't answer.

I want to ask him if he'd rather discuss it alone, but I remember I'm no longer an extra in the play of life. Ever since returning to New York City I've become one of the leads. Deep down I know, and have accepted, I've become a silent warrior capable of going where few men can. But today, I need to be careful whom I threaten.

Because the extras are always trying to take the places of the leads.

"I said—wouldn't you agree?"

Coming to grips with fact I'm doing all the threatening I need with my eyes, he begins to nod, realizing he wants no part of me.

"Yes," he finally answers, quietly, and then, "yes!" he goes on, with more certainty.

I loosen my grip, but don't yet let go. He looks at Perry.

"Perry—I apologize. I didn't mean to—I was just—"

"It's fine," Perry cuts him off. "Just leave us the fuck alone already."

I release Beck, and he scampers off.

Perry and I look at each other. We start chuckling.

"What an asshole," she says, giving Neo some kisses.

I pop a piece of a California roll into Perry's mouth, then another into my own. Then I feel my iPhone start vibrating in my inside tuxedo jacket pocket. I take it out. When I see the name on the caller ID, I freeze. Immediately I feel goose bumps cover my entire body; I feel instantly warmer.

"What's wrong?" Perry asks.

Without a word, I show her the screen.

Cobus de Bont.

A man responsible for me having the chance to regain my life while on the run in Europe.

A man who helped me get Perry back, and return her to her son Max.

A man most know as a European commercial real estate mogul, but who I know is one of the most corrupt, wanted men on the planet.

A man I owe a lot.

A man who owes a lot to me.

Perry's mouth drops open.

I answer.

"Cobus."

"Jonah."

"Can you hold on a second," I ask.

I hit the mute button and turn to Perry.

"Not here," I say, looking around.

I put the sushi plate down, grab Perry's wrist, and lead her away to an unpopulated corner of the terrace by the railing. I position the phone between both of our heads so we can both hear. I un-mute the phone.

"Cobus—how are you?" I ask.

"I'm well, Jonah. Thank you. Is this a bad time?"

Perry and I give each other a look.

"For you, Cobus, it's never a bad time," I say, keeping it light.

"Ha!" he responds. "Well, that's very kind of you to say. It has been a while, Jonah. In fact, I don't believe we've spoken since I returned you and Perry back to New York."

"No—I don't believe we have."

"How are you, Jonah? And how is Perry?"

"We're both great. Thanks."

"I don't just mean the fame and the accolades, Jonah. Don't get me wrong—I couldn't be happier that you were ultimately cleared and able to get your name back. Your whole life back. But how are you—really? How are you and Perry—really? Is she okay?"

I look at Perry, deep into her returning gaze.

How are we?

Are we as great as I know we both want to be?

I can't help feeling confused.

Cobus was always both caring and insightful.

But is this real concern?

"Really, Cobus," I say, my eyes still with Perry's, "we're perfect. And Perry is just great. To tell you the truth, we're in the middle of a charity event right now. And I'm the guest of honor. So, you know, it's not the best time to—"

"Say no more, Jonah. Really. I didn't mean to intrude on your evening."

"Not an intrusion, Cobus. Really. No way you could have known. Is there something I can help you with?"

"Actually, Jonah, I'm calling you from the Gulfstream."

The de Bont Beleggings corporate jet I know all too well.

"We'll be landing in New York City around midnight," he goes on. "Jonah, do you think you might be able to work me into your schedule tomorrow? There's something I'd like to discuss."

CHAPTER SIX

"I'm going to attend the autopsy which will most likely happen within the next thirty-six to forty-eight hours and notify the next of kin. Then I need to start with everyone who was on the deceased's shift, in terms of getting statements," Morante says. "I'm going to head over to Spectrum's headquarters this morning. I'll be discreet. Something I have no doubt they'll appreciate, considering the nature of what we're dealing with. We'll also run each name on the shift through the NCIC, which is the FBI's national crime database, and we'll go from there."

The Maybach just pulled away from Silver Rock. The sun is strong today, barely a cloud in the sky. Through the tinted windows, Manhattan rolling by, I see beams of sunlight slicing through buildings before stabbing the ground.

After the benefit last night, once back home, I filled Perry in on the previous day's happenings at Three Twenty One. We're talking with Morante on speakerphone.

"Speak with Trev Bayliss," Perry chimes in, "he handles all personnel issues."

"Trev Bayliss. Got it."

"What happened with Madame Martine?" I cut back in.

I look at Perry. Sexy yet sophisticated in a maroon Jacquard suit, ready to rock her day, she's reviewing her schedule on her iPad. A dead body and a possible high-stakes theft in our building, the

same night, and she took the news like I did. An initial ten seconds
of shock, a lost breath or two, then back to business. Whether it
was her usual pharmaceutical cocktail or her hardened nerves, or
a combination of the two, she was fast asleep in no time. Slept like
a baby.

She's been through so much.

We've been through so much. Seen so much.

Been prepared to process the unthinkable as almost common.

*Are we better for this? Or have we simply lost part of our souls be-
cause of it?*

"Good move setting me up not just as a detective but a personal
friend prior to my arrival. Madame Martine is one fiery woman."

"You have no idea," I respond.

Perry, eyes still on the iPad, chuckles.

"She took me through the entire sequence, the entire timeline,
just as she had you. I asked her if there was anything of interest,
anything at all, she'd thought of since speaking with you I should
know about. She said no. I asked her if she was sure. That's when
she said . . ."

Morante's voice goes into Madame Martine imitation mode.

"If I knew anything, Detective, that would help solve this, why
would I need *Joonah's* detective friend?"

"Sounds about right," I reply.

More chuckling from Perry, followed by, "She's awesome."

"I asked her who handles the office," Morante continues, "and she
said I should speak with Marilena."

"Marilena Ross," Perry and I say in unison. "Runs the office like a
well-oiled machine, whether Madame Martine is in town or not," I
complete the thought.

"Got it. Will head to Spectrum to speak with Trev Bayliss, then
I'll make my way back to the building to find Ms. Ross. Will check

in with you later. Oh—one more thing. I looked at the picture you sent me of the door handle and lock system on Madame Martine's office door—gave it my own firsthand eye test—and it's impossible to tell anything from simply looking. We're going to have to remove the lock and do a thorough evaluation as to how, and if, it was manipulated."

Once gone, I hit the intercom to speak with Dante.

"Yes, sir?"

"Dante, really. Stop with the—"

"Sorry, boss-man. Yes, Jonah?"

"After we drop Perry at the office, I'm having breakfast with Shawn at his office."

Shawn Magnus is the attorney who, along with his team, handles most of my contracts and agreements. His father Steven who's now retired, whom Shawn worked for, did the same for my father for like thirty years. Once I started Resurrection, I tabbed Shawn knowing he's as trustworthy as he is expert at his craft. Term sheets, purchase agreements, leases, vendor contracts, estoppel certificates—whatever. Whether we're drafting the documents or reviewing others' work, Shawn's team handles it.

"I know it, Jonah—Seven Forty Nine Third Avenue, I believe."

"That's right. After that I need to make an unscheduled stop before heading to the office."

* * *

At ten forty-five a.m. I walk into the Central Park South outpost of Sarabeth's, a charming Manhattan brunch staple for American comfort food. The space is airy and bright, from the combination of sun and artificial light bouncing between the pastel yellow-and-green walls. Before I utter a word to the hostess, I see Cobus seated at the furthest corner table in the back of the dining room. Our eyes meet. As I walk toward him, he stands up.

He looks exactly as he did the last time I saw him—in fact, as I saw him every day since I met him—morning, night, winter, summer. Perfectly tailored custom black suit, black button-down shirt, black necktie, and black shoes, to help shield his body from the rare skin condition, solar urticaria, which he doesn't actually have. Impeccably trimmed five o'clock shadow covering his face's dark skin.

His broad-shouldered, six-foot-two frame presiding over the room, he extends his hand to me. I take it. Unexpected emotions and memories roar through every cell inside me.

My time at Gaston's chalet in Switzerland.

Perry and Max being thrown into the black van in Amsterdam.

Bullets tearing into Andreu in Moscow.

Our respective grips firm, consciously posturing, I can't help thinking about all the black writing covering every square centimeter of his skin under the black suit. Tattooed words that could bring down many. Inked letters and numbers that represent the deepest, darkest secrets of all his "associates," should any of them ever be foolish enough to cross him.

"It's great to see you, Jonah. You look well."

"As do you," I respond.

All those years on the run I helped Cobus—which is not really his name—build his Netherlands-based commercial real estate empire. A young, hungry buck from The Hague looking to make my mark in the world was my front. Turns out the empire I helped Cobus create was his front for a completely different enterprise altogether. A more sordid, less legal one, I, to this day, still know nothing about.

Cobus de Bont is regarded in the business world as a titan.

Whoever this man really is, he's one of the planet's most crooked souls. Regardless, he helped me claw my way back to New York City.

I'm alive because of this mysterious man's promise to Gaston Picard.

I'm alive because of Cobus de Bont's respect for Ivan Janse.

I know to be wary of this man. A man I know to whom I owe my life.

"How is Annabelle? And the kids?" I go on.

"They're all fantastic. Just fantastic. Speaking of which—are you and Perry ever going to have a little one of your own together?"

I hope so.

"One never does know," I respond.

We unclasp our hands and sit down. Cobus already has black coffee in front of him. A waitress is immediately upon us.

"Good morning. Can I bring you something?" she asks me. "Perhaps some coffee?"

"Iced coffee would be great. A little skim milk, two Splenda. And I'd love an order of the chicken-and-apple sausage," I go on, realizing I'm famished as I'd barely eaten while at Shawn's office.

"And for you?" the waitress asks Cobus.

"I'm fine with just coffee. Thank you."

The waitress runs off.

"I'm really happy for the way things turned out for you, Jonah," Cobus goes on. "Clearing your name, then all that has happened since for you. I saw first-hand how smart you are. What drive you have. The unmatched, unwavering focus you possess. Focus that since the day I met you reminded me of myself."

"I appreciate that, Cobus. As much as to this day I appreciate you looking out for Perry, Max, and me."

"Gaston must have really believed in your innocence."

"Why do you say that?" I ask.

He looks away for a moment, doesn't answer.

He doesn't have to. If Gaston Picard hadn't believed in my innocence—allegiance to my father or not—he would have probably used Cobus to have me killed, not ensure my safety.

I change direction.

"I saw the article in *The Economist* a couple weeks back. I had no idea you were up to four major properties in Berlin."

"Once you landed me Feuerbach Turm as your closing act, Berlin became a sensible market to keep expanding."

Feuerbach Turm. The office building in Berlin we'd originally passed on two years earlier when I was still working for Cobus under the alias Ivan Janse in favor of the Freedom Bank Building here in Manhattan. A property I then secured for de Bont Beleggings at the final hour, once the deal for the Freedom Bank cratered, as Cobus' first acquisition in a market outside of the Netherlands.

"Looks like you've grabbed a few of the most prized properties in the central business district."

"What can I say, Jonah. For six years I worked side by side with one of the best real estate minds I've ever known. Heck—I even took Angelique, who you trained so well, on as my assistant after you left. Perhaps we learned more than we realize from each other."

Angelique, barely five feet tall and weighing no more than ninety-five pounds soaking wet, with more tattoo ink and metal visible on her body than actual skin, was my deceptively sharp assistant during my time at de Bont Beleggings.

The waitress returns with my iced coffee. I take it from her before she can place it down, and take a long sip.

"So what is it you want to discuss on such short notice?" I ask.

"It's time," Cobus responds.

"Time for what?"

"Time for New York City to become part of the de Bont portfolio.

Time to pick up where I left off once the Freedom Bank deal died with regard to entering the New York City market."

"Interesting."

Cobus gives me a puzzled look.

"Why is that so interesting?"

"I don't know—just figured you'd concentrate more on Europe now that you really got a hold on London and Germany between Berlin and Hamburg to go along with your control of the market in the Netherlands."

"You don't feel Manhattan makes sense for the de Bont portfolio?"

"I didn't say that. New York City will always be one of the prime markets for all serious players like you. All I said, based on your portfolio expanding in such a concentrated part of Europe, is that I'm surprised."

"Well, get over your surprise," Cobus semi-mocks me, a smirk sneaking onto his face. "I'll continue to slowly . . . *bleed out*—if you will—from the Netherlands throughout Western Europe, but I've been waiting to throw a few drops of blood across the pond for two years now."

Cobus takes a gulp of his coffee.

"So—what?" I go on. "You want me to identify some potential properties for you? Maybe introduce you to—"

"Actually," he cuts me off, "I respect your time too much to come here unprepared. We're both busy men. So we've been doing an extensive amount of homework on our end. I have a very strong sense of the properties I'd like to target."

"Is that so?" I ask, my tone all the explanation of my surprise I need this time.

"It is."

"Properties such as?" I go on.

"One Hundred Three Church Street, One Twenty One West

Forty-Fifth Street, and Eight Hundred Twelve Seventh Avenue—
to name a few."

Huh.

Three buildings that couldn't be more different from one another.

"Why those?"

"Strictly a long-term hold value play."

"And you did the research necessary to identify these
buildings—how?"

"Come on, Jonah, we both know my contacts throughout the
globe run deep. In real estate, in . . . other areas; in Europe, in New
York City. My abilities to gain crucial information are tough to
match. You, more than anyone, should know that."

The waitress places down my chicken-and-apple sausage.

"That being the case, Cobus, why then do you need me?"

I slice one of the links in half, and fork a bite into my mouth.

"Because you're the best, Jonah. And your firm, Resurrection—
which I've watched you grow into a burgeoning beast in what seems
like twelve minutes flat—is exactly the kind of firm I want to partner with here in the States. Perhaps even acquire."

In a perfect world, this is the moment where I would have choked,
reached for my iced coffee, and flushed the piece of meat down my
esophagus praying there was no need for a Heimlich.

But I know better.

If there has ever been a man to keep your composure in front of,
this is he.

"Is that right?" I move the conversation forward, my voice even.

I take another bite of the sausage.

"It is. So this is what I envision happening."

Cobus takes another swallow of his coffee, and places the mug
back on the table.

"You handle all aspects of the brokerage for us—in terms of our acquiring the properties we want, which optimally will be between three and four," he continues. "At the same time we hammer out a deal to have Resurrection handle all of the leasing and property management for the Manhattan de Bont properties. All the while, we begin to have discussions about how we might merge our two firms."

Yes—I owe this man my life.

But I repaid him by building his legitimate empire.

As far as I'm concerned, we're even.

This criminal and me.

We worked as closely together as two men can for six years.

And, in reality, I understand today I know so little about him.

What I do know is that I can never be joined with him again.

"With all due respect, Cobus, I—or for that matter, we, as I have two partners—are very comfortable with where we are today. Strong. Nimble. Growing. You, as much as anyone, understands what a good situation that can be. Why are you so sure we'd want to merge with, or be acquired by, anyone?"

"Because you're a smart man, Jonah. Why wouldn't you want Resurrection to become half of a two-headed powerhouse that reaches two continents?"

Get where you need to go, my father always taught me.

Worry about the mess later.

"Again, I'm not really sure that a partnership like you're envisioning is anything we're even thinking about at this point," I respond, "but truthfully, the issue is a larger one."

Cobus, his eyes never leaving mine, slowly uncrosses his legs, shifts in his seat, then crosses them the other way.

"Issue?"

I take another bite of sausage then wash it down with some more iced coffee.

"As much as I'd like to assist, Cobus, I simply don't have the bandwidth."

The murder of my father, the running, the different countries, the surgery, the abduction, the almost losing my whole life to finally get it all back and then some—I refuse to allow us to get involved again with Cobus. A man we know so little about, aside from the fact he's some kind of mystical criminal.

Own the words that come out of your mouth.

Always.

Fuck.

My mind drifts back to Mr. Esparanza.

"Between the deals we have on the table right now, all of our own property management issues, and a growing employee base and broker force," I go on, "it just wouldn't really be fair to you for me to say we can give you the attention an assignment of this caliber needs."

"I'm surprised, Jonah. Since when can't you make room for a huge payday?"

"Without a doubt the commission would be a nice one, Cobus, not to mention the leasing and property management fees we'd be talking about once everything is in place. But I can't let cash drive the issue here. Especially with someone like you, someone I wouldn't feel right taking fees from when deep down I know we wouldn't be giving this assignment the best effort we can."

Nice.

Turn it around on myself.

"That's it?" Cobus asks, his hands now in the air, palms up. "Just like that?"

"You sound locked in, your sights set. I don't want to waste your time. As I said, I'm happy to put you in touch with some very capable people if you want and I can answer any questions you might have about the properties you've identified. But the last thing I want to do is impede your efforts here."

He drops his hands back to his sides. A slight smile forms.

"Well, I appreciate the candor. As you know, Jonah, I don't like to settle for less than the best in my corner, so it's certainly my loss."

He leans forward.

"Are you sure there isn't *anything* I can do to persuade you?"

"Not unless you can add a few hours to each day."

I look at my watch.

"Sorry, I really need to run."

"I understand, Jonah. You're a busy man."

I reach down into my pants pocket.

"Stop it, Jonah—some coffee is the least I can do for you fitting me into your schedule on such short notice."

"Thanks. Remember, let me know if you need contacts or information, and I'll get you what you need. Perhaps we can grab a cocktail before you head out of town. When are you staying until?"

"Not quite sure," Cobus says after a brief pause. "Now that I need to shift gears, apparently a bit longer than I thought."

CHAPTER SEVEN

I HANG UP. I swivel my chair around and look out over my city as the sun begins sneaking away, its rays bouncing off spires and windows, pulling us into evening. I close my eyes for a round of my favorite game, but before I can even move my eyeballs behind my lids, Carolyn's voice comes through the intercom.

"Jonah—I have Norm Feller on line two."

I open my eyes, swivel back, and pick up the phone.

"Norm. How are you?"

"I'm great, Jonah. Thanks. You?"

"You tell me."

"Jerry appreciates the offer. Genuinely. Not only the dollar amount, but how much thought you obviously put into the project in terms of your vision. There is absolutely zero doubt you would create a gem of a property of which the Landis family can be very proud."

"I'm happy Jerry feels that way," I respond. "Can I assume he's accepted our offer?"

"Well—we're not quite there yet."

"Ah. Why not?"

"I'm sure you understand, Jonah, that in my position there are certain professional courtesies I must extend to the other bidders. I make my living as you do in this business. I have relationships I need to protect."

"Don't we all."

Here it comes.

"I took your number back to the other parties. Of course I didn't let them know it was you whose hat is now in the ring, but I let them know the number you offered."

"And?"

"I have ninety-six."

"Huh. Tell me, Norm. What's more important to your client—the right buyer, or nickel and diming? Before you answer, I should probably point something out in case there is any uncertainty on the matter. I have zero interest in doing business with those who see the value in the latter."

"Jonah, your track record speaks for itself. Jerry knows this. He also knows, as you do, the other players here are more than qualified. They too have bold ideas. Jerry is about the right buyer. That's why he wants to sit down with you again tomorrow, along with his attorney and me. We'd like to ask you some more questions before we make a decision."

I'm fine with this. The others came in too low anyway. I expected, and am prepared for, an actual bidding war; they should only know I'm prepared to move up another twenty million if need be. Instead, I get to go another round with them as a courtesy to Feller's "relationships" before landing this beauty for essentially what I offered.

"Understood, Norm, absolutely," I respond. "Who is Jerry's counsel?"

"Cassandra Lima. She's a partner with Ochs, Ochs & Stern. Are you familiar with her?"

Just what I need.

Fucking Cass.

"I am."

Carolyn walks into my office. She's carrying a large, blue box that immediately tells me whatever is inside was purchased at Tiffany.

"When are you all thinking in terms of meeting?" I continue.

"Obviously, the sooner the better. We'd love to squeeze it in to-morrow if you can."

Carolyn places the box on my desk.

"Do you need me for anything else tonight?" she whispers.

"No," I whisper back. "I'll see you in the morning."

"Dante is waiting downstairs," she goes on, "don't be late leaving, as you still need to stop by Silver Rock to pick up Perry."

I nod.

"I have an extremely tight day tomorrow, Norm. But I believe Resurrection is the right firm for this project. I'll look at my sched-ule and see what I can shuffle. I'll let you know sometime between now and when you wake up."

We hang up. I sit back in my chair and stare at the Tiffany Box for another moment. A little something from Perry, maybe? Or a client?

I stand up. I grab the scissors and cut the ribbon. I lift open the lid. Inside is a crystal William Yeoward Mediterine Bowl.

Filled with Shane's, my private security guard, decapitated head.

I place the tips of my fingers on my desk as if to balance myself, and close my eyes.

Shane.

I'm sorry.

I'm so sorry.

I look again. There's a Tiffany gift card stapled to his forehead. It reads:

De overtuigingskracht.

Dutch for "The Power of Persuasion."

* * *

Both of us entrenched in separate conversations, Perry slides her hand all the way up my thigh under the table. We're in the center of the main dining room at Catch, a chic Meatpacking District spot that serves up fresh seafood and a hot, trendy crowd. The vibrant space—a sleek fusion of wood, brick, and stone—is buzzing tonight as usual. Around the large, circular table with us are the principal partners of a huge law firm Perry just relocated into a non-Resurrection property. Two hundred thousand square feet averaging eighty-one bucks a square foot over the term of a fifteen year lease—a commission for us of a few million dollars for a few months' work. The least we can do is drop a couple grand of that on dinner for them.

I have no interest in the Cantonese lobster in front of me. All I can think of is the Tiffany Box with Shane's head in it in the trunk of the Maybach. Carolyn always keeps spare shopping bags by her desk, so I grabbed one for the box and had Dante stow the "gift" away when I left the office. My iPhone vibrates in my inside suit jacket pocket. I take it out. Surprisingly, it's a text from Perry.

I need you inside of me right . . . fucking . . . now . . .

I turn to her. Before my head even stops, she's standing up excusing us. The hand that was just on my thigh now gently touches the back of my neck.

I follow closely behind her through the space toward the main entrance. Her hand, reaching back, has hold of mine as she leads me, our fingers laced together.

"Per," I start in her ear, "I don't really think tonight is—"

"Stop it," she cuts me off, tossing the words back over her shoulder without breaking stride, her fingers tightening around mine. "The way those legal titans were all hanging on your every word as you explained the intricacies of using defeasance as a financial tactic—I couldn't be more fucking turned on right now."

Just before we reach the elevators we make a hard left down a narrow hallway. Immediately on our right is the men's room. I've come to love these covert, porno-style romps with Perry around New York City, The Hamptons, London—wherever the hell we might be—but tonight I'm just not there.

Cobus.

Shane.

Madame.

Esparanza.

Fuck.

I'm having trouble focusing. I don't want to disappoint Perry. Not because I'll then need to deliver tenfold later on tonight—with that, I'm fine. I don't like to disappoint Perry for one simple reason.

I don't like to disappoint Perry.

She needs to have this.

To feel this.

Control.

Life.

Power.

Energy.

She spent three years thinking all was lost.

She needs this.

I know the drill all too well. Perry stops just shy of the door, takes a half step left, pretends to answer her cell, and I slip by her. I quickly scope the bathroom. Clear. I hand the attendant a Benjamin. And tell him he's to stand guard outside, telling all comers they are to use the men's room upstairs as someone got sick and this one is being cleaned.

The door closes behind us. The instant the door greets the doorframe Perry spins around, grabs my ass hard—her nails digging into my skin through my suit pants—and kisses me. She breathes in deeply as our lips meet. I wrap both of my arms around her waist and pull her in hard.

Her eyes are closed. Mine are open.

"Per," I manage out of the corner of my mouth, "I want you. I do. I always want you. I just—"

"Shut up," she pushes out quickly.

"Per, you don't understand. I can't really—"

Her right hand reaches up and grabs me under the chin, as if I'm a child whose attention she's trying to secure once and for all. She pulls back sharply, her face retreating no more than an inch.

"Are you not hearing me?" she says.

Are you not hearing me?

Stop.

She reaches behind her, grabs one of my hands, pulls it back in between us, and down, under her black stretch leather dress and up between her legs.

She moves her lips to within a millimeter of mine, buries her stare into my eyes.

"What don't you understand about the fact it's time to take care of your girl?"

She turns around, sultrily walks over to the sink, bends forward over it—five-and-a-half inch spiked heels thrusting her ass high in the air—and locks eyes with me in the mirror. She whips her hair forward over her right shoulder, so not a strand is obstructing her back.

"You going to leave those stiffs sitting at the table all night—or are you going to come over here and unzip me?"

I take my suit jacket off, toss it on the table littered with mints, candy, eye drops, and other items used to solicit a tip, and come up behind Perry. Still in my pants I push myself against her from behind, my manhood teasing her. Bypassing the zipper I reach down with both hands and pull the form-fitting dress up over her waist, unpeeling the mouth-watering fruit.

My left hand, lovingly, reaches around her and grabs the front of her neck.

In the mirror, I see her eyes close.

"It doesn't have to be every time we're out," I whisper in her ear, "you're not alone."

Her eyes reopen.

"Get inside me. Now."

I kiss her neck. Then whisper in her ear again.

"I'm here, Per. Not just in this moment, but—"

She reaches down, behind her, and starts to unzip me.

"Jonah—seriously. I need you to—"

"Just listen to me for a second, Per."

In a blink Perry stands up, spins, and smashes an open-handed slap across my face.

"I don't want a fucking therapist right now, Jonah. I want my man. Love. My love. And I want it now."

So many things I want to say.

I say nothing.

A tear starts to roll down her cheek.

"I want us so close—right now—that God couldn't separate us. Why do I have to explain that to you?"

CHAPTER EIGHT

8:45 A.M.

The silent, streamlined brushed-steel elevator throws me up to the fortieth floor of Eleven Seventy Eight Avenue of the Americas— one of the monster billion-dollar behemoth properties on Sixth Avenue in the '40s. The European-style modernized cab, going about thirty miles per hour, is so sturdy it feels like it isn't moving. The doors open. I step out.

The Ochs, Ochs & Stern headquarters are warm, contemporary. The rugs and ceilings are nice earth tones of cream, beige, and brown. The walls and doors are all glass so clean it's hard to realize they're there.

"Mr. Gray?" One of the two women behind the reception desk asks, already standing up.

"I am."

"Right this way."

I follow the conservatively dressed receptionist and her size eight hips down a long transparent corridor. The only vibrant colors in the space are from the large-scale photographs of gorgeous floral arrangements alternating every hundred feet or so on each wall.

"Just you this morning?" she asks, turning to look back at me without missing a step.

"Aren't I enough?"

I enter the conference room. Cass, Landis, and Feller rise from their seats in unison. The receptionist takes my coat, and I walk toward my hosts. The conference room is like a giant ice cube. Running the length of the long space is a rectangular table made from the same glass as the walls surrounded by what must be thirty-five to forty ice-blue Davis chairs from the Fenix Series. Also running the length of the table, suspended from the ceiling, are three intermittently spaced gray microphones for the communications system.

The only thing not very ice cube like—or contemporary, or warm, or anything else for that matter—are the hunting weapons lining these particular long glass walls. Rifles both new and antique, knives of all shapes and sizes, harpoons, bows, arrows, pistols, crossbows, even a cutlass or two, you name it.

Each of the men are in their respective uniforms: Landis in the flood-ready jeans and button-down, Feller in the shiny navy suit. Cass, on the other hand, is the liquid gold to their hot dog grease. Literally. A bronze goddess who looks more likely to be flitting around Madame Martine's digs than handling the commercial real estate affairs for monsters and saints alike.

Cassandra Lima.

Standing almost five foot ten, Cass looks like she could be either Israeli or South American—which makes perfect sense. Her mother is a Jewish woman from Jericho, Long Island, where she was raised into the snobby intellectual before me, and her father is one of fifteen siblings in a Brazilian family from São Paulo, Brazil. Either way, she's gorgeous in a way that flat out disarms on impact. Her flawless skin is bronzed to perfection. Her dark, thick hair is shiny and rich, lush like the tail of a champion racehorse. And her huge, almond-shaped eyes are so green they leave emeralds envious. Women hate her because the moment she enters a room they become second fiddle. Men hate her because even in their dreams they can't have her, let alone handle her.

Perry hates her because my second year working at PCBL—when Per was still married and I was a young, arrogant animal destroying everything in Manhattan nine and higher on the hotness scale— Cass, a hard-working associate at the firm where she's now partner, was part of my fall 2005 ass rotation.

"So—should I be prepared for a scalping?" I begin.

A firm's executive conference room/war room adorned with memorabilia to give a subconscious home-field advantage.

Old school?

Definitely.

As transparent as it is amateur for a seasoned power-beast?

Absolutely.

"Actually, Jonah," Feller begins, "Christian Ochs is the son of Seamus Ochs, who—"

"Was not only a hunting enthusiast, but a hunting legend in the Midwest," I cut him off. "Not my first rodeo in these parts, Norm."

"Jonah, Cassandra Lima," he goes on.

"No need for the introduction," I explain.

No handshakes today. Time for a little disarming of my own. Sure, I have respect in this world that I've both taken and earned. But nothing earns the respect of other men more than letting them know you've been with a woman who wouldn't even throw her shredded, sex-torn panties on them.

I kiss her somewhere between her cheek and lips—closer to the corner of her lips—hand on her waist.

"How've you been, Cass?"

She keeps her demeanor even, tight.

"Jonah."

Crossbow—what?

I can literally sense Lurch's dick growing in his pants.

"So I'm surprised this isn't already my project to turn into a New

York City icon," I go on. "But I understand you have some further questions for me."

I see a quote from my father, tacked to the corkboard of my mind.

The moment one person can sense a particular deal has trumped all for you, is the moment leverage is a word you should forget you ever learned.

Damn Pop.

Miss you.

You didn't deserve that. No matter who you were.

I look at the Perregaux World Time—the watch that reminds me every day of everything I've been through—strapped to my wrist.

Gold bars.

"I hate to be short, but I have a lot of other business to tend to this morning," I continue further.

They motion in unison for me to sit. I do. The four of us are huddled tight at the end of this huge conference table, four ants at the corner of a chocolate bar we're about to devour.

"Any partners?" asks Cass.

"Partners?" I ask, a repeated question of my own. "As in, another firm?"

"Is this strictly a Resurrection deal? What's the story with financing?"

I laugh. Both to send a message, and because, well, it's funny.

"Didn't realize I was part of your interview," I say.

"Excuse me?" Cass says.

"You trying to earn Jerry's business?" I go on.

"What the hell does that mean?"

My iPhone vibrates in my pocket. I take it out and look.

Morante.

Finally.

"It means you need to read a paper or two, sunshine. I have three partners. Resurrection. And Resurrection. And Resurrection," I say, texting back *with others; call you in a bit*, before returning my phone to the pocket it came from.

"Don't be an asshole, Jonah. What about—"

"When Resurrection closes, Resurrection closes, Cass. The banks? The hedge funds? They're all just along for the ride—because they want to be in with the cool crowd. I keep the financial folks in my world for networking purposes and the art of scientific leverage—not to mention their famous clients feeling like they have a part of the Resurrection action they can boast about at Oscar parties. Nothing more, nothing less."

My iPhone vibrates in my pocket.

"Excuse me," I say, reaching for the mobile.

A text from Perry.

Has she eye-raped you yet?

She has, I text back. *But that was nothing. She just blew me in the bathroom between bites of a croissant.*

She texts a smiley face icon, with *what I'd do for you to be taking a bite of my ass right now.*

I look at Cass.

"Perry sends her best."

"I imagine she does," she responds. "Now, getting back to—"

"What else would you like to know?" I go on.

"Two years, Jonah. Two years. Now I know how capable you are, and I'm all about the Twenty Twenty shit and what not. But—"

"I'm sorry—the Twenty Twenty shit?" I cut her off.

She sighs.

"I know you're all over this city, Jonah. Putting new feathers in your cap at an astonishing rate while continuing to build your firm, all of it. But truthfully, this is something that worries me, and I get paid to look out for my clients."

I know where she's going, but I keep myself even. I want to hear the words come out of her mouth.

"I'm not following."

"Then let me just say it, Jonah. It seems these days you're always on TV or being quoted in publications or attending the opening of a new restaurant—I am concerned this project wouldn't get the attention from you it deserves. Of no fault to you," she goes on, feigned honesty infused with concern in her voice. "I can only imagine how much you—for that matter you and Perry, and Jake—have on your plate."

"Ahh . . . I see," I respond, slowly, carefully shifting my weight as I switch my crossed legs. "Just so I'm clear—you are possibly advising your clients to go in another direction because you are concerned for me, for my workload. That's sweet. Really."

"Jonah—"

"Really, Cass. I hope you can do better than that. What's really going on here?"

"You have some stiff competition," she changes direction. "I mean, one tenant sounds all nice and tidy. But we all know the benefits of diversifying a property with multiple tenants and staggering lease terms."

"Which is?" I ask, leaning forward and resting my chin on my bridged hands.

"Which is balance, Jonah. Which is stability and prudence in an uncertain market."

"This market is uncertain?" I ask, chin still resting on bridged hands.

This is a world-beater woman with South American blood flowing through her veins. She does *not* like being talked down to.

"You know damn well it is, Jonah. Any market—"

I straighten up.

"Look, like I said, I have a brutal morning. You want to bring me here and talk staggered leases, stability, whatever—pretend a thriving tenant just handed hundreds of millions in financing that I control is a problem—do your thing. Whatever makes you happy," I say spreading my hands out in front of me, prophesizing. "But I'm not sure I can do business with people who think they should have this much say over a building they are—how best to say this—not going to own any more. It all sounds a little too arrogant for me. I'm not in the business of egos. I'm in the business of creating value, and being paid to do so. All too often people seem to think those two concepts hold hands. They don't."

"Jonah, please," Landis tries to break in, standing up. "I think what Cassandra—"

"Actually, Jerry, I think it is you who needs to keep listening. To me. Not to her. Because this is big boy real estate deal-making time. Not listening to your paper-pushing attorney who's never been in the trenches."

He sits back down.

"No matter who buys this building," I go on, "the only thing the Landis name will have to do with any of it is if they did—or did not—let it end up in the hands of the right firm, the right people, to transform this parcel, uphold the family legacy, continue on with the true spirit and vision of this monumental neighborhood. Projects? Please. We're Resurrection. You go in another direction, I forget about this in a day or two because someone needs us to put our vision into transforming or forming commercial real estate magic in Gramercy or on Wall Street or in Columbus Circle. Don't get me wrong, you have a good attorney on your side," I say, looking eyes with Cass. "But are you all looking simply to make a deal? Or are you all looking to hand your family name—your family legacy—over to a firm like Resurrection, driven by leaving its mark as opposed to simply improving year-end numbers?"

My iPhone vibrates. I look at the screen and stand. Feller and Landis do the same. Not Cass. I hold my free hand out, palm down, eyes still on my little screen. They stop mid-stand and fall back into their seats.

I look at Landis.

"You have my offer. More importantly, you have my vision."

I look to Cass.

"Cass. Nice seeing you. I trust you'll be in touch."

* * *

The Maybach coasts along Fifty-Ninth Street. I watch the buildings on the south side of the street pass by, but my eyeballs don't move, don't lock on anything. They're not seeing. I can't stop thinking about what's about to happen.

What I've been pulled into.

"Jonah, I need to just say," Dante says through the intercom, his voice pulling me from my thoughts, "Everything is so hot, so you. Those lines? And all the different pieces and ensembles? I just love all the colors—some muted, some just the right amount of high-light-y-ness, it's all so just . . . uh! I mean, holy shit . . . wow. Talk about tight?"

"What are you talking about?" I ask, pulling my eyes back into the car.

"The Assiagi haul. You know, boss-man, the first batch of your new wardrobe I dropped off for you last night. The new season. In fact, I love today's suit choice. That tie is so hot."

The Ship stops in front of Sarabeth's, just as it did a day earlier. I look through the window. Dante gets out, comes around, and opens my door.

"Wait here?"

I look at the front of the restaurant.

Fuck.

I want this to be the end with Cobus.

But I know we've just begun all over again.

"Yes. Pop the trunk."

CHAPTER NINE

SHOPPING BAG IN hand, Tiffany Box in tow, I enter the restaurant. Cobus, in his usual uniform, is at the same table he was yesterday. He stands up as I approach, extending his hand, as if we don't both know I have a severed head with me.

I shake his hand. I put the bag at his feet.

"I always appreciate a gift. But I'm afraid I can't accept this."

In a blink, his expression goes from warm and welcoming to cold, unyielding, stone.

"I believe we both know you already have."

One breath. Hyde turns back to Jekyll.

"Jonah, please. Sit," he goes on, gesturing to the table. "I thought you might be hungry, so . . ."

I look at the table. An iced coffee just as I take it, and a steaming plate of the chicken-and-apple sausage I like is waiting for me.

I remove my Assiagi overcoat and hang it over the back of my chair. We both sit. Cobus reaches forward, lifts his coffee mug to his lips.

"He had a wife," I say, my voice low enough that I make sure no one within earshot can hear us.

"Kids?"

"What?"

He slurps a swallow, puts the mug down, and leans back.

"I said—did he have kids?"

"No. No kids."

"Well, then. See that? Sometimes you get lucky."

I steer my eyes left as a breath shoots through my nostrils.

"Kidding, Jonah," Cobus goes on, "Lighten up. You, if anyone, knows I always do my homework."

I move my eyes back to his.

"Why?"

"Because I'm on a schedule. And I needed your attention."

I jerk forward.

"I get that. Why, as in—"

Realizing my voice has elevated, I reel it in.

"Why, as in, why not just make sure you get me alone and punch me in the face or something? Why not just ask me again with a little more—"

Cobus drops a fist on the table, garnering the attention of both surrounding patrons and staff.

"Because I. Don't. Ask."

Like a true dissociative identity disorder sufferer, he throws a finger in the air and grabs the eye of a waitress.

"Excuse me," he goes on, "can I trouble you for a little more coffee?"

Everyone reengages in his or her previous conversations, lives, tasks. Cobus looks at me.

"Have you forgotten who I am?"

"How can I forget, when I'm still not really sure?"

He says nothing.

Touché.

"I gave you everything I had," I say. "I helped you build the real estate empire that covers for whatever life it is you actually lead. I gave that to your family. I gave that protection to your *kids*."

"You lied to me from the moment you met me, Jonah. Think

about that. Every single word about who you are, where you came from. For six years."

"You know why. I was running for my life! I was innocent—as we know—but I had no choice but to run! And hide! And plan! No matter what I said, or what I did, I was always your soldier. I was always loyal. Day, night, rain, or shine, I was all in. No matter what my real fucking name was."

"You say it as if I don't know this. You do remember that I was the one who watched your ass every step of the way as a favor to your father's friend, as you pursued your vindication, no? That in essence I was the one who *literally* saved your life on multiple occasions, so you could reclaim this life you're leading right now?"

"I never asked you to."

"Your father essentially did. By having Gaston Picard feel indebted to him. By leaving Gaston to—"

"You needed to help Gaston. You said it yourself. You simply could not run the possibility of one of the world's most renowned money managers—your money manager, for both of your empires—falling victim to an association with a global fugitive. Me. You needed me to get my life back. That was the only way Gaston kept his. And both of your lives could move forward unchanged."

"And what does any of this have to do with the fact that if not for me, Perry is still silently rotting away in Moscow?"

I look away.

Cobus stands up from the banquette, grabs an empty chair from the next table, slides it as close to me as it can go, then sits down.

I return my eyes to his. He moves in close, puts his arm around my neck, and pulls me even closer. I can see the tiny red veins snaking through the whites of his eyes.

"I didn't end up on the run because of a squabble with my Russian half brother. That was you," Cobus goes on. "I didn't ask the woman

I love to take her young child and join me across the Atlantic to embark on an unknown life in harm's way. That was you. I didn't have to live with not knowing if Perry and Max were alive or dead after they were abducted before my very eyes, on my own watch. That was you."

He retracts his arm just enough for the palm of his hand to stop on my neck. He squeezes, not hard, just enough to remind me of his presence.

Past, present, and future.

"Three years, Jonah. She lived in solitude for three years—captive, a prisoner—not knowing if her only son was dead or alive. You got her there. Me? Well, without me looking out for you, neither of you would have made it out of Moscow alive. This life you're living? This rebirth as your past self, only the celebrity version?"

Cobus removes his hand from my neck. He holds it out in front of us, and, palm up, touches his thumb to the tips of his other fingers. He then spreads them all apart with vigor as he simply says:

"Poof. All gone. Because it never started."

I agree silently by saying nothing.

"We both know the scariest part of you receiving the gift at our feet, Jonah."

Indeed we do.

It's the reason I wouldn't think of telling Morante, or any other member of the authorities.

"Where the rest of that body surfaces could definitely prove to be a difficult explanation for someone," he continues. "Wouldn't you agree?"

I'm in this.

Whatever *this* is.

Time to sharpen my nerve.

Time to sharpen my senses.

Time to get where I need to go.

"So, let's discuss the properties you mentioned," I change direction. "You want to talk buildings—get after it like we used to—then let's start talking."

Clean up the mess later.

Cobus straightens up. He gives me a stern eye.

"You sure you've got yourself in order? Because all it takes is one question for me to know whether you're on board—as you're portraying—or not."

Teeth clenched, I turn to him, and again lock eyes.

Own it.

Always.

Every—single—word—that comes out of your mouth.

"One Hundred Three Church Street, One Twenty One West Forty-Fifth Street, and Eight Twelve Seventh Avenue," I say. "You still want to ask me if I remember the buildings you mentioned yesterday?"

Cobus smirks devilishly, stands up, and takes his original seat across from me.

"These buildings are all very different, Cobus. From location to size to tenant roster," I go on. "This all being taken into account, I need to ask the obvious question."

"Which is?"

"Why the need for so much useable basement space? Something each of these properties has a uniquely large amount of?"

The corner of Cobus mouth curls up. His eyes squint.

"The obvious," he says, chuckling. "That—my friend—is why you're like no other. That's the Ivan I remember meeting in Amsterdam."

To hear him refer to me as *Ivan* sends a chill down my spine.

Ivan Janse. The name I chose once my physical transformation was complete at the hands of a surgeon in Switzerland. A physical transformation that gave me the years I needed to piece together all I needed to reclaim my life.

He takes a sip of his coffee, and continues.

"As you know, Jonah, the basement space is all well utilized in each of the three properties, which translates to some nice additional rent. And for the time being that works just fine for me."

"So then why the need?"

"Because I may want to absorb some of it for myself one day. And in such an instance, I'd still like to be able to accommodate my tenants' needs."

"Absorb it. Why? For what?"

"A longtime friend asked me for help last year. When he did, I saw an opportunity. Now—I warn you—it is a bit on the unusual side for me in terms of investment, as you'll be the first to attest. But I figured—why not. You only go around once. And wouldn't you agree we've all had times we're thankful someone was willing to stand behind us?"

"What's the investment?"

"Bang."

"Excuse me?"

"Bang," Cobus repeats.

He pulls out his iPhone, pulls something up, and slides it across the table to me. It's a website. I scan it.

"As in, 'Bang Steaks and Burgers,'" he goes on. "Based in Bucharest."

Bucharest. The capital of Romania.

"Best burgers and salads you've ever tasted," he goes on. "Shakes, too. And, unlike anything else like it, you can order fantastic quality steaks!"

"Chicken and rosemary aioli burger," I mumble as I read, "skinny burger, pear and bacon salad, tomato and white cheese . . ."

I look up, and slide him his phone back.

"A Romania-based fast food chain that serves steaks along with fries and onion rings?" I continue. "You think New Yorkers—spoiled with some of the best steakhouses on the planet—want to pay for the fast-food version with a shake?"

"That, my friend, I'll leave to my business partners to determine."

"The currency in Bucharest—the Romanian leu, I believe."

"Correct."

"How many leu does one of these fine steaks cost?"

"Eighty-eight for a fillet."

"In U.S. dollars?"

"Twenty-three. Half the price of the same cut—and, most importantly, same quality—in a typical steakhouse. Not bad in a world of quickly increasing cattle prices. No?"

"You're in the restaurant business now, Cobus. I would hope you understand there's a lot more that goes into the price of that steak sitting on our plates than just the cost for which it was paid."

"Such as?"

"Such as the cost of the real estate in which it is being eaten."

Cobus brushes off the meandering conversation.

"Anyway, again, all just speculation at this point to be left to my partners. I just want to not only provide the immediate solution should they decide to jump—meaning provide the necessary retail space as well as 'back of the house' basement space while still being able to accommodate the storage needs of other tenants—and collect the rent if they do. As the lead investor I'd be covering myself on multiple fronts. Wasn't it you who on a number of occasions reminded me the best leaders know when to let others lead?"

CHAPTER TEN

I SWEEP INTO the office. The receptionists give me a warm welcome as I blow by them with a quick return "hey." My overcoat, taken off in the elevator, is slung over my left arm. My right hand holds my briefcase handle. Upon sight of me coming down the hall, Carolyn stands up behind her desk. She follows me into my office.

"Is Jake here?" I ask.

"He is."

"Good. Tell him he needs to drop whatever he's doing and meet me in my conference room now."

"Perry?"

"I'll get her," I say, dropping the briefcase and coat on my couch.

I walk into Perry's office. She's sitting behind her desk, cracking up, speaking with Natey-Boy who's across the room on her couch. Minus his suit jacket with sharp braces perfectly complementing his thickly knotted tie and slicked back hair, Landgraff is looking quite comfortable. Slumped backward on the couch, right leg high as his eyes as it crosses the left knee, I'd even say he's lounging.

"Something funny?"

Landgraff perks up when he sees me and sits up straight.

"Our young buck Natey-Boy was just telling a funny story about a past conquest. A hot, horny little Ukrainian ex-gymnast with an inverted nipple who—"

"Fascinating," I cut her off.

I turn to Landgraff.

"Shouldn't you be working?"

"I, uh—"

"Oh relax, Jonah. We were talking about how we're going to present to Lennox next week and we digressed to some naughty talk. You do remember you and I used to do the same way back when you started at PCBL—don't you?"

I do.

Look where it led.

"You two need to finish this later," I say, disregarding her comments. "Per, I need you now."

Perry and I walk into my conference room. Carolyn closes the door behind us. Jake, no jacket, loosened tie, and open top collar button, is using two chairs facing one another as a recliner. In one hand is a spreadsheet he's intensely reviewing. In the other is a soft-shell crab tempura hand roll that looks like an ice cream cone.

I hit the button and cloud the glass wall.

"Isn't it a little early for sushi?" I ask.

"It's never too early for sushi," he responds, his eyes never leaving his spreadsheet.

"Who even makes rolls this early?"

He shoots me a, "Really? We going to go there?" look.

"Anyway, we have a new assignment," I go on.

"Oh shit," Perry sighs as she sits down across from Jake.

Jake, mid-bite, finishes and swallows as he puts his spreadsheet on the table.

"What's going on? What assignment?"

I sit down at the head of the table, for no other reason than it's the closest one to the button I just hit for the glass.

"I just met with Cobus de Bont. For the second time in two days."

"Cobus? Your boy from across the pond? He's here?"

"He is."

"Did you know he was coming to New York?"

"I did not."

"What's the assignment?"

"Cobus wants to start expanding in the Manhattan market. And he has pretty clear designs on the properties he wants. He wants us to handle the acquisitions, then he wants us to look after all the leasing and management affairs."

"Which properties?"

"Buildings like One Hundred Three Church Street and One Twenty One West Forty-Fifth. And, Eight Twelve Seventh Avenue."

"Did he say why he specifically wants these properties?"

"He did. For the amount of useable basement space."

"The basement space?" Perry chimes in.

"We'll get to that," I say.

"So—what could possibly be the problem with that?" asks Jake. "We know all the players—whether they're willing to sell at this very moment or not is a very different story—but we know them all quite well and we stand to make a boatload of cash. Unless I've missed something, isn't that why we all walk in here every morning?"

It's time.

Perry and I glance each other's way, not trying to conceal it from Jake.

"What am I missing? Why did Perry say 'shit' when she sat down?"

"It's not just what you're missing, Jake. It's what the whole world is missing. Something we need to make sure remains that way."

"Bro—remember, it's seldom I'm the smartest guy in the room. What the fuck are you talking about?"

"The Cobus de Bont you see, the world sees, is the self-made

Dutch commercial real estate mogul who I helped to build an empire. In the movie they're making about my life, in the book, when the story is told in all the magazines and papers and all that shit—he's the guy I worked for who, as you and everyone knows, gave me the shot. He believed in me. And gave me the opportunity to start a new life in Amsterdam as Ivan Janse so I could plot getting my life back."

"But?"

"But . . . there's a part of the story that's been left out. A part of the story Perry and I need to fill you in on. A part of the story that always remains between the three of us, and no one else."

"Jonah—seriously—you're freaking me out. What's going on? Who is this guy?"

"That's just it. I have no idea."

"You have no idea."

"That's right. I have no idea."

"He's not Cobus de Bont."

"Oh, he's Cobus de Bont all right. But only in terms of how the world knows him. De Bont Beleggings—his firm, his life—it's all just a front. Legitimate as it is, and I know as I'm the one who helped him turn it into an empire, it's all just a front."

"A front for what?"

"I have no idea. Whoever Cobus de Bont really is—white-collar kingpin, drug lord, organized crime syndicate boss—he's a criminal on a global scale. A criminal who has everyone from politicians to law enforcement to financial institutions in his pocket, will kill anyone or anything in his path, and answers to no one."

Jake looks at the half-eaten sushi roll in his hand, looks at Perry then back at me, and slowly puts his snack down on his spreadsheet.

"You know all this for sure?"

"We do."

"How?"

"One time in Amsterdam, then a couple times when I finally made it back to the States before heading off with Cobus to ultimately spring Perry from Moscow, I should have been killed, or captured. The only reason I wasn't is because Cobus was watching. How, with whom—I have no idea. But he was always watching from the second I stepped foot in Amsterdam and was ready to step in and crush whatever was blocking my path. Because he wanted to protect me? No. Because he had to protect me. He needed me to get my life back before I got pinched or maimed whether I was innocent or guilty. He needed to make sure Gaston Picard—the Swiss banking mastermind responsible for the financial management of both his empires—couldn't be tied to a global fugitive like me. At all costs. Cobus de Bont, as the story goes, wasn't just the guy I worked for with the private jet shuttling me around the world as I fought—unbeknownst to him—to reclaim my name and life. He was *literally* committing crimes of his own just to keep me safe and give me every chance to get home. All nothing more than a matter of due course for him to mitigate risk."

"But how do you know all of that for sure?"

"Cobus told me. On the way to Moscow to get Perry, the stakes incredibly high on so many levels, he told me. Because he wanted me to finally know I was only alive because he had allowed me to be. His way of letting me know I guess—no matter what happened from there—that I was indebted to him. And I guess he's now come to collect."

"Now, when you say crimes," Jake goes on, "are we talking about—"

"It doesn't matter," I cut him off. "Just have a look at this."

I open the camera roll on my iPhone, bring up one of the pictures, and slide the phone to him. He takes one look at the screen, starts to fumble the phone but recovers before dropping it, then covers his mouth with a trembling hand.

Shane's severed head sitting nicely in the bowl in the Tiffany Box.

I took the picture, along with another, in case I might need them before I returned my gift to Cobus. This just happened to be another use I hadn't seen coming. Jake doesn't have the strength to return the phone. He simply sets it down.

"Why didn't you ever tell me this?" asked Jake.

"Because I hoped there would be no reason to. To be honest, I never thought I'd hear from Cobus again knowing what he let me in on about his life. Seems I may have miscalculated."

"Why wouldn't he use someone else? Find another firm who just knows him as Cobus de Bont?"

"I've been asking myself that same question."

"And?"

Carolyn comes through the intercom.

"Jonah, you have Waterman calling in five minutes."

So many names.

"Waterman. Help me."

"Bloomberg. They want some bites from you for the piece they're doing on the financial district occupancy levels."

"Right. Bloomberg. Did they ever send the questions for me to—"

"I sent them to you yesterday at 4:05 p.m. Will resend them right now. Will you be on the call or do you need me to try and shuffle them?"

"No, no shuffling," I say, looking at my watch. "Too much going on. I'll be on the call."

"And?" Jake repeats himself.

"We all know a million and one unforeseen things can come up in a real estate transaction. Someone else will be able to rely on that reasoning should they not be able to get him what he wants. But not us. My knowing who he is, what he's capable of, and the fact I have respected that to the fullest these past two years by not breathing a word of it, is precisely why we're the perfect team for him to align with. Not only does he know we're the best, he knows I understand failure simply isn't an option."

"We can't just go to—"

I'm already shaking my head.

"Absolutely not," I snap back. "Cobus already made it clear to me if I even think of fucking around with him the rest of Shane's body shows up with my name somehow all over it. And knowing what he's capable of, that will just be the beginning until he gets what he wants."

"Christ, Jonah. I don't know if I have the stomach for this."

"I've seen you eat leftover foie gras at three in the morning. Your stomach will be just fine."

"So what now?"

"Until I know what he's actually up to, we have to play his game."

"Which is?" Perry finally jumps back in.

"Going after the specific properties he wants. I'm sure the basement space is why he needs these buildings. Just not for the bullshit reason he gave me."

"How are you so sure?" she goes on.

"Because I surprised him. The first thing I asked him when we started discussing the buildings he had designs on was 'why properties with so much basement space?' I could see in his eyes he didn't see me putting that together so fast."

"What did he say?"

"It's because he invested in—get this—a Bucharest, Romania-based fast-food chain that is exploring expansion into New York City. And if they do, they want to be able to use basement space for

the 'back of the house' while still being able to offer tenants basement space for storage and such. He was certainly quick with his
answer. But I know in my gut I've got a leg up on him."

"You don't believe him?"

"Oh, I believe he's an investor in 'Bang Burgers and Steaks,' something easily verifiable. What I don't believe is that they're coming to
the States anytime soon."

CHAPTER ELEVEN

Dante steers The Ship toward the Upper West Side. Neo is sprawled out on his side on the seat next to me. His eyes are closed as my left hand massages his belly. We're on the way to the vet for a checkup. The groomer, a walk on a nice day—Neo's always cool with Perry or Dante or anyone else in the close group for those tasks. But not for the vet. Ever since the first day I had him as a ten-week-old puppy, he shook like a leaf at the vet. Still does. So taking him myself is the least I can do for my favorite guy.

I'm on speaker with Perry and Jake, continuing the conversation.

"Look, I know we're all swamped, but as discussed we need to start the process. Let's start feeling them all out—and I'm thinking bringing another building into the mix as a backup."

Anything come to mind?" asks Perry.

"Three Thirty Four West Thirty-Fourth," I respond.

"Love it," Jake says. "So we'll be working four deals."

"Huge basement space and Baron wants to unload it," I go on, referring to Mitch Baron, an attorney friend of ours who recently inherited two properties when his uncle passed away. "He's playing the part of being thrilled to be an overnight owner, but Mitch has always been one to let the guard down a bit after a few cocktails. He's a high-powered corporate litigation attorney with a demanding wife and two kids. There's a reason he's been watching pricing in this city like a hawk. Because he wants no part of this. He knows selling these two buildings means his grandchildren will be set. Then he can go back to his passion—chewing companies up then shitting them out in the courtroom."

"Lovely," Perry says. "And in approaching the other three, I'm thinking I should be the point with Bobby."

Bobby Sturner is the owner of One Twenty One West Forty-Fifth Street, a half-a-million-square-foot property that stands thirty-two stories tall. Bobby is not your typical owner. He's a thirty-six year-old, broken glass-edge sharp, Harvard Business School trained, commercial real estate *player*. He was an investment banker at Goldman Sachs who amassed a small fortune by the time he was thirty—just in time for the real estate crash of 2007.

Like my father always said, it's about making your luck.

Hitting the lottery—that's blind luck. Bullshit luck. It's not real.

But through hard work we can all put ourselves in the position to truly get lucky. And that's exactly what Bobby had done. He took his small mountain of money, left the investment banking world, and began looking for commercial properties on the cheap from owners looking to get the hell out of Dodge. Through a disciplined approach of using aggressive yet responsible leverage he proceeded to target one building a year to acquire. Once he did, he spent the year molding said property into the peak performer he knew it could be. Each year, with each acquisition, everything from the market conditions to nuances in the commercial real estate financing world saw shifts. Some were subtle. Some were not. In each case Bobby used information and patience to stay ahead of his competition. He'd whip the building into shape, and if he couldn't get the building filled he'd get it damn near close. Then, he'd move on to the next.

Bobby Sturner is hungry, flies solo, and is in this game for the long haul.

"Yes, definitely Perry to handle Bobby," Jake chimes in. "You can see the dude literally undressing her in his mind every time he sees her."

"Huh. I thought it was because Per brought him his two largest new tenants in the last year."

"Don't worry, my hunk, he must think being around a girl who craves a brilliant man who can go all night might turn him into one."

"Is that right?"

"You know it, stud. How about Minnie? Who's going to deal with her?"

"Definitely Jonah," Jake says.

"Yeah, I was thinking me. Our families have the history."

"Phew—nice. She makes me nuts. The laugh, the bad breath, it all . . . just . . . it's all so . . ."

"Didn't I already say I'd—"

"Yes, you did," Jake cuts me off, "which leaves me to deal with Gary for Eight Twelve Seventh Ave. But I gotta tell you Jonah, HG just bought it, and we all know they're not exactly in the business of flipping buildings."

HG. Hunter Gaines, one of the largest REITs in the U.S.

"Come on, big boy, feel him out and get creative. There's always an angle. Everyone has an Achilles' heel. And anyone can be out-smarted. Besides—since when don't you like a challenge?"

* * *

We're in the waiting room at the vet's office. Neo, wide-eyed as he waits to confront his nemesis Dr. Crowder, is sitting straight up on my lap. I know we have a few minutes so I take out my iPhone, look through the contacts, and touch the screen.

"Jonah—fucking—Gray. To what do I owe this great pleasure?" asks a shrill, high-pitched, *New-Yaulk* proper accented voice.

"The pleasure is always mine, Minnie," I lie. "How have you been?"

Minnie Peretsky is the heiress to a huge commercial real estate portfolio in Manhattan. Though she's barely five feet tall, has pale, loose skin, a nose too big for her face, and messy, thin, curly red hair, Minnie enters any room—and talks to men—as if she's Sofia Vergara. She has two brothers, but one of them is an elementary school teacher and the other runs the family's restaurant empire in Chicago, so in New York, Minnie, no doubt approaching fifty now, runs the show.

"Freaking amazing, Jonah. Would you believe my little Chelsea is about to go to college? Brown, of course, just like her father. Who, speaking of that asshole, we finally decided to make the big move and get divorced now that all three will be out of the house. About fucking time already."

"Wow. I'm uh—well, good for Chelsea. That's really fantastic, I'm sure she worked hard to get there."

That, or the Peretskys built an addition to the library.

"As for the other," I go on, "I'm sorry to hear that. For you and Rick. That can't be easy."

"Please—he's the worst. Did you know he's been shtupping his assistant for like ten years? I only ask because apparently anyone in the world with a pulse who lives outside of my townhouse knows. Christ . . . the things I think about doing to him when I see him sleeping..."

There's a brief, creepy pause.

"Anyway," she springs back to life, "guess that means it's finally time for you to get your shot with me!" she says with a couple snort-capped laughs. "But enough about me and the torrid love affair we'll have behind that gorgeous Perry's back. What's on your mind?"

"One Hundred Three Church Street."

One Hundred Three Church Street is a steel-frame construction, one-million-square-foot, twenty-five-story building built in the late 1950s in Downtown Manhattan. The Peretskys built it with an equal partner whom they bought out in the late '80s The location is awesome; it has direct access to a bunch of subway lines and is walking distance from others, as it is also to the PATH and ferry. Today the building is worth about six-hundred bucks a foot. Which means, give or take a little loose change, a price tag of about six hundred million dollars.

"What about her?"

"I heard you might be willing to part with her."

I had never heard such a thing.

"Pfft—please," she scoffs. "She's the mother of all cash cows, Jonah. Whom could you have possibly heard that from?"

"Not important. I was informed you were willing to listen to an offer last year because you'd been told it would be a premium number from a very eager buyer. Which, unfortunately from the number you were presented, meant neither turned out to be true. I figured it was at least worth corroborating with you, as I know you'll always at least listen when quality people have something to say. But I guess whomever passed that on to me was mistaken."

"Indeed they were. But I must say, Jonah, I like the bravado. Adding a bold building like One Hundred Three Church to Resurrection's portfolio on the heels of all the deals you've been closing? Ballsy, kiddo. Definitely ballsy."

"I appreciate that, Minnie, but it's not for us."

"Oh?"

"It's for a foreign buyer who has my firm handling their affairs."

"Who?"

"I don't have the executed brokerage agreement in place yet, so I can't disclose. Anyway, that's why I figured I'd ask about the rumor I'd heard—because you know I'm real, therefore you know there is a select group of individuals I would ever attach my name to—"

I don't let her hear me swallow.

"—And bring to the table. These folks I'm talking about now? Speaking your language, simply put—they don't fuck around."

"Which means what?"

"Which means they don't throw words around like premium and eager unless they mean them."

Silence.

Just as I expected.

Because I don't care who you are. Very few can pass up the thought of a six-hundred-million-dollar payday.

"Humor me, Jonah. After all, you're the one who just said I'm a smart enough woman to always listen. I wouldn't want you to make a liar of yourself. Has anyone on your end talked numbers yet?"

"We haven't. At least, not substantially enough to the point I'd even think of floating a figure. Even a ballpark."

"Well, if you do have that discussion, give me a call. I'll let you give me the number. Under one condition."

"Which is?"

"You deliver the number to me in person over the dirtiest of martinis. Because unless I see a price that will blow my skirt up over my head, which I doubt could ever be the case, how could I ever pass up a chance to get you drunk and take advantage of you?"

I feel a grimace spread across my face.

* * *

I drop Neo, pumped to have yet again survived his annual checkup, back at Silver Rock to an awaiting celebratory feast of grilled chicken.

I return to the Maybach. Dante is manning the open rear door. Before getting in, I stop to read a text from my longtime best friend, L. He's responding to my inquiry—*Are we a go?*—from a few minutes ago.

We are. See you there.

"Where to, boss-man?" asks Dante as I get in.

"Meatpacking District."

We head west through Midtown. As we do my iPhone rings. It's Detective Morante.

"Detective. Thanks for checking in. What's doing?"

"A few things. First, I attended the autopsy earlier as discussed. According to the coroner it was an open-and-shut cardiac arrest. The window of when the death actually occurred has been pegged between 8:45 and 9:45 p.m., and apparently this guy was long overdue for anywhere from a triple to a quintuple bypass. When I brought this news to Mr. Esparanza's next of kin, his wife, I learned he was not only a slave to anything fried but his idea of exercise was lifting a few *cervezas* to his lips before bed. So no big surprises there."

"But the way he was found. The shoes. The fingernail."

"The autopsy just makes clear the cause of death. My job is to figure out the circumstances surrounding said cause of death."

"Gotcha. Right."

Call waiting. I recognize the number, but it isn't attached to a contact.

"I'm sorry, Detective, can you hold on for one second?"

I swap.

"Jonah Gray."

"Jonah. Pirro. Do you have a second?"

I have him attached in my contacts to his cell. This is the number coming from the flagship Manhattan Assiagi boutique.

"Actually, I'm swamped, Pirro. Is this something that can wait until later?"

"I'm just calling to make sure you're happy with the first wardrobe delivery. That everything's to your liking. I hope it's okay we prepared it before the contract was actually signed."

"It is. It's all great. And I believe the contract was received by Carolyn, so we should have that turned around quickly. I'll let you—"

"The suits, the shirts, all of it is up to snuff?" he cuts me off.

"Yup—all good. So if you'll—"

"Don't overlook the accessories, Jonah. I made sure to include new belts and shoes we've introduced for this season. Just to make sure we didn't miss a single element. Seriously, I can't stress the belts enough. The leather we—"

What doesn't this guy understand about "I'm swamped?"

"Belts and shoes," I repeat. "Got it, Pirro. I need to take this other call, so I'll be sure to reach out if I have any questions."

"Great, Jo—"

I swap back.

"Sorry, Detective."

"That's fine. Anyway, I spoke with Trev Bayliss. He explained to me that for a building this size an overnight crew consists of anywhere from nine to twelve workers. This particular crew had twelve, but one was out sick which means eleven people were on hand— ten not counting Mr. Esparanza. I have all of the crew members' names and we're running them through the NCIC as we speak."

CHAPTER TWELVE

THE SHIP EASES to a stop by the curb on Gansevoort Street.

"You have forty minutes until you're due at Strip House," Dante says through the intercom. "Shall I have Carolyn—"

"We'll make it," I cut him off, my eyes glued to the building that has become my newest love affair.

Dante springs from the car and opens my door. I get out, stand up, my eyes never leaving the building as the world springs from different shades of gray to color. Jason, as always, is bustling. My eyes look up a bit, reach out, and slowly trace the building's scaffolding from west to east.

"Jonah!"

I turn my head left. L, my closest friend since childhood, is standing in front of the auto body shop next door. He waves me over. L's dressed casual in overpriced jeans, an untucked button-down, and brown leather shoes. As I get close his head turns and he surveys the building in front of him—the auto body shop—just as I'd been examining Landis' property.

"I was out with this new girl last night," he says, as I'm still a few strides removed from reaching him.

"Not exactly where I thought we'd be starting, but why not. And?"

I come to a stop beside him. Me staring at L, L staring at the building.

"Fucking brutal. Was set up with her. She turns out to be *maybe* a six on her best day. You know I hate setups. But the source was my cousin Ali who you know I trust—and who you know would be offended if I'd said no—so I sucked it up and agreed to do a cocktail. Let's just say it wasn't ten minutes before I went to my new 'go to' get out of jail line."

"And what is the new line these days?"

L turns his attention to me, we guy-hug, then he continues. "I ask the girl to tell me something unusual about themselves. When it's my turn, I explain that I love asparagus because I dig the way it makes my pee smell later on."

"Unfortunately I know better than to ask if you're kidding."

"Not at all. Grosses them out—they want nothing to do with me. And I get to avoid having to be the bad guy. Beautiful."

"What time did you meet her?"

"Seven."

"So I'm guessing by seven thirty you were already getting cozy with one of your regulars."

"I wish. Just my luck, she says, 'next time—Bar Americain. Best asparagus salad in the city. This way we can—"

"Ahh! Stop there!" I blurt out, my hand up.

"I know. Right?" he says.

I put my hand back down to my side.

"Seriously. What's the matter with you?" I go on.

"Come on, Jonah. Neither of us has the time for that conversation."

I look at the auto body shop.

"So let's get to it."

L's line of vision joins mine. Just a baseball's chuck away from the nucleus of what has become one of the busiest intersections of retail and restaurants in Manhattan is this beaten, broken, one-story red-brick building with three roll-down garage doors—which at this moment are all up. Across the top of the façade is a simple white, tin, rectangular sign with "Laskowski Auto" cursively written in scratched, faded blue paint.

"The owner's name is Roddy Laskowski. He took it over from his father in the early nineties. Roddy's probably in his mid-forties. Definitely on the gruff side, but a good guy. I've known him for years. He's done some work for me on my rides."

The meat distributorship warehouse that's been in L's family for generations is just a couple blocks away. Therefore with typical L bravado, L sees himself as an authority on all things Meatpacking District. In the world of commercial real estate there are a number of factors that lead to a select few becoming true experts, real power players. But as my father always said, there are the things that separate even the power players from the straight-up assassins.

The assassins always have a hidden arsenal.

An arsenal, no matter how hard anyone ever looks, that will never be found.

"Who gives a fuck, Jonah, if opening our eyes every day is a gift or a curse," Pop would say. "What matters is your eyes are open. See what you need to see. Learn what you need to learn. Know whom you need to know. Everyday. Unmatched knowledge is key for becoming ultra successful. But with unmatched knowledge and resources, you can own the motherfucking world . . ."

An image of my father sitting in his kitchen having breakfast when I was a kid pops into my head.

Then, oddly, I see an image of Perry from this morning in the office.

"Tell me about Roddy," I say.

"I told you. His father used to—"

"Not Roddy the auto body shop owner, L, Roddy the man. Does he have family? What's he like?"

"Dude's divorced. Has been for a while. He has kids. He may have two, but I'm not sure. I know he definitely has one."

"What's he into?"

"Loves to booze. And loves the ladies. Been out with him a bunch of times. Guy's a freaking hound."

I look at today's watch on my wrist—an F.P. Journe Tourbillon Seconde Morte valued at about a hundred grand. It's one from the collection I inherited from my father. I rotate his watches on a weekly basis to have a piece of him close to me. The only outsider in the rotation is the Perregaux World Time I acquired in Amsterdam a couple years ago before returning to New York City. That one reminds me of all I went through to get myself—and Perry—back home.

I look back at L.

"Let's meet Roddy Laskowski."

We step inside the building through one of the garage doors. Immediately we're enveloped by loud banging, clanging, and the whirring of drills and car lifts going up and down. The space is surprisingly cleaner and more organized than I imagined. The concrete floor, though grease streaked, is smooth, shiny. There are yellow lines painted to designate the different workspaces around each car lift, like where the cubicle walls would extend up from if this were the bullpen of an office. By each lift there are multiple well-kept tool chests. The ceiling is definitely on the dated side, but there's new, high-end track lighting, and multiple black video surveillance domes.

Within ten seconds of our entrance a man dressed in jeans, Nikes, and a black Polo comes around a silver Range Rover being lifted into the air and heads toward us. He's tall—like six four or something—with slicked-back black hair and bold facial features that fit with his oversized head.

He sticks his hand out well before reaching us, as if it's now guiding him.

"Roddy—nice to see you," L says.

They shake hands.

"Same. How's the new Panamera Turbo S I've seen you tooling around in?"

"An absolute monster. Love that baby."

"Just be careful on these streets," Roddy goes on, taking his hand back and now addressing both of us. "I mean, is it just me, or has avoiding huge potholes in this city begun to resemble avoiding land mines in Afghanistan or some shit?"

"Roddy—Jonah Gray," L changes direction.

We shake hands.

A lot can be learned about a man or woman from their handshake. Roddy's is strong, firm. Like mine.

"Jonah, nice to meet you."

"Likewise," I reply, staring through his eyes, taking a peek into his soul.

Our hands separate. His sight shifts over my shoulder to The Ship outside by the curb.

"Christ. That's some fucking ride."

"Thank you. Gets me where I need to go."

"I'm guessing it gets you a lot more than that. What'd that run you? Like—"

"Roddy," I cut him off, "I don't mean to be blunt, and I really appreciate you taking some time for me this morning. But I'm on a tight schedule today."

His eyes move back to mine.

"Of course. You're a man who likes to get right to business. I should have known from the suit."

"So L tells me this business has been in the family for some time."

"That's right. My father—"

Even though L gave me the history, I listen to Roddy's longer version out of courtesy.

"So tell me about the actual building," I say.

"What would you like to know?"

"You said your father moved his shop here from Newark in 1969. Was the building already here?"

I don't actually care about the answer—which I already know. The point of the question is to better gauge his attachment to the place.

"Nope. He built it—helped with the actual design and everything. This way he could have the shop organized exactly as he liked it. My father was, you might say, a bit tight like that. Liked all his shit lined up exactly as he wanted it, and could care less about what anyone else had to say about it."

I can't help but chuckle.

"Sounds like your father and my father would have been friends."

"Don't get me wrong," Roddy responds through a chuckle of his own, "the man knew how to run a shop. Taught me everything I know about cars and business. The man was just a major ballbuster."

"Roddy, can we step outside?"

The three of us exit through the middle garage door. The sun blasts us. I take my sunglasses from the inside pocket of my suit jacket and put them on.

"I want your building, Roddy."

There's a pause. Roddy looks at L, then back at me.

"What do you mean you want *my building*?"

"Exactly what I said. I want your building. And I'm prepared to pay you handsomely for it."

"My business isn't for sale."

"I don't want your business. I just want your building."

"In that case my building's not for sale."

In the words of Stan Gray, "Everything's for sale besides air. And it's only a matter of time before some genius or crook figures out how to bottle that."

"What—like to be my landlord?" he goes on.

"Not exactly."

"Then what?"

"I can't actually disclose the purpose. Let's just say—"

"It really doesn't even matter," he cuts me off, putting his hand up. "This business, this shop, it's all I know. I'm not ready to hang it up just yet."

"Who says you have to? There are plenty of other places to open up shop in this city."

"Come on—don't try to push that by me. Garages like this are a dying breed in Manhattan for just this reason. The bigwig real estate types like you see way too little revenue coming from such valuable land. We both know there aren't other one-story garages for me to just move my shop to. The other ones around this city only exist until the owners buckle under the pressure to sell out so big development can move in."

Huh. Roddy's a bit more astute than I planned on.

"There's always a way, Roddy."

"Meaning what?"

"Meaning when it comes to real estate, I get creative. And I wouldn't have come here without a plan."

"He's not kidding, Roddy," L jumps in. "No one, *no one*, thinks like this guy."

"What kind of plan?"

"We'll get to that. First—here's my offer to think about. Three thousand per square foot for the thirty-four-hundred-square-foot plot of land—equaling ten point two million dollars. On top of which I'll throw in one point three million for the building that I'm going to tear down immediately after signing. That's an eleven-point-five-million-dollar payday, plus a guarantee from me to help you relocate and keep growing this business. Not a bad testament to your father's name, and what he started."

CHAPTER THIRTEEN

DANTE DOCKS THE Ship in front of the Strip House—a steak-house—on West Forty-Fourth Street. I walk through the front door.

"Good afternoon," the statuesque hostess says, "may I—"

I see Jake already seated inside. He's waving to me. He's already with fork and knife in hand and a napkin tucked into his collar to shield his chest.

"I'm meeting my partner, who I see. Thanks."

I walk past the bar, which is on my left, toward the dining room. The interior, screaming of Venetian red throughout, is a beauti-ful union of old-world glamour and contemporary flair. Original Studio Manasse prints of 1930s burlesque stars cover the walls, and gorgeous, wide, crystal chandeliers hang overhead. As I near the table I unbutton my suit jacket.

"I don't care what anyone thinks—The Palm, Smith & Wollensky, Old Homestead, Keens, whatever—this place has the best steak in the city," Jake says. "Don't you think?"

I sit down. It's two fifteen p.m. The place is only dotted with patrons as the lunch crush has passed. A waiter approaches immediately.

"May I get you—"

"Bring him a glass of cabernet," Jake says.

"Actually, no," I jump in immediately, my eyes on Jake's already half-empty wine glass. "Still too much of this day left. Just some water for me."

"And perhaps something to start?"

In front of Jake is an appetizer order of scallops in black truffle butter and edamame succotash, which he's barely touched.

"I'd love a shrimp cocktail. Thanks."

"Right away, sir. I'll be back shortly to give you the specials and take your main course."

"So why the urgency for the two of us to chat?" I start. "Wait, let me guess. You're back on the idea of a website that allows people to order customized blow-up sex dolls—where customers can set dimensions, upload photos, the works—and you want me to invest."

"You know that's a good idea," Jake says through a quick, short, forced laugh.

I look again at his half-empty wine glass.

"What's on your mind, partner?"

Jake thinks as he assembles his words. He straightens up. He puts his fork and knife down. He takes another sip of wine.

"I'm nervous."

"Don't be."

"Why not?"

"Because I have it under control."

"*You have it under*—" Jake cuts himself off, looks around, and reels in his voice. "You have it under control? It was you who took the picture you showed me, correct?"

"It was."

"And you're not scared shitless? For Perry, for yourself, for all of us?"

"I'm not. I mean, yes, of course, I am a little, but, if—"

"If what?"

I take a deep breath.

"I know who we're dealing with. I'm not sure yet *what* we're dealing with, but I know the man. I know Cobus. He doesn't want to hurt us. He simply wants what he wants, and knows I understand failure is not an option."

He looks around and leans forward toward me.

"So what am I missing? If that's so clearly understood, then why the need to cut Shane's fucking head off," he asks in a tight-lipped whisper.

"Because that wasn't about motivation alone. Yes, motivation was a part of it, but this is more complicated. The vehicle used for motivating me, if you will, was because I offended him."

"Offended him? How?"

"By turning him away on his initial asking. In Cobus' mind, my willingness to help should have never been a question. And to tell you the truth, his thinking along those lines isn't entirely wrong."

"Why?"

"Because I owe him."

"I thought you two were square. I thought the two of you—"

"Not just for my life. For Perry's life."

"I understand that. He looked out for you, which meant by default Perry as well. When Max was abducted, Perry took off on her own to Switzerland to join Gaston and get his help locating Max. She learned almost immediately through Gaston's contacts Max was alive and safe with his father in Manhattan, at which time you decided together she'd be safest tucked away at Gaston's chalet until it was time to go home, which would be soon enough. And when it was time, true to his word, Cobus got you both back here safe and sound."

"For the most part, that's right. But not exactly."

"Not exactly," Jake repeats. "What *not exactly?* What do you mean?"

"I mean the last three years before we returned, Perry wasn't at the chalet in Switzerland with Gaston."

No response. Jake looks confused.

"I know you, and everyone else, thinks she was," I go on. "Yes—Max was back in Manhattan. Only neither of us knew this. In fact, I had no idea where either of them were."

He shakes his head.

"I'm not following. What really happened?"

I swallow hard. I look down at the tablecloth. The memories, though five years earlier, are still as fresh as they are awful. I lift my eyes back up to Jake's.

"One afternoon the three of us walked through Amsterdam. It was a gorgeous day. It was really crowded. There was a World Cup qualifier match versus Scotland so the place was teeming with people. I sensed we were being followed. Before I could even blink, we were literally sprinting through the crowds from our pursuers. Out of nowhere, a black van screeched to a stop in front of us. More guys jumped out, grabbed Max and Perry, wrapped them in their big, burly arms, and were pulling them toward the van. We were all so shocked, and frightened. Perry's voice, laced with sheer panic, was screaming for Max. As I fended guys off I caught glimpses of Perry and Max kicking and screaming. But every time I took a step toward them another set of arms or fists came at me. I remember even biting off a part of one dude's face then spitting it out just to get myself free, get some space."

"Jesus Christ, Jonah," Jake says.

I take a sip of water, and continue.

"I'll never forget the sound of that sliding door slamming shut. The van peeled out and I ran after it as fast as I could. Gunshots came from behind me and hit the van. At the time I had no idea if the shots were aimed at the assailants or me, so I just kept running.

I ran all the way home. I learned later the shots were from Cobus' protectors of me who at the time I didn't even know existed. But I'll never forget the sound of the sliding door slamming. It still haunts me. It still wakes me up at night. Even in that moment something about it was so . . . I feared and sensed something was so . . . final."

"You couldn't go to the cops," Jake correctly deduces. "In the States you were still a fleeing murder suspect. In the Netherlands you were a fraud who would have been extradited."

I nod. I clench my jaw.

"It was so hard. To have that happen in front of my own eyes, on my watch, and not be able to do anything about it was so hard. At the same time, I knew maintaining my cover, and getting home, was the only chance any of us would have. I had to have faith and keep it together. I had to get home."

"What happened? Where was she?"

I shake my head, pissed to have to even think about it, and drop a fist on the table that sends all the silverware and everything else bouncing. My water topples forward. Neither of us give it a thought or look. A waiter starts toward us. I throw an authoritative hand in the air expressing him to leave it alone, and keep his distance.

"Fucking Andreu Zhamovsky."

Andreu Zhamovsky. My scumbag, Russian half brother, whose plan to steal treasured Fabergé Imperial Easter Eggs I foiled. And had sent to prison for embezzlement in the process.

"It turns out a few years after we were gone, and after apparently paying his way out of the Russian prison system early, he came looking for Perry to get to me," I go on. "Her asshole husband explained that not only did he think his wife was running with me, but we had Max. Andreu made a deal with him. Should he ever get a bead on where his wife, son, and I were, he was to let Andreu know. And for that he'd make sure asshole husband would get his son back."

"Don't tell me. Somehow the stars aligned."

"You have no idea. Like some insane cosmic clusterfuck. Asshole husband's brother was traveling in Amsterdam and was sure he'd seen Perry even though there had been some minor adjustments made to her appearance. To be sure, he followed her, and that's when he saw Max too. So the brother called asshole husband, asshole husband called Andreu. But there was a problem. According to the brother in Amsterdam, Perry and Max were with a guy, but it wasn't Gray. Why?"

I cover my face with my hand, and then move it away as if I'm unveiling myself.

"The surgery," Jake says.

"The surgery. Once asshole husband said there was no Gray, Andreu said there was no deal. Asshole husband pleaded with him—he was desperate to get his son back. So the two came up with a solution. Now—think about the abduction I described. What do you think that solution was?"

He says nothing as he processes my words. He leans back in his chair.

"Perry."

"Correct. They didn't even try to take me. Asshole husband would get his son back. Andreu would hold on to Perry for as long as it took for me to show up and lead him to the Fabergé Imperial Easter Eggs he'd been trying to get a hold of with his mother."

"So where was Perry all that time?"

"In complete isolation in some remote wing of a Zhamovsky estate in St. Petersburg. For three years she had no idea if I was alive. More importantly, she had no idea if her own son was alive. She had no contact to the outside world whatsoever. All she had were her thoughts. Thoughts that soon enough became suicidal. Thoughts she refused to let get the better of her because she felt in her soul her boy was still alive."

"My God," Jake says slowly. "Poor Perry."

"She's been through so much. She put so much on the line. For me."

"She loves you, bro. She knew what she was doing when she ran with you. Look, it's awful what happened, but there's no way either of you could have—"

The waiter shows up and places my shrimp cocktail in front of me.

"Are you two ready to order?" he goes on, placing a couple napkins on top of the spilled water.

"We need a few more minutes," Jake says.

The waiter leaves us.

"I know," I say in response to where Jake was going, putting my hand up. "But it doesn't make it any easier to think about every day. What she went through because of me. Her days running into nights running into days—all alone. Anyway—once I landed in Moscow, Andreu didn't go lightly. His crew beat the crap out of me something awful. It was Cobus' crew who ultimately busted Perry and me out of there. Without him, no shit, I don't think we would have left Moscow alive."

"I don't get it. Why the secrecy?"

"Because that's how Perry wanted it. The flight back from Russia on Cobus' Gulfstream, even though we'd been separated for three years, she was so quiet. She told Cobus and me about her isolation—what the space she was in was like, how seldom she ate, the minimal contact she had with humans—but mostly she just stared out the window. No doubt remembering thousands of memories she only wanted to forget. That first night back in the States, we were trapped somewhere between stunned and relieved. And we were both exhausted. We passed out. But in the middle of the night I woke up. I could feel Per staring at me. I sat up. Her eyes were filled with tears. She told me she was so scared. I asked her of what. She said of having to reflect on, and confront, what she had just been through."

"Understandable," Jake says.

"Agreed. I told her we'd get her the best help money could buy. That she could take as long as she needed. She said she wanted to get back to living, but that whether I realized it or not my story—our story—was about to become a big one. And unless she could confront her ordeal—and these newfound demons—on her own without having to share them with the world at the same time, she didn't think she'd be able to recover. So I gave her my word we'd keep that part of the story quiet. And not only did Cobus cover our asses, he has kept this secret as well."

"Just unbelievable," Jake goes on.

"Like I said. I owe him."

"Has Perry ever fully opened up to you about all of it? Everything that happened?"

"She visits with her therapist often, so I'm guessing she's dealing with it all in her own way. But I don't know. And I don't push. She knows I'm here if she needs me."

She does know.

Doesn't she?

"You know, I don't want to say anything out of line. But ever since you two returned Perry's been—she's been a little, like, she's been—"

"Different," I save him from squirming any further.

"Yeah. Different. She's always been edgy, and sharp as anyone in the room, but I don't ever remember her being full-throttle twenty-four-seven."

"I know," I concur. "Believe me, I get it. It's like she won't stop for even one second because in that second she might have to relive one of the memories she's running away from."

"She's always been intense," Jake continues, "but there was always a softness underneath that kind of, like, balanced her out."

Now I'm the one beginning to fend off unwanted memories. I look at my watch.

"We need to order and get moving," I change direction.

"So Cobus isn't as scary as I thought," Jake takes my cue.

"Oh, he's scary all right, but I like to believe he and I have a mutual respect for one another that is unlike any other between two people. Trust me, that's our saving grace, so long as he never perceives us to be crossing him. He ever thinks we're fucking him, it will be a different part of our bodies than our heads that shows up in a box somewhere."

CHAPTER FOURTEEN

CAROLYN FOLLOWS ME into my office.

"Jim Cramer's producer called. They asked if you're available to do an in studio piece tomorrow night about REITs on *Mad Money.* Now, tomorrow you have a three-thirty p.m. meeting with Marcus and Polow that shouldn't last more than an hour, but you and Perry aren't due at Eleven Madison Park for Diskin's dinner party until eight. You'll have plenty of time to stop home and freshen up. Fine?"

"Fine," I answer, though I'm barely listening.

I hit the speakerphone button on my phone. I punch in Perry's extension.

"Hey, handsome."

"I need you."

"Shall I disrobe now? Or is it in bad taste to traverse the hallway naked?"

"I mean I need to discuss some business with you. Is your puppy around?"

"My puppy?"

"*Natey-Boy* Landgraff."

"Ha ha."

"Bring him."

I press the speakerphone button again, disconnecting us.

"Here," Carolyn says, handing me a stack of phone message

memos. "The phone hasn't stopped—guessing you're not picking up your cell. Two of those are from Cass Lima."

I drop the stack of notes on my desk without looking at them. Just as Carolyn exits, Perry enters.

"I have a project for your boy."

"He doesn't need a new project," Perry responds as she sits in one of the chairs facing my desk, and crosses her legs. "In case you forgot, I have him working on a little project of my own. The pitch we just scored for a three-hundred-thousand-square-foot requirement next week."

"And?"

"And what?"

"Since when can't our soldiers handle more than one assignment at a time?"

"Why Nate? Why can't we put someone else like Kleger or CJ on it?"

"Because it has to do with my Meatpacking District assemblage deal. I need to know it's going to be handled properly out of the gate. Landgraff's like us. He can handle it. He *wants* to handle it. Besides—Kleger and CJ each have deals potentially closing any day now, which means cash in our pockets. I want them locked in."

Perry's eyes, trained on me, narrow.

"There's more," she says.

Strategy.

My father once said, "Strategy, psychology—when it comes to business, what's the fucking difference? The best way to manipulate your foes is by first controlling your friends."

Natey-Boy Landgraff knows I'm watching him. He's sweet on Perry—he doesn't want to be, but he is. The innate *guy* in him can't help it. I can see it in his young, hungry eyes. Subconsciously he wants to please her. And what better opportunity for him to do so than by pleasing me?

"Isn't there always?" I respond.

Landgraff, hair perfectly slicked, tightly dressed minus the suit jacket, appears in the doorway.

"You want to see me?"

"Come in, Natey-Boy," Perry says, her eyes still locked with mine.

He does as she says and stops in front of my desk.

"Have a seat," I say, gesturing to the empty chair next to Perry's also facing me.

He sits down.

"I know you're preparing for the Lennox presentation next week, but I need you to do something for me. And I need it done fast."

"You got it, Jonah. What do you need?"

"I need an auto body shop."

"An auto body shop," he repeats.

He looks at Perry, who shrugs, then looks back at me.

"Like—you need a recommendation?"

"No. I mean I need an *actual* auto body shop."

"May I ask why?"

"Doesn't matter. I need one. If it's vacant—great. If it's not, find out what it will take to get the tenant out of there."

I can see Landgraff's wheels turning.

"What about somewhere like Long Island City? I know there are a lot of—"

"No. Needs to be Manhattan."

"Come on, Jonah," Perry interjects. "Those buildings are a dying breed in Manhattan. The only reason a handful of them remain is because the people who own them refuse to go anywhere. Which is exactly what you're looking to make one of them do."

"Actually, two of them should Landgraff find what we need. But we'll get to that. For now, just focus on the requirement. Get creative. Look at geographically undesirable, outskirt lots with rundown one and two-story buildings as potential conversions. Find out which operators of the existing auto body shops are willing to expose their price—because we know they all have one. Look into the properties' history; look for building department violations, back taxes owed, whatever might be used for leverage. And, again, only in Manhattan. Can you do that?"

"Of course."

"Good," I say. "Then get on it."

"Did you get a chance to speak with Sturner?" I ask Perry as Landgraff leaves.

"Just briefly. I told him I want to speak about One Twenty One West Forty-Fifth. He asked if I had a tenant. I told him, 'not quite.'"

"What did he say?"

"That he was crazy today, but he could meet me for a cocktail tonight at seven thirty at the West Side Smith by Lincoln Center. Which works for me. I'd rather tell him we want the building in person so I can see his millionth."

The *millionth*. What Perry, Jake and I refer to as that first millionth of a second reaction someone has to unforeseen news where their expression gives up their true feelings before their poker face can kick in. No matter how good that poker face is, everyone has a millionth. And only a very select few even know it exists to identify.

"You free for a cocktail at seven thirty?" she goes on.

My iPhone rings. Cobus. I hold it up for Perry to see, hit Accept, then hold it to my ear.

"Cobus."

"How we doing, Ivan?"

I hit speaker and put the phone on my desk so Perry can listen.

"Doing just fine."

"Is going back to Ivan fine, or do you prefer Jonah? I'm just so used to calling you Ivan that, well, as you might understand—"

"Up to you," I cut him off. "Two names. Same person."

"Is that right?"

I pause. I don't answer.

"I received your brokerage agreement," he continues. "I thought we were closer than that. Do you really want me to sign that document?"

"I thought the goal here was to make this as . . . usual as possible," I respond, speaking in code, replacing "usual" for "legitimate," my eyes locked with Perry's.

"Two honest men work together, documents mean nothing," Cobus changes direction. "Two dishonest men work together, documents mean nothing. Isn't that right?"

"As right as anything in business," I answer.

Another test. A brokerage agreement protects me—my team, my firm—with regard to any deal we secure. Cobus knows this as well as I do. Want? Absolutely. Need? Where we're going, I know our union is way beyond words on paper.

"Trash the brokerage agreement. Ivan Janse? And Cobus de Bont? We work on honor. We work on history."

I swallow.

"Your partner Jake," he continues.

I'm surprised.

"What about him?"

"I feel very comfortable in my relationship with you and Tess—I mean, Perry."

Tess. Perry's name while we were incognito in Europe. He's driving the connection, history home. Duly noted.

"But Jake. I know he's your third. And I know—I've learned—he's essentially family to you. I just want you to know he checks out. I'm fine with him should he keep in line with our mutual goals."

Cobus and I have never had one conversation about Jake.

Perry's jaw drops.

"Suggestion," Cobus goes on, "fill him in, if you haven't already, as to how—*intense*—I am about my business."

CHAPTER FIFTEEN

I FOLLOW PERRY into The Smith, a loud, bustling spot where thirty-somethings gather for cocktails and solid American fare. We both initially focus on perhaps the most annoyingly narrow bar space in all of Manhattan to our right, but out of the corner of my eye to the left—past the host station—I see a navy suit jacket-clad arm extend straight into the air to get our attention. I touch the small of Perry's back, and we change direction.

"Perry, nice to see you," Sturner says as he stands from the table.

Few men can keep from letting their eyes give Perry an up and down—and Sturner's no different. Only a guy like Sturner doesn't care. He wants Perry to notice. He wants me to notice *him* noticing. For a guy like Sturner, this moment of power strokes his ego. For Perry and me, it's all just part of the dance. Perry is smart enough to understand in this initial moment she can begin to get a deal to swing her way based on a guy's subconscious desire to be around her, smell her, dream of fucking her. Once she has them right where she wants them? She destroys them with her mind, which would have been more than enough to work them over in the first place.

Sturner drinks Perry in. Skintight, silver metallic silk Lurex pants paired with a gray silk satin blouse show off her perfect form. No doubt he's trying his best to imagine what her already gravity-defying ass looks like at this very moment lifted by her beige BB Leather Point-Toe Manolo pumps.

"You too," responds Perry as they exchange a cordial kiss hello.

"Jonah," he goes on, extending his hand to me. "Always a pleasure."

His grip, eye contact, and expression suggest two things. He's wavering between happiness and disappointment I've accompanied Perry. But he isn't surprised.

We unclasp hands.

"Please," he says, gesturing for us to sit, then grabbing the waiter's attention. "What does everyone want?"

"I'll go with a Prosecco," Perry says just as the young server steps to the table.

"And I'll do a Belvedere, rocks, twist," I add.

The waiter scurries off. Sturner washes back a sip of his previously ordered neat whiskey.

My iPhone vibrates. Morante. *Spoke with Marilena as the Madame suggested. Breakfast tomorrow?* I text back, *Yes. Brasserie. E. 53rd St.*

"So," Sturner starts in, "Perry, I was surprised when you called and said it wasn't about an inquiry for space."

"Why would it have been?" Perry responds with a question of her own. "You're doing a fantastic job over there. Correct me if I'm wrong, but I think you only have that oddly shaped, four-thousand-and-change-square-foot space on the fourth floor. And since when would I be handling such a small requirement?"

He tips his glass Perry's way.

"Fair enough. So, then, why the call?"

Here it comes.

Watch his eyes.

"We have a buyer for the property," she goes on.

His eyes are on Perry.

Mine are on his.

I capture his "millionth." In it, I see something I hadn't anticipated. A twinkle.

He's excited by the prospect of selling.

Why?

Just like that, his poker face falls into place.

"A buyer that isn't Resurrection?"

"That's right," Perry responds.

"What makes you think I'd part with a 98 percent leased property in such a strong submarket?"

"Hmm. I'm thinking a boatload of cash?" she goes on.

"I'm looking to build a portfolio for the long term. A long-term that includes a little something called the Hudson Yards development not too far from this building. My attainable price per square foot literally goes up every day."

"Let's not get carried away, Bobby. Best case scenario, Hudson Yards is still a couple years out."

"You'd never know it by the way prices have been skyrocketing for anything on the West Side between Meatpacking and the Fifties."

Sturner pauses.

"Who's the buyer?" he goes on.

"We can't say," Perry replies.

"Why not?"

"Because our client doesn't like to be in others' mouths. They're very private and prefer their identity remain confidential until they truly believe they can obtain their mark. Anyway—it doesn't matter. The buyer is a powerhouse. Let's just say, all due respect, if they represent a master's degree in real estate, you're still in the second grade."

Perry shifts in her seat. As she does, I see Sturner's eyes get a nice look down her blouse.

"Is that so?"

"Something like that," Perry responds with a giggle. "Anyway, I love how it sounded."

Our drinks are placed in front of us. We pick them up, clink each other, then clink with Sturner. Each of us takes a healthy sip.

"It's not like you, Jonah, to be so quiet," Sturner says.

My father once told me, "Shut your mouth and listen. Because no one ever learned anything while talking."

"I'm just thinking about what you were saying regarding pricing," I say. "Our buyer loves your building because of the location—he's really keyed in on that portion of the city. But while I know they will be willing to pay a serious premium for the property, I also know they have no interest in paying prices that reflect perceived value two years down the road. Resurrection pays only what current market conditions dictate. And I always advise my clients to do the same."

Plant the seed.

If you really are looking to sell, you'll come out nice.

If I misread you, you now have no choice but to pay attention.

"Well, as I said, I have no intention today of selling this property. Unless someone gives me a real reason to even entertain such a thought, the property remains mine."

"Huh. Interesting," I say. "Exactly as I thought."

I feel Perry staring at me like Sturner is.

"What is so interesting?" Sturner asks.

I've seen your millionth.

I've seen a little piece of your soul.

"Your choice of words. 'No intention today of selling.' 'Unless someone gives me a reason . . . the property remains mine.' You know what all of that adds up to?"

Sturner says nothing.

"What you *didn't* say," I go on. "The simple words—'the building is not for sale.'"

I down the rest of my cocktail and stand up. I look down at Sturner, reminding him of the existing hierarchy. My expression goes stern.

"Which makes sense, considering a wise man once told me all

buildings are for sale," I go on. "Sometimes their owners just need to be reminded as such."

My eyes still on Sturner, I extend my left hand to Perry. She takes it and stands up. A little lesson for my little friend of what it really means to have the attention of a woman like Perry.

"Thanks for taking a few minutes," Perry says.

"Now, if you'll excuse us, we have a dinner meeting across town," I say. "But I do hope we have the chance to speak again soon."

Sturner pauses, then he stands up and extends his hand to save face. On the way out I hand the waiter a Benjamin to cover the round.

* * *

The second we exit the restaurant, Dante jumps from the driver's seat and opens the rear door for us. The block is a busy one directly across from Lincoln Center; three restaurants in a row—The Smith, Cafe Fiorello, and Épicerie Boulud—all with sidewalk seating. "Jonah, marry me!" a woman yells. As we move toward The Ship, Perry and I ignore the stares and pointing as we've gotten used to doing. "You kick ass, Perry," another woman shouts. "I want to go shopping with you!"

"Bet you do, sweetheart. That blouse is so Two Thousand Twelve," Dante says as we duck into The Ship, cracking Perry up.

The door closes behind us, leaving the city sounds and voices behind in an instant.

"He didn't need any reminding his building's for sale," Perry says.

"No. He didn't."

"I wonder what's going on with him," she goes on.

"Boss-man, confirming I have us headed to Daniel on East Sixty-Fifth," Dante says through the intercom. "Have you there shortly."

My phone rings. I hold it up so Perry can see who's calling.

"Have fun," she says, teasingly.

"Madame Martine. How are you this evening?"

"How do you think, Joonah?"

"I assure you, Madame, we're on top of this. It has only been a day or so, so—"

"There is no *only*, Joonah. Not with a prototype for a fragrance of this magnitude missing this close to launch! I have trusted you, Joonah. I *need* this handled!"

Out of the corner of my eye I see Perry, faced away from me watching the passing city, pop a pill. She washes it down with a swig of Poland Spring.

"Madame—I need you to trust me. Haven't I looked out for you from the moment you and I, together, decided you being in my property was the right move for you?"

She sighs.

"Yes, Joonah, you have. That is why it would be such a shame if this cannot be rectified before it is too late. I would be so disappointed. Tell your detective friend he better get to the bottom of this fast. Or the press may find out inadvertently that a prototype of my greatest creation yet curiously went missing just before the launch—right out of my own office. Nothing personal, Joonah. Because nothing can ever be personal when running an empire. Wouldn't you agree?"

CHAPTER SIXTEEN

2:52 A.M.

Still in my suit pants and dress shirt, minus the jacket and tie, I'm sitting in my home office at Silver Rock. My top button is undone and my sleeves are rolled up. The room, like all in the townhouse, has a thirteen-foot ceiling lined with the same magnificent neo-classical molding surrounding the windows and doorway. Though much of the property built in 1888 has been renovated over the years, the office shell remains true to its old-world roots while everything within is contemporary—a seamless, blended contrast of time. Night light coming through the windows mixed with the light from my 27-inch iMac screen is all that illuminates the space.

Neo, like a little eight-pound horse, is asleep on his side on the desktop next to the computer screen, all four legs sticking straight out. His chest rhythmically rises and falls with each breath. Every once in a while he goes into a twitching frenzy while dreaming.

Sitting in my black leather executive chair, my eyes move left away from the screen. All I see are colorless shadows, outlines, in front of me. I look straight ahead over my sleek desk, past the accessory chairs facing me, past the black leather sofas and Cuoio Collection coffee table, all the way to the rear-facing wall adorned with three dormant, vertically placed, sixty-five inch LED TVs.

I'm looking all the way to that rear wall.

All I'm seeing is the map I was just looking at on my screen.

The house is so silent, I hear the zone's AC—on auto mode—kick in.

I look back at the screen, at the map of Manhattan I've been studying, processing, for the last hour. Using Google Maps I've made each property Cobus is focused on the central figure, placing it in the center of the screen. I've been zooming in and out, I've been rotating right and left. I minimized the map at one point and, using Wite-Out tape, I connected all the properties to see if a pattern emerged. None did.

I look down into my lap. My eyes widen at the fact I'm holding a pair of scissors in my right hand. I feel warm liquid running down my left forearm. There are two fresh gashes in my flesh, the snaking blood black in the nighttime glow.

Why is there so much blood?

Is it because the cardiologist has me taking aspirin every day?

I look at the box of Kleenex on the far corner of my desk. Instead of reaching for it, I lift my forearm to my mouth. I lick the blood away with my tongue.

*　*　*

5:22 a.m.

Fresh from the shower, my left forearm wrapped tight in gauze and my waist wrapped in a towel, I walk past Perry's walk-in closet toward my own. As I do, I hear her iPhone vibrate against the cherrywood top of her closet's center island. I look, and see the screen has beamed to life.

I take a few steps toward it. There's a new text. It's from Natey-Boy. Landgraff.

It simply says, *Call me as soon as you get up.*

I continue on into my closet. I take a bottle of water from my fridge and down it in one shot. I let my towel fall off me. Surveying my Assiagi arsenal, deciding what to wear and hearing Pirro reminding me to pay special attention to the "sensational accessories," I can't keep my mind from veering to the map of Cobus' target buildings I'd been surveying all night.

Standing in front of my full-length mirror, I put my shirt on before anything else and begin buttoning it. I start at the top, and work my way down. Once I hit the fourth button I notice Perry in the mirror, behind me, standing naked in my closet's entryway.

"Good morning, beautiful," I say, my eyes locked with hers.

She starts toward me.

"You never came to bed. I don't like it when you don't come to bed."

"Was studying—more like obsessing over—the buildings Cobus has us targeting. I spent the night on Google Maps. I can't for the life of me figure out the real reason for these buildings with the unusually huge basements."

Perry reaches me, drapes her left arm up around my neck, and comes around my right facing me. She looks into my eyes then looks down at my left forearm.

"My lesson in cutting bagels while tired in the middle of the night. Fumbled the knife into my arm."

Her eyes come back to mine. She kisses me deeply. She gets on her knees. And takes me in her mouth.

* * *

6:19 a.m.

I settle into the back of The Ship and take out my iPad. I bring up Google Maps. I lock in on Berlin, and begin investigating the properties acquired there since my involvement with de Bont Beleggings ended.

"Strong look today, boss-man," Dante says through the intercom. "Love you rocking the mauve tie. Takes a *real* man to show a color like mauve who's boss."

Staring at the screen, I say nothing back.

* * *

7:28 a.m.

I'm in my office. My iPhone rings. It's Cass. I answer.

"You were always an early riser like myself," I say.

"True—but not the point. I figure I'd better get you early as I can before you begin your day of interviews and such. Did I just read a book about you is being published by FSG? How much time does that take sitting with an editor?"

"What's really going on, Cass? I want you to drop this act."

"Nice show yesterday. My client truly believes this is another deal you can take or leave. My days going to sleep and waking up with you tell me otherwise. I know you want this deal."

"Ah. You still think of us going to bed and waking up together. Which no doubt means you still think of what happened between the actual going to bed and waking up. Which no doubt is why I'm still on your mind first thing in—"

"Don't be a pig."

"Where are you going with this, Cass? And?"

"I'm concerned for my client, Jonah. We know—"

She pauses, then goes on.

"I know what you can do with this property, this project. But as I said yesterday, I don't know if I'm really confident it would have your full attention."

"All due respect—why does that matter? Asked another way, why should you care one way or another? You're their attorney."

As the words roll off my tongue, I see what I've been missing. Cass knows I am, in fact, the right buyer. And she hates this. Because, like a little schoolgirl, she hates that we didn't work out. Now is her chance to get back at me. By making this difficult for me via feigned concern.

Let the games begin.

"I care because Jerry Landis trusts me. He's not just looking at this as a windfall. He's looking at this as something that needs to honor those in his family who came before him. He wants to make sure it ends up in the right hands."

"As you made clear yesterday," I remind her. "And you need to make sure, if you are—hypothetically—to go to bat for me, that I am one hundred percent the right buyer," I go on.

"The other visions presented, Jonah, are anything but cookie-cutter. On the contrary, they are quite formidable. And coming from firms with more downtown development under their belt. Believe it or not, others can be in your league of savvy."

"Take out your calendar," I say.

"Why?"

"Because you seem to be very familiar with the other visions presented to your client, but I haven't told you mine yet. No doubt you heard what I laid out secondhand from Landis and Feller. But I feel you owe it to them to have the full picture, crystal clear, from my mouth, in order to properly compare all the offerings on an even plane. Wouldn't you agree?"

You want to play?

Let's play.

"I do," she concurs after a brief pause.

"Then let's figure out when, in the next forty-eight hours, you and I can sit down, face to face, just the two of us."

* * *

8:38 a.m.

I walk into Brasserie, a sleek, French mainstay on East Fifty-Third Street. The space feels clean, almost sterile, and is bright; the décor is somewhere between the interior of a spaceship and a restaurant where that spaceship might be traveling. As I descend the central, mildly sloping staircase into the main dining room, I notice Morante seated in one of the booths off to the left.

"Jonah," he says as he stands and extends his hand.

"Detective," I say back, shaking his hand firmly. "Thanks again for your assistance."

He nods. We sit down.

"I guess the rich like fancy even for breakfast," he says, looking around.

"What I like, Detective, is great service and close to my office. And I hope you're hungry—they happen to make the best smoked salmon Benedict you've ever had."

A waiter arrives.

"Good morning, gentlemen, something to drink?"

I look at Morante.

"Coffee would be great, black," he says.

"And I'll do an iced coffee," I add, looking back at the waiter. "A little skim milk, please."

I look again to Morante.

"Should we just do the whole order?" I ask. "In the interest of time?"

"I actually ate, so I'm fine. But if—"

"Please bring us an order of the smoked salmon Benedict and some mixed berries," I cut him off, looking back at the waiter.

"Very good," the waiter replies, before scurrying off.

"So," I say, "how we doing?"

"With regard to Mr. Esparanza, we had an interesting hit when the NCIC database results came back. There's a kid on the crew he's been working on with a breaking and entering in his past. Twenty-eight years old. His name is Alan Billings. But he goes by James Billings—James being his middle name. Anyway, this is probably how he got through Spectrum's screening process. He's been employed by them for four years. And he's been on the same crew as the deceased for seven months."

"Has he been a good employee?"

"According to Bayliss, he has."

"What's the story with his past crime?"

"It took place nine years ago in Pittsburgh. Did a couple years of time. He probably decided to relocate and start fresh as a result. Anyway, I'm going to look to get a statement from him first. But I plan on getting statements from everyone on Mr. Esparanza's shift in quick order. The faster you get information in these instances, the better."

"Gotcha. Moving on to Madame Martine, did you get a chance to speak with Marilena?"

"I did."

"And?"

"And—that is one tough, tall woman with a mountain of disdain it seems not only for her boss, but everyone she works with."

"Whoa. I knew she was tough, but I just figured she ran a tight ship for Madame. Funny, she and I always got along pretty well—"

"Which is exactly where I was going," Morante cuts me off.

"I'm not following."

"As much as it seems like she can't stand anyone, she was beyond tight lipped with me from the outset because she knew I was a cop. But when I brought your name up, with regard to your connection to Madame Martine and your desire to help get this right for her not just as a tenant but as a friend, something happened. Something

. . . changed in her tone, in her demeanor."

"I dealt with Marilena a lot when we were building out their new office space. As I said, Marilena runs the show when it comes to handling that office. Madame Martine had her essentially managing the build-out down to every last detail. It was a few months of us in very close contact. The space coming out perfect was very important to Madame, so I was very hands on even though I'd usually have my chief of property management, Harvey West, overseeing such a project."

"Whatever it is, I have a feeling she'll open up more to you. The key is asking her the right questions."

"What do you suggest?" I ask.

"I want you to pay Marilena a visit on your own."

CHAPTER SEVENTEEN

I WALK INTO Three Twenty One Park South, listening to a voice mail from the wife of my missing security guard.

"Hi, Jonah, it's Victoria Concord. I'm sorry to bother you, but Shane hasn't checked in with me, and I'm a little concerned. I know his work schedule with your traveling can get a little hectic sometimes, but it's not like him to not call or text just to keep me in the loop. Please just tell him I'm looking for him. Thanks."

The concierge and I exchange greetings as I head past his desk, toward the elevators. I jump in one waiting in the lobby.

The doors open on the eighth floor, and I get off. The reception desk is straight ahead.

"Good afternoon, Mr. Gray," the young, perky, fashion-y receptionist says as I approach.

"Good afternoon. Is Ms. Ross in?"

"She is. Let me ring her."

Less than a minute later Marilena appears in the reception area. Standing over six feet tall in her heels, she's a force in every way. She's a slim yet ripped, feminine yet high energy, alpha girl. She has long, straight auburn hair, fair skin, and emerald-green eyes. Today she's wearing a printed silk wrap dress that shows off her dazzling legs.

"How are you, sweetheart?" she says, greeting me with a Euro-style, double-cheek kiss.

"I'm well, Marilena. Thanks. All good with you?"

"Just the usual insanity of keeping this place together. Not to mention a little bottle of perfume that seems to have gone missing. Which, I'm guessing, is the reason you're here."

"Is there somewhere we can speak for a minute?"

Marilena and I walk through the space to her office, which, like Madame Martine's, is more a combination office and apartment. She closes the door. Overhead hangs a dangling crystal chandelier. I walk past the long, weathered Ralph Lauren leather couch and sculptor's table and bookshelves stocked with old volumes. I stop at the floor-to-ceiling window facing Park Avenue South and watch the activity below.

"Can I have Jessica bring you something to drink?"

Jessica is Marilena's assistant.

"No—thanks. I'm fine."

I hear Marilena walking behind me. I turn around. She's walking to the chair behind her desk. She sits down, crosses her legs, and gets comfortable.

"Were you in the building, *Mr. Gray*? Or was this a special visit to see me?"

I walk over and sit in one of the chairs facing her desk.

"I wasn't in the building. I made the trip here so I could speak with you. I'm troubled by what happened. Madame Martine owns this company. But we both know you run the show."

Marilena nods gently.

"I care about Madame," I go on. "I care about all of you. I take great pride in the fact your firm trusted me enough to make this move."

"We love it here, Jonah. You've been great."

"I appreciate that. But if this is what Madame believes it is— some type of corporate espionage that would entail a serious breach in this property's security protocol—I will have failed as a landlord. Terribly."

Marilena crosses her legs in the opposite direction.

"How can I help?" she asks.

"Tell me where there may have been a breakdown. Tell me about the other night. Was anything unusual going on?"

"Not at all," she answers, matter of fact. "It was a night like any other around here. Everyone left around the same time they usually do. Trust me—I keep tabs on everyone."

"I don't doubt it. How about Tiffany? Was she on her usual schedule?"

"She was. Once the bottle had arrived and she put it in Madame's office, she tended to some more work then was gone around seven fifteen or seven thirty. The same time she leaves every night."

"And she's the only one—aside from Madame and Laurent— who has a key to Madame's office."

"Correct."

"So Tiffany put the prototype in Madame's office after it arrived."

"Correct."

"Huh."

"Huh—what?"

"How long has Tiffany been Madame's assistant?"

"Almost three years. Why?"

"I just find it odd that Madame leaves the third key with her assistant, and not you."

"Why would you find that odd? I only run her freakin' life," Marilena exclaims, before biting her tongue. "Like I said, it was really an ordinary night around here, Jonah. You must have all sorts of cameras in this building. Have you looked at the video of that night?"

"We're in the process of reviewing it now."

I pause, then change directions.

"Did I ever tell you what happened to my mother?"

"No."

"She passed away when I was five years old. Breast cancer."

"I'm so sorry."

"Thank you. A lot of years ago now."

"Were the two of you close?"

"We were. I remember eating jelly donuts and playing Go Fish with her every Saturday morning."

"Those sound like lovely memories."

"They are. I feel lucky to have them. It was hard losing such a loving parent at a young age."

"I can't imagine."

"I think that's one of the reasons I'm so concerned about this. Don't get me wrong; I treat all of my tenants with the utmost care and respect. But I have a special place in my heart for Madame Martine. You see for me, it isn't just about getting that bottle of perfume back. It's about making sure Madame feels safe. As she should."

"Of course, Jonah."

"If you think of anything—anything—from that night, Marilena, please pick up your phone and call me."

* * *

Jim Cramer stands about fifteen feet from me, speaking into a camera.

"We can't talk about The Market these days, without talking about REITs. Some of them are straight up on fire! Makes sense, right? The economy seems to slowly yet steadily be finding its legs again, and as businesses grow they need more space. My guest today is not only recognizable because of his story, he happens to be one of the best minds in the New York City commercial real estate game. His firm Resurrection Realty is a private company—which, viewers, means you can't buy stock in it—but it's growing at a furious pace and is considered one of the gems in the sector. Simply put, when Jonah Gray talks shop, everyone listens."

Cramer turns toward me, starts walking in my direction, and extends his hand as he sits down with me at the desk.

"Mr. Gray, welcome to *Mad Money*," Cramer goes on as he joins me at the desk and sits. "Always a pleasure to have you with us. How are you?"

"I'm well, Jim, thanks for having me."

"So, again for those watching, Resurrection Realty remains a private company."

"That's right."

"Word on the street, Jonah, is there are a number of firms finding you and your portfolio quite attractive. Any interest in merging with another player?"

"Perhaps one day, but we're happy with where we are for the time being."

"Check. Okay—let's get down to it. REITs are exploding. What's going on?"

"Well, like you said, Jim, as businesses grow they need more space. But it's more than that. A lot of money's been sitting on the sidelines for a long time that's coming back into play. That's why we're seeing more development in major cities like Manhattan than we've seen in years."

"What makes you a good landlord? Not *you* you, but you as in landlords as a whole. What separates one from the next?"

"We're a service industry, Jim. Companies have a lot of choices when it comes to their real estate needs. I think a number of landlords have really learned to raise their game in this respect. In terms of it not just being about providing space, but attending to the tenants' needs. Making them feel safe. Putting amenities in properties that add real value. Tending to needed repairs and such in the most timely manner possible. Keeping tenants informed of things happening in the property that may affect them—even if it's only a possibility, and even if it may only happen for a few minutes. Real estate has always been about location. Today it's no different. What's different is the ability to service, and respect, the tenants—in essence, the clients."

"It isn't just about the inner workings of a building, or a firm even, all working together internally that creates superior product," Cramer deduces. "It's about how those nicely aligned parts will translate outward—to those it needs to reach."

Whoa.

To those it needs to reach.

Thanks, Jim.

"Correct, Jim. Location, respect for your tenants and employees, and top-flight service equals true value in commercial real estate."

"Who do you like in the space today? Who should investors be looking at?"

"I'm a big fan of what Martin Wild is doing with Marcus Enterprises right now. They're positioned beautifully for taking..."

* * *

The Ship docks on Madison Avenue between Twenty-Fourth and Twenty-Fifth Streets. Dante jumps around and opens the door for Perry and me. We step out and head towards the entrance of Eleven Madison Park, where we have a dinner party.

Midway between the sidewalk and the entrance I notice someone in my peripheral vision coming toward us. My head snaps left.

Cobus.

"Jonah, Perry—good evening," he says.

"Cobus," Perry gushes, "it's great to see you," she goes on, giving him a huge hug and kissing both cheeks.

Perry knows this man is dangerous. She also knows he saved her life.

She's playing her role. Yet part of her is genuinely happy to see him.

"As it is you," he says back, gently holding her hands down low.

"How's Annabelle?" Per goes on. "And the little ones?"

I subtly look around. At the corner of the street is a parked black Mercedes S600. A very large man in a dark suit and sunglasses, even though the sun has nearly set, stands outside the vehicle, hands clasped in front of him below his waist. Though I can't see his eyes, he appears to be staring straight at us.

"They're great. Thank you. Annabelle asks for you."

He gestures toward me.

"Both of you," he adds.

What's going on?

How did Cobus know we'd be here?

"Jonah," he goes on, extending his hand.

We shake.

"Cobus. What brings you to this part of town tonight? Checking up on me?"

"Hardly. I knew I'd be close by tonight and it dawned on me that while you and I have had the opportunity of catching up, I hadn't seen Te—I mean, Perry," he responds, looking back at her.

Again.

Our history.

"I appreciate you taking the time," Perry says to him. "I owe you my life."

"Your man came after you, Perry, guns blazing. I simply backed him up."

Perry looks at me and takes my hand. Both of us knowing had Cobus not needed me to remain alive, we'd have been dead in Moscow.

"How'd you know where we'd be tonight?" I ask.

"I called your office earlier. I spoke with Carolyn."

Odd.

For too many reasons to list, Carolyn knows to never give out my schedule.

"Anyway, since I have you for a moment, I'd love an update as I'm going to be behind closed doors most of tomorrow," Cobus continues. "You making any progress with my buildings?"

My buildings.

Message received.

"We've made contact with ownership in each instance and we're going from there. I didn't realize there was any urgency here."

"We're in the business of buying and selling office buildings, Jonah. Urgency permeates our lives. You know as well as anyone—there's always someone waiting in the shadows to take what others covet."

"Life, buildings, whatever," I respond.

"Life, buildings, whatever," he repeats. "My official entrance into the U.S. market once and for all is long overdue. With prices soaring as they are, I need to lock myself in now. Can you blame me?"

"I—"

"Wait—don't answer that," Cobus cuts me off. "Why wouldn't you want us to move fast—that's how Resurrection keeps getting richer, stronger. An ambitious buyer with deep pockets. One might even say I'm your dream client."

CHAPTER EIGHTEEN

IT'S THE MIDDLE of the night. I'm in my office. As usual the lights are low. The night is still inside and out. I remain in the day's suit minus the jacket, tie, and shoes. Again, I'm poring over a map of Manhattan on my computer screen, a bird's-eye view that shows all Cobus' targeted properties. This time, though, the screen is split in two. Manhattan on the left, a map of Amsterdam's South Axis on the right. The two cities, like most, differ vastly from one another. Manhattan is Manhattan—both main office space districts, Midtown and Downtown, are a golf ball's throw away from each other, and the market as a whole is shoved together like commuters in a rush hour subway car. But in places like Amsterdam there are a few main districts with office properties, and they can be miles away from one another. The South Axis is the most important office space district in Amsterdam, and de Bont has numerous holdings there.

"To those it needs to reach," Jim Cramer said on set this evening.

Like last night, I'm looking at both maps studying the buildings on each in relation to one another. But tonight I also have my eye on what the buildings in each city are near. Each building individually, the buildings as a whole—what the properties are near.

Nothing.

I stand up, walk over to my briefcase that is on the couch, take my MacBook Air from it, return to my desk, set it down next to the desktop screen, fire it up, and sit back down. The desktop screen is big, but with the two maps it's hard to see everything I'm looking at on each. I also want to look at the cities where de Bont Beleggings has more recently acquired property. Germany. First I bring up a map of Berlin's most central borough—one comprised of what used to be both East and West Berlin—*Mitte*. I know de Bont has holdings here, but I'm not sure of the exact addresses off the top of my head. In an effort not to use precious screen space, I take out my iPhone and bring up the de Bont Beleggings website; the site contains a page listing their holdings. Once I have the addresses I manipulate the window, or Berlin map, to take up the left half of the screen, and I mark the de Bont properties with tiny squares of Wite-Out tape.

I open another window, bring up a map of Hamburg, and size this window for the screen's right half. I go through the same process—iPhone for addresses, locate properties on laptop screen, mark with Wite-Out tape squares. I sit back in my chair. The laptop screen is smaller than the desktop, but I have all four maps lined up, buildings marked on each, in front of me.

I study them. Left to right. Right to left. I study them.

If there's a pattern, I don't see it.

If the buildings in each city are close to something in particular, I don't see it.

I need another map. I stand up again, walk to my briefcase, take out my iPad, return to my desk, prop the iPad screen up to the left of the laptop—which is situated to the left of the desktop, and bring up a map of Rotterdam. No research necessary here—I'm very familiar with this market as I helped Cobus build his presence here. I quickly mark the properties with the Wite-Out tape squares, sit back, and study the three increasing in size screens.

What is it about these particular buildings? Is it all of them? Some of them? Should I be able to see what I need to studying these maps? Does the answer lie in properties—or something different altogether—nearby? In other buildings? In other—somethings?

This time I'm able to finally draw a conclusion. On my desktop, over the maps, I bring up my email. I compose a new one to Carolyn.

First thing, please call Frederick.

Frederick manages my air travel.

I need the G550 tomorrow night.

The G550 is the Gulfstream private jet I own.

I'll be traveling to Sciphol.

Sciphol—Amsterdam's main airport.

Alone.

*   *   *

8:48 a.m.

Perry and I are in my office. We're sitting on the couch. Perry looks like she just stepped off the pages of Vogue in a Hérve Léger Bare Combo Jacquard Bodycon Dress and BB Metallic Leather Manolo Blahnik pumps.

"You sleep at all last night?" she asks me.

"Not really."

"Damn. And you could *still* perform like that in the shower at the crack of dawn."

"Once I heard that water going, and thought of your naked little ass in there, figured why not—we both needed to get clean to start our day."

"Don't you mean get dirty?" Per says, her eyes on me while she takes a sip of coffee.

I look at my watch.

"I have a call with Duggard at nine thirty. Hopefully I can finally lock in his renewal. Want to listen in?" I ask.

"Love to, but I have an appointment."

"With?"

Perry pauses.

"A doctor's appointment."

"Ah. Liz?"

Liz is Perry's therapist. She's extremely well regarded in the world of psychology, and a friend of mine from high school. Once we returned from our time overseas, I asked Liz if she could squeeze Perry into her already packed caseload. Thankfully, she was able to.

I want to go there.

I can't go there.

Because she'll bring me there when she's ready.

Won't she?

Natey-Boy enters my office, iPad in hand. Like me, he's minus his suit jacket, but also like me he's tight from his perfectly knotted tie down to his brilliantly polished shoes. He looks at Perry first, trying desperately not to let his eyes linger too long. He barely succeeds. Then he looks at me.

"Good morning," he says as he slowly walks toward us. "You wanted to see me?"

"Sit, gorgeous," Perry says.

He looks at me.

Why did you text Perry yesterday at the crack of dawn?

"Go on," I assure him, "sit."

He does.

"I know I just threw this new project at you," I go on, "but remember, all you need to do is tee this up for me. Something. Anything. Just tee it up. And I'll hit that motherfucker off that tee and all the way to the green. Understood?"

"Of course, Jonah."

"Good. So—has anything popped onto your radar?"

"Actually, I think I may have something."

Of course you do. Because you're me not that long ago. A young animal looking to do one thing more than impress those you need to impress. Win.

"Let me have it," I say.

"It's in Manhattan, which I know is criteria number one. But it isn't currently a repair shop. I mean—isn't one exclusively."

"Exclusively?" I ask.

"It's a gas station. Now there's also a two-car garage on the site used for oil changes, tire changes, things like that."

The current configuration won't work—the site will need to be razed and the kind of garage Roddy is used to operating out of will need to be constructed. Does this make things more difficult? Yes. But it's very workable.

"Gas stations have been prime acquisition targets these last few years. That's how few sites remain in Manhattan for new development," Perry jumps in. "Where is it?"

"On the corner of First Avenue and Ninety-Third Street, right by the FDR."

"Is it currently in use?" I ask.

"It is, but the lease is coming up and the owner of the site won't even get a chance to jack the price on the operator. The guy who owns and runs the station wants out."

"I'm not surprised," I say, "the oil companies may be profit-generating beasts, but the margins in the actual gas station business are thin. It's a grind business. If the volume isn't there, it can be brutal. Tell me about the actual site. Gas stations are notorious in this city for being on oddly shaped parcels."

"This one is on basically a rectangular lot," he says.

Gas stations can be tricky acquisitions because of the environmental issues. There's always the possibility of contamination from underground wells that may have leaked. The bad news—a potential nightmare for rezoning for residential. The good news? We're not looking to rezone, as we'd be dealing with a similar use. Could actually be a nice, tidy fit.

"Who's the owner?" I ask.

He opens his iPad, swipes, and taps in his security code.

"I'm not sure who the principal is, but the owner of the site is a company listed as Biscayne Property and—"

"Fucking Anshel!" Perry and I exclaim in unison, me throwing my iPhone in the air and letting it land on the couch.

Perry starts cracking up.

"Just what we need," she says between cackles.

"Did I . . . Is there . . ." Landgraff stammers.

"Go on, Junior!" Perry implores Landgraff. "Ask who Fucking Anshel is!"

Landgraff looks from Perry to me.

"Anshel Greenbaum is old school," I explain. "He's one of the biggest old-money owners in this city—office properties, residential, mixed-use, all kinds of real estate."

"So why is he 'Fucking Anshel', and not just 'Anshel'?" Natey-Boy astutely asks.

"Because few people in this city hated my father as much as Anshel Greenbaum. They battled a bunch of times, and while Anshel is a man used to getting what he wants, my father put his face in the dirt more than once. Anshel hated my father. Which means by default he hates me."

"So what do you want me to do?" Landgraff asks.

Esparanza.

Cobus.

Madame Martine.

Do I really need this?

Why not. Fucking Anshel has had this day coming.

And I could use a way to release a little steam.

"I want you to keep looking for other options. But I also want you to set up the meeting. Let his office know you're a potential buyer—and nothing else. Pose as a potential station owner slash operator. Under no circumstances do you mention Resurrection. If he knows you're connected to me, he won't meet with you. His office will ask what it is in reference to. When you tell them the address they'll try to pass you off to one of his underlings; tell them your father—your boss—only meets with principals therefore you need to meet with Mr. Greenbaum. Not Anshel—respect—you always refer to him as Mr. Greenbaum. Got me?"

"Got you."

"Good. Get that meeting."

CHAPTER NINETEEN

10:10 A.M.

As I approach the closed door to Jake's office I hear faint music behind it, which in reality, I learn, is blaring when I turn the handle and enter. Some type of indie rock band it sounds like. Speaking is a waste of breath. I hold my hands out, sign language for "What the Fuck?"

"GELATINOUS SHITE!" Jake screams to me.

"GELATINOUS WHAT?" I yell back.

"SHITE! GELATINOUS SHITE!"

He air guitars for me for a few seconds—lip bite and all—then he taps his computer keyboard and turns it way down. Jake is minus jacket and tie with his top two buttons open, like always these days unless he's out of the office, or, if *in* the office, in the company of contemporaries or clients. His cheeks are flushed.

"Scottish indie punk band. My college buddy Carol manages bands, says they're really up and coming. Nice, right?"

"Is Carol a guy?" I ask.

"He is," Jake responds dejectedly. "I know—brutal name. I think getting into the music game was the only way he could get laid."

"Gelatinous Shite? That's really this band's name?" I go on, pointing to the speakers. "It's disgusting."

"What it is, my friend, is genius. Gelatinous Shite! Kids love crazy nonsense."

"How do you know what kids love?"

"Hey," Jake changes direction, "how's this for an idea—genetically engineered dark-meat-only chickens. Since, you know, the dark meat is so much more tasty. And, of course, for the more health conscious, the flip side—genetically engineered white-meat-only birds. Nice, right?"

I have no words. I just stare.

"Do you know any—what would I need for something like that—chemists?" he goes on.

I notice what I think is some kind of sandwich on his desk.

"What's that?" I ask, pointing.

"Cronut, bitch," he says with some urban sauce on his words.

"One of those things from downtown?"

"Damn straight—right out of Dominique Ansel's Soho bakery."

"Don't people line up down the block for those things?"

"They do. Which is why I had Jesse go downtown to wait in line for it."

Jesse is one of our young soldiers who's been in a bit of a slump.

"My way of letting him know if he can't get deals closed, he's of no more use to me than an errand boy," he goes on. "Anyway, you need to try these things. Simply—fucking—amazing. A heavenly marriage of a croissant and donut. Only I take it one step further. I slice mine in half—"

He slices his flat, facedown palm through the air for effect.

"—Then add ham, Swiss, mayo."

My right hand subconsciously covers my stomach.

"Dominique would be proud."

"No doubt. I actually emailed her a picture of this and other past creations. I haven't heard back from her yet."

"Just a heads up," I switch gears, "I'm going to Amsterdam tonight. I've been racking my brain for what Cobus might be up to—mapping the buildings he wants, mapping his portfolios in other markets, hypothesizing, postulating—I simply can't for the life of me figure out what he's up to. That's why I have to go back. I need to figure out what I'm missing."

Jake leans back in his chair and clasps his hands behind his head.

"Does it really matter? I mean, at the end of the day, according to you this needs to happen. Cobus hasn't given us a choice. A certain severed head and body to potentially follow tells us that—and it sounds like that's just scratching the surface for this dude. So looking at it from the opposite direction, wouldn't we almost be better off not knowing what he's into? That way we could at least claim ignorance if we ever had to?"

"It's not that simple. This isn't about saving our asses should Cobus go down. He's protected on a whole different level. He has governments in his pocket, municipalities, the works."

"Then back to my original question. Does it really matter?"

"It does. I need to know if others are being hurt by whatever is actually going on. Because now we're a part of that."

"What if you figure it out—and don't like what you find?"

My father always said, don't worry until you have a reason to.

"We'll deal with that when we get there. Anyway—I'm going solo, and the plan is to be there and back in twenty-four hours. I'm wheels up tonight at nine, which, between the flight length and time change, has me there at roughly six thirty a.m. tomorrow. Only you, Perry, and Carolyn know, and I want it to stay that way. Anyone asks where I am, I had to go out of town on last-minute business and I'll be back in a day or so."

"Done."

I look at my watch.

"We calling Gary?"

Gary Albert. Chief Acquisition Officer for Hunter Gaines, the

REIT that owns Eight Twelve Seventh Avenue, the Cobus target Jake is the point man for.

"We are."

"Where are you with him?"

"He knows we have a client who wants the building. I told him we were willing to come to the table with a number truly reflective of the market. He said while this isn't one of the properties in their portfolio they see as 'having been maximized in terms of value,' he has an obligation to his shareholders to listen. Once he said that, he'd laid out my angle. And not the one where I tell him unless he unloads the building to me, the world learns his wife sleeps with hot-shit retail broker Julie Kaye."

"No," I say, genuinely surprised by this nugget.

"Yes," he mouths to me while nodding his head yes.

I point at the phone.

"Let's get to it."

He hits the speakerphone button. Once there's a dial tone, he dials the number.

"Mr. Albert's office," a perky voice answers.

"Hi, Karen, it's Jake Donald."

"Yes, Mr. Donald, Mr. Albert is expecting you. One moment."

Three seconds later he picks up.

"Jake."

"Gary. What's happening over there at HG this morning? Have you guys put a man on Mars yet in your quest to take over the galaxy?"

"Not quite, smart-ass. But I did manage to walk on the surface of the Jacuzzi water at the spa yesterday. A couple old guys in towels were pretty freaked out. Does that count for anything?"

"Nice," Jake says, chuckling. "Gary, I'm here with Jonah."

"Jonah, how are you?"

"I'm well, Gary, thanks. All good by you?"

I genuinely like Gary Albert. He's one of the good guys—a fifty-something man who's gotten to the level he has with honesty and hard work. And he's no bullshit. If there's a deal to be made, he'll let you know. If there isn't, he'll let you know. If you do a good job of swaying his thinking, he'll let you know. If that's not going to happen, he'll let you know.

Unfortunately, guess he's not that solid in bed . . .

"Everything is just great. So as I said, Jake, I'll always listen when it comes to a property or properties in our portfolio. But as I also said, we're really not looking to call it a day with Eight Twelve. We just feel we still have too much upside with the property. That said, tell me what's on your mind."

"We have a real buyer who wants to put into play a real number."

"Who's the buyer?"

"I can't say yet. They are very private—both in company status as well as personality—and like to remain that way until they believe a pursued deal has strong likelihood of becoming reality. What I can tell you is they are a foreign player. And they are eyes-deep in cash."

"What is the number they are offering?"

"Before I throw it down, let's remember HG purchased this building just shy of nineteen months ago for five hundred thirty a foot for a total of three hundred eighty-four million and change, a number many would say was right on point in terms of the market at the time."

Eight Twelve Seventh Avenue is a forty-story office tower totaling seven hundred twenty-five thousand square feet. Simple math: 725,000 (Total Building Square Footage) x $530 (Price per Square Foot) = $384,250,000 (Purchase Price). If we are able to acquire the property the total square footage will probably go up slightly from seven hundred twenty-five thousand, because in New York

City—and only in New York City—buildings seem to grow when they change hands. Just part of the game.

"I appreciate the refresher, but I remember the price, being that I made the deal."

"I wanted to preface our offer with this reminder to make it immediately clear our number represents more than a hundred million dollars' profit in less than nineteen months. Our buyer is willing to pay six hundred eighty-five per foot for a total of four hundred ninety-six million and change."

"That's definitely a nice number, guys, but it's probably a tough sell over here. As I said we still believe we have upside in this property and can realize even higher gains in the next twenty-four to thirty-six months."

"Aren't you 97 percent leased?" Jake asks.

"We are. But between the under market leases rolling over in the near term and the Hudson Yards development, I can't help but—"

"With all due respect, Gary," Jake cuts him off, "Hudson Yards is almost twenty blocks lower than, and more west than, this property. Besides, we're talking about a forty plus percent ROI in less than nineteen months and a near guaranteed stock price bump."

My iPhone vibrates in my hand. Morante. I hold it up and point to it.

"You good?" I mouth to Jake.

He nods yes. I get up and head to the hallway, Jake and Gary's voices quickly fading behind me. The last thing I hear is Jake saying:

"What might your shareholders say about you passing that up?"

CHAPTER TWENTY

"Detective. How we doing?"

"I was able to get statements yesterday from more than half the crew Mr. Esparanza worked with, and something interesting happened. One of the girls I spoke with could barely sit still. Rosa Rivera. Pretty Spanish girl who can't be a day over twenty-five. When I asked why she was so nervous, she said because the police made her scared. That was all. I asked her why the police scare her, she just said they did. And that she didn't like talking to them."

"Fake nails?"

"Indeed. Fake nails."

"Light blue?"

"Bright red."

"Okay. So what about talking to her was interesting?"

"What was interesting was when she said she didn't know what happened. Before I even told her why we were speaking. I pressed her a bit after that, but she clammed up real hard. Then she asked if she had to talk to me anymore. When I said, technically no, she didn't; she was done."

"So what now?"

"I'm going to try and get the rest of the statements today. And when I speak to Mr. Billings, I'll be sure to remind him of my familiarity with his past. See if I can shake something from the tree."

"I've got something I think as well," I change direction. "When

I was speaking with Marilena about that night—if everything went on as usual—she said to me with all the cameras the building has I must have already looked for myself in terms of people coming and going. Like she was fishing. Or going with the reverse psychology approach. Or both."

"What did you tell her?"

"That we were still in the process of reviewing the video surveillance from that night."

"When we watched it, it was just as we were told—correct? Tiffany left at seven thirty, then Marilena was the last one out from their company just before ten."

"Correct," I confirm.

"Then go back and watch it again," Morante says. "It makes more sense for you to do it on your own—as you'll better recognize those coming and going from the building. And possibly something that was missed."

* * *

I walk into Hillstone on the corner of Fifty-Third and Third. As I descend the stairs into the basement restaurant, I see an already seated Minnie wildly waving her hands. Like she was literally staring at the stairs until she saw me.

"Minnie," I say as I reach the table, leaning down and kissing her bony cheek. "I figured a lady such as yourself would lunch somewhere like the Twenty-One Club."

"Fuck you, fancy boy. I had a craving for the spinach dip. You have a problem with that?"

"Not at all," I say, unbuttoning my suit jacket and sitting down. "It's the exact breath of fresh air I needed. I love this place. In fact—the best way to order the grilled chicken salad is with honey mustard instead of their usual peanut dressing. A pretty girl I once knew told me that."

"Well, look at you," Minnie responds, acting surprised. "Just a regular guy."

"If it were up to me, Minnie, lunch and dinner every day would be at Corner Bistro."

"You realize you're getting me hot being all down to earth and such, right?" She goes on, "Would it help my chances of getting a couple of your fingers my way under the table if I said I wasn't wearing any panties?"

"Not one bit," I say, matter of fact. "But it's always flattering, Minnie."

"Damn Perry. I figured, but at least it was worth a shot. By the way—I'm really not wearing any panties. Not because I thought you'd diddle me or anything, I just like the feeling of a brisk breeze on my crotch. With no obstruction. Straight-up air on cooch."

And you have no idea why your husband screwed around? You're like a fucking cartoon character.

"Interesting," I muster, completely clueless how to respond.

"Girl thing," she says, thankfully waving off the discussion. "We drinking?" she goes on.

"Not me," I answer, "I still have a lot of ground to cover today. But you go ahead."

Minnie flags the waiter over.

"What may I bring you?"

"Two glasses of pinot grigio," she says.

"Minnie, really, I—"

"Don't be a candy-ass," she cuts me off. "Our fathers used to down multiple martinis over lunch. No?"

I nod yes to the waiter, looking to move on, and he scampers off.

"So, Jonah, why this newfound interest in one of my best holdings?"

"As I said, the interest is a client's. Not mine. And I always go to bat for my clients, as you know."

"How serious are they?"

Let's hope not deadly.

"I think I'll let the number they're offering for the building answer that."

"I'm all ears."

"Six hundred and fifty per foot."

"You're right. That's a serious offer."

"Personally, I think it's a bit high, but the buyer wanted to show you two things—he has the means to play, and he wants to do this fast. It would be a record for the neighborhood, and six hundred and fifty million dollars in your account."

"Give or take a hefty commission for you."

"Which I deserve," I shoot back, "for making everyone happy. Then I go back to targeting properties for Resurrection."

"Must be a special client if you're handling this brokerage and not leaving it to the brokers working for you."

You might say that.

"Minnie, I want to be frank," I shift, leaning toward her. "I love this deal."

"Of course you do. Not only would—"

"No," I cut her off, leaning forward, placing my hand on hers, "I love this deal *for you*. And not just from the financial standpoint."

Sorry, Minnie.

Game time.

"What are you talking about?"

"I'm talking about that fact I have zero interest in property downtown on the water at this point for Resurrection. For the same reasons, as your friend, I'd love to see you get out of this property."

"What are you talking about? Why?"

I sit back in my seat.

"Look what happened with Sandy. Look how that storm tore downtown up. Do you not feel you were lucky to be spared? Do you not feel you could have just as easily been a property owner downtown dealing with huge problems?"

"We were definitely fortunate, Jonah. But—"

"Fortunate? Please. Years later buildings all around you are still dealing with issues from black mold to tenants running for the hills to structural foundation damage. Fortunate? I'd say more like spared by the grace of God."

"That may be, Jonah. But storms like that don't often come this high up the coast."

"True—but you're talking about the past, Minnie. Look at what's happening in the world today. Asia, South America, the States— life-altering storms are happening more and more frequently. And the experts in this field are all in agreement on one thing. This trend is going to continue. Me? I have no interest in investing in property that statistically puts me in a higher risk bracket for natural disasters. Too many people who trust me do so because they believe I have their best interests in mind. I owe it to them to steer clear—no offense—of a building like this one."

Minnie hangs on every word. The waiter places our glasses of wine down. To keep Minnie with me, and show her good faith, we clink and I down a healthy sip.

"I see an opportunity for you to not only shed what could one day become a huge headache, but be paid handsomely to do so," I go on. "Minnie—a smart businesswoman like you makes this deal. Every day."

I can see her wheels spinning.

"Isn't this advice you should be giving your client?"

"It is. That's why I told them they need to be mindful of the fact certain issues can arise that can affect the water table."

She smiles. Because, who doesn't like knowing the one in the middle has seemingly taken a side.

"Make this deal, Minnie," I continue. "It's the right move. And with this kind of cash on the table? It's the only move."

CHAPTER TWENTY-ONE

6:05 P.M.

Fuck.

Should I be doing this?

"How are you, sunshine?" I say, kissing Cass gently on her cheek.

"Sunshine, is it?"

"It is when we're not in a conference room with you trying to kick me in the balls."

"Business is business, Jonah. Besides, when did you become as sensitive as you are rough?"

"I've always been both. If you need a refresher, remember me waking you up at three in the morning."

Cass blushes.

"I thought we were here to talk business, Jonah. For me to get a firsthand account of your vision for my client's site."

"We are. And we will. First, what are you drinking?"

We're at the bar in Arlington Club, one of the few swank spots on the Upper East Side. The vaulted-ceiling, earth-tone space serving up the unique combination of steak and sushi is bustling. Cass always looks beyond fine, and this evening's no different. She's dressed in a black, form-fitting pants suit she's no doubt been wearing all day.

I catch the bartender's eye and order us a round. I turn back to Cass.

"Off the record, you look phenomenal," I say.

Damn, haven't I learned?

"Let me guess . . . *hot yoga! It's changed my life!*" I go on mockingly, my voice a few octaves higher than usual.

"Asshole," she counters, smiling. "Yes, I mean—no, no hot yoga, but yes, I've been exercising, or working out, or whatever."

"Yeah, well, whatever you're doing, it's working. I've seen that ass live. I can only imagine how it might work a Stairmaster into submission."

"Stop it, Jonah," Cass cuts into me, playfully slapping me on the knee. "Your days of seeing my ass live are long gone. And what would Perry think if she heard you speaking like this?"

"She hears me speak like this all the time."

"I mean to me."

I know this girl. I don't answer. Because I know my silence—right now, in the wake of this discussion—is all she wants to hear.

Does this make me awful?

Human?

Shit!

"Anyway, on that note," she continues, "sometimes we can't have what we want simply because we want it. Turning this now, of course, to our potential deal since you gave me the perfect lead-in."

The bartender places our drinks in front of us. The best tequila in the house over a couple rocks for me, a glass of sauvignon blanc for her. We clink glasses.

"Cheers," we say in unison.

"It's nice to see you," I go on.

"You too," she replies.

We both go to take our first sip.

"How nice?" I ask, just before letting the liquid pass through my lips.

She finishes her sip.

"Stop it, Jonah."

She returns her glass to the bar.

"Stop what?"

"Stop taking me back to a time when we sat across the table for dinner. Not business."

"Don't be so serious. We had fun."

"Yes, we did. Unfortunately while that's where we ended for you, I thought we were building something together."

"We were young, Cass."

"Screw that. Too easy an excuse for you. At least have the backbone to say you were scared, or you still had too many girls you wanted to fuck, or we all know boys mature slower than girls—anything but 'we were young, Cass.'"

Score.

Desired nerve struck.

"You want honesty? 'D.' All of the above."

We both take a sip of our drinks.

"Now was that so hard?"

"No," I answer. "Now I'd like an honest answer from you. Then we can get on with our business."

"What's the question?"

"Did you come here thinking strictly business? Or were you equally looking forward to the possibility of sitting here, at this bar, having these cocktails, talking about anything *but* business?"

As she thinks, her lips part. She touches the tip of her tongue to the bottom of her front teeth.

"Why don't you at least ask me a question you don't know the answer to."

My phone rings.

Perry.

"What's happening, beautiful?" I ask, my eyes locked with Cass'.

"A few things, actually."

"Go."

"Dante is at the house right now. I decided to let him handle your packing for me, since—you know—he does love focusing on how his 'boss-man' dresses. And because I'm stuck in the office with Natey-Boy working on next week's presentation since he had no choice but to spend all day on your new requirement. I hope that's okay with you. That . . . and the fact Dante's probably in your underwear drawer at this very moment."

"That's fine. Just remind him about the fact I need to wear—"

"Wear only Assiagi," Perry finishes my sentence. "I know. I already gave him the rundown. Once he's done he'll be back to you and waiting out front. It won't be long. Keep your eye on the time."

"What's next?"

"Natey-Boy wants us to have dinner with him and his girlfriend. I think we should. Admit it, Jonah—he's you back in our days working for Tommy. He's been killing it for us. He's earned a night on the town with us."

What's really going on here?

"Besides," Perry continues, "I saw a picture of her and she's a freakin' smoke show. You'll love staring at her for a little while."

"You know his having dinner with us, no business or clients involved, will undoubtedly send some waves of envy rolling through the office."

"I do."

"And?"

"And I say good. Let it. Competition is as healthy as it is necessary. Within the walls as well as outside of them."

Spoken like a true power-beast.

"Then let's do it."

"I'll leave a note for Carolyn."

I mouth "I'm sorry" to Cass, and put my finger up indicating I'll just be another few moments. She gives me the, "of course, take your time" face.

"I'm just finishing up here," I go on, "anything else?"

"Yes. I need to go to Miami for the night. Malkoff is down to the Southeast Financial Center and Wells Fargo Center and wants me to help him make the final decision between the two."

Malkoff is Justin Malkoff, who manages the real estate affairs for U.S. based KoolBev, one of the largest beverage conglomerates in the world. KoolBev is a large client of ours, and they are relocating their Southeastern headquarters.

"Of course. When?"

"Not sure yet, but definitely within the next few days."

We finish the conversation and I return to Cass.

"Everything okay?" she asks.

I take a nice sip of my tequila.

"Everything is just fine. So, you ready to hear my vision for your client's site?"

When it comes to real estate, there is always one player who can make or break any particular deal. Usually it's the owner or the final decision maker on the buyer side; perhaps it's the broker or the engineers hired to inspect a property who present a case for structural issues and such. In this case—it's the seller's attorney who between her pedigree and hotness has a serious hold on her client. And, unfortunately for her, the problem isn't just that there's ample room here for her to let a personal situation drive the potential business for all of us.

The problem for her is that I'm aware of this.

"I am," she answers.

"Great. Before we start, turns out Perry needs to head out of town

for a night later this week. Should I give you the full picture now—
or should we split the discussion into two sessions? I wouldn't want
us to have to rush through it . . ."

Don't. This isn't right.

Or is there no choice?

Time will tell.

"Don't play with me, Jonah."

We each down the last swallow of our drinks. I gesture to the
bartender for another round. Our eyes again locked, I make sure my
chin is confidently high.

"Why not?"

CHAPTER TWENTY-TWO

"JONAH, WE'RE LOOKING at twenty minutes or so until we begin taxiing," Ken, the pilot says.

"Great. Thanks."

Ken disappears into the cockpit. The G550 is a luxurious private jet on the larger side, comfortably able to carry up to fourteen passengers intercontinentally. Tonight, amongst the polished mahogany and brass finishes, it's just me. Settling into a big, plush, caramel leather chair about mid-cabin, I stare out the window at the personnel and odd-shaped airport vehicles coming and going, preparing us for liftoff. Soon Jennie, my usual flight attendant, appears from the galley.

"Good evening, Mr. Gray. May I bring you something to drink?"

Jennie is a tall, sultry brunette with a scratchy, soulful voice. Every time I see her I think she's more country western star than flight attendant. Yet, once again, here she is.

"Do we really have to do this every time?" I answer her question with one of my own, returning my eyes to the cabin, to her. "Jonah. Please. Call me Jonah."

"Of course, Jonah."

"Thank you."

I check the time. 8:45 p.m. Five hours and change flight time plus a six-hour forward time difference equals me needing to get a few hours of sleep.

"Do we have any tequila on board?" I continue.

"Will Gran Patron Platinum do?"

"It will. Tall glass. Just a couple rocks."

"You got it."

I take my MacBook Air out of my briefcase and fire it up. I had hoped to finally get a look at the Three Twenty One Park security footage from the night in question on the way to the airport but got stuck on several calls. As I log into the web-based surveillance system we use for all Resurrection properties, and choose the appropriate building, Jennie places my cocktail down along with a plate of cheese, grapes, and crackers. I thank her and take two huge gulps of the tequila.

I decide to go back to the night in question, and watch the main entrance of the building, working backwards from the time Marilena supposedly left. Just as I had previously seen, at 9:55 p.m. Marilena exited the property, alone. I cue the time up to begin an hour earlier, at 8:55 p.m. I press play.

As I watch I see nothing out of the ordinary. Traffic is thin this time of the evening, as most have long gone for the day. There's a stretch of fourteen minutes at one point when no one comes or goes. Still, I watch as though I'm viewing the most eagerly anticipated Hollywood blockbuster of the year. I barely notice when the jet barrels down the runway and takes off.

"May I bring you another?" Jennie says once we're airborne and cruising.

I look at my empty glass.

"Please," I answer.

I look back at my computer screen. When I do, I see something as interesting as it is unexpected. I hit pause, but I've already missed him. I rewind a few frames and let it play again. Yes, it's him. I rewind again and hit play. This time I hit pause at exactly the right moment.

Greg Shand.

The founder and owner of Spectrum Global.

Spectrum Building Services, the cleaning company Mr. Esparanza worked for that cleans our buildings, is one subsidiary of Spectrum Global. Global handles all of the competencies a building might need from the cleaning services to the security guards to even the messenger centers—a subsidiary called Spectrum Swiftly. It's literally one-stop shopping for commercial property owners to cover all bases. We use Spectrum for all of these services throughout our entire portfolio.

I look at the time he entered the building. 9:29 p.m. Shand owns a small empire; his company employs over five thousand people. There's no doubt a guy like this has a streamlined hierarchy in place to handle all day-to-day building-related affairs, from the menial through management level oversight. So why would he show up at this particular property, at this time of night, on a date where not only a member of his overnight cleaning crew died, but there may have been a security breach?

Jennie places my fresh cocktail down. Before touching it, I take out my iPhone. Until we're further out over the ocean I should still have service. I call Morante. He doesn't pick up. I leave a voice mail.

I look back at the screen. Greg Shand. I move forward again with the footage to see when he exited the property. Like I've seen now multiple times, out comes Marilena at 9:55, alone. Just as alone as Shand is when he exits at 10:22 p.m. I rapid-fire a few grapes into my mouth. Then like a college kid, I down my huge glass of tequila in one shot without coming up for air.

* * *

"Jonah, it's time to wake up," I hear.
I know that voice.

And it's not Jennie.

My eyes, heavy, slowly open in spite of a hangover just settling in. I'm lying on the soft, charcoal leather couch across from where I was sitting earlier. I can see my laptop still on the table where it was earlier, the screen dark while in sleep mode. The cabin is softly lit. Outside the windows the world is still black. All I hear is the whirring of the two Rolls Royce engines. We must still be midflight.

Then why wake me?

"Jonah, it's time to wake up," I hear again.

Cobus.

I look up through groggy eyes. He's standing over me. His eyes and expression are stern, dead serious. As I take him in, he takes a few steps backward so I can see more of him. He's wearing his suit pants, but the shirt is gone. His hairless torso is lean, shredded, each muscle from his stomach up to his shoulders then down through his forearms and hands as if cut from stone. From his waistline up to his neck, right where the top of his collar rests, he's covered with finely written, intricate, orderly ink. There are words, names, numbers, as if his body is some sort of journal or ledger.

The last time I saw these tattoos was when they were first revealed to me. Two years ago, on a private jet from New York City to Moscow. We were going to find, and retrieve, Perry. And Cobus—or whoever this man really is—was explaining to me I had only survived my journey because he had my back.

"Who are you?" I remember asking.

"You'll never have my name. And you don't want it," he answered. "There are a number of large organized crime syndicates in this world. Let's just say one of them answers to me."

I look left. Then right. No sign of Jennie anywhere. I look back at Cobus.

"How did you get here?"

He dismisses my question, and gives me one of his own.

"Do you remember this writing? Do you remember what it means?"

He told me on that same flight.

"Insurance," he said. "Dirt. Bargaining power. Though few can get to me—or even know my true identity—there are a lot of people who want me brought down in this world. I'm very careful about who I get in bed with. But when I do decide to deal with someone, there's nothing for buying loyalty like showing them their name, next to an account number I know they use for money laundering, tattooed on my body. Or maybe their name next to an address that represents a safe house where a certain missing person is buried in the concrete foundation. My connections run deep—in business, in government, in the underworld. No one will ever get to me, and they know that. This—what you see—is my way of letting those I allow into my world, whether they like it or not, know there is no turning back. And they'd better be looking out for my best interests. Because it doesn't matter whether it's the authorities or another crime syndicate. There isn't a database in the world that can bring down the house more than my body should it fall into the wrong hands."

"Do you remember," Cobus asks again, his voice louder now. "And do you remember that photographs of this writing—photographs of every millimeter of this body—are with the proper people in case of a day I might end up in hands other than those of my choosing?"

"Yes," I respond. "I remember."

Without another word he steps back to me. He reaches down, grabs a fistful of the shirt where it covers my chest, and sits me up. With his left hand he grips the back of my head like it's a softball as he slightly turns his torso right. He pulls my face to within three inches of the rear end of his external oblique muscle, on the side of his body just above his belt.

"What do you see?" he asks through clenched teeth.

I see Jonah Gray tattooed on his body in black ink. Beneath it, I see Ivan Janse. Under both names, there's more writing. I squint as I try to make out what it says.

"You owe me, Jonah," he continues, his voice tainted now with a slight growl.

"We're even," I reply, still trying to make out the words.

Damn.

Why can't I read this?

Are these words written in script?

Stop moving.

Fuck!

He squeezes his fingers tighter around my head. I reach back with my right hand and grab his wrist, still trying to make out the words under my name.

My names.

"You. Owe. Me. Jonah. Now stop worrying about things you needn't worry about. Get back to New York. And get the fuck to work!"

* * *

"Jonah, it's time to wake up," I hear.

Lying on the plush, charcoal-gray leather couch across from where I sat at the beginning of the flight, I flinch backward as my eyes open.

"I'm sorry," Jennie says, "I didn't mean to scare you. It's just that we're about thirty minutes out of Schiphol, and I know you like to freshen up, change, and have a little something to eat before touchdown."

Schiphol. Amsterdam's international airport.

The cabin is filled with sunlight. Across from me I see my laptop still on the table where it was earlier, the screen dark in sleep mode. I look around for Cobus, realizing immediately he's not here.

"I have your fresh clothes hanging right over here," Jennie goes on.

"Right. Thanks, Jennie," I say, my voice raspy as it sputters to life.

I look at the clothes hanging on a hook on the wall about twenty-five feet from me.

"Some coffee, perhaps? Or some ice water?"

"I'd love an iced coffee. Just a little skim milk. Thanks."

"Of course."

Jennie heads off to the galley. I look at my watch. It's 7:55 a.m. in the Netherlands. My first instinct is to call Morante and tell him what I saw on the footage. But I realize this will have to wait until later as 7:55 a.m. here means 1:55 a.m. back home.

I stand up. When I do, I feel a terrible pain in my right thigh. Without taking another step I undo my belt and lower my previous day's suit pants to my knees. There's a bunch of thin, centimeter-long stab wounds—maybe twelve or fifteen of them—in my right thigh near the previous cuts. I touch them gingerly with my right hand. As I do, out of the corner of my eye, I notice one of my sterling silver collar-stays on the ground next to the couch I was sleeping on. With my right hand I reach up and touch my right collar. Sure enough, the collar-stay slot is empty.

I pull my pants back up, pick up the collar-stay, and head to the bathroom. The door closes behind me and I splash my face with water. I—Jonah Gray—stare into the mirror. Only to see Ivan Janse—the man I was known to the world as my last time in Amsterdam—staring back at me.

Jonah Gray.

Ivan Janse.

Once this jet's wheels touch that ground, it's going to take both of us to get what I need.

CHAPTER TWENTY-THREE

AFTER FINISHING WITH the customs agents who've come on board, I deplane. There isn't a cloud in the sky. It's a beautiful day in Amsterdam. Sunglasses on, I descend the stairs leading from the G550, my left hand holding my briefcase handle. Fifty feet away there's a Mercedes AMG S65 waiting for me. A chauffeur is standing next to the rear door, which is open.

"*Zuidas*," I say once we're both in place and the car is moving.

Zuidas means South Axis in Dutch. The South Axis is the most important business district in Amsterdam, where the most prominent contemporary commercial real estate properties stand. De Bont Beleggings—Cobus' firm—has numerous holdings there. Including the Vinoly Tower. Where the company is headquartered.

Where I used to go to work every day.

"Vinoly Tower," I continue.

I look at the Perregaux World Time. 8:39 a.m. The distance from *Schiphol* to *Zuidas* is a little over fifteen kilometers, or about ten miles. It's rush hour. Which means, from past experience, a trip that should take eleven or twelve minutes will take between twenty and twenty-two.

We leave the airport grounds, and head east on the A4. My eyes pass over the lush green fields dotted with billboards, and the smallish buildings here and there lining the landscape, but I see none of it. My mind is filled with all kinds of memories, while my heart is filled with all kinds of mixed emotions. Eight years of my life were spent in this country. Eight years on the run, rebuilding my life with a new identity, with two objectives in mind. Clearing my name. And returning Perry and Max home safely. In the two years since I've been back in New York City, I never thought I'd see Amsterdam again.

I hoped I'd never see Amsterdam again.

At 9:01 a.m., the buildings of the *Zuidas* come into sight. On my right I pass the postmodern Meyer and van Schooten designed ING House, world headquarters of ING Group. Nicknamed *de kruim-eldief*, or the dustbuster in English, the iconic structure built like a table on angled steel legs looks more like a spaceship than an office building. Soon up ahead I see the glass, patchwork-looking façade of WTC H—the twenty-five story tower of the country's World Trade Center site. I see the contemporary, Pi de Bruijn-designed Symphony Office Tower—home to high-profile tenants such as the Holland Financial Centre, Arcadis, and Prologis. Symphony—the third tallest building in all of Amsterdam—is one of the most distinctive looking in the *Zuidas* due to its fusion of different brick types mixed with arresting colors and terraced facades. Off to the left, across the highway, is the glass Akzo Nobel Tower completed in 2011. I think of home when I see the Erick van Egeraat-designed, twenty-four-story office tower called The Rock. Its expressive design looks like it would be right at home on the downtown portion of Manhattan's West Side highway.

I have the chauffeur stop about a hundred feet from the building. He opens the door. I get out. The door is closed behind me, but I don't move. I spend a few moments just staring up at the structure. And going over the plan in my mind.

Vinoly Tower looks like a giant glass and steel 'L', the top of said L appearing to have a couple giant cracks running down the exterior of the building that are actually staircases. Having left my briefcase in the car, I start toward the target, blending right in with everyone taking part in the morning rush. I move into the plaza with the herd, past the row of parked bicycles and motorcycles, toward the main entrance. But I don't enter. I keep walking. In my favor is the fact I know every single thing there is to know about this property. Something I'm counting on.

Once I'm out of the field of view of the main entrance security cameras, I stop, turn, cross my arms, and look up at the building. But I don't just look up. I act as if I'm *studying* the façade. Why? In case someone—anyone—has noticed the soul that has strayed from the pack and appears headed for the side of the building. To anyone looking at me now, I look like I must in some capacity work for, or with, the landlord.

After about thirty seconds I start walking again, my arms still folded and my head down as I walk, an appearance of being deep in thought. Fifty more feet, further yet from the masses, I stop and do it again. Thirty seconds later, again I'm on the move. I finally round the corner that takes me to the back of the building.

Immediately I head toward the service area of the structure. As I walk past the loading bays, concerned that even though I've been gone a couple years someone may recognize me, I pretend to be speaking on my cell. This, in conjunction with a slight turn of my face away from those moving about, helps me shield myself.

Past the commotion, and the last truck being unloaded in the fourth bay, there's a ramp up along the wall that leads into the building. I head right for it. I literally hear my father's voice in my head.

"Anyone can belong anywhere, at anytime. Just play the part."

As I near the top of the ramp and approach the door, I see my potential obstacle. I tuck my cell away. Next to the door, face high, there's a small panel with both a keypad and a small camera—a facial recognition access system I helped integrate into the de Bont Beleggings portfolio a year or so prior to my exiting the firm. Hoping I was never removed from the system I subtly look around, then position my face in front of the camera as I feel I'm clear. A simultaneous beep and green blink of a light on the panel lets me know I'm a go.

Once inside, very familiar with my surroundings, I head straight for the service elevator that will take me to the basement. I hit the down button; the doors open immediately as it is idling on the ground floor. I step inside, hit "B," and begin to descend.

The elevator stops. Quietly, carefully, I step out of the cab, my head still straight, my eyes still forward. Immediately I'm surprised by what feels like the cold steel tip of a gun against my left temple. I stop in my tracks.

"*Kan ik u helpen?*" a deep voice asks.

"Can I help you?" in Dutch.

"*Ik geloof dat je kan,*" I respond, calmly, my Dutch still intact as if I'd spoken it five minutes ago. "*U ziet—*"

I feel it happening.

I feel myself going to that place few can go.

A place I've been.

A place I need.

Mid-sentence, like a flash of lightning as my assailant is processing my words, my left hand shoots up and grabs the wrist holding the gun like a magnet to metal. In the same motion, my right hand comes across in front of me and grabs my new friend's balls like a bear trap. There is no need for an increase in pressure. I'm squeezing as hard as I can on impact.

"Aaahhh!"

"*Laat de knop los,*" I snarl. "*Nu.*"

"Drop it. Now."

Grip still on his balls like a vice, I pull back showing him I *will* separate his testicles from his body. The gun falls away, clattering on the concrete floor. I drop my forehead into his nose, shattering the bridge. He falls back into the wall, his hands cupped over his face. A spider web of blood starts streaming through his fingers, down, around, into his mouth, and down his neck as if a faucet has been turned on.

How did he know I was coming?

Was he watching, and waiting?

Was someone else?

I pick up the gun. Glock 42. Serious piece. I put the tip between his eyes. This is a commercial building, so tenants have the ability to access their basement storage space at their leisure without guns being put to their heads.

"How did you know I was coming?" I go on.

Blood streaming steadily, he says nothing. I jam the tip of the Glock into the skin between his eyes so hard it pins his head against the wall. I keep pushing.

"Aaahhh!" he groans again, the blood in and around his mouth bubbling as the air comes through his lips.

"How?" I press.

Through squinted eyes he summons the strength to stare me down like a man. Then, for a split second, he can't help from keeping his eyes from looking up over my shoulder at the ceiling. Knowing the property as well as I do, there's no need to inquire as to the object of his interest. It's a security camera.

Is someone on the way?

Is he just hoping someone is?

I can't chance anything. I'm guessing I have minimal time. I can stay and question a man whom I'm seemingly going to have to break to get answers from, or I can have a quick look around. Choosing the latter I step back to my new friend. Then crack him across the side of the head with the Glock, knocking him to the ground.

"Get what you need," Pop always said. "Clean up the mess later."

Writhing on the ground, smearing blood on the clean, smooth, polished gray painted floor, still cupping his nose, he turns onto his back. When he does, I kick him square across the face, laying him out cold.

I move forward into the basement. I can tell immediately the configuration is different, something I imagine has been done since I've last been here in order to accommodate whatever it is Cobus has going on. I can go right or left, but choose to go down the corridor running straight from the elevator, as if dividing the basement into two sides. Immediately I notice it used to be longer. I come to a wall about a hundred or a hundred and fifty feet closer than I did in the past. Again, I can go right or left. Knowing the footprint of the building it is clear to me this has been done to create a more efficient use of potential useable square footage. Or, in simpler terms, create more space.

About forty feet down each hallway, facing one another, I see two doors. I decide to go left. Walking briskly, Glock in my right hand held up in front of my chest, my soles against the painted concrete create a series of small rapid-fire echoes. When I reach the doors, I first look at the one on my left. It's a brushed steel door with a simple knob with a keyhole in the center. There's a small signage plate next to it that says "Devinshire Technologies"—a tenant who's been in the property, and has had storage space in the basement, about seven years. I look at the door on my right, directly across the hall. The door is exactly the same. Only this one, along with the simple knob, has two additional locks that clearly use very different keys. And there's no tenant signage plate.

Knowing it's a long shot I still reach for the knob, which is locked as suspected. Not a second later, back where I came from, I hear the elevator doors open. Immediately I hear footsteps coming. And while I can't be sure how many people there are, what I am sure of is that it's definitely more than one.

There are stairwells leading up and out in all four corners of the basement. But because of the reconfiguration, I can't be sure they are still accessed as I remember. My best bet is definitely heading back to the elevator and going from there, but that's out. From my calculations, heading back that way would have me running square into whoever this is at the moment I turned right, and they turned left.

Knowing there's no way of keeping my footsteps quiet, I take off, away from them, continuing down the hallway. Immediately I hear their pace pick up to match mine. I reach the end, and can only go right. I turn, but before sprinting on, I look back. Just as I do, two guys, dressed in dark suits like the original dude I dropped at the elevator, come around the corner where I'd made my first decision to go left. They, too, have guns. And they know where I am, as there was no slowing down for a directional decision.

They're coming.

I take off. Even in my haste, I notice the intermittent brushed steel doors lining both sides of the hallway. Just as I can hear my pursuers approaching the turn behind me, I come to yet another right or left decision. No time. My sense of direction telling me to go right leads me back into the belly of the beast. And that to go left keeps me moving toward daylight.

As I push off my right heel, they turn the corner behind me. Each fires their gun, missing me, as I disappear. Finally, up ahead, I see an "Exit" sign. I blast through the door underneath it, barely breaking stride, and bound up the two flights of stairs three steps at a time. I come to the ground-floor landing, holster the gun in the rear waist portion of my pants under my suit jacket, and exit the property.

Within seconds I realize I'm at one of the front corners of the building. Immediately I blend into those walking through the plaza in front of the structure. Moving fast enough to create distance from my new friends, but not too fast as to draw attention to myself, I never look back. Soon, I'm back in the car, and we're heading out of the *Zuidas*.

CHAPTER TWENTY-FOUR

"*BEWEGEN. NU,*" I bark to the driver from the back of the Mercedes. "*Sneller!*"

"Move. Now. Faster!"

I'll stick with the English translations going forward.

We take off down the street. I turn around and look out the rearview mirror. Once outside, it seems my two new friends barely chased me. I turn back around and face forward. Within sixty seconds we're going west—the opposite direction we came in—on the A4.

What the fuck just happened?

How could they have known I was coming?

Was the security guard in the basement waiting for me? For Ivan? For Jonah?

Did he come at me simply because I wasn't recognized as a tenant?

The plan for the morning was to take a quick tour of Cobus' properties—more specifically, the basements in Cobus' properties—in Amsterdam. But the plan had apparently just changed. Without question there would now be a portfolio-wide alert put out about me, if there wasn't already. Which meant forget another basement—I'd be lucky to get within a hundred feet of another building.

Is it Cobus himself who alerted them?

If yes—how?

The email to Carolyn—is he monitoring my email?

The conversations with Perry.

Is he listening in on my cell?

Is he listening to my office?

Breathe. Slow down. Think. The plan now changes—because it has to.

"Central Station," I say to the driver.

The city of Amsterdam proper, often referred to as the "Venice of the North," is actually ninety or so small islands connected by approximately twelve hundred bridges. The chest cavity of the city is a series of half-moon shaped canals that tighten as you get closer to the heart—*Dam* Square and the city's main train station, Central Station. I see the driver nod to me in his rearview mirror. He takes the next exit off the highway. We need to change course and go north. No doubt he's looking for the s108.

Leaving Europe without an understanding about what Cobus is up to—has us up to—is not an option. So if I can't see his buildings in Amsterdam, I'll hit another city in the de Bont Beleggings portfolio. The Mercedes makes its way deeper and deeper into the city. The sprawl of the contemporary *Zuidas* and highways gives way to a more intimate, old-world cornerstone of European history. I swallow as a wall of memories crashes over me like a wave in the ocean. The streets lined with different color and height canal houses; the canals lined with different shaped and styled houseboats. I lower the rear windows to smell, and feel, the flowery air flow through the car, through me. We pass what seems like an endless collection of seventeenth-century footbridges for traversing the canals. With each that slides by I wonder when the last time was my own feet walked over it. And I remember other bridges not within eyeshot but close by—like the *Magere Brug* with its stone façade painted an unusual white, or the barred windows under the *Torensluis* Bridge that reminds passersby it was part of what was once a prison—I had crossed with Perry, and Max.

Soon we're headed north on *Oudezijds Voorburg*, one of the valves going straight into Amsterdam's heart. The car stops in traffic directly in front of the red bricks of one of Amsterdam's finest hotels—Sofitel Legend The Grand Amsterdam. I take out my iPhone to call Carolyn. After pausing, I power it off and put it back in my jacket pocket.

"Does your mobile have international access?" I ask the driver.

"It does."

"May I borrow it?"

He hands me his Vodafone-powered Samsung Galaxy S5 Gold. I hand him five hundred Euro in cash.

"I need twenty-four hours before you replace it. Can you do that?"

"You got it, Mr. Gray."

I jump out of the car, briefcase in hand, and continue north to the corner. I come to *Damstraat* and make a left. The narrow street through the old city is jammed. Tourists, mostly, on the cobblestone sidewalks stream in and out of all different types of restaurants from the casual dining of the Carne Argentina to the fast-foody New York Pizza.

Heading west now I text Carolyn's cell phone: *Calling you in 30 secs from int'l cell. Please pick up.* I continue at a brisk pace down *Damstraat*. Thirty seconds later I call.

"Jonah. What is this number?"

"Doesn't matter, Carolyn. I'm sorry to wake you in the middle of the night, but there's been an urgent change of plans. I'm about to take a train to Rotterdam, so I need you to have the jet meet me there as soon as possible, as I may need to leave in a hurry. And I need you to handle this via your cell phone only—no email, no landline. Got it?"

"Understood, Jonah. Where will you be going from Rotterdam?"

"Hamburg."

"Hamburg it is. Is everything okay?"

"Everything is fine. Until I return, you can get me on this number. If Perry or Jake asks anything, be sure to explain my whereabouts only if no one else is around, verbally, and quietly. No discussing any of this with them on their cells or email. All correspondence via our usual avenues is to remain strictly business."

"Got it, Jonah. I'll have the Gulfstream move to Rotterdam immediately where it will be ready and waiting to be wheels up at a moment's notice. All I need from you is a simple text once you're on your way to the airport."

"You're the best. Till later."

I hang up just as I come to *Dam* Square at the end of *Damstraat*. One of the three busiest and most well-known squares in all of Amsterdam, today is no exception. People are coming and going on foot and bikes in every direction. There are children, elderly, people from near and far. On the circular, plateaued steps encircling the white travertine National Monument, people are sitting and chatting with coffee and breakfast while others quietly read a book or newspaper.

I check my watch. 10:01 a.m., which means 4:01 a.m. at home. I cross the square and come face to façade with the neoclassical Royal Palace, a building that served as city hall from 1655 until 1808 when it was converted to a royal residence. I turn right onto *Damrak*, a busy thoroughfare, and head north toward *Centraal* Station. With each step I take, the amount of people coming and going from the city's hub swells. On my left I pass everything from souvenir stores to a Subway to a small casino to a sex museum.

About seven hundred fifty meters later I see that I'm upon *Centraal* Station. The scene in front of my destination can be a bit daunting for those not native; it is a serious labyrinth of intersecting streets, trolley rails, crosswalks, and street signs that seem to flow in no particular order whatsoever. People zigzag at a constant clip via foot, automobile, trolley, and bicycle. Being that I spent almost eight years of my life in this city, I barely pause as I step off the curb. I perfectly time my line clear through the chaos, like a mosquito flying between raindrops.

Paranoia has me not even wanting to use a credit or debit card for fear of being tracked. There are vending machines for tickets servicing only those stations in the Netherlands—so people don't have to wait on the lines with those sorting out more complicated itineraries—but while they accept cards they do not accept cash. Only Euro coins. Hence, the change machines.

I make my change and head straight down the main corridor, passing a HEMA store, a Starbucks, and a Heineken boutique selling not just the beer but all sorts of branded Heineken clothes and trinkets. It isn't long until I hit a bank of the yellow automatic ticket vendors. The next train for Rotterdam leaves in eighteen minutes. I slide in just shy of twenty-five euro for a first-class ticket, in order to have more space around me, and wait for my little yellow ticket. Once I have it in hand, I head straight for Track Four.

I find the first-class cabin and walk toward the front. There aren't many people making the trip from Amsterdam to Rotterdam this morning, as I immediately not only take count of five but also size each one up in terms of threat level. Nothing too thought provoking. An older couple trying to make sense of a map they're holding up, and three kids way more into whatever app it is on the iPad they're hovering over than my presence. I settle into one of the wide, soft gray chairs facing another just like it. There's a small table between the two seats jutting out from just below the window.

I place my suit jacket over the opposite chair, put my briefcase down next to the chair I'm sitting in, and take out my iPad. I look at the World Time. Three minutes until we get moving. Knowing the ride should be about an hour and seventeen minutes I calculate my arrival time. My eyes move back to the tablet, and all the photos I have to swipe through—shots I took in my home office of all the marked-up maps I had lined up.

My eyes stop on the map of Rotterdam. In the two years since my time working with Cobus, his holdings in the Netherlands had grown considerably. But while growth in cities like The Hague and Utrecht have been minimal, the bulk of the growth has taken place in Rotterdam.

Why?

What's so special about Rotterdam?

Or Hamburg, Germany? Where for some reason de Bont Beleggings' growth has been significantly more robust than the more valuable real estate in Berlin?

I look up as I see movement at the rear of the first class cabin. Someone has joined us. He's somewhere in his thirties and tall, probably six foot two or three, with an athletic build and dome-bald head. He's wearing sunglasses. He's dressed in jeans, a tucked-in white button-down open at the collar, a navy blazer, and nice, brown, tie-up leather shoes. He's talking on the phone, a *De Telegraaf*—Amsterdam's most widely circulated newspaper—under his arm. He never looks my way as he takes a seat.

Subtly, I watch his every move as he gets settled.

Ninety seconds later the train pulls out. I think of the gun in my waist. Acting natural, I return my attention to my iPad. After ten minutes or so more of poring over my maps and notes, I close the iPad and return it to my briefcase.

I glance at Dome-Head. He's reading his paper. I turn and look out the window at the passing countryside keeping him in my peripheral vision. The green fields gliding by seem endless. They're dotted with farmhouses adjacent to the parcels being cultivated. Interfering with nature at one long stretch are power lines running adjacent to the rails. Thirty minutes in we pass a turbine farm so vast I can't see where it ends, harnessing wind for energy.

There it is. I feel it in my gut, in my balls, Dome-Head just glanced at me. How could he possibly be following me? When—literally—I have no idea whose phone I'm even using?

Only Carolyn and those managing the jet know I'm on my way to Rotterdam.

Frederick?

I shake my head, giving myself a "snap the fuck out of it." There's no way this guy can possibly be tailing me. As we're rolling into the stop for The Hague, I decide to play a little game just to give myself piece of mind.

When the doors open, I don't move. After about twenty seconds I act as if I'm just realizing this is my stop. Hastily I start gathering my things. My stomach almost drops out of my body when Dome-Head casually stands up, folds his paper, and heads to the open door by him.

No.

How is this possible?

At the last second I act again. I pretend I'm confused when I see the platform sign *"Den Haag,"* as if I made the wrong decision to get off at this stop after all. I make the move back to my seat. I glance in the direction of my fellow passenger. Sensing I'm possibly onto him, he hesitates. Then, gets off.

I watch him. Not twenty feet away from the train, he takes out his phone, dials someone, puts it to his ear, and looks back.

CHAPTER TWENTY-FIVE

As we approach Rotterdam I put my suit jacket on and get ready to rock. The gun in my waist is a welcome awkwardness, my own little posse should I find myself in a pinch. I look at my wrist. 11:58 a.m. It's almost an acceptable time to call Morante, but not quite yet. Anyway, it will have to wait, regardless. I had planned on my stay in Rotterdam being a short one. But it may even be shorter than anticipated.

The doors open. I spring from the steel tube, my eyes darting everywhere behind my sunglasses. Adrenaline coursing through my veins, I don't notice, or feel, any eyes on me.

Yet.

My destination is clear. I cut the straightest line I can through the crowd. Rotterdam Central Station underwent a complete renovation between the years of 2008 and 2013. This is my first time seeing the result; for a nanosecond I slow down as I need to gain my bearings. Once I recognize I'm navigating an aesthetically contemporary version of the previous layout, I ramp back up to full pace.

I exit the station. Directly in front of me is Millennium Tower—*Millenniumtoren*—a thirty-five-story, WZMH Architects-designed skyscraper completed in 2000. The building is mixed-use. It has office space, apartments, and a hotel. Cobus acquired it in August 2013.

Millennium Tower would be the obvious choice. Without breaking stride I turn left and head toward another property in *Weena*,

or the Central Business District of Rotterdam, *Weena* Tower—
Weenatoren. I see the rounded façade of the thirty-one story tower
a bit down the road. With each step I take, with each breath, the
reality of the situation grows more intense.

Who's watching?

Who's waiting?

I feel a thin layer of sweat come to the surface under my collar.
My gut's telling me full steam ahead—fighters get cut, and keep
fighting. My brain's reminding me of words once spoken by my father—words that have been my saving grace all these years:

"You want to run into a burning building? You *need* to run into
that burning building? Just remember to put on fireman's gear.
Then run into that fucking burning building."

My gait still strong, my wide eyes behind my sunglasses slam into
double duty surveying my immediate surroundings with intense
precision while scrutinizing every pair of eyes that pass me. "Optical
juggling" I've come to refer to it as over the years. I'm getting closer
to *Weena* Tower. The thin layer of sweat is getting thicker.

On my left, as I pass *Delftse Poort*, the street before the block with
Weena Tower, I notice something. A DHL truck. Just as I look, the
driver is returning to the vehicle.

I make the left. In the fifteen seconds it takes me to reach him,
he's opened the back of the truck and climbed in. I startle him as I
come up on him.

"Excuse me—I hate to bother you, but I work in *Weenatoren*, and
we're waiting on an envelope that will make or break a deal this
morning. I'd love to get a jump on the contents of that envelope."

A quick once-over by the tall, thin, ginger-looking dude is all he
needs to decide I'm legit.

"Sure. What's the name of the firm?"

"*Houthoff Buruma*."

The Netherlands-based law firm I remember has been in the building for years. He heads about two-thirds back into the truck and starts looking on a shelf about waist height. I casually look over each shoulder.

"Who would the envelope be addressed to?" he asks.

He stands at the sound of the rear doors closing, his arms drop to his sides. I'm standing in front of him, briefcase on the ground next to me. He takes one clumsy step toward me. Before his foot hits the ground I've pulled the piece from my waist and have it aimed at his face. His better sense takes hold. He stops, hands out in front in submission.

"What do you want?"

"Your keys, your clothes, your truck. Along with this gun, I have a nice stack of euros. So this can go one of two ways."

* * *

Four minutes later, Ginger having already left for his day off in my clothes, and with a little extra spending money in his pocket, I sit in the driver seat and turn on the ignition. I catch myself in the rear-view mirror, and pull down my DHL baseball cap lower over my eyes. My briefcase is behind my seat, tucked away safely out of sight under some packages.

Found me some fireman's gear.

I turn the truck around and head down *Delftse Poort*. I make a left on *Weena*, then the immediate left on *Poortstraat*. The side of *Weena* Tower, leading toward the rear of the building where the service area is, passes me on the right. Though Cobus acquired this property after I'd already returned to the States, I did a number of deals here during my time with de Bont Beleggings. I'm intimately familiar with the property.

As I approach the service and loading bays area of the property, I scope out the right place to park my new truck. Close enough to the entrance into the property, and out of the line of any other potential trucks or traffic. Preparing for a possible hurried departure, I turn the red-and-gold box around and reverse into my spot. Then I text Carolyn: *Leaving for airport in T minus 10 mins.*

The activity at the building appears to be business as usual, which doesn't surprise me. While no doubt all de Bont properties have been put on high alert for my possible presence, Cobus simply can't afford to take drastic measures like increasing security levels unannounced or having an army on hand. This would bring questions and concerns from tenants, which would lead to more eyes on his properties, all of which I know he doesn't want. For me this all means one thing: a double-edged sword. I'm probably not dealing with an increase in the amount of people after me. Yet at the same time I'm most likely dealing with security measures designed to seamlessly operate in the building's background so as not to disturb the tenants, but all now on high alert for me.

My sunglasses are still on. My gun is under my DHL polo shirt in the back of my waistline. I take out my new cell, hold it to my ear, feign speaking on the phone, and get out of the vehicle. Before I grab any packages, I lock the door, put the keys in my pocket, and head over to the building employee overseeing all coming in and out of the service area. The phone hopefully squashes any chance for unnecessary conversation, especially since I'm a driver who's never been seen at the property before.

"Excuse me—can I quickly use a bathroom before I unpack the truck?" I say, pulling myself from my faux call.

"You got it," he says, more interested in something he's reading on the paper in his hand than me. "It's just inside," he goes on, pointing, "around the corner to the left."

Exactly. Right by one of the building's internal staircases. Cap still low, along with my chin to avoid the cameras, I head in. My face is hidden pretty well, but whether someone can see my face or not a random DHL deliveryman wandering around a property is likely to draw attention this morning. I know I have to move fast.

I walk casually up the ramp at the end of the loading bays into the building. I reach the bathroom. Someone from the property's engineering team—I know from the black embroidery above the breast pocket of his white work shirt—is coming straight at me. I hate losing the time, but I continue on into the bathroom.

I jump into a stall and lock the door behind me. I do nothing but listen to my surroundings. I'm the only one in the bathroom. Thirty seconds later I head back out. I open the door to the hallway. To my left is a woman walking away from me. I turn right and duck into the stairwell.

When I hit the basement level I put my ear to the door. I don't hear anything. I open it just a crack. Still I hear nothing—no voices, no feet walking—nor do I see anything. I step out into the hallway. Chin and baseball cap brim still low I head left down the hallway. Like all de Bont properties the building is kept clean with an almost antiseptic feel, as tenants often need to access their storage space. The walls are white; the concrete floor underfoot is painted a glossy gray.

I walk briskly. No storage yet. I pass some mechanical rooms, then a workshop. I come to the end of the hallway and make a right. On my right I pass a lounge/changing room for the building's engineering team. Finally, I come upon what I'm looking for. Both sides of the hallway become lined with interspersed brushed steel doors. Each door I pass has a single, simple knob with a keyhole in the center and the name of a tenant on the wall next to it on a signage plate. I come to the end of the second hallway. I can go right or left. Again, I go right.

More tenant storage. Until about halfway down the hall I come up on a door exactly like the ones I saw in Amsterdam. It's brushed steel like all the others I've passed, but with two more locks that use different keys and no signage plate on the wall. I look across the hall. There's another door just like it about twenty feet down. I look back at the door ten inches in front of me. I look down at the doorknob. Thanks to a certain Swiss plastic surgeon, who decided to throw in a little something extra during my transformation in 2004, I never have to fear leaving fingerprints, as I no longer have any. I turn the knob. Nothing.

I step back. I look quickly in each direction. I look back at the door. I'm so close. Leaving without seeing what is on the other side is not an option.

Get what you need. Clean the mess up later.

I gear up, and kick the center of the door hard as I can. Nothing. I kick closer to the knob. Nothing. I back up as far as I can, my back literally up against the wall behind me, and barrel forward, launching myself shoulder first. Nothing. It doesn't even budge or rattle within the doorframe. I exhale loudly and look at the floor.

I'm pretty deep within the basement. I'm already teetering on having been in the bathroom a suspicious amount of time. Some sort of cavalry is inevitable at this point.

Fuck it.

I've got a jet to catch.

I step back, pull the gun from my waist, and fire three shots in rapid succession—one each into the center of the knob and two locks above. Each explodes. I kick the door by the knob and it blasts inward.

I step into the room. I'm not quite sure what, if anything, I was actually expecting. But I never would have guessed this. The space is large; I'm guessing a fifteen-hundred-square-foot white, sterile, box. Half the room is empty. The other side is filled with two kinds of items, each perfectly stacked in rows to the ceiling. I step to the first item. It's these black steel drums that look like huge tuna fish cans. Each has a label on it. The letters "Rh" followed by a circular navy-and-gold emblem. And each has a tamper-proof seal.

Rh.

What could that possibly be?

I move to the other item in the room. Rows of gray plastic containers impeccably stacked to the ceiling. These too each have a tamper-proof seal, and a label, "Ir," followed by a gray symbol that resembles a regular G and a backwards G backed up to one another.

Rh.

Ir.

Huh?

I hear footsteps in the distance. I straighten up. My ears sharpen. Definitely more than one pair of feet. And they're moving fast.

Fuck.

Here we go. I take my phone out to snap pictures of the labels, only to see a Samsung Galaxy in my hand I'm not familiar with. My iPhone is still in my briefcase. I look at the phone. Shit. There's simply zero learning curve time built into this situation. Only instinct time. I jam the phone back in my pocket.

Playing "I got lost on my way to the bathroom" isn't an option. Even if they didn't hear the gunshots, which I doubt, the shredded door tells the story. Figuring they'll be expecting me to hide somewhere in the room, I go for the same element of surprise tactic waiting for me back in Amsterdam. Fast and silent, like a lynx, I move next to the door.

I brace for the mayhem about to ensue. Immediately I think of the pain about to be inflicted on whoever confronts me. And, surprisingly, I envision the pain I may endure myself. Pain that may seep into my skin, into my bones, into my core. My lip curls up in a sneer.

Have I already accepted the pain that may come?

Do I desire it?

Do I deserve it?

Is this why I cut my own flesh?

I slip my middle finger through the gun's trigger guard, and wrap the piece into my fist like a pair of brass knuckles. I cock the wrecking ball back to my cheek ready to unleash it the second I see flesh. As the footsteps get closer and closer, the warrior in me bubbles to the surface of every cell in my being.

The footsteps stop.

Slowly I see the beginning of a profile slink into the room. I let my fist rip, smashing through my new acquaintance's jaw with such fury, the only thing keeping shattered bone from scattering is the skin holding it in. Another soldier comes rushing in behind his fallen comrade. As he crosses the doorframe's threshold, I round-house kick him in the gut, instantly knocking the wind out of him. He buckles over; when he does, I let my fist fly again, but at the exact moment I destroy his eye socket, a blow catches me on the side of the face. I stumble backward into the room, my hat and glasses flying off in the direction I'm moving.

Just as I look again at soldier number three who hit me—a thick, bald, burly dude in the same black suit as all the others—he smothers me like a wet blanket on a fire. We go crashing to the ground. He ends up on top of me with a left arm bar under my chin. My right arm free, I send the wrecking ball into the side of his head. He buckles but doesn't break. Blood instantly starts running from his left ear. As I do everything I can to jar myself loose or gain some type of leverage, he gives me a good shot across the face with his right fist. But in the effort to throw the punch he leaves himself exposed for a split second—all I need to knee him square in the balls.

His body tenses up as his face winces in pain. I flip him over, and unleash the wrecking ball, spreading his nose across his mug in an explosion of blood. He screams in agony, cupping his hands over his face. I stand up, line up, and deploy the wrecking ball once more into his balls for good measure.

In a blink, I round up my glasses and hat with my left hand. As I move to flee the scene, Soldier Two is on one knee swimming in disbelief and pain. But Soldier One, his jaw visibly altered, is back up. Only his gun is twenty feet away. I step right to him, stop a foot away, and point my weapon straight at his groin.

"We still fighting here? Or are you going to step aside?" I ask.

Arms raised, he moves out of my path. As I walk by him, slowly, our eyes locked, I lick the blood I feel flowing from my split lip. I smile, exposing my blood-smeared pearly whites. At the moment I begin to pull my eyes from his, I surprise him with the butt of my gun meeting his crippled jaw again. He goes down, a primal scream pouring from his throat before he hits the ground.

Before exiting back into the hallway, I bury my heel into Soldier Two's eye socket again. He hits the ground in a heap. I can't take any chances as I make my way back to the truck.

I've got a jet to catch.

CHAPTER TWENTY-SIX

GLASSES AND HAT back on, I'm jogging as I make my way back through the basement to the stairwell. Images randomly shoot around in my head like they're falling from a smashed piñata. The labels with the letters. Cobus. Neo? Cobus' thugs—are they part of the security team of the building he pays off to protect the basement? Or are they a different team altogether?

I see Madame Martine. And Cass. Eduardo Esparanza. I shake my head to push these images aside. First things first. I need to get out of here. As I retrace my steps, gun ready to go in my hand, I'm pleasantly surprised to see there isn't any backup yet for the three soldiers I dropped. I make it to the stairwell. I've still seen no one.

I slowly open the door. Seeing it's clear I carefully head back upstairs. I crack the door—still no one apparently waiting for me. The taste of blood in my mouth from my lip reminds me to take the bottom of my shirt and dab away as much as I can. I take a deep breath, and replace the gun in the back of my pants' waistline. Then head back out into the hallway.

Acting casual, like the DHL deliveryman I am who just took a leak, I exit the property the way I came in. I walk past the guy who directed me to the bathroom; he pays no more attention to me now than earlier. My vision locked on my truck, I pull my keys out. I unlock the door, get in, close the door, turn on the ignition, and take off.

I make a right off *Poortstraat*, back onto *Weena*. One thing is certain—the basement storage space Cobus is looking for back in the States isn't for a burgeoning restaurant empire. It's for Rh. And for Ir. Which is—what?

Another question gnaws at me. After I pummeled three of his boys, why was there no further backup?

I head toward the Hilton Rotterdam, which is less than a mile away. Knowing from which direction the cabs like to come to get in the taxi line, I park the truck around the corner from the front of the hotel. I place the keys up in the sun visor, grab my briefcase, and get out. Then I flag down a taxi before it rounds the corner to get in the queue.

"Where are we going today?" asks the chipper, older gentleman of a driver.

"Rotterdam The Hague Airport."

There is one main commercial airport, situated between Rotterdam and The Hague, that serves both cities. It's about twenty minutes from the former, thirty minutes from the latter. Which means I'll be in the car for a bit.

"What airline today?" asks the driver as we move into traffic.

"We're not actually going to the main terminal," I respond, as I fish my iPhone out of my briefcase. "We're going to the second terminal. Where the private aviation is."

Curiously, I don't hear anything back. I look up. Driver's eyes are on me in the rearview mirror. I'm guessing as soon as he drops me off he'll be contacting DHL to see if they have any job openings for drivers.

"You know where that is?" I go on.

"Yes—yes, of course," he finally responds.

All true New Yorkers own a unique ability to immediately make it clear to taxi drivers, simply through body language, they want to be left alone. The younger, punk version of myself used this ability often. Over these last years, I like to think I've seen and learned enough to keep said competency at bay. But today, I let it shine through as I have things I need to tend to, and I'm simply in no mood for small talk.

I look at my watch. 12:32 p.m., which means 6:32 a.m. at home. I power on the iPhone, which I haven't checked since I fell asleep in a tequila-drenched stupor on the jet. I need to see who's called or texted me, and while I have no intention of communicating with anyone about the current matter at hand, business as usual correspondence needs to carry on.

I scroll through the list of texts I've missed, stopping only on those I feel need attention. One from Jake: *Gary Albert and I had numerous conversations deep into the day. We sweeten the number, he believes he can at least begin a dialogue internally.* One from Pirro: *Hi Jonah, I sent some more accessories (you are going to LOVE these belts) and shoes to your house. Enjoy!* One from Cass, in the middle of the night: *Thanks for tonight. Yes . . . I think we should spend another night discussing your vision for this deal . . . let me know . . .* Perry: *We're all set for dinner with Landgraff and his girlie girl.*

I don't love that Perry is texting me about things we would be discussing this early in person. On the other side, by six thirty a.m., between early workouts and getting a jump on work-related correspondence, we're often in different parts of Silver Rock. And at least both are work related. I keep going.

One from L: *Call me. Important. We're going out with Roddy.* Another from Perry: *Just got a call from Joy Wells. Apparently they know about the Madame Martine situation. Being reported tomorrow.*

Joy Wells is a journalist at the *New York Times*, and close personal friend of Perry's for years.

Shit!

I locate Madame Martine's mobile number in my phone. Still worried about if and how Cobus is tracking me, and, or, how I, or my entire team, is being monitored, I decide to make the call on my new Samsung. Completely paranoid? Absolutely. But I've learned the hard way over the years a little paranoia often goes a long way.

"*Bonjour—*"

"Madame Martine, I told you we are doing everything we can possibly do in order to—"

"I want to believe you, Joonah, but this situation has still not rectified itself, and I am very close to the release date. I simply cannot take the chance of it being leaked to the public before I desire, and having this launch screwed up because of it. I trust you can understand this."

"But do you really think bringing this to the press will really stave off a botched launch?"

"I have no idea what you are talking about, Joonah. But, you see, with a brand such as mine there is tremendous loyalty. No matter what it turns out has happened with the fragrance—in terms of who has taken it, and for what reason—there will be sympathy for us. And whatever would come before the actual launch would be irrelevant."

"Madame, please. As I promised you, we are doing everything we can on our end to get to the bottom of this. I hope you would believe, out of respect to our relationship and the commitment I've shown you and your firm, that I am treating this as a top priority. And it has only been a couple days."

"I do trust you, Joonah. But this doesn't change the fact this situation is still unresolved. No matter how hard your team is working on it, or not."

"I *will* figure this out, Madame Martine."

"Then get to it, Joonah. The clock is ticking."

I hang up. I text Perry back. *Call Joy and tell her the situation is in hand; a mix-up with imminent resolution. There's nothing for her to look further into.*

Fuck it. Early or not, I need to speak to Morante.

"Detective Morante."

Thankfully he sounds as if he's been up for hours.

"Detective, it's Jonah. Sorry to call so early."

"Not a problem, Jonah. I'm an early type. Already been to the gym and just walked into the office. What is this number?"

"International cell. Tending to some business, but I'll be back in town by tonight."

"Ah. Got it. So, you want to go first, or should I?"

"You."

"I spoke with Mr. Billings," he dives right in. "He said he had no idea what I was talking about. I brought up his past, a certain breaking-and-entering situation that got him some time back in Pittsburgh, and I wondered how his employer might feel about learning he'd gotten this job by altering his name. He pleaded with me not to tell them. I asked him again if there was anything he wasn't telling me. To which he answered, no."

"Did you believe him?"

"I did. He was visibly upset, and in a moment where I could see it in his eyes he only wished he had something for me. It was clear the emotion that washed over him was fear of losing his job. Nothing else."

"I can't help thinking about both of these situations occurring on the same night. Is it possible Mr. Esparanza is simply collateral damage of whatever happened in Madame Martine's office? Whether he—or someone close to him—was in on it, or not?"

"Anything's possible, Jonah. We still need to get deeper with each to put it together. Something of interest that Billings did mention

was that Rosa Rivera—the young, skittish girl who said she didn't
know what happened before I even told her why I was questioning
her—and another young girl on the same crew were often together,
and both slackers. And that the night following the night of the
incident, Rosa wasn't at work. The other girl, Kristen Fuller, came
up clean both on the NCIC search as well as when I spoke with her.
I'll be speaking with both of them again today."

"Got it."

"How about you," Morante goes on. "You have a chance to look
at that footage again?"

"I did. And I saw something really interesting. I decided to start
at the time Marilena left the building, and work backwards. Like
the previous times we watched, Marilena takes off, alone, at 9:55
p.m. So next I cued the time to start running an hour earlier, from
8:55 p.m. By this time, like later in the evening when Marilena left,
traffic in the property is thin as most have long since left for the day.
There's even a stretch of like thirteen or fourteen minutes when I
don't see anyone. Until 9:29 p.m."

"Who did you see at 9:29?"

"Greg Shand."

"First time I'm hearing this name. Who is he?"

"He owns Spectrum Global. And at 9:29 he enters the building."

"Spectrum Global. Isn't that the company Mr. Esparanza worked
for?"

"No—that's Spectrum Building Services, a *subsidiary* of Spectrum
Global. Global is the parent company that owns all the subsidiaries
handling all the different competencies within the buildings—from
the security guard company to the company cleaning the marble
and steel to the company handling the messenger centers, Spectrum
Swiftly. It's literally one-stop shopping for commercial real estate
owners to cover all bases. All started and envisioned by the majority

owner, Greg Shand. He entered the property, as I said, alone at 9:29 p.m. And left alone at 10:22, almost an hour later."

"Huh," Morante sighs while absorbing what I'm telling him. "That would be like you showing up at one of your properties late at night to check if the guys scheduled to maintenance an elevator had arrived."

"Exactly. It is without question a guy like Shand has a streamlined hierarchy to handle the affairs of his company in each property on a daily basis, from the menial through management level oversight. Seems a little too coincidental to me Shand would show up this late, on this particular night, at this particular property, when two of his subsidiaries ran into serious problems. Wouldn't you say?"

"I have the login credentials," Morante says. "I'm going to go have a look at the footage one more time. Should I go have a chat with Mr. Shand?"

"I'd prefer if I can," I reply. "I've known Greg a long time, and I'm an important client. He'll simply refer you to his counsel. But me, he'll have to answer."

"Sounds good. Oh, Jonah, before you jump off, I have a question."

"Shoot."

"I got a call from my friend Roger Burress in the Special Investigations Division—he works on the Missing Persons Squad. Shane Concord was reported missing by his wife yesterday. Roger figured he'd mention it to me since your and my relationship is well known, and Shane works for you."

Damn. Works. Present tense.

"You remember the last time you saw him?" He continues. "Or where he may have gone? Roger is just getting his ducks in a row, but I told him I'd reach out to you since he has a few people before you on his list and, as you can imagine, every second matters when it comes to missing persons cases."

I turn away from the phone for a second, so Morante can't hear me swallow, then re-assume the position.

"Shane's really missing?" I feign shock. "My God."

I pause, letting out a big, audible sigh.

"*Really* missing?" Morante inquires.

"Shane's wife, Victoria, left me a message that he hadn't checked in with her. I just figured it was miscommunication between them. No, I'm not sure when the last time I saw him was. Since the circus surrounding Perry and me has slowed down a bit recently, I haven't needed him at my side twenty-four-seven. It's been more of an event-by-event or appearance-by-appearance basis."

"So you haven't seen him since he was manning the floor Esparanza had been found dead on. I'm sure you know Concord was one of us—NYPD. Good guy. Dedicated. I got a chance to say a quick hello to him when I stepped off the elevator before you got back from Madame Martine to meet me."

Fuck—I forgot about that.

"I haven't. Harvey West, who oversees property management for the Resurrection portfolio and you met that morning, called Shane, as he figured I'd want him to."

Sorry, Harvey, but casting a wide shadow buys me time. And we both know you have nothing to do with this.

"Harvey, like all my immediate top brass, has Shane's contact information," I continue.

"Did you know him well?" Morante goes on. "Personally?"

"Not really. Was strictly business. So I wouldn't have the faintest idea where he might have gone."

CHAPTER TWENTY-SEVEN

TEN HOURS AFTER landing in the Netherlands, I re-board the Gulfstream. Jennie, walking through the cabin with a tray of sandwiches, stops midstride when she sees me. She looks me up and down.

"We're about twenty minutes until we taxi. Why don't you freshen up. I'll pull you a fresh suit."

I toss my glasses and DHL baseball cap onto one of the seats, step into the bathroom, and strip off the DHL shirt. I rinse my face. The icy cold water is refreshing. It stings my split lip, which I like, welcome. Without drying my face, I just stare at myself in the mirror, water dripping everywhere.

Shane's disappearance coming to the surface was only a matter of time. Now it just adds to the spinning carousel of chaos that has once again become my life. There's Perry's upcoming trip to Miami, and my *follow-up meeting* with Cass on behalf of Landis. There's Minnie Peretsky, Greg Albert, and Bobby Sturner—and the fact I, in conjunction with my partners, am looking to get them all to sell to a psychopath. A psychopath who may just bury me if I don't come through.

I need to get Roddy Laskowski into line, which in order to pull off means I need the right site. Which just may mean a meeting and some subsequent strong-arming of Fucking Anshel, which is not exactly what I need at this particular moment. Madame Martine.

Esparanza. Morante. Marilena. Greg Shand. All of this on top of keeping up appearances, both literally and figuratively, while running the hottest boutique commercial real estate shop in the city.

My mind and body, both willing as always to forge ahead relentlessly, feel tired. They are both craving something—the way they used to crave coke when I was a younger power-beast, the way I craved and devoured Life Fuel Energy Shots during those four sleepless days and nights before the heart attack. My history, Perry's present—all of this should lead to me being straight up scared of any and all substances. But it doesn't. And I'm not. I have to get where I need to go at all costs, and fatigue inhibiting my mission never has been, and never will be, acceptable.

What does this make me? Fearless? Reckless? Determined? Senseless? Protective? Loyal?

Again I splash my face with freezing cold water. Again I stare at myself, letting it drip.

Is it pain that I'm craving?

Because it invigorates me?

Because I deserve to have it find me?

* * *

In a fresh Assiagi suit minus the jacket, and all the Assiagi accouterments from head to toe, I sit in the same seat in front of the same table I did last night. I look across to the couch. My eyes on my briefcase, I call for Jennie. She peeks her head out of the galley.

"Yes, Jonah?"

For all the same reasons I won't touch my iPhone for anything out of the business realm, I want no part of my laptop or iPad. Have these devices been part of Cobus' monitoring scheme? Has he watched me reviewing and manipulating maps of cities like Berlin and Rotterdam and Manhattan? How? Who around me could have ever given him access to these devices?

"I spilled water on my laptop so it's completely screwed. Do you have one I could borrow for a little while?"

"I do. Is an Apple MacBook Air okay?"

"Perfect. My weapon of choice."

Jennie disappears. I hear her going through what I presume to be her bag. She returns twenty seconds later, MacBook Air in tow.

"Thanks so much. I really appreciate it," I say, extending my hand to take it from her.

"Not a problem," she says as she hands it over.

I place it on the table and power it up.

"Is there a password?"

"Nope. Nothing to hide," she responds in that hot, sultry voice.

"Too bad," I say, eyes still on the booting machine. "Nothing like a little naughtiness."

She giggles then pauses.

"We've got about five minutes till wheels up. Can I bring you anything for while you work?"

I'd love a line. Or a Red Bull. Or a punch to the face.

"Just some ice water would be great."

"Coming up. Flight time this afternoon will be about one hour and fifteen minutes."

Once the machine is powered up and ready to go, I jump in with Google. I have nowhere to start but the beginning. I type in the letters "Rh," just as I saw them—capital "R," and lowercase "h." I hit search.

My iPhone rings. It's L. I don't answer. Instead I dial him back on my new Samsung Galaxy.

"Hello?" he says, hesitation in his voice.

"It's me."

"What number is this? Are you out of the country?"

"I had to take off for a quick trip—which I'd appreciate you mentioning to no one, and I'll explain when I see you. What's up?"

"Fucking Mister Jet Set. I love that shit. You on the private jet?"

"L—no time today. We can talk toys later. What's up?"

"My sense of timing, punk ass. I popped in on your new friend to ask a car question right at the time he was seething from a fight with his ex-wife. I told him he needed to relax with some booze and ass, and that I'd take him out tonight. All you gotta do is call me, ask what's up, I give you the 'I thought you and Perry had a charity function' bullshit, you pop over to meet us—done and done. You work him over Jonah Gray-style."

"I like it. Nice."

I look at the World Time and crunch the time like a computer. By the time we lift off, it will be about 12:25 p.m.—7:25 a.m. at home. An hour and change flight time to Hamburg will bring me to 1:30 p.m. and 8:30 a.m., respectively. I know exactly which building in Hamburg I'll be going to see, and it's only fifteen minutes from the airport. I don't plan on being in Hamburg any more than an hour or so—3:30 p.m. and 9:30 a.m. Eight hours flight time gets me home today at 5:30 p.m. Aside from some serious jet lag issues, I should have no problem going out tonight with L and my new friend Roddy.

"Once you know the plan, text it to me on this phone," I go on. "And I'll call you later."

"You got it, bro. Over and out. Too bad about that *Page Six* bullshit. Not used to seeing things written about you and Perry there unless it's what party you two were at, who you were with, and what you two were wearing."

Page Six is the gossip page in the *New York Post*.

"What does it say?" I ask.

"You haven't seen it? Bro, what went—"

"*Just,*" I cut him off while closing my eyes, "read it to me."

"Hold on."

Ten seconds later he's back with the paper.

"It's a small paragraph on the left. Right above one about DiCaprio being spotted downtown at The Electric Room with some of his boys and a new ten on his arm. Like that's fucking news."

"L. Seriously. Just—"

"Right. Just read it. The headline is 'REAL ESTATE POWER PLAYER JONAH GRAY IN SECURITY SNAFU.' Then it goes on to read: 'Word on the street is security detail in one of Mr. Gray's Park South properties may have fallen asleep on the job. It seems the prototype for a new Madame Martine—the legendary perfumer who recently moved into a Resurrection Realty property— fragrance has gone missing. Foul play? Inside job? Either way, it seems Mr. Gray may have some explaining to do.'"

"Gotta go. See you tonight."

Without waiting for a response I hang up. I go straight to my contacts. I find Dawn London, the publicist for me personally as well as for Resurrection. I dial on the iPhone, since it's business, and if Cobus is watching and, or, listening as closely as I think he may be, he already knows about this situation.

"You were my next call, sunshine."

Dawn London is a young, sharp publicist who's as good at spin and crisis management as she is with promotion. The girl could convince you an old lady with the right of way, crossing the street, run over by a motorcycle gang, was at fault as easily as she could convince you everyone needs flavored toilet paper.

"*Page Six* is just one outlet who has this news," I say. "According to Perry, the *New York Times* knows about it too. I'm guessing they're about to try to dig deeper."

"Is the situation in hand?"

"It will be. For the time being, I'd like to release a short statement."

"I've already drafted it and upon your approval will release it on your behalf. I want it kept short, owning the situation, vowing resolution, and expressing that Resurrection is working with all parties necessary—including the vendor under contract to handle security in Resurrection properties—to rectify the situation. I want it made clear you hire an outside company to handle the expertise of security, whereas your expertise is real estate."

She goes on to read me the statement.

"Sounds right on all around," I confirm.

"Do we want to name the firm who handles security? Give everyone interested an actual name to start looking into?"

Absolutely. But I can't. Not until I've spoken with Shand from Spectrum Global. I need to keep him in a good place.

"No," I respond. "I'm not in the business of throwing people I do business with under the bus. People want to dig, let them start digging."

I hang up and return to my Googling. "Rh." Restoration Hardware's homepage is the top result. Under that is something called the Rh blood group system on Wikipedia. I click on the result and begin reading: "The Rh blood group system (including the Rh factor) is one of thirty-three current human blood group systems. It is the most important . . ."

I go back to the search results. The next one down is RH Contemporary Art, a multichannel platform looking to bring the work of international artists to a global audience. The address is on West Sixteenth Street in Manhattan. Could this be it? Art? Doesn't feel right—not with those tamper-proof drums that were all exactly the same size. I keep going. Next: "What is Rh Incompatibility? Rh incompatibility is a condition that occurs during pregnancy . . ." Nope.

Next: RH–Yahoo Finance, the stock ticker quote for Restoration Hardware. I keep going, then move on to the second page of results. Everything is still about Restoration Hardware or blood. Page three, more of the same with a few new results mixed in that seem equally way off-base. Page four and on gets more and more random, with nothing seemingly on point whatsoever.

As the jet barrels down the runway and lifts off, I decide to move on to the gray plastic containers. I type in "Ir"—again, exactly as I saw it—into Google. The first result is Ir Conjugation—Conjugate Ir in Spanish. The second one says: IR—Wikipedia. I begin reading the summary. "Ir or ir may refer to: iridium (chemical symbol Ir), the 77th element; ir, the Internet country code top-level domain for Iran; IR may refer to Iran, which has the . . ."

I keep going. Next up: International Rectifier—The Power Management Leader. I click on it. Some type of automotive company it seems. I click on "About Us." "International Rectifier Corporation is a world leader in power-management technology. Leading manufacturers of computers, energy-efficient appliances, lighting, automobiles, satellites, aircraft and defense systems rely on IR's power management benchmarks to power their next generation products." Huh. I click on the "Products" tab. There are multiple products listed under headings such as Power MOSFETs, Gate Driver ICs and Controllers, IGBTs, Motor Control Solutions—I have minimal, if any, understanding of what any of this means.

Doesn't feel right. On the gray containers Ir was printed in a very simple, black font, and there was that gray logo that looked like two G's backed up to one another. This IR—International Rectifier—has a very bold, red, unique logo. On each of the two labels back in that storage space the two letters were written very plain, simply matter of fact next to a unique logo. Ir was not the name of a company, nor was Rh. These initials have to do with what's inside those drums and containers, not who's responsible for getting them there.

I click back to my results and move on. Next, IR: Summary for Ingersoll Rand plc—Yahoo Finance. The summary says "View the basic IR stock chart on . . ." No need to go any further. Ingersoll Rand is one of the world's behemoth companies, and has brand names like American Standard, Trane, Thermo King, and ARO under its umbrella to go along with its well-known, red, bold, IR logo.

Spanish Verb Conjugation—ir—123TeachMe comes next, followed by IR—Proactive Performance Management Solutions. The summary says, "That's where we come in. Where others see disaster, we see solutions. Customers in over 60 countries rely on IR Prognosis to optimize systems and help . . ." Another Ir company. I move on.

More entries related to Ingersoll Rand and Spanish verb conjugation. I move on to page two, then three, and find the same with yet more companies appearing with the initials Ir from IR Illuminators to Indian Railways to IR Mobile. Soon we start moving into articles past and present on which professional athletes have hit the IR List—Injury Reserve—in their respective sports.

I sit back and take a deep breath. I turn and look out the window just as we blast through a thin layer of clouds into the clear, endless, blue sky. My father crosses my mind. As much as I want to ask what he would do with all the shit dropped into my lap, I hate myself for still wanting his advice this many years after his death. I loathe him for betraying my mother all those years ago. I love him for being my brutally honest father. And for the fact his huge balls showed me the way to an iron backbone.

My eyes move to my briefcase on the couch across from me. I stand up and walk over to it. I reach inside, into one of the side pockets, and pull out a business card I've had in my possession for ten years. "Agliani Brothers—New York City's Most Respected Tailors" is embossed in red on the front of the nice, thick, white stock. The address is 149 West Forty-Eighth Street. I flip the card over. Handwritten is another address. "9009 Pettit Avenue. Queens, NY." I'm not looking at it because I need to remember the address—this has been seared into my memory from the moment I saw it. I'm looking at it because I want to remember who it's from, what it means.

I return the card to its rightful place in my briefcase. I retake my seat. Then put my eyes back on the screen, and keep going.

CHAPTER TWENTY-EIGHT

THE JET DESCENDS toward Hamburg. I've spent an hour scouring the Internet to get nowhere. Staring at the screen, I close my eyes in order to play back my encounter with the storage room. I start with stepping back, firing three shots, and blowing the door in. I step inside. All over again I feel the surprise at what's in front of me. The black, steel, tuna-can-looking drums. The gray plastic containers. The labels. The navy and gold logo on one, the gray, backed up 'G's' on the other. The initials. "Rh." "Ir." As I remember one more detail about both storage vessels, my eyes open.

The tamper-proof seals.

I type in a new search. "Rh Hazardous." The first result is: Series HHT – Hazardous Area Humidity/Temperature—nothing worthwhile. Number two is something to do with residential homeowners in Knoxville, Tennessee. Number three is also a no. Next, rhodium—Chemical Properties, Health and . . ."

I click the fourth entry. A water source company called Lenntech is giving the rundown on the chemical properties of an element called rhodium. Atomic Number: 45. Atomic Mass: 102.91 g mol-1. Electronegativity according to . . .

I pause. Atomic number 45 means this is where it is found on the Periodic Table of Elements. I can swear on this hour since I've boarded the jet and begun my search I'd seen something that had to do with the Periodic Table. I begin hitting the back button, and retracing each step, or page, taken.

There it is. The second result under the initial "Ir" search I'd quickly passed over, and dismissed. IR—Wikipedia. I begin reading the summary again. "Ir or ir may refer to: iridium (chemical symbol Ir), the 77th element . . ."

Holy shit. Goose bumps erupt all over my body. I finally may be on to something. "Rh" is something called rhodium, the forty-fifth element on the Periodic Table of Elements. "Ir" is iridium, the seventy-seventh element on the Periodic Table. All of which means . . . absolutely nothing to me. I Google the Periodic Table. It appears on the screen, and I can't help but to have a flashback of sitting in Ms. Dann's high school chemistry class staring at Kristen Wernack's gorgeous hair and absurd ass. I find the forty-fifth box for rhodium in the center of the grid. Iridium, the seventy-seventh spot, is literally right below rhodium on the next line down.

Okay. So I have rhodium, and iridium. And still not a clue what either of them even is. I Google rhodium. The first result is the entry in Wikipedia: "rhodium is a chemical element with symbol Rh and atomic number 45. It is a rare, silvery-white, hard, and chemically inert transition metal. It is a member of the platinum group. It has only one naturally occurring isotope, 103 Rh. Naturally occurring rhodium is usually found as the free metal, alloyed with similar metals, and rarely as a chemical compound in minerals such as bowieite and rhodplumsite. It is one of the rarest and most valuable precious metals."

I keep reading. Approximately 80 percent of all rhodium mined is used as one of the catalysts in the three-way catalytic converters in automobiles. And "because rhodium metal is inert against corrosion and most aggressive chemicals, and because of its rarity, rhodium is usually alloyed with platinum or palladium and applied in high-temperature and corrosion-resistive coatings." From here it goes into more detail, the chemical properties, isotopes, occurrence, mining and price, and so on.

"Jonah, we'll be landing in five minutes," Jennie calls from the galley. "Can I get you anything before we land?"

"No thanks, Jennie. I'm all set."

Five minutes. I move on to iridium. The third entry down is the Wikipedia page for iridium. I click it. "Iridium is a chemical element with symbol Ir and atomic number 77. A very hard, brittle, silvery-white transition metal of the platinum group, iridium is generally credited with being the second densest element (after osmium) based on measured density, although calculations involving the space lattices of the elements show that iridium is denser. It is also the most corrosion-resistant metal, even at temperatures as high as 2000 degrees C." I keep reading, and quickly learn facts like iridium is obtained commercially as a by-product from nickel and copper mining and processing, and that it is used in applications from the production of certain long-life aircraft engine parts to electrical contacts for spark plugs to high-temperature crucibles.

I sit back, look up at the ceiling of the cabin, and process. Aircraft parts? Catalytic converters? Both metals are rare, both metals are extremely resistant to high temperatures. Is Cobus building something? Why all the locations in different cities—and why cities like Rotterdam, Hamburg, and now New York? What do these three cities, along with however many others Cobus has in the mix, have in common?

Without hesitation, or concern whether Jennie would care or not, I clear all of the browsing data on her computer. As we near touchdown, Hamburg comes into view through all of the windows, surrounding me as if the city's about to swallow me whole. I power Jennie's computer down.

* * *

Sitting in the back of the Mercedes waiting for me at the airport, I head toward my destination. This time I left my briefcase on the jet, tucked away in the closet with my clothes. I'm not intimately familiar with Hamburg. According to the driver, our ride heading south into the heart of the city, though only seven and half miles, will take about twenty-five minutes because of congestion and traffic lights.

The property I'm headed to is called the Emporio Building, located at *Damtorwall* 15. Completed in 1964, the twenty-two-story, glass-and-steel property designed with an international feel has been a fixture of the Hamburg landscape for fifty years. The previous occupant, Unilever, moved to a new corporate headquarters in the Hafen City District on the River Elbe in 2009, and the property underwent a massive renovation, completed in 2011. It is de Bont Beleggings' most recent acquisition in Hamburg, purchased earlier this year.

I have both phones with me. Does Cobus know I'm here? Or am I just some guy the security team has picked up on lurking around their buildings? Have they passed my image on to the top levels of security and management—or has Cobus himself been given images and, or, video footage of me on de Bont properties? I want to hear Perry's voice. But if he is monitoring me, or us, the way I'm sensing he is, I don't want him knowing Perry and I are on different continents.

I take out the iPhone. I have business to tend to. Keeping Cobus at bay, if that's where he is, means I need to stick to handling my affairs as if I'm in Manhattan, and all is on course.

I dial Minnie. I've set the table, one with all the fine china and sterling silver flatware a woman like she expects, and she's been given ample time to gaze at it. Now it's time to play my game. The one that taunts her. Teases her. Threatens to do one of two things.

Either pull the tablecloth out sans the finesse of a magician, or flip the damn table altogether.

Minnie Peretsky is a real estate owner.

But she's not, nor will she ever be, a real estate player.

Big difference.

"I like you being my first call, Jonah."

"Good morning, Minnie. How are you?"

"Just stepping out of the shower, literally dripping wet. How hot is that?"

I gag.

"You're even frisky in the morning," I quip.

"I'm always frisky, Jonah. Unfortunately I'm guessing you didn't call for a little a.m. phone sex."

"That you're right about. I called regarding the offer I've put on the table on behalf of my buyer."

"What about it?"

"It still stands, exactly as presented. But I wanted to give you a heads up that my client has now decided there are a couple of other properties that may work just as well for the portfolio they're trying to develop. And one of the owners involved is looking to unload."

Minnie says nothing. She's staring at the table. Time to grab the corner of the tablecloth.

"Now in my gut, I believe One-Hundred Three Church is still their property of choice," I go on, "but if I know this client—and I *always* know my clients—they'll move on to choice two in a heartbeat if they believe the primary target is not an easy catch and close. These are not emotional buyers. Pure strategists. And once they're in buyer mode, they like to move fast."

"So—what exactly are you telling me, Jonah? Five seconds after getting me to sit on the can, now I need to shit or get off the pot?"

Such a lady.

"What I'm telling you, Minnie, is that I respect you as a friend and a businesswoman. I trust you'll do whatever is in the best interest of your loved ones, and the future of your family. If that entails taking this opportunity that I've presented, then that's something—yes— you'll want to let me know sooner than later."

I hang up with Minnie, and keep going down the checklist. Business as usual. I text Landgraff. *How we doing—meeting with Fucking Anshel a go? Other options?* I keep going down the list. Cass. Without question she has Feller and Landis eating out of her hand—those two old-timers are no match for a siren like this woman. But that's the thing about a *true* siren according to classical mythology—the art of seduction is used as a tool to lure, capture, and ultimately destroy. In my gut I feel Landis is waiting on Cass' guidance to make a move forward, not Feller. But with a woman like Cass—a true blend of smarts, beauty, cunning, fortitude, and sexiness—one can never be certain who's playing whom.

I decide to call Feller. As the broker, I reason I should check in with him as opposed to going straight to the owner, Landis, as a sign of respect. At least make the guy feel like he's doing something to earn this commission. But before I check in with him, there's another piece of the puzzle I need to slide into place. I find Jason Eder's number in my contacts. Do I have plans to relocate his restaurant? Absolutely not. But everyone involved—from Cass to Eder to Feller to Landis—should they talk need be reminded that's exactly what I'm going to do unless the new ownership of this site falls into place. Fast.

"Jonah. How are you?"

"Can't complain, Jason. How's everything on the restaurant front? Any new word from Feller on ownership?"

"Nothing new. According to them, they're still just trying to set- tle on the right group to purchase the site."

"Indeed they are. And, as you know, Resurrection is one of the parties in the mix and I intend on obtaining that site. That said— real estate is real estate, and one never knows what might happen. Therefore, it is time we have a look at some sites. There are a number of opportunities that aren't officially on the market but that I have access to. And a couple of them I believe could be extraordinary should we have to go in that direction."

"Sounds like the right plan, Jonah. When can we look?"

We lock in a time to go investigate the sites, end our call, and I email Carolyn the details. Now it's time to call Feller. I find his number, and dial.

"Norm Feller."

"Norm—Jonah. How are you this morning?"

"Doing well, Jonah, thanks."

"Great. Just wanted to check in and see how you, Jerry, and Cass are doing in terms of coming to a decision."

"We're still weighing all options. Apparently, we may have another suitor. So, while we know we need to keep things moving along, I need to make sure we have all the offers possible on the table before Jerry can make that ultimate decision."

"Of course, Norm. I understand. Just to keep you up to speed, I got together with Cass last night to go over the vision I'd presented to you and Jerry. Since she's part of your decision-making process, I thought she should have this straight from me in order to have as much information as possible when it comes to evaluating Resurrection's offer."

"Great, Jonah. Thanks for letting me know. I agree Cass hearing your vision from you, as opposed to from us, puts us all in a better position to evaluate properly."

"You got it, Norm. I figured she mentioned to you and Jerry we were getting together."

"Nope, she didn't mention it."

I pause.

"Norm, can we have an off-the-record conversation? A conversation that once we hang up, remains only between the two of us?"

"Absolutely, Jonah. What's on your mind?"

"Cass and I had a very frank discussion. Now I want to preface this by saying I think it's always best to be up front when emotions as well as this much cash are on the table—so I have zero issue with Cass' openness. In fact, I asked for it. And I appreciate her willingness to indulge me."

"Her openness in terms of—what?"

"In terms of where Landis' head is at, and where both she and the team—right now, at this point—are leaning in terms of who's the right buyer. Now I get it, Norm—it's your duty, your obligation to your client—to tell me that all is still apples to apples, and we're still technically in the 'evaluation' stage. But since Cass was candid with me, I'd like you to be with me as well. What's the thinking behind the choice you're leaning toward? And what ultimately solidifies that choice?"

"The thinking behind who we're leaning toward is this—"

CHAPTER TWENTY-NINE

AT MY DIRECTION, the driver stops a half block away from the *Emporio* Building on *Jakobikirchhof.* The day is overcast in Hamburg, there's a mild bite in the air. Pistol in my rear waistline, I exit the back of the Mercedes and head for the property.

Being unfamiliar with this building absolutely has me feeling at a disadvantage. It also has me essentially plan-less. I decide my best bet is to hide behind my sunglasses while pretending to be deep in conversation on my phone, and stroll around the exterior of the structure. The goal is to blend into the city, another businessman headed from one part of the *Neustadt* neighborhood of Hamburg to another, all the while finding and surveying the situation with the property's service area and loading bays. When I see what's going on, I can devise a plan from there.

Once I round the corner toward the rear of the building, the loading bays are within eyeshot immediately on my right. There are all the usual suspects for this area of a commercial building— trucks backed into place, loud noises, and the expected building personnel all in their required uniforms. Only there seems to be an unusual amount of security today. Up high on the platform, near the entrance to the building, are three guys all in dark suits. Three guys dressed exactly like those I'd encountered in Amsterdam and Rotterdam.

I look back over my left shoulder, keeping my nerves in check while pulling my face out of their sight line, to see if any traffic is coming along my left. When I'm clear, I continue on a forty-five degree angle from the direction I'd just been moving once having turned the corner. The property is now at my back as I walk away.

Fuck.

What now.

Rhodium. Iridium. How? Why? What does it all mean? Are these elements where it all ends, or begins? The only way to truly gauge the danger I'm in, or the danger I've put my partners and possibly other members of the New York City commercial real estate community in, is to find out as much as I can. I'm so close. Just one more glimpse in one of these basements may be all I need. A glimpse I know may be a costly one.

I'm so close.

I remember words from my father.

"Without the battles, no wars can be won."

Once I'm about a block away from the property I make a left and circle back around. I lift my chin, clench my teeth, and decide there's one last hand to be played. During my surveillance walk I noticed an entrance to a parking garage underneath the building. It's manned with a lone dude in a booth, but he's barely paying attention. Tenants have a magnetic sticker in their windshield that lifts the parking control barrier arm. Guests push a button, which gives them a ticket that lifts the same arm.

Look the part. Be the part. Always. If you need to belong, then belong.

Sunglasses in place, cell to my ear, purpose in my stride, I enter the mouth of the garage as if it's just another day walking to my car. The attendant never looks my way. Then, twenty feet in, a voice from behind stops me dead in my tracks.

"A little far from Manhattan, aren't we?"

A chill shoots up my spine. I turn around. Cobus. Dressed as always from head to toe in his usual black suit, shirt, tie, and shoes, his five o'clock shadow and dark hair perfectly manicured as if he's just come from the salon.

Cobus.

"I mean, is this a coincidence, or what?" he goes on, moving toward me. "Or—wait—is it really true there are *no* coincidences? Meaning, is this actually any less of a coincidence than, say, that perfume prototype going missing the same night that overnight cleaning crew worker died in one of your properties?"

Whoa.

How the hell does he know that?

"I would have been here sooner, and met you in Amsterdam, had my jet not been behind yours," he continues. "Amazing. Few people realize how much opportunity there is in South American cities like São Paulo—but it all comes down to what we each see value in, Jonah. Isn't that right?"

"South America, now. You in the market for larger than usual basements there as well?"

"I figured my security team is . . . *equipped* to handle any type of outsider who tries to infiltrate our properties," he continues, brushing off my response, "and that I could finish up with my affairs. Unfortunately, I forgot just how crafty you can be. Deducing you'd still be saved within our facial recognition security systems? Becoming a DHL delivery man in Rotterdam? Impressive as usual. The error is mine, as I should have expected as much."

I don't speak. My eyes dart this way and that to see if we're alone, but if anything is clear at this point, it's that I'm not even close to alone whether I see others or not. My eyes settle back on his.

"You do realize, Jonah," he continues, "I could have you thrown in jail in either Amsterdam, Rotterdam, and now Hamburg with one simple phone call. Trespassing, assault—I mean, what's gotten into you?"

"We both know you won't do that," I respond.

"Oh, no?"

"No."

"What makes you so sure?"

"The one reason you came to me. I don't have the option of failure—as you've made quite clear—in the game of commercial real estate where failure is always on the table. We both know I can't deliver from a jail cell any more than I can dead. But don't you think our history deserves more respect than what you've given me?"

He stops once he reaches me. We're face to face.

"Respect?"

"I'm not a fucking moron, Cobus. Extra huge basements to handle the affairs of a growing restaurant chain? Really?"

"You're saying this isn't true?"

"I'm saying this isn't true."

He pauses.

"So, then, answer me this. One way or the other—does it matter?"

"It might."

"In what way?"

The situation has truly become a scary one. How the fuck does he even know I'm here? Right here, in this garage, in Hamburg, Germany, at this very fucking moment? I've literally only been communicating with Carolyn about this itinerary, and have been doing so offline.

Jennie? The pilot, Ken? The people who manage the jet? The drivers Carolyn has been setting up to meet me at each destination?

Fuck!

"I don't want to be involved with anything that hurts others," I go on.

"You're handling my affairs in Manhattan. A hired gun. Nothing more. Nothing less."

"Our history, Cobus—the aboveboard part of our history—is widely known because of my story. I'm far from just a hired gun. This shit ever gets out—what you're really involved with, and that I helped you bring your bullshit to New York City—I'll be fucking ruined. Perry, Jake, everyone who works with and for me will be done."

"Well, then, I guess you'd better make sure not only you get this done, but you do so quietly. Wouldn't you agree?"

I try to reason with him; return us to a different time when we worked, built his real estate empire, together.

"Cobus, if you just tell me what it is you're really trying to—"

He puts his hand up.

"Jonah. Stop."

Our faces are eighteen inches apart. He takes a deep breath.

"When you look at me, Jonah, what do you see?"

Monster. Criminal. Psycho.

Ally. Savior. Confidant.

My past. My present. My future?

"I see a man who gave me the opportunity to rebuild my life. A man I helped build a real estate empire he can use as a legit cover for a criminal existence. A man with whom I'm even."

"Let me refresh your memory," Cobus comes back without a second's hesitation. "You and me? We're nothing more than two men who from the moment we met one another lied through our teeth about who each of us really is. You had a lot to hide. I had even more to hide. And, as far as you seeming surprised that I walked into this garage behind you, have you so quickly forgotten that I monitored your every goddamn step for six years in Europe, as a favor to Gaston? That I was there to save your skin on multiple occasions?

Literally keep you from ending up six feet under because my people were there—watching—when you didn't even know it?"

"I never asked for your help."

"But Gaston Picard—believing in your innocence as a favor to your father—did. So you received it. Without it, you would have been killed three times over, not given the opportunity to clear your name and rebuild your life. But you know what, Jonah? Do you realize what all of this means?"

"What?"

"None of it means a thing. All of our past—everything that has happened between us right up to this very moment—none of it matters one bit. You're a more—"

Cobus looks away for a second, as if to catch the right word from thin air, then back to me.

"—*emotional* person than I am. I helped you, and I appreciate how you helped me. Yet, if I'm being truthful, I feel you pledging yourself to me, and my growing business, the way you did was payment of a debt due me whether you knew it at the time or not. But beyond that? Beyond a certain amount of respect I may have for you? I don't care much beyond that, about you, anyone, or anything. Outside of my wife, my kids, and my affairs, everything is downright irrelevant. This way life remains simple, and I can focus on exactly what I need to without distraction. Much the same as why I dress the same every day. You say we're even? We'll never be even. But, again, this doesn't matter. None of it does. What matters is everything that happens from this moment forward."

Cobus steps even closer to me. He holds up his iPhone.

"All you need to keep in mind, Jonah, is one thing," he goes on, "that you worked for me then, and you work for me now."

A video begins playing. As the contents of the footage unfold before me, I can feel all the blood rushing from my head like it's in a race to my feet. Shane's thick, burly, decapitated body, in a suit like he wore every day just as the last time I saw him, is lying on a steel gurney.

"If I'm not happy with the fruits of your labor, this body ends up wherever I see fit. With evidence of contact of this body with you, or whomever I see fit. Do we understand one another?"

I nod. He puts his phone away.

"Stop wasting time, Jonah. You should be in Manhattan right now landing me those buildings, not flying overseas to make things your business that aren't. You've got a jet to catch. And that creepy-little-freaky-thing Minnie right where you want her. Which means you're dismissed."

My instinct is to spread his nose across his face with my forehead, then drive my fist through his chest so hard it comes out his back. Instead I keep my inner gladiator in check. Holding so much in—so much I want to say, to do—I clench my teeth and walk out the way I came in. There's no doubt I'm in a world of shit. But there's also no doubt about something else.

I don't care if you're Cobus de Bont, the President, or anyone else. No one "dismisses" Jonah Gray.

CHAPTER THIRTY

LIKE AN ARROW from a bow, The Ship is launched from the Lincoln Tunnel into the West Side of Manhattan. Neo, jumping all over the backseat in excitement to see me when I got in twenty minutes ago at Liberty International Airport, is already curled up and asleep in my lap. I look at the World Time. Five fifty-five p.m. My eyes move to the darkened city, made even darker by the tinted glass between us, floating by. Silhouettes of buildings, passing cars, and random construction and development sites are dotted with popping lights of all colors.

I'm exhausted. I didn't sleep one minute on the flight back. Unfortunately I didn't investigate the rhodium and iridium situation any further, either. The unexpected meeting with Cobus has my paranoia at such elevated levels I felt he might have been monitoring me inside the jet, or even somehow monitoring Jennie's computer. Jennie, who for the love of God, may have been part of his eyes and ears for all I know these last twenty-four hours. I literally stared out the window for seven hours and change, broken up here and there with a tequila over rocks to mellow my nerves.

We make a right off Thirtieth Street onto Ninth Avenue.

"Meatpacking District in T minus six minutes," Dante says through the intercom. "I'll return Neo home to Silver Rock, take Perry to her dinner meeting, then return to you and wait outside for when you're ready."

"Thanks, Dante," I say, my eyes still on the black-on-black passing city. "But stay with Perry. I'll find my way home."

"You got it, boss-man."

I take out my iPhone. Time to put the plan into effect. Before I do, I see I have a new text from Landgraff. I open it.

Hey Babe—with Natey-Boy and playing around on his phone. He was about to text you he got the meeting with Fucking Anshel. I decided to steal his thunder.

I dial L.

"Jonah—what's up. my brother?"

"You tell me?" I say, reciting my first line of the script. "I just finished up a meeting and I'm downtown. You around for a cocktail?"

"I thought you and Perry had a charity event tonight?"

"Tomorrow night. You in your office?"

"I'm not—I'm actually grabbing a drink with Roddy."

"Oh—then go ahead, do your thing. I didn't—"

"Hold on," L cuts me off.

We've been best friends since we were little kids. Roddy doesn't stand a chance. This is all beyond seamless for us. I hear L explaining the situation.

"Come meet us," L goes on.

"You sure? I mean, if Roddy—"

"It's fine. Come meet us. Roddy just said he's been thinking about what you proposed, anyway. And that he has some questions for you. We're at the Standard Hotel bar."

"Great. Just need to make one quick stop and I'll see you soon."

Neo opens his aging eyes, lifts his head, and looks up at me. I pick him up and hold him so we're nose to nose. I kiss his little face. He kisses me back. I smile for the first time in what feels like days.

* * *

I have Dante drop me at the Apple Store on Ninth Avenue between Fourteenth and Fifteenth, just a couple blocks from where I'll be meeting L and Roddy. Unsure exactly how it is Cobus is tracking me and, or, monitoring me, one thing is certain: he's fully on to me. He made it clear he knew I was on my way to Europe before I'd arrived—and only stayed in Brazil because he figured his security could deter me. Which, I believe, is all he wanted and what he ultimately got—my being deterred—as opposed to my being captured or seriously injured. At the end of the day Cobus wants me in New York getting him his buildings—nothing more, nothing less. He knew I was going to Europe, and he knew I wasn't going to just accept the "larger basements for my restaurant investment" bullshit. He knows me way too well. Which leads me to believe he had whatever system in place he was going to use to track me, and possibly all those close to me, before he ever made that first call to me when Perry and I were at the ASPCA event. With every second that goes by, it's becoming more and more evident this is a more elaborate setup than I realized.

Did he somehow get someone into my office do his dirty work with regard to all my devices? Maybe manipulate them all when I was in a conference room or something? There are times when my phone is on my desk near my desktop, and my iPad and MacBook Air are merely feet away in my briefcase. Same for Perry, and same for Jake. Did he get someone into Silver Rock posing as a cable guy or Con Ed worker, someone to make a quick detour into Perry's and my offices to handle the computers? Fuck if I know. What I *do* know is this is a man who has goddamn *governments* in his pocket; a man who watched my every move for six years. And, without a doubt, he's watching.

Am I losing it? Overthinking all this? Possibly. I know to be supremely wary of this man. But I also refuse to stop trying to understand what he's up to. I need a research machine I know he hasn't, somehow, had access to. I go inside, buy a 128-GB iPad mini, have it set up onsite, then head to the Standard on foot.

* * *

I open the red door marked "848"—for Eight Forty Eight Washington Street—and enter the Standard Hotel main bar, new iPad in hand. The predominantly white space with dropped, bulbous, interspersed hanging white light fixtures and brown, cream, and white tiled floor is crowded with all the usual suspects: Wall Streeters, Asian and European tourists, and young hipsters. Eyes move my way as I enter the space, something I'm used to and, like always, simply let wash over me. I spot L and Roddy at the far end of the bar.

I move through the crowd. As I'm shaking hands with a banker I know from UBS, L spots me and waves me over. When I reach him we guy-hug.

"I really hope I'm not intruding," I say, moving my attention, and outstretched hand to Roddy.

"Not at all," Roddy responds, taking my hand and shaking it firmly. "I'm actually happy this happened, because I have some questions I would have ended up asking L to pass on and it would have turned into a game of telephone, which hardly ever ends well."

He turns to L.

"No offense."

"None taken," L says. "I know I'm an idiot."

"Can I get you something?" asks a very tattooed, very thickly bearded bartender.

"Most definitely," I respond. "What's the best tequila you've got back there?"

"Like—best? Or ridiculous best?"

"Ridiculous best."

"I just cracked a bottle of Rey Sol Anejo about an hour ago."

"Done. Pour some over just a couple rocks for me."

"You got it."

"Fucking baller," L says throwing back a swig of Belvedere. "I love it."

I turn my attention back to Roddy.

"So—what questions can I answer for you?" I ask.

"When we initially met, you said you had a plan. What exactly did that mean?"

"Simple. Once you accept my eleven-point-five-million-dollar offer, I move mountains to find you an equal or better site to run your business—which, I must admit, in hopes you'd entertain my offer, is a process I've already begun. Typically that would now be your financial obligation to secure the new site, and I'd make sure to find a relocation spot we could make a sweet deal on for you to come out ahead dollar wise. But, in this case, I'm prepared to do something unusual. If you want to pocket the cash I pay you, I'll buy the new site we decide upon myself and you can simply be my tenant in the early going. You can let me worry about all the upkeep and issues that accompany being a landlord. I'll even put in an option for you to buy the property from me if you want. Real estate holdings, as we know, is what I do, and do very well. This way you're holding all the cards in terms of what hand you'd like to ultimately play regarding your new real estate situation."

"Sounds like a nice start," Roddy says, nodding. "What next?"

"The actual relocation. I have a team that is second to none in terms of handling the logistics of a move like this in the most efficient, effective way so as to limit the intrusion this move would make on your business. My team would begin with a detailed analysis of your operation, gaining as much of an understanding as possible not just of what the operation does as a whole, but how the different competencies of your company work together. This way, with your input and our newfound knowledge about your business, the best possible approach can be determined for physically moving the company, in terms of what aspects of the business need to be moved with others, which aspects of the business need to precede others in terms of reaching the new location, things of this nature. My team would make this as seamless as possible, with as little downtime for your operation as possible. If you'd like, I'd be happy to put you in touch with other firms we've recently relocated to get their opinion on how we handled the process. I truly believe you'll be more than satisfied with what they have to say."

"Sounds like you've done this before."

"Once or twice," I say with a smirk.

The barkeep hands me my cocktail. I toast with the others and down a healthy sip, followed by another.

"So tell me, Roddy," I go on, "at what point did others approach you about buying your building? Before we first spoke at your shop, or since? I'm guessing the latter."

Roddy's eyes squint slightly as he calculates how best to answer this.

"What makes you say that?"

"You're taking this more seriously. I hear it in your questions. I see it in your eyes. Something changed your mind. I'm guessing a conversation you must have had with someone, in terms of seeing this as an opportunity as opposed to an insult. What did they tell you? Did they remind you about the inconveniences a couple years of construction right next door would bring? Or were they so bold as to explain someone, sooner rather than later, would come along and figure out a way to push you out?"

Roddy takes a swig of his cocktail.

"The construction," he finally says.

L laughs.

"I figured. I also figured others wouldn't be far behind to come see you if they hadn't already. Which is why I made sure my offer, no matter who else came to the party, would be the best."

"Is that right?"

"It is," I answer.

"Then if you're so sure, why offer me the choice to lease the new property you'll buy, with an option to purchase? Didn't you devise that play during this conversation, as further security, based on your new assumption I've been speaking with others?"

Fucking Roddy. Not bad.

"Perhaps. But I'm still confident my offer was your best."

Roddy doesn't answer. He just lifts and tips his glass to me. I do the same.

"I'm interested in your offer," Roddy goes on. "And should you show me some sites that may just work, I may even become very interested. Let's leave it at that for now."

"Consider it left."

At that moment, behind me, I hear someone call my name.

"Jonah! Hey, Jonah!"

I turn around. Jacob Geller, a talented but obnoxious young hotshot architect I've worked with on a few projects, is coming toward me. Dressed like his usual eccentric self, his thick brown hair is teased high like he's in a punk band, he's wearing dark framed glasses I don't think he needs, his polo shirt collar is up, his skinny jeans stop four inches above his naked ankle, and his burgundy loafers are perfectly shined.

"Jonah—hey, it's been a while," he says once he reaches me.

"Jacob. How are you?"

His eyes take glossy to a new level. I introduce him to L and Roddy.

"So, what can I do for you?" I go on, insinuating that unless there's a specific question I might answer, I'd like to get back to the people I'm here with.

"Nothing specific," he slurs, "I just wanted to say hi. And that I'd love it if we got a chance to work together again."

"That would be nice," I lie.

Working with Jacob is often like working with a child. He thinks his talent level gives him the right to treat deadlines as arbitrary, and the clients' tastes as inferior. Jacob Geller and I clashed often while working together. So this somewhat surprises me, as I never had a problem setting his ass straight.

"Hey. Uh—man, that piece today in *Page Six* was too bad. That must have, you know, kinda sucked. You know, since you really get great press usually."

And there it is. Jacob Geller has developed some beer muscles under his corny outfit and relishes a chance to get a jab or two in for the times his immaturity forced me to wield my tongue as a sword.

"Which *Page Six* piece?" I ask.

Before Geller can answer, I step away from the bar to reposition myself, and "accidentally" catch his feet in a vicious sweep. His feeble little legs are cut out from underneath him, and he hits the tiled floor with a thud.

"Ahh!" he screams, his hands immediately moving upward to clutch his head.

"Damn," I exclaim, surprised by such an unfortunate accident.

As others around us gasp at Geller's swift hitting of the deck, I reach down to assist him.

"Fuck, Jonah."

"Sorry about that. Caught you as I was moving away from the bar."

My left hand grips his right elbow with such force, his eyes widen like I just punched him in the gut. When they do, I make sure they're staring right into mine. And he can see the glimpse of my soul he wants no further part of. The part that could snap his elbow like a twig.

"Let me help you up," I go on.

I grab a fistful of his yellow-and-black polo shirt with my right hand. But before lifting him, my balled fist pins him to the floor so hard if I push even just a little bit more, there's a shot it goes through his breastbone and I end up holding his beating heart.

"You ready to get back on those children-sized feet?" I ask in a firm whisper.

Unable to speak, eyes still locked with mine, he nods up and down fast.

"Awesome. Then let's get to it."

In one swift motion I lift Geller back to his feet. As he tries to shake it off, and hold together a semblance of dignity, I tussle his hair even more than it is.

"There we go," I keep at it, "back on his feet."

For good measure, I give him a casual yet solid, brotherly, open-hand slap across the face.

"I knew you weren't such a pussy," I go on. "Sir!" I call, getting the bartender's attention. "Get this man a shot of the Rey Sol Anejo."

"You got it."

I look back at Geller.

"Not every day can be champagne and victories, can it?" I ask. "I'm sorry—did you say something about *Page Six*?"

"Damn, Jonah," he says, rubbing his cheek with his left hand while rubbing the back of his head with his right, "if I'd gotten a chance to finish, all I was going to say is that I hope it's nothing too serious. And that whoever wrote that got their facts wrong."

"Doesn't matter. I don't concern myself with nonsense."

"Fucking gossip journalists," Geller goes on. "If only they realized the *actual* story is often what surrounds what they think is the story."

This statement catches me. I don't know if it's because the words are so simply profound, because my mind is so locked on this Cobus situation, or both. But it makes me think. Are the buildings Cobus chooses, coupled with rhodium and iridium, the driving force behind what markets he enters? Or is it something about these particular cities that ultimately determine where he needs to buy new properties?

Which way is this working?

As Geller slinks away, I sense L moving closer to me.

"Remember, bro, I've been next to you since we're little kids," he whispers in my ear. "I know who you are."

"What's that supposed to mean?"

"Let your plans be dark and impenetrable as night, and when you move, fall like a thunderbolt."

I turn and look my lifelong friend in the eyes, our noses almost touching.

"Sun Tzu," L goes on, in a firm whisper, "*The Art of War.*"

CHAPTER THIRTY-ONE

I WALK INTO Silver Rock. Caught somewhere between buzzed and drunk, I head straight for the elevator and up to the fifth floor. When I step off, Neo is coming down the hall toward me. I pick him up and we exchange kisses.

"What are you still doing up?"

I put him down. He trots ahead of me back toward the master bedroom, no doubt wanting to get back on his favorite chaise and go back to sleep. The hallway is dimly lit. As I follow him I take off my suit jacket and loosen my tie.

Upon entering the bedroom, the lighting the same warm glow of the hallway, Perry enters at the exact same moment from her closet. She has nothing on but a pair of black panties. Without a word she walks over to me, wraps her arms around my neck, and kisses me.

"I missed you," she says, her words slurring.

Her eyes are having trouble focusing. She reeks of alcohol. Immediately, I'm sobered up.

"I missed you too."

"What the hell went on over there? What's going on?"

"We can discuss it in the morning."

"How was L's friend?"

"Roddy."

"Right, Roddy. Is he budging?"

"Actually, I believe he is. Something else we can discuss in the morning. How was your dinner with Gardner?"

Peter Gardner, the CEO of a software firm looking for a new home.

"Went well," she says, her words muffled from her face being buried in my neck. "I brought Natey-Boy with me. Figured he could use some education about how the big kids get shit done."

I take her arms, and gently move her away from me. I throw my jacket and new iPad on one of the room's chairs.

"You seem to have Natey-Boy Landgraff with you a lot," I can't help saying.

"We're working on, like, a ton of shit together, Jonah. He's making things happen the way we used to back when we wanted to get ahead. Why shouldn't I reward the young buck with some face time?"

She clumsily waves her right hand in front of her face.

"When we're talking about this face," she finishes her thought, concluding with a chuckle. "What's wrong," she goes on, coming toward me again, "someone jealous?"

As she almost reaches me, she loses her balance. I catch her.

"Christ, Perry. What'd you mix with the booze tonight? Xanax? Some Oxy?"

"Fuck you, asshole!" she screams, slamming her fists into my chest.

She steps back.

"You don't get to judge me, Jonah."

"I'm not judging you, Perry. I'm *worried* about you!"

"Well, don't be. I'm a big girl who can handle her shit."

"Is that right? Is binge drinking and pill-popping handling your shit?"

"You bastard," she whispers, eyes squinted.

I want to help.

Please. Take this chance.

Open the door.

"I just want to understand this, Perry. Only because what you're doing—it isn't sustainable. You have to know that."

"What I *know*, Jonah, is that few perform each and every day the way I do. Isn't that what matters? That my effort translates into positive revenue for your company?"

"*Our* company, Perry. There are three of us, three partners. You owe it to us not to become the fucking junkie you're turning into."

"How dare you," she growls now, eyes still squinted.

Don't do this.

You.

Me.

Don't do this.

"But it isn't even about that," I go on, as if I didn't even hear, or care about, her last words, "it isn't about Resurrection. It's about your health. It's about the fact I want to spend the next fifty years together. It's about, I mean, you have a son, Perry."

"You think I don't know that?" she screams. "You think I don't know I have a son? He's all I think about every second of every day when my brain isn't stuck on business or how I look or you!"

I shrug off the last part of that sentence.

"What do you talk about with Liz?"

The therapist.

"I mean, do you address this shit? The constant pills? The booze? What you're trying to escape?"

"What I'm trying to *escape*?"

Clearly incensed, Perry steps to me, and points a finger in my face.

"I was a FUCKING HOSTAGE, JONAH, FOR THREE YEARS! THREE YEARS!"

"I know you were. I was the one who almost died getting you the hell out of there."

"You were the reason I ended up there! Without my son, not knowing if he—or you—were alive or dead!"

"Let's not forget, you were married to a cheating pig asshole of a husband who you chose to take your son away from. I never asked you to run with me, Perry. I gave you the opportunity. But I never asked. I never would have put that pressure on you."

She stands down.

"No, you didn't. But I ran anyway. I believed we were supposed to be together, I believed in you, and I believed it was the best thing for Max. And look what happened. Your twisted half brother kidnapped me. Then he locked me away in some corner of one of his family's estates in Russia. They literally treated me like an animal. Food was pushed into my room. Days and nights ran into one another. Do you remember me telling you about my sleep? That I was so scared to sleep, and so scared what might have happened to the two of you, my spinning mind would keep me awake for days at a time, only for me to crash out of exhaustion?"

Her glazed eyes stare into mine. Wanting her to keep speaking, keep opening up, I say nothing. I just nod.

"The times I feel the worst, Jonah," she continues, "are the times I think about that part in my life. How scared I was. And, unfortunately for me, those times are every goddamn second I'm awake and my mind isn't occupied by something. Work, fashion, fun, whatever. I need intensity the same way I need numbness. For me, I don't know if I'll ever be able to find that place in between again where everyone else gets to live. That place where I used to live."

"We need to get you back there, Perry. Max may be a college-aged kid at this point, but he still needs his mother. He's always going to need his mother. Look at what an amazing young man he's turned into. That happened because of you."

"You know, it's funny," she goes on. "I used to pray every single day that the door to my room or little apartment or whatever the hell it was would open, and you'd be standing there. Then I'd wonder if it was so I could wrap my arms around you . . . or kill you."

She starts toward me again.

"Once I saw you, and saw you were alive," she continues, "everything I always felt for you came rushing back. I felt safe again. And I knew right there and then I wanted to see you again so I could hold you."

"Do you still feel that? Do you still feel safe?"

"I don't know what I feel, Jonah. I truly want to get back to that person I was before Europe ever happened. Whether that can really ever happen again, I guess time will tell."

"Did something else happen to you there, Per? Is there anything you never told me?"

She pauses.

"You know I was held against my will, for three years, tormented by my own thoughts. What could be worse than that?"

I open my arms, inviting her in.

"What's the matter, *boss-man*? Can't handle this version of me you're stuck with?"

She reaches me, and starts unbuttoning my shirt. We kiss deeply as she does. Falling into one another, and the emotion of the moment, my clothes being taken off morphs into my clothes being torn off. As my belt and pants are unbuckled and begin sliding down, the pistol in my waistline I've forgotten about falls to the ground. It bounces around aimlessly, randomly, on the carpet like a football, and into Perry's shin.

"Ow! What the fuck was that?"

She looks down. In the room's soft glow she sees the pistol on the floor. She puts her arms in the air, turns, and walks away.

"Jesus Christ, Jonah. Does this shit ever end with you?"

I watch her perfect form head toward the bathroom as she keeps talking.

"And you wonder why I'm so fucked up. I think I've had enough for tonight," her voice tapers off as she disappears.

CHAPTER THIRTY-TWO

THE SHIP SAILS north on the New Jersey Turnpike, leaving Liberty International Airport behind. Neo stands, his hind legs on my thighs, as his front paws secure his balance against my chest. Holding his precious little face with my two hands, I kiss the top of his head.

"You got it, boss-man. Standard Hotel it is. As for Perry, her dinner is scheduled uptown at Ouest."

I look up and reply.

"Thanks, Dante."

As the words come from my mouth, something passing on my right catches my attention. Out the window, past the confines of the highway in the near distance, are shipping containers stacked what must be three or four stories high. Though it's night, they are well lit up as the Port of New York and New Jersey is not exactly the type of operation that has a closing time. The metal boxes are of all colors, albeit each a bit faded from years of wear and tear: red, blue, yellow, orange, green, and white. Some have writing on them, others don't. My eyes move back to Neo.

"Oh, boss-man, before I forget, if—"

My eyes open. I look at the clock—3:52 a.m. Perry is sound asleep next to me. I sit up in bed. My mind is foggy from my crazy recent schedule and the booze, but I hold on to remnants of the dream I was just having. The shipping containers. I didn't think much of seeing the Port of New York and New Jersey—a sight I've passed hundreds, if not thousands, of times in my life—earlier that night. But for some reason I'm thinking about it now.

The Port of New York and New Jersey.

One of the biggest ports in the United States.

Quietly, I get out of bed. Just wearing my underwear—silk Assiagi boxers, of course, handpicked by Pirro—I grab my new iPad and head to the elevator. Just as it opens Neo appears next to me, looking up at me with his loving little eyes. I scoop him up, hit the button for the first floor, and the doors close behind us.

The kitchen is dark, aside from streaks of light from the moon and street lamps sneaking in through the windows. I place Neo on the island in the center of the room, which is topped with a slab of gray-and-white veined Italian marble. Since he's up I decide to give him a little snack. He sits and waits patiently. First I put his water bowl up next to him, and he starts in for a drink before I've even rested it down. Next I take some of his grilled chicken from the refrigerator, cut that up, and place that down for him as well.

I sit on one of the counter stools surrounding the island, flip open the iPad cover, tap in my four-digit code, open Safari, and go to Google. I type in a search for the "largest United States Ports." Immediately a list comes up—it's a bit outdated, from 2012, but I have no doubt it has changed very little if at all since then. The list is categorized as CARGO VOLUME AT U.S. PORTS, 2012, SHORT TONS. The largest is the Port of South Louisiana, followed by the Port of Houston, Texas, and then the Port of New York and New Jersey. The port right by Manhattan is the third largest in the United States.

I type in a new search. "Largest Ports Europe." The first entry is a Wikipedia list of Europe's busiest ports. I open it up.

"Holy shit," I say, as I drop the iPad on the island and my hands move to my head.

Neo looks at me then goes back to his snack.

I'm amazed by what I see. The busiest container port, in all of Europe, is the Port of Rotterdam. Second? The Port of Hamburg. I don't see anything for Amsterdam. I Google, "Ports Netherlands." Sure enough, there it is. It's not one of the largest, but as the second largest port in the Netherlands behind Rotterdam it still does a serious amount of volume.

Ports. Rhodium. Iridium.

What the fuck?

Surprisingly, my mind goes in another direction. I see Cobus yesterday in Hamburg. I'm remembering something he said.

"Amazing. Few people realize how much opportunity there is in South American cities like São Paulo—but it all comes down to what we each see value in, Jonah. Isn't that right?"

I Google "Largest ports in South America." There it is. The Port of Santos, in Santos, São Paulo, Brazil, is the largest, and second busiest, port in South America.

I look at Neo. He's slurping down some water to wash down his chicken. I stand up and walk around the island, slowly, thinking. What does this all mean?

My mind goes back to Europe again. I'm in the storage room, in Rotterdam, staring at the labels on the drums and containers. There are the letters. There are the symbols.

Drums. Containers. Ports. Labels.

I remember a thought I had on the flight from Rotterdam to Hamburg.

These initials have to do with what's inside those drums and containers, not who's responsible for getting them there.

I sit back down and again pick up the iPad. Rhodium and iridium are precious metals—which mean they are mined. I Google "Largest producers rhodium." The first result is titled RHODIUM

MINING STOCKS, COMPANIES, PRICES, AND NEWS. I
tap it. Just like that, a page from a site BlastInvest appears listing
the company names of precious metal producers, along with the exchange they're on—meaning which stock exchange in which country—the current price, and the change in price that has occurred
during recent trading. I open a second Google window, and type in
the name of the first company. Eastern Platinum. The company is
based in Vancouver, Canada, with a green symbol that is an outline
of Africa, with the country South Africa highlighted in yellow since
this is where their mining efforts are predominantly located. I move
back to Google window one, and look for the next company on
the list. Northam Platinum Ltd. I return to Window Two and look
them up. Based in Johannesburg, South Africa, Northam's logo is
their name in chunky silver letters.

This doesn't seem to be going where I'd like, but I forge ahead.
I move on to company number three. This one, also based in
Johannesburg, South Africa, is named Jettis Resource Platinum,
Ltd. This entry, it appears, is much more interesting. And not just
because it turns out Jettis Resource is the world's leading producer
of platinum supplying 38 percent of the world's supply, as well as a
huge chunk of the world's rhodium and iridium. Because their logo
is the same navy and gold one on the labels accompanying "Rh" on
the black tuna-can drums.

Holy shit.

Cobus is in bed with some of the world's leading precious metal
suppliers?

Why?

How?

I look at Neo, and can't help finding it odd he's already having
another huge drink from his bowl. He doesn't usually drink this
much water. Nonetheless, it makes me thirsty so I get up and grab

a bottle of water from the fridge. I sit down yet again and decide I need to power through the rest of this list until I hopefully find the company attached to the other logo.

Vale S.A.—a Brazilian multinational diversified mining and metals corporation with a simple green and yellow V logo. Stillwater Mining based in Billings, Montana, is next. Stillwater is the only platinum, palladium, and other related metals producer in the U.S. Their logo, though charcoal gray, is three long S's side by side, so I keep going.

Lonmin out of the UK—no. African Rainbow Minerals also based in Johannesburg—no. Pan African Resources—no. Glencore—no. Glenroche Mining Company . . .

And there it is.

The charcoal-gray G's backed up to one another. Glenroche PLC, based in Zug, Switzerland, is one of the world's leading precious metals and coal producers with operations in nineteen countries across Africa, Asia, Europe, North America and South America. The company has a market capitalization of thirty-three *billion* dollars. And they, too, are connected to a criminal.

How?

Why?

CHAPTER THIRTY-THREE

At 8:40 a.m. The Ship pulls up to the corporate headquarters of Spectrum Global on West Thirty-Ninth Street. Housed in an old, red-brick, Garment District building, Spectrum and all of its related subsidiaries' operations take up nine of the building's twenty-one floors. Fifteen years earlier, when Spectrum began as a simple commercial janitorial services company, they most likely got a great deal to take some space as American garment firms were being forced out of business as clothing production went overseas. Since then the firm has grown exponentially, not just within their original expertise, but with the acquisition and integration of other companies hence competencies such as security services, marble and metal cleaning services, carpeting, messenger centers, and so on. To be split between nine floors is never an ideal scenario for any firm. But Spectrum, like many other companies, would likely admit there are worse problems to have, as this one is simply a sign of accelerated growth.

Shand, like myself, is a go-getter, someone in the office early. While I figured the best time for a surprise visit is on the early side, I didn't want it to be too early where I'd risk missing him. I walk into the old, simple lobby that takes me back to the 1920s, and stop at the concierge desk.

"Good morning, sir. May I help you?" an older gentleman in his Spectrum Building Services blazer asks.

"Yes, I'm here to see Mr. Shand. Is he in yet?"

"In fact he is, he just arrived about twenty minutes ago. Is he expecting you?"

"He's not."

"May I have your name?"

"Jonah Gray."

"His assistant just walked in a few minutes ago as well, so why don't I ring up to her? In the meantime, may I see your ID?"

I get off the elevator on the second floor. I step through glass doors with the Spectrum Global logo, as well as all of the related subsidiaries' logos, on them, and enter the white, sterile reception area. The space is quiet as the day has just begun ramping up. A woman is getting settled behind the reception desk that seats another three or four. I approach her, but as I do, a fifty-something woman with red hair, a conservative pants suit, and giant glasses that should actually be described as goggles, comes through an adjacent set of double doors off to the side.

"Mr. Gray, Angelina," she says, extending a hand.

"Nice to see you," I reply, taking her hand and shaking it.

"Please follow me, if you will, to the conference room. May I bring you some coffee or tea? Perhaps some juice or water?"

"No thanks, I'm fine."

"Please," she says, leading me through the door from which she just came.

The conference room, like the reception area, is essentially white, basic, clean, and functional. In the center of the room is a long, light-color wood conference table that can accommodate twenty-five to thirty people, with multiple plugin points for computers, projectors, chargers, and the like. Around the table are white leather Allsteel Acuity task chairs. The walls are lined with black-and-white photographs of the different Manhattan properties Spectrum is in.

"Jonah," Shand says, charging into the room. "It has been a while."

"Indeed it has," I say. "How are you?"

"Thankfully I'm well. The kids are healthy and getting older. Does anything else matter?"

He stops in front of me and we shake hands. Greg Shand is six feet tall with an athletic runner's body, silver hair, strong features, and an ever-present smile that frames his oversized, cloud white, shiny veneers.

"I'd have to say no on that one."

"What about you and Perry? You two ever going to add a little superstar to the mix?"

"I guess time will tell," I say, giving one of my cookie-cutter answers for this all-too-often-asked question.

"Coffee? Juice? Did you eat?"

"I'm good. Angelina already asked me. I'm fine."

"Then, let's sit and get down to it."

Motioning with his hand, he offers me a chair.

"It's always nice to see you," he goes on, sitting as well, "but obviously I'm not surprised by this visit. I want to begin by saying I really appreciate your keeping this quiet as we all figure out what happened."

"It's beneficial to me as well," I remind him, "so no need to thank me. We believe we're making headway with the police in determining what happened to Mr. Esparanza. And I must say, on behalf of myself as well as the investigator handling this, we appreciate the access we've been given to your employees and their files."

"Of course, Jonah. Please, something like this happening to someone while they're on the clock for my firm is extremely troubling, and something I'll always take seriously. Have you come up with anything concrete?"

"We think so, but I'll leave that to the investigators handling it to confirm. I just don't want to misspeak about any of the facts. How about from your end? I imagine you've been doing an internal investigation?"

"Of course."

"And?"

"We've done interviews with everyone on this shift as well as others who sometimes join this shift, and apparently no one is offering any knowledge beyond the man simply must have had a heart attack."

"On this vacant floor?"

He puts his hands up.

"I know—I don't understand it either. Maybe he wasn't feeling well and went to find some quiet space for himself. Who the hell knows?"

"You know, I'd love to believe this was simply a death-by-natural-causes situation. But if any of us thought that was the case, you and I aren't having this conversation."

"Why can't it be that?" he asks.

"What do you mean?" I ask, puzzled.

He pauses, collects the right words to match his thought.

"A man has died from a heart attack. Do the circumstances surrounding that really matter? You know—in the big picture of things?"

I think I know where this is headed, but, appalled as I am, decide to play Shand's game.

"You mean—as far as, what's the difference if the surrounding circumstances included one or more other people leading to said heart attack? He can't be brought back to life, and no one else got hurt?"

"Something like that."

Scumbag.

"Unfortunately the detective investigating is smarter than you know. He saw the body in the exact manner it was found. A manner that clearly illustrates someone else was there."

"So why can't someone come forward from that night's crew and . . . say . . . give some story that in a very benign manner corroborates the way the body was found?"

"Does this person, or story, exist?" I inquire.

"Maybe," he says, with a shrug.

Wow. Dude is willing to give one of his workers a few extra bucks to make this go away. Justice be damned. For there is truth to be shunned.

He stands up, and starts walking, slowly, around the table.

"All I'm saying, Jonah, is that we both have a lot of reason to see this thing go away. A cleaning crew member on the overnight shift dying mysteriously in one of your buildings—that my firm cleans—is detrimental to us both. Now I'm not saying any of us yet absolutely knows what transpired."

He stops and looks at me.

"All I'm saying," he continues, "is that it's always—*possible*—someone hasn't yet come forward with a perfectly logical story which makes all of this go away."

"And what about that story explains why no one called management, or the home office, or the police when no one could find this guy?"

"Ah. You mean the fact he complained he hadn't been feeling well to some of his coworkers earlier in the evening, so they just figured he'd left and let the home office know on his own."

"This happened?" I go on.

"I'm not sure," he comes back, "but it's always *possible* that in the flow of tending to their work as opposed to all of the little conversations going on someone simply forgot about hearing this . . . until now. I mean, let's not forget, all it would take is one person forgetting they heard a man who ended up having a heart attack say he wasn't feeling well."

"I guess there are still all types of potential scenarios that may play out," I concur.

"Indeed!" he says happily lifting his arms, palms up. "All I'm saying is that we'll just need to let this play out. But that there is still a real chance this might go away in a manner that leaves both you and me—and, more importantly, our firms—unscathed."

"Assuming, of course, this isn't connected to the other situation that occurred in the property that evening. I mean—let's be honest, after that little *Page Six* nugget yesterday, I'm already dealing with a bit of PR damage control."

"Connected? How would that possibly be?"

"I have no idea one way or another. Which is why, as you said, we'll have to just let this play out."

"Now we've gone through the footage, Jonah, thoroughly, really limiting the search time to the thirty minutes before and after the time the prototype package was delivered. This is when, according to percentages, the most likely scenario would have been for the theft of something this tightly secured to have happened. No one— *no one*—unaffiliated with this building, that firm, or who was registered for the day as a visitor according to protocol, entered or exited the building during that window."

"What about a bigger window? Did you check the few hours before and after the alleged theft as well?"

"We did, but we're really of the belief the focus needs to be on that 5:46 to 6:46 window, the hour surrounding the 6:16 p.m. delivery of the bottle. My top security experts have been at this a long time. And if this is what they tell me, I have no reason not to listen."

"So—what are you saying? That you're of the belief this prototype was misplaced, or must be somewhere still in the building?"

"I'm saying those are certainly possibilities, along with another theory. The bottle may have never been here at all."

"Excuse me?" I say, shaking my head. "I'm not following."

"One of our theories is that there was never any bottle."

"But there was a package delivered at 6:16 from Paris, just as described. I've seen the records of the delivery."

"We are in agreement the package was delivered. But we believe it may have been nothing more than an empty box."

"An empty box? Why?"

"What could be better marketing than a story of a much-anticipated product swiped by a rival for fear of how spectacular it is? Since this has happened, I've done my homework on Madame Martine. And her company is not foreign to spectacular methods of gaining attention."

"There's spectacular and there's extreme."

"Since when do they have to be mutually exclusive? Besides, both the individual who accepted the package into the building as well as her assistant, Tiffany, said they saw a package—and Madame Martine herself has expressed the package was to remain unopened so she would be the first to lay eyes on the actual prototype in the morning. The package was seen. An actual prototype, or bottle, or whatever, was not."

I just don't see it. I've come to know Madame Martine quite well. Aggressive marketing, possibly. Lying to my face, doubtful.

"Well," I say, standing up, "I guess until we know anything for sure, we'll have to both make sure everyone keeps at it. After all, as you've said, there's a lot at stake for both of us in terms of this being handled properly."

"Agreed, Jonah," he says as he comes my way. "Let's be sure to keep in touch as this all plays out."

He reaches me and we shake hands again.

"Thanks for coming by," he goes on.

We turn and start walking, me following Shand out the way we came in. Just before we reach the door, I stop.

"Oh, before I go, there is one more thing I was wondering about."

He too stops and turns to me.

"Which is?"

"We saw in the security footage you came by the building at 9:29 p.m."

I'm sure to mention the word "we," so he gets it I'm not the only one with this information. I'm also sure to give him the exact minute in question. Because anyone understands there's no ballparking when it comes to looking closely.

"And left at 10:22," I go on. "Do you usually come by properties in the evening?"

I watch closely.

In his *millionth*, I see fear.

In his *millionth*, I see disappointment.

He holds it all together. He forges ahead, still well in character.

"Not usually, but sometimes. More so nowadays as we've been expanding and gaining new clients. Of course I have a terrific management team in place, but sometimes I can't resist the urge to hit the pavement and check on things myself. You know, keep everyone on their toes."

He doesn't miss a beat.

"I figured as much," I respond, keeping it light, "I too have trouble not checking up from time to time on things I've left to others. So—on a night like that—will you typically stop at one property, or do you check on a few?"

There's a bit of a pause before he answers this question.

"Usually a few."

"Like two or three? Or like five or six?"

Against his will, his face becomes a bit harder as he thinks.

"Anyway," I go on, cutting his thought process short and letting him off the hook, "not a big deal. Was just curious."

I turn and open the door.

"How's Julie?" I say as I walk away, throwing one last question over my shoulder.

Julie is Shand's wife.

"Oh—didn't I mention she's great when we sat down?"

"Nope. You said you were well, and the kids were thankfully healthy."

CHAPTER THIRTY-FOUR

THE SHIP PULLS up in front of my office building. Dante opens the back door and I step out. Morante is waiting outside for me.

"Any word on Shane?" I ask, going with a preemptive-strike strategy.

"Not yet, but our guys are all over this. A missing person is bad enough. But a missing officer and man who served this country? That's a whole different level."

"Absolutely," I respond.

Fuck.

This is not good.

"NYPD won't rest until we find Shane Concord. I can promise you that," he goes on. "So? Were you able to meet with Shand?"

"I was."

"And?"

"And something is definitely up."

I fill him in.

"How about you?" I go on. "Anything new?"

"Yeah. The girl Billings said Rosa is tight with—Tori—I was able to track her down again. I pressed her a bit this time; told her if she wanted to alter her statement to what she *actually* knows, now would be a good time. No answer. I explained that I had good reason to believe that she and Rosa were up to something that 'falls outside of the business description of the overnight cleaning crew.'

Ballsy little firecracker—she told me to fuck off. That's when I explained to her that if she, or Rosa, or the two of them together, were withholding any information whatsoever about what happened to Mr. Esparanza, there would undoubtedly be hell to pay, starting with obstruction of justice. She was freaked out and remained hardened, but blurted out, 'Rosa didn't hurt no one! That's not what this is about!'"

"Whoa," I say, surprised.

Morante continued, "'Is that right?' I said. 'Well, then, Tori Bolton, what *is* this about?' No answer. 'Why wasn't Rosa at work the night after Mr. Esparanza passed away?' Still no answer."

"So what now?" I ask.

"Rosa gets the full court press."

Morante holds up a large, yellow envelope.

"There's something else."

He hands me the envelope.

"What's this?"

"You tell me. Open it."

I do as he says. Then I slide a photograph from the envelope.

"Recognize her?"

My eyes bug out of my head. I can't believe what I'm seeing. I return my eyes to Morante.

"What time did she enter the building?"

* * *

I step off the elevator and head straight for my office. To keep anyone who was hoping to approach me about this or that at bay, I allow my gait's pace to explain now is probably not a good time. As Carolyn sees me coming down the hall, she bounces from her desk and meets me halfway.

"We're being inundated with calls, Jonah," she says before even reaching me. "Me, reception—anyone and everyone wants to be the first to get some one-on-one feedback from you about this possible Madame Martine security breach."

"What have you been telling them?" I ask, my stride unaltered.

Carolyn, as she's done so many times before, turns on her heels, heads in the same direction I'm going, and meets me stride for stride.

"That the only comment you have at the moment, while the situation is properly and expeditiously being handled, is the one already issued by your publicist, Dawn London. I've also given those exact words—typed out—to the girls handling the calls coming into reception."

I turn to her as we move briskly down the hallway.

"Of course you did," I say, "that's why I love you."

"My ability to read your mind is merely one of the reasons why you love me, but we can leave that discussion for the one at a later date surrounding my Christmas bonus," she says, deadpan. "I assume there won't be any further comment on the matter until it has been resolved one way or another, so please let me know ahead of time if that's going to change," she goes on.

"Of course."

"Your interview via phone with Pimm Foxx is scheduled to begin in forty-three minutes. Can you still make it, or would you like me to tell his producers that they'll need to find someone else today?"

Pimm Foxx, the host of *Taking Stock* on Bloomberg TV. I look at my watch.

"Will there be any security bre—"

"They provided me with the line of questioning last night," she cuts me off, "which I in turn forwarded to you."

"I didn't have a chance to review it," I admit.

"The material appears to be strictly related—"

This time it's me who does the cutting off.

"I could care less about the material. They keep it real estate and market focused, there's no discussion I'm not prepared for. But it may be a good idea to let them all know that if the conversation does move into one about this *alleged* security breach—that I have already commented on publicly through my publicist—it may possibly be the last time I do their show."

"Understood, Jonah."

We turn right at the end of the hallway in unison and keep walking.

"Dinner tonight," she goes on, "you and Perry are all set for eight o'clock with the little ones at Dirty French."

"The 'little ones,'" I repeat, and chuckle, "I like that. Funny."

"I aim to please. I'll let Dante know the plan. Is there anything else at the moment?"

"No."

"Then I'll go call Mr. Foxx's producers."

Just as Carolyn breaks off from me and heads back in the opposite direction, I enter Perry's office. She's sitting back in the chair behind her desk, reviewing some documents.

"What's up, stud?" she asks, without ever moving her eyes away from the paper to me.

"There's actually an email I'd like you to have a look at. Check this out."

I hand her the new iPad that hasn't left my sight. I've written something in the body of a new email I've opened, an email that doesn't have a recipient entered into the outgoing address line. The words I've typed read: *Just respond "Interesting!" Then stand up and follow me out of the room without another word.* Perry does exactly as I've said. She follows me to Jake's office.

"Not a shot," Jake, standing behind his desk, barks into his office's phone, which is obviously on speaker. "Come on, Gary—really?"

"I told you, Jake, we see a lot of upside in this property—one *you* brought an offer to us for when I made it clear we are not looking to part ways with this asset in our portfolio."

"I see your point, Gary. I do. But *seventy dollars* per foot over a number we've come in with that already shows a premium? You really think there's justification for that type of a counter?"

"I told you I believed your offer was at a real enough number and I would take it inside the walls. When I did just that this morning, the response was collectively that the type of counteroffer I've presented is all that would make sense. And, to be clear, I'm in agreement."

"With a counter that represents a price over *fifty million dollars higher* than the price we offered," Jake says, sarcastically, as if he needs confirmation.

"Correct. And here's why. In our forecasts, drawn up with very heavy weighting toward the surrounding area growth with regard to this particular property, we don't foresee selling until six to seven years down the road. Yes—the number you presented is a premium, but that's for today's market. Six or seven years down the road we both know whoever owns this building has an asset worth well more than the five hundred and fifty million dollars we're talking about today. If we're even going to entertain this type of an exit, we'd have to do so in a manner that allows us to enjoy even a sliver of the further upside we'll be passing on."

"All due respect, Gary, we're in the business of making deals reflective of market conditions today," Jake says on cue, just as Perry and I said to Sturner the other night. "I mean, what if King Kong shows up next year and decides the Empire State Building isn't really where he likes to troll for ass, because he's really more an Eight Twelve Seventh Avenue type of ape?"

"All due respect to you, Jake. While we appreciate the concept of making market-reflective deals, we're one of the largest commercial real estate firms in the world who butters their bread by way of heavily devised strategy. If someone wants to knock on our door and ask us to alter that strategy, they need to understand they're going to pay us to do so."

Jake, now staring at Perry and me, says nothing.

"Seven hundred and fifty-five dollars per square foot, for a total purchase price of five hundred and sixty-six million and change," Gary Albert continues. "You want to start talking from this number, then we'll talk. But while six hundred and eighty-five per foot may have gotten you in the door, that's as far into the building as that number's going to get you."

Albert hangs up. Jake, still standing, sighs. He reaches down, picks something up off his desk, and pops it in his mouth.

"Was that a marshmallow?" I ask.

"'Twas. Just needed something sweet to follow up the salty taste of the bacon, egg, and cheese I just stuffed down my throat before that call. What's up?"

"Check out this email," I say, handing him the iPad as I'd done with Perry.

"Interesting," Jake says, worry in his eyes.

The two of them follow me out of Jake's office, back through the hallways, and onto the elevator.

CHAPTER THIRTY-FIVE

WE WALK OUT of the building, the two of them silently following me like trusting schoolchildren trailing the cool kid. There's a bite in the air, yet there isn't a cloud in the sky, so the sun still warms us. We cross Park Avenue. Now on the west side of the street, I stop and face them.

"What's going on?" Jake asks, squinting from the sun and using his hand as a visor over his eyes. "What happened in Europe? And why are we talking out here?"

"We'll get to the latter. Let's start with Amsterdam. Once I landed I knew exactly which building I wanted to check out first. When I got there, getting into the building wasn't an issue. The problem was the gun put to my head the second I entered the basement."

"They knew you were going to be there?" Perry asks.

"At the time I wasn't sure. After seeing what was going on in the basement, it became very clear to me there were extra security guards at each property manning the basement. A separate security team that has nothing to do with the rest of the property, just protects the other situation going on with these buildings."

"Wait!" Perry exclaims, shaking her head, putting her hands up. "You said you had a *gun* put to your head. How did . . . is that, I mean—"

"I took care of him. Left him wishing he'd never met me."

"Is that how you got the split lip?" Perry asks.

"I have no idea. This was just the first clash with his thugs."

"Jesus, fuck!" Jake says, putting the hand not being used as a visor on his head. "The first clash with his thugs?"

"Guys—that's not what's important. Let's not lose focus here."

"Jonah, if there are men looking to—"

"Per! Seriously! Let me speak!"

She quiets down.

"The basement was one I had previously known very well. From the second I was moving through it on my own I could tell it had been reconfigured. Soon it was clear to me. Some of the storage units were for tenants—marked as such, with their respective firm's nameplate next to the door—while others were not. And the ones that were not, the doors had multiple serious locks."

"Did you try to get in one?"

"I did. No luck. Not in that building, anyway."

"Meaning?"

"I got the hell out of there. When I did, and found myself in a cab, that's when all of the questions started flooding me. How did they know I was coming? *Did* Cobus himself in fact know I was coming? Or did his security detail simply pick up on someone heading to the basement who didn't belong there? I started getting extremely paranoid—so paranoid, in fact, I gave the driver cash for his phone because I was thinking maybe someone was even listening to my calls. I didn't know what the fuck was going on."

"So, where did you go? Back to the airport?"

"And leave with nothing? Fuck that. On my new phone I called Carolyn and told her to have the jet meet me in Rotterdam where I was going via train. On that train, I'm pretty sure there was someone tailing me. But I made it to the building I had in mind in Rotterdam. When I did, I finally got a glimpse into what my old friend is up to."

"Which is?" Jake asks.

"Rhodium. And iridium."

"Rhody-what?" Perry asks.

"Rhodium and iridium. In the building in Rotterdam, I was able to get into one of the multiple-lock storage rooms in the basement. When—"

"How?" Jake asks.

"Huh?" I respond.

"How did you get in?"

"I shot my way in. With the gun I lifted from the dude I left unconscious in Amsterdam."

"The gun that bounced into my shin last night," Perry adds.

"That bounced where?" Jake quips. "Forget it," he goes on, both hands now on his head as he spins away from us. "Forget I asked."

"Anyway, both are precious metals—expensive precious metals like gold and platinum, just less common or known to people like us."

"They were both in the room?" Perry asks, the conversation now just us as Jake is still ten feet away catching his breath.

"They were. The rhodium was in these black, tuna-can-looking drums and the iridium was in these gray plastic containers. Stacked rows of each, every drum or container having a tamper-proof lock or seal."

"How did you know what was in them?" Perry continues, as Jake rejoins us.

"Each had a label. The label for the drums had the letters "Rh" on them, and the containers each had a label with "Ir" on them. The letters are the initials for each from the Periodic Table of Elements. Along with the letters on each was a logo or symbol, and it turns out each logo was from one of two of the leading precious metals mining companies in the world."

271

"Holy shit," Perry pushes out in a whisper.

"Holy shit is right."

"How do you know all of this?" Jake asks. "What the initials meant, who these companies are, any of it?"

"One part motivation, two parts time on a private jet with Wi-Fi and Google at my fingertips. Wait, there's more."

"Of course there is," Jake sighs.

"I woke up in the middle of the night. For some reason, my mind was stuck on the Port of New York and New Jersey, more importantly the shipping containers, I'd passed on the way into the city from the airport last night. I've never given this place much of a thought in all the times I've passed it in my life, but last night it reached out and grabbed me for some reason. So I started doing a little late-night research."

Perry starts whispering to herself, looking off into the distance, crunching information in her head.

"Wait! I got it! I learned when I studied abroad that Rotterdam has the biggest port in Europe. And I know Amsterdam and Berlin have sizeable ports, while the port right here—the Port of New York and New Jersey—is one of the biggest in the country. That's how he picks his cities to expand his portfolio!"

That's my girl.

Stay with me.

I need both of you to stay with me.

"Boom. You got it," I say.

"But wait," Perry says, returning to seriousness. "What exactly is happening with these materials? Who's pulling the strings—Cobus or these companies? And why?"

"That I haven't figured out yet. But before I left Europe I decided to make one more stop. I boarded the jet and we headed to Hamburg, another city where Cobus has been expanding, and another city with one of the most significant European ports. Again, I knew exactly which building would make the right litmus test. Only I never made it into that building."

"Why not?"

"Because Cobus himself was waiting for me. He knew I was coming."

"To Hamburg?" Jake asks.

"To Europe. To Amsterdam. Which brings me to why we're speaking out here. The little conversation he and I had in a parking garage in Hamburg left little doubt he's not just watching, closely, but he was well prepared to keep an eye on me—on all of us—well before he ever got here."

"How is that even possible? How do you know?"

"The only person I spoke with about changing my itinerary and heading to Rotterdam was Carolyn—and that was in a car I'd never been in before, with a driver I'd never seen before, on a phone that wasn't even mine! Either Carolyn is being monitored, or Jennie from the jet or, Ken, the pilot or—*someone*—gave him that information. I have no idea. But it's more than that. He mentioned to me what's going on with Madame Martine and the dead guy at Park South, as well as my dealings with Minnie. And not just the business side of it, but the fact she's a creepy little sex freak. These are simply things I've never remotely had a discussion with him about. Which means he's either listening to our calls, or watching our emails and texts, or—fuck me if I know—all of the above. Going forward, unless the three of us are standing somewhere like this, alone, away from everything, we don't talk about any of this. We keep everything business."

"Okay, now I'm officially freaked out," Perry says.

"Don't be. You can't be, or we're done. None of this is because Cobus wants any of us to get hurt. It's solely about his getting these buildings that he wants, and knowing that we're doing everything in our power to make that happen every step of the way. What's going on with Park South, my Meatpacking deal—none of that matters to him. All that matters to him is getting the buildings he wants. So we keep doing everything we can to make our client happy."

"And then what?" asks Jake.

"The next thing I have to do is figure out the rest of the story—as Perry said—who's pulling the strings, and how. Which means I need to continue my research. And reach out to certain people without his knowing, something else I need to figure out."

"How are you going to do any more research? You said yourself he's probably monitoring everything including every computer, iPhone, iPad, all of it. And if he's watching so closely and has now been adamant about you keeping your nose out of his business and on these deals, then—"

"This is my research machine, which I used last night in the kitchen," I say, cutting him off and holding up the new iPad. "Nothing more, nothing less. I bought it last night myself after I landed before meeting L and Roddy. It hasn't been out of my reach since, and it won't be until I know everything going on. From here out, we keep everything via text, email, cell conversations, even verbal discussions in our homes and office—and The Ship—about business. That's it. Nothing about Cobus or this situation. That's to be left to me."

We turn and head back toward the building. Jake stops at a vendor to grab a hot dog. Perry and I cross the street.

"Is my going to Miami still important?" Perry asks.

"More than ever," I respond, still staring straight ahead.

"Then I think I should go tomorrow night. Get it over with."

"I think that's a good idea."

CHAPTER THIRTY-SIX

THE SHIP STOPS in front of Twenty Two Penn Plaza, a brick shithouse of an office building built in the 1930s near Penn Station, on the corner of Thirty-First Street and Ninth Avenue. Dante opens the door. Perry, Landgraff, and I step out.

"Don't go anywhere," I say.

"Of course, boss-man. I'll be waiting right here."

I look at Dante.

"We won't be long."

The three of us enter the weathered, tired lobby that hasn't seen a facelift since the '80s.

"May I help you?" asks the older fella at the security desk.

"Yes, we're here to see Mr. Greenbaum."

"Is he expecting you?"

"He is."

"And who may I ask is visiting?"

I look at Natey-Boy.

"Nate Landgraff."

The security guard scans the computer screen in front of him.

"Here you are. Go right on up. Tenth floor."

* * *

The elevator doors open on ten. We step off. The first door we see has the name "Biscayne Property and Holdings" on it—the name of Fucking Anshel's company—along with the names of twelve or thirteen other companies the family owns, most of which I'm guessing are shells.

I open the door and enter the office, Perry and Landgraff behind me.

"Yes, may I help you?" I hear from a raspy, cigarette- and coffee-stained voice.

The overweight receptionist, who can't be a day younger than eighty, is hunched over her desk wearing some kind of floral frock, her hair in a bun, and glasses that look like they're from the '50s. It's 2016 and she's *actually* smoking a cigarette; there's a fan directly above her in the ceiling that sucks in the smoke the moment it escapes the nasty white stick.

"Nate Landgraff here to see Mr. Greenbaum," I say.

"Have a seat in the conference room," she says, giving zero direction as to where the conference room might be. "I'll let him know you're here."

Turns out the conference room is right behind us, off from the reception area. Like the lobby, and the reception area we just traversed, this room is dated, tired. The blue carpeting has worn thin in the more trafficked areas, the glass table has nicks and dings along the edges, and the credenza against the wall is of the maroon and Formica persuasion that screams "Greetings from the 1970s!" The three of us settle in, and take seats around the table.

"Unless I ask you to, you don't say a word," I say to Landgraff. "Your work here—while well done—is literally finished."

Moments later an older, shrinking man, wearing old everything from his beige suit to his yellow shirt to his brown tie to his orthopedic shoes, and a yamaka, enters the room. His son, Moishe, a guy who resembles his father—only the six-foot-tall, athletic version of him, also wearing a yamaka and a much nicer suit—trails him.

"Wait, what is this?" Fucking Anshel says upon sight of me.

This one's for you, Pop.

"Business," I respond. "This here," I say pointing to Natey-Boy, "is Nate Landgraff, who set this meeting up with you. The man who, ultimately, will make the commission from the deal we're all about to do. This is Perry York, my partner, and I'm—well—I don't think I need any introduction."

"How dare you! You want to trick me into a meeting with you? Who the hell do you think you are?"

"In the essence of time, looking to bypass the bullshit that would have come with me trying to get this meeting on my own, yes, I back doored my way in. You have a gas station site on the corner of First Avenue and Ninety-Third Street, right by the FDR. I need that site. And I'm prepared to do whatever it takes to get it."

"You bastard. You think you can walk in here—*into my house*—and tell me what *you* want, and what *you* plan on having, like you own the place? You're no different than your dirty pig of a father—an arrogant, no-good, fuck!"

"Ouch," I say, clutching my heart with my hand. "Do you actually kiss your ugly stick-beaten wife with that mouth? Or do you save that tongue just for friends?"

"Get the hell out of my office!"

"You heard my father," Moishe says, starting toward me, "time for you to go."

Careful, Moishe.

Don't you know what to do when a shark swims by?

"I just came here looking to do a little business," I say, not even thinking of standing up. "Since when aren't we all interested in making a little money?"

"I don't do business with scum like you," Fucking Anshel growls.

"You're a slum lord, Fucking Anshel. So if I'm scum, what would one call you?"

I turn to Moishe, now not five feet from me.

"You touch me," I say, my voice as razor sharp as my squinted eyes, "I knock your jaw across the street."

Moishe stops in his tracks.

"You can leave on your own, or I can call security who will in turn call the police," Sonny-Boy says. "Up to you."

I look back at Fucking Anshel.

Time to pepper them with some body blows.

"Go ahead. Call security. In the meantime, I'll tell all of you one of the little tales my father once told me about the Greenbaum empire. The one about the apartment complexes in the outer boroughs like Brooklyn, Queens, and the Bronx. The one about all the violations related to those properties hidden via kickbacks. In fact—let's make that story a bit more interesting. Why don't I call *my* contacts in the Department of Buildings, and have them start investigating every nook and cranny that has to do with these buildings since the beginning of time. How do we think that might go?"

"You're no different than your father. An animal."

"Damn right my father was an animal. An animal that, as I understand it, lunged forward and tore a nice hunk of flesh out of you once or twice."

Mix it up with a couple jabs.

"My guess is that you never hated him for playing dirty," I continue, "you hated him because he played the game better. Rest assured, those times doing battle gave him more than a bit of insight about you as well to go along with all the rumors that already existed about what a shady piece of shit you are. You know what I call you? What my father used to call you?"

No answer. Fucking Anshel just puts his chin in the air.

"What I just called you a few seconds ago. Fucking Anshel. We don't refer to you simply as Anshel, we actually use the extra breath to put a 'fucking' in front of your name. Because it's worth it. Because that's who you are. And my understanding about you, Fucking Anshel, is that you're not just a cheap owner, but you don't even know how to give a proper kickback. You see, that's what all you old-school idiots living in the new world don't understand. Guys at the Department of Buildings would much rather have a chip to play with someone like me down the road than a couple greasy, crumpled bills in their hand from a cretin like you. Because they're never going to need something from you *thirty years ago*. But they may just need this or that from me in the future."

"What the hell do you want?" Moishe chimes in.

"I told you what I want. The gas station site on Ninety-Third and First. And I'd watch your fucking tone with me, Moishe. Because I'm guessing you, like Daddy, would rather the proper authorities never get wind of the fact the Greenbaum clan all like to live in their conjoined rent-stabilized apartments paying prices from the 1930s because they're all still in the names of the elder generations."

I look back and forth between Fucking Anshel and Moishe.

"Am I wrong?" I go on.

Neither says a word.

Catch him with an uppercut to the jaw.

"That's what I thought. You see, my father was a lot of things, but one thing he wasn't was shortsighted. He kept dibs, and took notes, on more personalities in this city than is an actual number of people most individuals will meet in a lifetime. Through the years he told me—over dinner, over cocktails, in between sessions of berating me—where all of the bodies are buried when it comes to people like you. Why? Because he wanted me to be impressed, as I usually was, when he stuck it to those who we now both knew had it coming. Little did either of us know his life would be cut short. And I'd be the primary beneficiary of all those conversations."

"You little—"

"Save it, Fucking Anshel," I say, as I stand up.

Time to drop him with a crushing overhand right.

"This is how it's going to go down. By the end of the day, I want the most recent Phase One Environmental Report done on the property in my office."

A Phase One Environmental Report is a report prepared for a real estate holding that identifies potential or existing environmental contamination liabilities.

"Also by the end of the day," I continue, "Natey-Boy over here will get you the price we'll be paying for the site—a number that will be fair, and nonnegotiable. From there I'll have my attorney draw up a purchase agreement. We all walk away with something solid, and you and your family don't get publicly shamed in front of both the world and your synagogue, and, simultaneously, thrown out on the street. Sound good?"

* * *

An hour later, I'm on the roof of our headquarters, One Hundred Five Park Avenue, alone. Standing on what is essentially the fiftieth story of a forty-nine-story-tall building, the unimpeded sun pounds me. My Assiagi handmade metal and horn sunglasses, handpicked compliments of Pirro, shield my eyes. My tie is loosened, my top button undone. I can see all the way south to Freedom Tower, north to Four Thirty Two Park Avenue, the recently completed, eighty-three-story condominium building that is one of the tallest such residential properties in the world, west to the Empire State Building and One Penn Plaza, and east to the Chrysler Center where I used to work when I was with PCBL way back when.

On the iPad I'm researching Jettis Resource, the company that mined the rhodium I saw in Rotterdam. I'm not exactly sure what I'm looking for, but I can't help thinking the more I learn about these companies, the more I'll have a shot of understanding the relationship between them and Cobus.

My phone rings. Carolyn.

"What's up?" I answer.

"The producers from *Closing Bell* just called. Because of all the action with the REITs today, they'd like to have you on today live from your office to answer questions from Bill and Kelly."

Bill Griffeth and Kelly Evans, the hosts of CNBC's *Closing Bell*.

"Am I okay to give them the green light to have a crew come in later to set you up?" she goes on.

"Does my schedule give me the room?"

"It does."

I look at my watch.

Business as usual.

"That's fine. And do me a favor, let them know before—"

"Beforehand that there are to be no security-related questions," she cuts me off. "Way ahead of you."

I hang up. Before my phone is back in my pocket, it rings again. Without looking I pick up, figuring Carolyn forgot something.

"What did you forget?"

"Forget?" I hear.

Cobus.

I take a deep breath. I turn around, my view shifting from north to south.

"I thought you were my assistant. What's going on?"

"You tell me, Jonah. How is everything moving along now that you're back in New York, focused on my deals? I mean—the opportunity to make these types of commissions simultaneously hardly comes along every day. Isn't that right?"

Don't patronize me, asshole.

Resurrection, like de Bont Beleggings, is in growth and acquisition mode.

And we both know I'm better at the real estate game than you'll ever be.

"The deals are moving ahead, some, as expected, proving to be more challenging than others. Again, been a while since brokering deals for commissions has been me and my partners' bread and butter. But who can say no to the right client?"

"That's what I like to hear. How about an update on each deal?"

I take him through the basics of where we are with each, focusing more on Perry's and Jake's deals. He's made it clear he knows all about mine with Minnie.

"You know," Cobus says, after my quick review, "there may be a way for Jake to close that gap between the price he offered and the one Mr. Albert came back with. And close that gap quickly."

I swallow. My hand instinctively checks for the gun in my rear waistline, under my jacket.

"And what is that?"

"We both know exactly what that is. And it has to do with the fact his wife enjoys the company of other women."

It's now crystal clear I'm not the only one being monitored, watched, listened to. These are both—the info about Albert's wife and the difference in where each side is number-wise about a sale price—things Jake said to me in person, in the confines of his own office.

Cobus, again, is using the moment twofold. To make me understand just how closely he's paying attention. And to remind me there are to be no limits whatsoever in getting him where he needs to go. No matter what that means, or who might get hurt.

CHAPTER THIRTY-SEVEN

I STEP OFF the elevator on the eighth floor of Three Twenty One Park South.

"Good afternoon, Mr. Gray," the receptionist says, "May I help you?"

"Actually, I'm looking for Tiffany. Is she in?"

"Of course. Let me call her for you."

Thirty seconds later Tiffany, wearing black, skintight leather pants, a white, silk blouse, and standing nearly six feet tall on her black, suede, ankle-strap pumps, greets me. As always, her long, dangling ponytail bounces from side to side behind her with each step.

"Hey, Jonah," she says, kissing me on the cheek. "Madame Martine isn't here. Is there something I can help you with?"

"There may be. Is there somewhere we can talk?"

"Of course. Follow me."

We walk through the space, into a small conference room by Madame Martine's office.

"Can I have someone bring you some coffee? Or maybe some water or juice?" she asks, while offering me a seat with her hand.

"No thanks, Tiffany. I'm all set."

I unbutton my suit jacket, put my iPad down on the glass table in front of me, and sit down casually as to help her feel at ease.

"All right, then."

She sits as well.

"What's up?" she continues.

"As you know, Tiffany, we're doing everything we can to sort out what happened the night Madame's prototype was taken. Myself, the police, Spectrum Global who owns both the security and cleaning services company in the building—we're all working hard to figure this out. And we're trying to do so in a manner where reputations stay intact, businesses go on, and hopefully everyone can walk away from the whole mess quietly, and unscathed."

"Of course, Jonah. I completely understand."

"Good. So, then, I need you to indulge me once again. I know we've been through it before, but tell me again the sequence of what happened from the time the package with the prototype was delivered until the time you left."

"Sure. As I told you before, the package arrived at 6:16 from Paris, and I immediately placed it on Madame Martine's desk. And then I locked it in her office."

"Right. And only you, Madame, and Laurent have keys. Correct?"

"That's right."

"What time did you leave the building?"

"Seven twenty."

"Tiffany, I don't want to make waves with anyone, but I'd like to talk about something with you off the record. Just between us."

"Okay."

"It seems like Marilena has a problem with Madame Martine. I mean, truthfully, it seems like she has a problem with everyone here—including you. Why do you think that might be?"

Tiffany pauses, chooses her words carefully.

"I'm kinda happy you're bringing this up. Look, I like Marilena. I respect her. She definitely has a high-pressured job. But as much as I really didn't want to say anything, she's been even more uptight since this whole thing happened."

"Do you think she might be hiding something?" I go on.

"I guess she could be."

"Do you think, maybe, she finds it insulting that she—from what I understand—essentially runs this office, and doesn't even have a key to Madame's office?"

"Maybe."

"I mean," I go on, "whoever tried to get in there didn't have a key, or the door handle and lock area wouldn't have been scratched up like that. Right?"

"Makes sense," she concurs.

"But if then, hypothetically, Marilena was somehow involved— why? What could possibly be the reason? Right? I mean, why bite the hand that feeds you in such a vicious manner that it could severely impact the future of the company and even possibly land her in jail in the process?"

"I have no idea," Tiffany says, shaking her head. "I guess one never can really understand what's happening in someone else's head."

I take a photograph out from the large, yellow envelope I'm holding, and slide it over to Tiffany.

"Could this be Marilena entering the building?" I ask.

She looks at the picture. Confused, she looks at me, then back at the photo.

"When was this taken?"

"At some point that night. Again—do you think this could be her?"

The picture is of what appears to be a woman entering the building, turned away from the camera, with a jacket on, hood up, and the arm of sunglasses wrapped back around over their ear.

She studies it a bit harder.

"It's hard to say," she says, leaning back in her chair. "It looks like it could be anyone."

"Exactly. That's why we always make sure the cameras we have on-site at all of our properties have significant range. This way, sometimes cameras can pick things up that other cameras don't—even though other cameras may be much closer to what we're trying to see. You see this?"

I take another picture out from the large, yellow envelope. I look at it as I continue speaking.

"This picture was taken from another camera across the lobby. All we had to do was zoom in on the image in question."

I slide the picture to Tiffany. It is a picture of the same person from the first photograph, at the same time, only from a more frontal angle. She studies it, speechless.

"We both know, Tiffany, clear as day, that's you. Only now with a different jacket on, hood up, and wearing sunglasses. This footage is from that same night at 7:48 p.m. Which means you're reentering the building twenty-eight minutes after you originally left. Why?"

Tiffany swallows then slides the photo back to me.

"I won't sugarcoat it, Tiffany. This has the potential to get real bad for you, real fast. What's going on?"

* * *

The Ship stops on Ludlow Street on the Lower East Side. Perry flashes me one last photo on her iPhone Max sent of him and his friends. She leaves her jacket on the back seat as Dante opens the door for us just steps away from the entrance to the restaurant.

The moment we step into Dirty French, a happening, French-infused eatery where bistro cooking meets haute cuisine, the energy is as palpable as the crowd is beautiful. Eclectically furnished with everything from a wall-length carnival mirror to a Julian Schnabel ink-splotched French flag above the bar to neon-pink spray-painted ceramic roosters, the spot is funky, sexy, electric, and ready.

Perry, as always, looks traffic-accident-causing hot. Tonight she's wearing a Michael Kors Strapless Eyelet Jacquard Jumpsuit with the same designer's Janey Runway Leather Platform Sandals. Not even three steps inside, every eye in the place already on us, Perry is approached by Lillian Vanu, an editor at *Vogue*, about a Power Women spread they'll be doing with the likes of Marissa Mayer and Maureen Chiquet she'd like Perry to be a part of. I don't make it much further, running smack into Jan Fleming, a hedge-fund animal, who's been asking me for six months to invest with him. Eventually we make it to the bar where Natey-Boy Landgraff and his girlfriend are already having a cocktail.

"Holy shit, you're fucking gorgeous," Perry exclaims, wrapping her arms around Landgraff's girl.

She's not kidding. The woman is no older than thirty, no shorter than five foot eleven, with a strong, slender frame and powerful yet pouty features framed by long, flowing, blond hair. She's also dressed to kill, wearing a short, cobalt, Alice + Olivia Kasia Croc-Embossed Leather V-Back Dress and Alexandre Birman Strappy Metallic Snakeskin Cage Sandals. The color of her toenails matches her dress, which matches her eyes. Her legs go on forever, and her ass is the kind you stare at just a little longer than you probably should—no matter who's watching.

"Hey, *Natey-Boy*," Perry goes on, separating from her new friend and tussling Landgraff's perfectly slicked hair, which no doubt makes him nuts.

"This, uh, this is Victoria," Landgraff says, his voice showing signs of nerves. "Victoria, this is, um, this—"

"It's Perry and Jonah," Perry cuts him off, laughing. "Stop being so serious, Natey-Boy. Take a look around. Wouldn't you say it's time to loosen up?"

I offer my hand to Victoria to keep things moving along.

"Victoria, Jonah. Nice to meet you."

"Nice to meet you too," she says, taking my hand.

I then move my hand to Landgraff, which he takes.

"Nice job getting that meeting today."

Stroke the ego.

In front of his girl.

Make him believe he's worth it.

Because in him I see shades of me.

At that moment, the maître d' appears telling us our table is ready.

* * *

"I see a couple of us don't have drinks," the waiter says to Perry and me once we're seated. "May I bring you both something from the bar?"

"What's the beautiful girl drinking?" Perry asks, her eyes on Victoria's cocktail. "Seriously, I'm tempted to ask you to stand up and twirl so I can look at your ass again."

"The lady is drinking what we call a 'Belmondo'. It's Blanco Tequila, Pear Eau De Vie, some ginger, a little—"

"Whatever. Looks yummy," Perry cuts him off. "I'll have that."

"Of course. And for you, sir?"

"Give me your best tequila over just a couple of rocks."

My phone vibrates at the same moment my iPad chimes. A text from Jake. *Just got an email from Woodlock. They're out. Not kidding. They're citing security concerns because of this Madame Martine shit. Calling them now.*

Not good. Woodlock is a branding agency who's been a tenant in one of our Park South properties for ten years. Jake has been handling the negotiation to renew them, and their hundred and ten thousand square feet, for another twelve years. Losing them would be a punch to the gut. Not just because keeping them, and their cash flow, should have been a reverse tomahawk slam dunk, but because of what their leaving would say to the marketplace.

"Holy shit," Perry gushes, again, "I can't get over how fucking hot you are!"

"Well, I don't know," Victoria says, a bit uneasy by all the fawning.

"Stop it! Seriously! You're insanely beautiful. But, I mean, in all seriousness—I'd expect nothing else from our little Natey-Boy. He's a natural. A real estate fucking killer, if he keeps it up. Right, lover?" Perry goes on, turning to me.

"Possibly, one day," I respond to the unexpected question. "If he keeps his nose down and his ass out of trouble. I guess we shall see."

"*Shall?*" Perry says, half-mocking me. "Shit, babe, I think someone had a long day and needs to loosen up."

"I, um—I'm just, you know, doing all I can do make deals and learn from the two of you. And Jake. That's what I'm here for."

"Stop being so modest, Natey-Boy, you've been crushing it. You're what we call a rising stud."

"How about you, Victoria," I say, looking to change the direction of this conversation. "Are you a model? Or in fashion?"

The waiter returns with our cocktails. We all hold our glasses up, clink them, and toast one another.

"I am in fashion, but on the opposite side of the camera," Victoria answers. "I'm a photographer."

"Stop it." Perry says. "Now I fully have a problem with you."

"And what is that?" asks Victoria.

"A photographer? Looking like that? You're now officially hotter than I am!" Perry goes on, standing up now, "Come on. I'm stealing you down to the bathroom for a little bit."

What is she off to take? And why does she need more?

Where does this lead?

Stay with me, Per.

Stay with us.

Once standing, Perry takes another huge sip of her drink, a little of it escaping her lips and running down her chin.

"I need the real dirt on Natey-Boy. Like if he takes care of you the way my man takes care of me," Perry continues, "and I don't mean spoiling you with hot little outfits like that Alice + Olivia little number, if you know what I'm talking about . . ."

As the two scamper off, over Landgraff's shoulder, I see Perry take her new friend's hand.

"I appreciate you spending time with me like this, Jonah. Out on the town together. It means a lot. I hope you know, I take the opportunity you've given me at Resurrection seriously every day. I only want to get better and better."

I take a nice sip of my cocktail.

"Then keep doing just that. Getting better and better."

"If you don't mind me saying so, Jonah, it was wild watching you in that meeting today with Mr. Greenbaum and his son. I want to be able to assert myself like that one day. Just be able to step on whomever gets in my way and have all the right ammunition to just get going like a bat out of hell."

"Is that how you see me?" I ask. "Like a bat out of hell? Reckless? Unforgiving? Single-minded?"

"No. I mean, you know—I mean, I did say that, but not because . . . not because, if—"

"Forget it," I cut him off.

Not because he's necessarily wrong. Because I can't stand watching him flounder.

"I told Fucking Anshel we'd have his number to him by the end of the day. So what are we going with?"

Landgraff pauses.

"You want me to set the number?"

"You saying you can't?"

"No. Not at all."

"Did you look at the comps while investigating?"

Comps—industry jargon for comparable parcels, or deals.

"Of course I did."

"Then?" I prod him.

"Comps say it should change hands somewhere between eight-and a half and ten million dollars. So I say, since you made it clear he'll be taking what you offer, you go in on the low side with . . . um, Jonah—I, uh," he stammers as he drops his eyes and points, "Are you okay?"

I look down. With my right thumb and index finger I've been pinching the top of my left hand so hard there are ten to fifteen fresh, small, bleeding wounds. I take a napkin, dip the end in some water, and dab at my hand.

"I'm fine."

CHAPTER THIRTY-EIGHT

3:02 A.M.

I'm in the kitchen, sitting at the island, on the iPad. I have the lights on at a warm, soft glow. Neo, standing on the island having a snack, taps at his bowl. He wants more water.

"You got it, pal." I say, standing and walking to the fridge. "Thirsty little fella these days, aren't you."

I open the fridge, take out a bottle of Fiji, and pour the contents into his water bowl. Before getting back to work, I pick up my iPhone and send an email to Neo's vet.

Hi, Dr. Crowder. Neo seems to be drinking a ton more water than usual. Is this normal? Thanks.

I get back to my research. Now I'm reading up on the second of the two companies from the labels—Glenroche. First I go through the history of Zug, the Switzerland-based company. Next is detailed information about the areas of mining and expertise Glenroche takes part in, followed by an outline of the firm's different locations around the world. Next I read about the company's operations, then its relationship with other mining firms, and the bios of senior management. I keep going through more and more Google results about the firm.

What's this?

In 2009, 6500 troy pounds of Glenroche iridium went missing from the Port of Antwerp in Belgium.

Iridium.

Missing.

Another port.

I keep reading. As I do, I can't help asking myself, "What the hell is a troy pound?" I open another Google window, enter "troy pound" in the search box, and get the following:

"Troy weight is a system of units of mass customarily used for precious metals and gemstones. There are 12 troy ounces per troy pound, [1] (373.24 g) rather than the 16 ounces per pound (453.59 g) found in the more common avoirdupois system . . . [2] Although troy ounces are still used to weigh gold, silver, and gemstones, troy weight is no longer used in most other applications."

Huh. So—what kind of numbers are we really talking about? In the search box I enter "Current iridium pricing." A page from a site BlastInvest I've already seen in my research comes up. This page shows the pricing per troy ounce as of this day not just for iridium but other precious metals like rhodium, palladium, and ruthenium to go along with the more known ones like gold, silver, and platinum. As of today, iridium goes for $570 per troy ounce.

I open the iPad's calculator to calculate the dollar amount of this 2009 heist had it happened today. I type in the current price, 5-2-0, hit the X button, and type in the number of troy ounces in a troy pound, 1-2. The result is 6,240, which means a troy pound of iridium, today, is worth $6,240. I hit the X button once more to get the price for the amount actually stolen, and type in 6-5-0-0 for 6,500 troy pounds.

40,550,000.

Holy shit.

That heist, today, would have been worth more than forty million dollars.

Looking back at my BlastInvest page, I can't help but notice the price per troy ounce of rhodium is literally more than *twice* the price of iridium, checking in at $1,175. I do the same math a second time. Had this heist happened with rhodium, today, it would have been worth more than ninety-five million dollars.

I spend some more time reaching throughout cyberspace in order to gain as much clarity on this topic as possible. We're not talking front-page Business Section news, but with enough digging I find a number of articles from different papers around the world in the last few years. Articles that all have one thing in common: one of the major rare metals producers having fallen victim to a shipment gone missing—from ports. There's one from German newspaper *Süddeutsche Zeitung* in 2013 about 7,500 missing pounds of ruthenium. Another from the French Weekly *L'Express* in 2013 about missing rhodium. Another yet from 2012—Dutch newspaper *Algemeen Dagblad* reporting on 5,500 missing pounds of iridium. The deeper I dig, the more articles I find.

Could this be what this is all about? That Cobus isn't connected to these firms at all, but is somehow stealing these materials? And, if so, for what?

* * *

5:45 a.m.

I'm in the shower. Just standing here under the water, arms at my side, as the water washes down over me. How do I protect everyone? How do I figure this all out, and make it—whatever *it* may be—right?

I think I hear music. Why would that be at this time? Just as I question if it's real or in my head, it gets louder until it reaches a rock concert-like level. *Foo Fighters.* I reach for the shower door handle. But as I do, it opens from the other side. Perry, wearing nothing but the white, satin babydoll she slept in—which she doesn't take off—steps in with me. Within seconds she's drenched, the satin becoming a second skin, as she kisses me deeply. I reach down with my right hand, pick up her left leg by the back of her knee, and wrap it around my waist. My left hand holding her ass, pressing us together, she arches her back away from me letting the water soak her face. I kiss her neck with the hunger of a ravenous lion, a lion hungry to feel flesh as opposed to eating it.

I lift her up. I turn us around, and pin her to the wall. Her leg still wrapped around me, she reaches down, takes me in her right hand, and starts stroking me.

"I can't take it. I can't fucking take it," she pants, as the song begins to reach its crescendo. "Now. I need you inside me *now*!"

I spin her around, and enter her from behind.

Grabbing her hair in my fist, I arch her back until she's almost upright so I can get more of her neck again. In sync as we always are, we can't help going faster, and faster, and faster. As we do, so does the music. As we hit our stride, Dave Grohl starts screaming all around us:

I never wanna die! I never wanna die!
I'm on—my knees—never wanna die!

"Don't stop, Jonah!" Perry yells. "Don't stop! Don't ever stop!"

* * *

Thirty minutes later, I'm standing naked at one of the sinks in my bathroom shaving. Neo, sitting on the gray-and-white swirled marble countertop next to the sink, is watching me as he often does. Halfway through, part of my lower face still covered in shaving cream while the rest is clear, I stop. And just stare at myself.

My eyes drift over the topography of my body, from self-inflicted wound to self-inflicted wound. Sliced forearm. Stabbed and now bruising thigh. Gnarled hand.

This pain.

This pain reminds me I'm alive.

This pain reminds me I'm mortal.

After fifteen seconds or so I lift the razor to my face again. I place it on a portion of the skin I've already made smooth, just above the lower jawline where it leads to my chin. I press the razor to my face harder than necessary then drag it down, taking a nice slice of skin off. Instantly blood flows from the wound, mixes with water, and races down my chin and neck to my chest.

Neo starts barking.

I don't move.

Staring in the mirror, I just watch it flow.

* * *

Standing now in my closet, having just put on my Assiagi belt as I finish getting dressed, I text Cass. *Sorry for the short notice, but turns out tonight's a good night to keep this moving forward.*

Four minutes later she responds, *Why? Perry off to Miami tonight?*

I respond, *Turns out, she is.*

Immediately I see, *Where and when?*

CHAPTER THIRTY-NINE

STANDING BEHIND ONE-WAY glass, I watch Morante put the screws to Rosa. She's sitting on a metal chair in front of a metal table. He reads from the piece of paper in his hand.

"Tori, in her own words, said 'Rosa didn't hurt no one! That's not what this is about!'"

Rosa, wearing jeans, a blue zip-up sweatshirt over a white t-shirt, sneakers, and a baseball cap with her ponytail sticking out of the back, is pretty, young, and a bit unkempt. Morante puts the piece of paper on the table in front of her. Her eyes stay on the detective.

"So, Rosa?" he continues, "What, then, is this about?"

Rosa looks clearly torn. She's scared. She wants to talk as much as she wants to bolt. It's all over her face.

"Rosa, I'm doing you a favor by not having you arrested," Morante presses on, "but if you keep this silence up, I'll have no choice."

Morante takes a seat across the table from her.

"Tell you what," he goes on, "why don't I tell you a little story. One that I think may bring you around to opening up with me a bit more. You see, when Mr. Esparanza, the older man you worked on the overnight cleaning crew with, was found dead—dressed, with his boots placed perfectly beside his body at his feet—a small piece of something called polymethyl methacrylate acrylic was found in the room. Do you have any idea what this is?"

More silence from Rosa.

"I didn't, either. Turns out this is a fake fingernail—one that was painted a shade of light blue. Now, we can both see that you're wearing red nail polish today. And the first time we spoke, you were wearing orange nail polish. I notice these things. Red, orange—clearly neither is light blue. But here's where the story gets a bit more interesting. The piece of polymethyl methacrylate acrylic we found, the fake fingernail, was sent to a very specialized crime lab, the kind you see on those CSI shows and shows of that nature on TV. And guess what? It was confirmed for me late last night that there is in fact DNA present on that small piece of fingernail found at the scene where Mr. Esparanza was found. Now—whose DNA might that actually be? That's still yet to be seen. But this is why, Rosa, it's time for you to start talking. Because if that DNA turns out to be yours—DNA found on a raw, unoccupied floor of an office building with a dead man—the questions will become much more serious. As in was this murder? Was this manslaughter? Was it intentional? Was it not?"

Morante stands up. He stares at Rosa. She stares back, still silent.

"I'm going to walk out that door now, Rosa," he continues, "but if I do, this opportunity will have gone away. It will be time to take a DNA sample from you that will either exonerate you or have you arrested. If I walk out that door, Rosa, you'd better go get yourself a lawyer."

Morante starts for the door.

"You may think talking will send you down the rabbit hole," he keeps going, "but I promise you—if you're hiding something—it's the other way around. And there's no turning back once you're headed down the rabbit hole. I can promise you that."

"I was fucking him!" Rosa blurts out, just as Morante reaches for the doorknob. "I was fucking the old dude when he died. Everything was going, you know, okay, then we heard the elevator doors open.

He just got this frightened look—shit, I'm guessing we both did—across his face, and then he was just gone. Done."

Morante turns around.

"You were having sex with Mr. Esparanza at the *actual* moment he died?"

"Yeah. That's why you found him like that. I was scared. Once it happened, and I realized what was going on—you know, just how big the whole situation was—I kinda panicked. I just wanted to get the hell out of there, but I just . . . I . . . I, you know, I couldn't just leave him there like that all naked, and . . . anyway, I quickly dressed him the best I could."

"Did you hear anyone walking, or speaking?"

"Not at this point. All I'd heard was the elevator doors open, then close."

"Was this the first time you had been intimate with Mr. Esparanza?" Morante asks, as he returns to the center of the room and faces Rosa.

"I wouldn't exactly call it intimate," Rosa responds, "but, no. It wasn't the first time."

Morante takes his seat again.

"Help me understand this. What was the nature of this relationship?"

Rosa pauses.

"The nature of the relationship was money."

"He was paying you for sex?"

Rosa lowers her eyes and nods.

"Do other men pay you for sex when you're supposed to be working?"

Rosa returns her eyes to Morante.

"It's like this. We make, like, no money for the work we do. So sometimes when girls like Tori and I are working in a building where we know there's somewhere no one will be coming by—like a vacant floor—we offer up some extra services to the guys we work with. Anyway, that's all this was. I swear. I was giving him some ass for cash. That's when it all went down. We were fucking, and—"

"Where?" Morante cuts in. "Right there? On that cold concrete floor?"

"I had some towels for us to lay down on. After all, we *are* a cleaning company."

"Of course," he replies, sarcastically, "how foolish of me. Please go on."

"Like I said, we were fucking and that's when he just—he just— froze. Just like that. He just died."

"What happened, Rosa, is that he had a heart attack."

"I'm so sorry it happened. He was a nice man, I never would have done anything to hurt him."

"Then why not just come forward and explain all this?"

"And lose my job? And have a story like that about me come out—that I fuck guys for cash while I'm on the clock and one of them died? Look, I was scared. And in the heat of all of it I guess I wasn't thinking straight."

"What was with the boots? If you took the time to dress him, why not finish the job and put his boots on?"

"Because just as I was about to put them on—*that's* when I first heard people across the way talking. So I grabbed the towels and hid."

* * *

"I'm all ears," I hear Perry say as I turn the corner into her office, "Let me have it."

She's standing behind her desk, both fists down on the glass, in full power-player mode from her locked-in expression to her form-fitting geometric-print jacket and skirt suit. Jake is sitting off to the side on the couch.

"Even though I said I don't see parting with this property today," I hear Sturner's voice coming through the phone, as Perry locks her eyes with mine, "the number you've given me is compelling. One that I may be inclined to counter, under one condition."

"Which is?" Perry asks.

"I retain a minority ownership in the property of 15 percent. If this buyer is as top-notch as you claim, then I have no problem remaining a passive investor and riding the market a bit further at their direction. I want to be involved with the further upside on this property in some capacity. Plain and simple."

"I don't think this buyer will go for that," Perry says.

"It's nonnegotiable."

"Then they'll probably walk."

"Take what is the beginning of my counter to your client, Perry. If, and only if, they agree to this stipulation, do you get my price."

Just as Perry hangs up with Sturner, Carolyn comes through the phone's intercom. "Perry, is Jonah still in your office?"

"What's up?" I answer.

"Mr. de Bont is downstairs at the security desk. Shall I have them send him up?"

The three of us look around at one another as Jake straightens himself up on the couch.

"Yes. Please meet him at the elevator and bring him into Perry's office."

A few minutes later, Carolyn leads Cobus into the room.

"May I bring you anything, Mr. de Bont? Perhaps some coffee or tea?"

"No thank you, I'm all set."

Carolyn heads off as Cobus fully enters the room. Immediately he moves toward Jake.

"Jake, I presume?"

Jake, now standing, meets Cobus in the middle of the room.

"Cobus, nice to finally meet you," Jake says as they firmly shake hands. "Obviously I've heard so much about you these last couple years. I feel like I should thank you for helping Jonah find his way back to us. He's not just my partner, he's family."

Scared shitless, Jake just let us both know where he stands—where he'll always stand—in seven words.

That's loyalty.

"No thanks necessary," Cobus responds. "The world needs more Jonahs."

He turns and walks to Perry.

"And more Perrys. How are you, beautiful?" he asks as he kisses Perry on both cheeks.

"I'm well, Cobus. Thank you. A little stressed because of a certain new requirement, but other than that—"

"Since when are there requirements you can't handle," he tosses backward over his shoulder to Per as he turns and moves to me. "Jonah. How are we this morning?"

"Moving along," I answer as we're now face to face. "What brings you by?"

"I know you gave me the bird's-eye view of where our deals are yesterday, but I thought—since I was in the area—I'd get the up-to-the-minute specifics as to where each deal is right from the source. After all, a wise friend used to often tell me the words of his father, 'always get them in person.' Isn't that right, wise friend?"

I nod in agreement.

"Besides," he goes on, "I felt it was time I finally meet Jake, such an integral part of the Resurrection partnership. And a man after my own heart."

He looks at Jake.

"As I understand you, too, like to snack in the office," Cobus goes on.

He looks back to me.

"Oh, Jonah, before I forget, I just remembered on the elevator up I have an appointment at the Apple store in the Meatpacking District later today. My phone went a bit haywire on my flight in from Europe last night. The problem is, I'm not sure of the time and unfortunately—well—I can't use my phone to check. May I borrow your iPad for a moment, before I forget?"

The room goes silent, still, like someone just hit the "pause" button on our lives. He knows about the research iPad. He wants to see how far I've gotten.

Wait.

If he can see me using this machine, somehow, whether it's in my home or office—then why can't he see the contents of the pages I'm looking at?

What am I missing?

A few seconds later, Cobus extends his hand toward me. A snapshot of the gun in my waistline flashes in my mind. At this exact moment, thankfully, Carolyn pokes her head in the door.

"Jonah, I have Sienna on the phone."

Sienna is one of our housekeepers at Silver Rock.

"She said she's been trying to reach you," she continues, "but you're not picking up your cell."

"It's in my office. What's wrong?"

"It's Neo."

I feel the blood rush out of my face.

"What happened?"

"He's sick."

"Jonah, let me—" Perry says.

"No." I cut her off. "I'll handle this. Cobus, just tell Carolyn what you need, and she'll be happy to help you. I'll be in touch later."

My iPad in hand, I head out, leaving Cobus standing there empty handed.

CHAPTER FORTY

I STORM INTO Silver Rock as I'm reading the return email I just received from Dr. Crowder, Neo's vet. *Increased intake of water can mean a number of different things with a dog this age. Bring him in, the sooner the better.* The elevator opens on the fifth floor. Sienna, a portly British woman in her mid-fifties, is waiting for me.

"Where is he?" I ask.

"Come on."

I follow her down the hallway, into my bedroom, where Neo is laying on his side on his favorite chaise lounge. His eyes move when he sees me, but aside from the end of his tail wagging a bit there's no other movement. I get on my knees. I bend down and kiss his nose as I gently stroke his tiny head.

"So, my boy's not feeling well."

He sticks his tongue out and gives me a quick swipe across my nose. With the iPad in my right hand, I scoop him up with my left and cradle him to my chest.

"Come on, you're coming with me. Let's go see Dr. Crowder, and get you right."

* * *

Dr. Crowder, a forty-something, gay, extremely compassionate and caring man, has been Neo's vet his whole life. The two of us are talking alone in one of the exam rooms. Neo has already been taken into the treatment area of the facility.

"The preliminary intake exam leads me to believe, Jonah, that his kidneys are beginning to fail. But let's hold off on discussing anything definitive until we've run the full battery of necessary tests."

"I don't understand. He just had his checkup. Why wouldn't it have been noticed then?"

"Because—again, if this is what is happening—it most likely just began as recently as since he was just here. Most likely at the time the increased amount of water intake began."

"What exactly is the correlation?" I ask.

"He's having trouble holding water in his body. Hence the increased need to drink water, and, I'm guessing, go to the bathroom. Has he been peeing more often than before as well?"

I nod in confirmation.

"If this is what's happening, is there anything we can do to make him better?"

"If this is what we're dealing with, we'll start with his diet. When the kidneys begin to have issues, digesting protein efficiently becomes more and more difficult. So we'll need to gradually switch him over to a prescription food for senior dogs with lower protein concentration."

"Okay. Please help him. We've . . . "

I stop talking, as I hear my voice beginning to quiver while my eyes well up.

Senior dogs.

My Neo, still a puppy in my eyes, is a senior dog.

How has so much happened, over so many years, so fast?

"I know this is hard, Jonah."

"He's part of me, Doctor. We've been through so much. I need him."

"I get it, Jonah, how these animals become engrained in the fabric of our lives. That's why I got into this field in the first place. But we also need to keep certain things in mind when it comes to our animals. Neo's not a young dog anymore. He's not going to be here forever. He's almost fourteen and—"

"You've told me before a dog like Neo can live to sixteen or seventeen years old."

"Well, that's often true."

"Well, then—please. Do whatever you have to do to help him through this."

"Absolutely. Again, before we do anything, we need to see his final test results. But assuming this is what is happening—which I suspect to be the case—I want to keep him here for a couple days for observation while we change his diet and try to get his system back on track. We'll see how he responds, and go from there."

* * *

Before heading to the office, I stop at Silver Rock. I'm standing in the kitchen. I'm thinking about Neo, about how lucky I've been to have such a special little dog with me all these years. I look down at his water bowl, which is now back on the ground from the island by way of the housekeeping staff.

Looking at his dishes, I notice my messy little eater got some of his food in his water bowl. I pick the bowl up and walk it over to the sink to dump it out. Just as I reach the sink, about to pour, the top of the bowl catches the lip of the counter, and the water spills out backward onto my waist and groin area. When it does, something surprising happens. I hear a "zzzzzz" that lasts no longer than a second.

What the—?

It sounds like a quick electrical fizzle or sizzle. I drop the bowl in the sink then take on the awkward position of trying to bend as far forward as possible to see my own crotch. All I see is wet fabric.

I take off my belt and hold it up in front of my face. Today's choice is a classic black leather belt with a branded buckle, the cursive Assiagi A in sterling silver. As I study the accessory, something catches my eye. But it isn't the buckle. It's the portion of the belt itself—the last two inches or so—just before it meets the buckle. There are tiny rows of holes in the leather so small, yet so concentrated, one can't really see them with the naked eye unless holding it up like this.

With both hands I take the belt between my thumbs and index fingers, and start pressing, feeling around this couple-inch portion of the belt with the holes. It feels like something is in there, something flat, thin. I move my fingers down the belt a bit, away from the buckle, to see if I feel a similar *something* there too. I don't.

I walk over to the drawer where we keep things like pens, take-out menus, Scotch tape, Post-its, and pull out a pair of scissors. I cut the belt all the way through on both sides of the tiny holes, removing this couple-inch piece from between the buckle and the rest of the leather. Then I peel the back and front pieces of leather apart.

What I see is as astounding as it is mysterious, because I have no idea what I'm looking at. There are two tiny flat squares, one black, the other silver, that have been embedded within the leather behind the tiny holes. The black square is the larger of the two; it looks like it must measure around one inch by one inch. The silver one can't be more than ten millimeters wide or long. Nothing is written on either.

Just to make sure both are dead, whatever they are, I turn on the faucet and run them under water. Shocked, the water again turned off, I just stare at the two small wet squares now in the palm of my hand. I head upstairs to my closet. Once there, I study the rest of the belts I've received since making this little *deal* with Pirro. All the new ones have the little holes and, from what I can feel, the little squares inside. I look at a few of my older Assiagi belts. No holes. Nor can I feel any squares.

No. Fucking. Way.

Even though I think I'm starting to understand what's happening, I need to find out exactly what these are. And I know just who to ask. I put on another of the new belts and head back out into the city.

* * *

I walk into Three Fifty Nine Park Avenue South, another of the Gray legacy Park South properties in the Resurrection portfolio. The building, from size to age to tenancy type, is similar to Three Twenty One where the Madame Martine and Esparanza debacle is taking place just a few blocks south. I head right to the service elevator and hit B for basement.

I step off and walk straight. The floor is a shiny lacquered gray, and the concrete walls are painted a sky blue, which is chipping slightly. I'm headed toward the chief engineer's office. Peter Vitoli has been the man behind the operations in this property since the days of my father. Not only is he one of the best in the business for running the daily operations side of a commercial real estate holding, he is what some might term a "tech geek."

Peter needs his team to be able to remotely tap into and service up-to-the-minute machinery and surveillance systems at the drop of a dime. So, it is imperative he—as chief building engineer—stays on top of the latest technological advances with regard to the integration of computers into building mechanical systems, and the like, and trains his team accordingly. Peter, as a hobby, just happens to be known as one of the enthusiast types who takes his self-education of these things to the max. In fact, so much so that he's the main resource for the chief engineers in our other properties when they have a question.

As the whirring of the main boiler room comes and goes on my left, I turn right at the end of the hallway and immediately on my right is the entrance for Peter's office. Peter, a heavyset man with a heart as big as his love for all things Italian, thinning, slicked-back black hair, and a handlebar moustache, stands up upon seeing me. The thick, pork chop of a hand he offers me goes with the rest of his knobby features. We shake.

"What can I do for you, Jonah?"

Remembering that Cobus somehow knew about the iPad but couldn't actually see what it is I was doing on it, my fears of being literally "watched"—as in visually—at all times has subsided a bit. Confident that if he was having trouble seeing the iPad in my home or office this environment should be even less worrisome, I show the iPad screen to Peter.

"Since our window-replacement program is coming up next year, I wanted to see if you're familiar with these windows," I say. "Another owner just told me they're going with them because of their ridiculous wind-resistance capacity."

No windows. Instead is a note that reads, *This is not really about windows. When you answer me, please answer about windows as if this was a great suggestion, and we should absolutely look into this product as a possibility. Then I'll have another question for you. Answer now.*

Peter looks at me, his eyes both apprehensive and trusting. I give him a gentle nod of my head, as if to say, "Trust me."

"KnowlBin—great product," Peter says playing the part beautifully, as if he's done this before, "Yeah, your friend's not kidding. These windows are already on our short list."

"Good stuff," I go on. "So then, if I'm correct, these are the two different sizes we'll need for floors two through twenty-six, plus some specialty cuts for the retail-level windows."

I show him the iPad again. A second paragraph after the first reads, *I'm going to put two small, thin, squares in your hand. If you know what they are nod your head "yes," if you don't, then shake your head "no." If yes—I'm going to say something further regarding the windows then give you the iPad to write down what they are—the more information you can give me for each, the better. Now say "correct."*

"Correct."

He opens his hand. Without another word I hand him the silver-and-black squares. He gives them a look, and nods yes.

"Great," I say. "Then do me a favor. Write down for me here, the best you can off the top of your head, a list of which capital improvement programs are on the forecast for next year, and the ballpark timing for each. I need to have this information with me for a meeting I have this afternoon."

I hand Peter the iPad, he hands me back the two squares, and starts typing. A couple minutes later, iPad back in hand, I head back toward the elevator.

In the back of The Ship, on my way to the office, I open the iPad. I read what Peter typed for me.

The smaller of the two, the silver one, is a GPS product made by a company called Xelin—which I know because we attach these devices, or similar derivations of these devices, to some of our smaller yet more expensive pieces of equipment in case someone tries to steal them from the building. Xelin is known for making the smallest GPS products in the world. GPS means Global Positioning System; it's the kind of system behind the navigation system in your car or the mapping system on your smart phone. Anyway, this GPS chip is used for tracking whatever it is attached to. And the tracking location is usually kept in real time and monitored using a wireless, Internet-based system.

The black chip is a voice transmitter. I only know this because my sister used one—I think it was called The Secret Whisperer or something—to catch her husband who she suspected was cheating on her. Anyway, these things are tiny voice transmitters—or microphones/ recorders—and they are strong. They can even record a whisper from like thirty-five or forty feet away. The way it works is that each one of these devices, or squares, has its own SIM card in it and associated code. Let's say, for example, a code of 12345. The way the device is set into motion is by calling into the SIM card and entering the code— and now whoever is the one calling in has become its master. Anytime you want to listen in on that particular microphone/recorder, just call in and listen anonymously from afar. There's no distance limit as the listening in is done via cell, and when calling in there are no rings, no beeps, no clicks, no sounds—nothing.

I'm flabbergasted. The way Cobus has been watching and monitoring me—actually, I now believe, all of us—is by simply listening to me via these belts. It's actually pretty fucking genius. When a certain belt on any given day is on the move, Cobus knows via the GPS chip which microphone/recorder to call into. Then he, or whomever he has assisting, can listen in on me as often as they like.

My mind drifts to Pirro, but that will have to wait. To alert Pirro that I'm onto this is to undoubtedly alert Cobus, and the best thing I have going now is that I'm ahead of the game. The longer I can play dumb, the longer I have to put together a way out of all this.

The longer I have to protect everyone.

But how?

This is going to be tricky. I mean, Cobus could literally be listening to me right now as I'm reading the iPad—which now makes perfect sense as to why even though he knew I was using the iPad to continue my research, he was never able to see what I was looking at. The more I think about it, the more I can see how simple the underlying premise is: the best way to watch those working in collaboration is to listen to them. The best way to know what someone is saying about you when you're not in the room: listen to him. The best way to track someone who relies on others to coordinate his life: listen to him.

That's how he knew my itinerary changed in Europe. Even though I was being so careful about communicating with Carolyn, he was listening to my conversation with her. The same way he's been listening to our conversations about the respective deals. The same way he no doubt listened to my conversation with Perry and Jake about where I am with figuring out what he's up to.

Without question, Cobus is onto me.

And the fact I'm onto him.

Knowing me as well as he does, how tenacious and unwavering I can be, he can't be surprised I'm trying to put this all together. Yet he still came to me—*that's* how important it is in his mind he get these properties. He knows I have the best chance to deliver, and he truly believes I'd never cross him. No matter what I know.

So the question begs to be asked. If he was willing to go into this risking the possibility I'd learn about his other business dealings— where does that leave me if this all goes as he'd like to believe as planned? As a man he trusts enough to finally call us even, so long as I carry his secrets to the grave?

Or am I simply a dead man walking?

CHAPTER FORTY-ONE

In the play of life, my role has been cast.

Action.

Dante opens The Ship's rear door.

"Wait here," I say.

"You got it, boss-man. Although I thought there were errands I was supposed to run for Perry before picking you both up for a lunch meeting."

Standing on the sidewalk now, I look up at One Hundred Five Park.

"There's been a change of plans. I'm not feeling well—not sure if it's something I ate, stress because of Neo, or what. All I know is I have way too much shit going on right now to be out of commission. So I need to go home and use the afternoon to rest."

"Of course. I'll be right here. Sorry you're not feeling well."

"Thanks, Dante."

I hold the iPad up for him to look at. He's looking at a page from the tablet's Notepad. It reads:

Don't say another word. Just get in the car and wait. Once I come back down, I'm going to place the belt I'm wearing in the backseat and say to you "Let's make this happen." Once you hear these words, go to Silver Rock, take the belt upstairs, put it in my closet, and drive to the address I'm about to hand you.

At this moment I hand him a small piece of paper, with *Go to THE DEAL HOUSE* written on it.

"I'll be back down in a few minutes," I go on, looking him square in his eyes so he can see—and hold onto—the trust he's had in me from the moment we met.

I nod, as if to say "it will be okay," and mouth, "Trust me." He nods and returns to his station behind the driver's seat.

* * *

1:18 p.m.

As I ride up the elevator in One Hundred Five Park to our offices, I can't help but take a deep breath. I look down at my belt, still treading water somewhere between shock and relief. I look back at the doors in front of me that are seconds away from opening. In order to keep this game alive, there's still one more confirmation I need while I keep moving everything forward.

The doors open and I head straight for Carolyn. As she sees me coming, she stands up.

"How's he doing?" she asks.

"Too early to tell," I say. "Thankfully he's in good hands. We'll know more when the tests are complete."

"Oh, he's just the cutest little thing. He'll be okay, Jonah."

"Thanks. Let's hope so. Carolyn, I need you to shuffle my schedule this afternoon. I'm not feeling well. I need to head home and get some rest because between these deals we need to put in place for Mr. de Bont and everything else we have on the table, I need to get myself right."

"Of course, Jonah. As usual you've put yourself under an enormous amount of pressure, and now this with poor little Neo . . . totally understandable."

"Thanks, Car. Oh, there are some documents I need to review for one of Landgraff's deals. Can you pull these and put them on my desk?"

I open the iPad cover, swipe to the next Notepad page I've previously written, and hold it up for her.

Don't be alarmed, but don't speak right now. I need you—on someone else's cell from the office (say yours isn't working)—to set up Perry, Jake, and I for a helicopter ride NOW from the 34th Street Heliport to East Hampton Airport. On this same cell phone, arrange for a car to pick us up and take us to the house. Then I need you to reschedule Perry and Jake's afternoons as well. Trust me. Now—look at me and nod if you understand everything.

Carolyn, masking the fear in her eyes to about 90 percent, looks at me and nods. With my eyes I motion back to the screen. She looks. Under the paragraph she's already read, there's another sentence.

Read this aloud—"Got it, I'll have those waiting for you."

She does exactly as I say. As I head off to go find Perry, Carolyn takes off in the other direction.

* * *

Perry's office. As I enter, upon sight of me, she shoots up from the chair behind her desk and rushes over to me.

"How's our boy?" she asks, wrapping her arms around my neck.

Our boy.

How is Neo.

How are we?

"Hard to tell," I say, my arms around her waist squeezing her back. "Dr. Crowder thinks his kidneys are failing. But we're not there yet. He still wants to see the final test results before making any final conclusions. And even if what he suspects to be the case is a reality, we'll start with a change of diet and go from there."

I grab her arms, push her back a bit, and look in her eyes.

"He'll be okay," I continue. "He has to be."

She puts her hand on my cheek.

"He's so lucky to have had you all these years. Dr. Crowder loves him. He'll help him get better."

"I know," I say back, my voice cracking a bit. "Anyway, more on the little fella later. I actually just asked Carolyn to cancel my afternoon. I don't know if I ate something, or it's this Neo business, but my stomach is all over the place. I feel completely wiped. I'm going to head home and use the afternoon hopefully to sleep."

"Baby, I'm sorry," Perry says. "Can I do anything?"

"No, beautiful, you have enough to handle on your own. I'll touch base with you later on. Hopefully I'll be back to myself by then."

I open the iPad cover, swipe to the next note, and hold it up for Perry to read.

Don't say another word. In thirty seconds, head straight to the elevators and out of the building. I'll meet you outside.

Perry moves her eyes back to me. Wearing her "Holy Shit—not more craziness" expression, she doesn't move. She's been through chaos with me before. Which, whether she likes it or not, means she knows to trust me.

I nod. She pauses, but finally nods back showing me she's on it.

* * *

As I walk toward Jake's office, I see him enter the hallway from the bathroom. By the time he sees me, my left index finger is already to my lips. Getting it that I'm "shushing him," he uses a shrug and putting his hands out, palms up, to silently ask, "What's up?" Quickly I swipe to the next page and hold the iPad up. It reads, *Don't say a word to me right now, or to anyone else. Just meet me outside in front of the building in thirty seconds.*

Once he's read it, and he's looking at me, I widen my eyes and cock my head to silently ask—"Got it?"

His eyes now wide too, he nods. I leave and head directly to the elevator. Once inside and on my way down, I take out my iPhone and send an email. It's to Perry. It reads, *Feeling fine—needed to get out of the office because I set up a meeting for 4 o'clock at 318 Meadow Lane to show you know what, about what's going on, to you know who. Figured better to lay it all out for him to see there. Going home to change then heading straight off.*

* * *

Once back outside I head straight for The Ship. Perry sees me; she starts toward me, but I put my finger up as if to say "one second." She stops where she is. In stride, with my left hand, I unbuckle my belt and slide it around my waist, off me. With my right hand, which is still holding my now ever-present iPad, I open the rear door and toss the belt inside on the backseat.

"Dante?" I say.

"Yes, boss-man?" I hear through the intercom.

"Let's make this happen."

I close the door. The Ship takes off. Just as I motion to Perry it's okay to come over to me, Jake exits the building as well. Silently with his "what the fuck?" hands out, shoulders shrugged, he walks toward us.

"You can talk now," I say.

"Seriously? What the hell is going on?" Jake asks.

Perry grabs my arm and looks at me.

"What's happening, Jonah?" she asks, her tone and expression serious.

"We're going to the Hamptons. To The Deal House. Now. The three of us. Per—I just sent you an email. Open it and read it, but don't respond."

The Deal House is the name of the estate Perry and I are building on the water in The Hamptons.

"What are you talking about?" Jake goes on as he reaches us. "Why? I have a ridiculous afternoon coming up."

"As do I. And aren't I supposed to be in Miami tonight?" Perry says.

"Carolyn is on top of rearranging your schedules. And we'll be back for you to be on a later flight to Miami as I have things to tend to as well."

"Why the Hamptons? Why the new house?" Perry asks.

"I'll explain all of that once we're there."

"How are we getting there if Dante just took off?" she goes on.

"We're taking a helicopter. Carolyn is taking care of it, as well as the car that will be picking us up at East Hampton Airport."

I hail a cab. I look at my wrist.

1:28 p.m.

"For now," I continue, "let's just worry about getting to the Thirty-Fourth Street Heliport. Until we set foot in the new house, not a word about Cobus from here on out. The cab driver, the helicopter pilot, the driver who picks us up—you never know who is listening."

Pun intended.

CHAPTER FORTY-TWO

THE CAB PULLS off the West Side Highway at Thirtieth Street into the West Side Heliport parking lot, and we get out. Sitting on the westernmost edge of Manhattan, New Jersey is clearly within eyeshot just across the water.

"You handling Albert?" I yell to Jake above the rotor of the waiting Bell 206L4 we're walking toward.

"I was waiting for him to call me back when you pulled me out of the office," Jake screams back.

We settle into the chopper. Behind the pilot and copilot seats are four seats that face each other, two and two. Perry and Jake are sitting in the two seats backed up to the pilot and copilot. I'm facing them, able to see the backs of our navigating hosts' heads behind them. We each put on our microphone-equipped headset, designed to keep noise out while we speak to one another as if we're in a conference room. As we liftoff, none of us say a word. We each just stare out the window as the world drops away. The cars of the West Side Highway are quickly reduced to orderly insects. The buildings beneath us instantly become a distant grid of rooftops as we head east.

"I believe I have Minnie where I want her," I say.

Perry and Jake look at me.

"She's going to sell," I go on. "She's essentially there."

"Strong work," Jake says, nodding. "Although not exactly your most impressive sell to date, my friend. She loves you. You could sell her dog shit as the newest phenomenon in face cream if you wanted to."

"Nice," Perry says.

"Just saying," Jake shrugs.

"How about you, Per?" I say. "What are you thinking about Sturner?"

"I'm thinking—we both saw in his millionth he wants to sell that building. So why then want to hold onto a minority, passive interest in it if it's actually something you're comfortable unloading?"

"There could be an issue with the property he's been able to bury," I respond. "Why not pass that on to someone else, and participate in the inherent upside we all know he's right about with that building?"

Perry and Jake look at one another, then back to me.

"I'll call Gordon." Perry says.

Gordon Kadanoff is one of our insiders at the DOB.

"And start digging," she goes on.

* * *

2:50 p.m.

The gates at 318 Meadow Lane, in Southampton, New York, slowly swing open with the touch of a button on my iPhone. The driver carefully makes his way down the straight, pebbly driveway to the construction site. The Deal House, a sprawling, white, twenty-three-thousand-square-foot behemoth of a beach house combining Old World elegance with modern convenience on just over six beachfront acres, is almost officially a home after fourteen months of construction.

"Holy shit!" Jake exclaims. "I imagine we'll be doing some serious partying here!"

Truth be told, I've only seen the house a handful of times. This has been Perry's pet project. Another way to keep her mind continuously occupied. Which means another way I can try to give her what she needs, and doesn't just want. It would be an understatement to say no detail has been spared with this place. Ten bedrooms, all with breathtaking views of the Atlantic Ocean. Twelve bathrooms. Eight fireplaces with early nineteenth-century mantels. Coffered ceilings. There's an infinity-edge pool, Jacuzzi, tennis court, squash court, and wine cellar. There's a world-class kitchen, a gym, a theatre, and a sauna. Behind the house, on the water, there's a dock for our still undecided-upon yacht. There's even a koi pond on the property. When finished, the place will be no joke. My guess is the day we receive the certificate of occupancy, we could sell it for between sixty-five and seventy million and make a handsome profit.

The closer we get to the structure, the more we can see there's still some work to be done. A portion of the roof's shingles are not yet in place. Some painting still needs to be completed. Around the southern end of the house there's still scaffolding. The car stops. The three of us get out. Again, with the touch of a sequence on my iPhone, I unlock the front door. As we walk toward our new beach home, Perry and Jake walk a few paces ahead of me, Jake asking Perry questions about the place so fast she can barely answer one before the next is flying from his lips.

There's a text from Cass. *Where am I meeting you later?*

I look at the back of Perry, just a few paces ahead of me, then back at my phone.

This isn't right.

I need to retreat.

But I can't resist the urge to move forward.

Red Cat. 227 10th Ave, between 23rd and 24th. 8 pm. I write. *Proper business attire preferred.*

I step into the sprawling front foyer just behind Perry and Jake. While the outside of the house is not yet complete, the interior basically is. The entrance space is massive. It's a circular atrium with exquisite beige marble underfoot, white walls, and equally interspersed doors that lead off in different directions to different portions of the house. Between each door is a beautiful, white-framed mirror with traditional, shaded wall sconces on each side. In the center of the rotunda is a circular, pink-cushioned, antique French bench with ornate gold trim. Just past the bench, in the center of the room, a staircase begins ascending toward the rear of the house to the second floor. The ceiling above us is only half closed; the perimeter of the entry foyer is covered overhead, but the center is left open, so you can see where the staircase branches off to both sides at the top and comes back around. It gives off the understanding that the same type of central area, with doors leading in all different directions, exists on the second floor as well.

Jake starts clapping slowly.

"Wow, guys. Seriously. Bravo. Bra—fucking—vo."

We make our way down one of the hallways leading east, and eventually come to the kitchen, which is a chef's wet dream. The rear of the light and airy, stark-white room faces the ocean. Between the perimeter of space and the huge central island, all topped with white and gray-swirled Italian marble, there's more than expansive counter space. There's a farmhouse sink also custom-cut from the same marble, and the world's highest end appliances from a La Cornue Grand Palais Stove Range to a Mugnaini Wood-Fired Pizza Oven to a Wolf Warming Drawer. There's even a $2,300 Blendtec Stealth Blender. Yup, you heard right—a $2,300 blender.

Jake heads for the fridge.

"I'm starving."

"Don't think you're going to find much in there," Perry says, "considering, you know, no one's lived here yet."

Jake checks anyway. He opens the door, and upon sight of seeing not one item inside, closes it dejectedly.

"I need to sit down for this, then. I have no energy."

He takes a seat around the massive white, wooden table. I toss the iPad onto the island, take my suit jacket off which I toss over another of the chairs around the table, and remain standing. Perry remains standing too, resting on her elbows on the island.

"So—let's have it," she says.

"I figured out how Cobus has been watching me. Watching us."

I take them through everything. The spill. The "zzzt." The cutting of the belt. The GPS device. The voice transmitter/recorder. My visit to Peter Vitoli. All of it.

"You've got to be kidding," Jake says, his head in his hand as he's now leaning forward on the table. "How is something like this even fucking real? It's like we're living in a Robert Ludlum novel! Seriously, who does this shit?"

"That's why you put the belt in the car," Perry says quietly to no one in particular. "So he can't listen to us right now."

"This isn't a normal man," I remind them. "His connections go as wide as they go deep. Governments. Municipalities. God knows what crime syndicates. Politicians. Something like this, I imagine, is easy for a man like Cobus. And, as much as I hate to admit it, it's genius in its simplicity in terms of how wide a net he's able to cast."

"Goddamn Pirro. I want to kill that motherfucker," Perry seethes through gritted teeth.

"We'll get to him. For now, we need Pirro to keep thinking everything is fine because we need Cobus thinking we still have no idea we're being listened to. The second we let Pirro know we're onto all of this is the second Cobus gets wind of it. Besides—that's if Pirro even knows. I'm guessing this shit came from way over his head. Assiagi is an Italy-based company. My guess is someone owed Cobus something; he's friends with someone at the top there who's just as shady as he is—who knows. Either way, it's irrelevant at this point. We leave Pirro as is."

"So why are we discussing it out here? Why the trip out east?"

"Because I need to confirm that the belts are the only means of surveillance. I've gone over everything in my mind in terms of what he knows and when we may have spoken about it or I may have spoken about it, and while I think it's all about his being able to hear me, there are a couple things I just can't be sure of. We're out here because I wanted to lure Cobus somewhere he'd want to see what's going on—not just hear about it—the way he wanted to see my iPad this morning that he knows I've been researching him on."

"So, again, why here?" Jake asks.

"Because the city is too dense. Out here I can lure him somewhere and easily see if he's taken the bait. I put the belt in the back of the car and the same way I communicated with the two of you earlier—writing on the iPad—I communicated to Dante to drive it to Silver Rock and put it upstairs in my closet. If Cobus was listening to me earlier, he thinks I'm home resting right now which would mean, A—I wouldn't be speaking, and, B—the GPS wouldn't be moving. But, if he *is* actually also monitoring my, or all of our emails, and digital correspondence, he'd have picked up on my email to Perry when we were leaving and sensed something was going awry, bringing his ass out here. Something, unlike if we're in Manhattan, it wouldn't be hard to see. Per—read the email I sent you aloud."

Perry looks at her iPhone and with a couple taps of the screen opens the email and begins reading.

"*Feeling fine—needed to get out of the office because I set up a meeting for 4 o'clock at 318 Meadow Lane to show you know what, about what's going on, to you know who. Figured better to lay it all out for him to see there. Going home to change then heading straight off."*

"Nice," Jake says, "you used the address instead of calling it 'The Deal House.'"

"Exactly," I concur. "And alluded to talking about something with someone that reeks of trying to be sly about looking for help with a certain unspoken situation, and doing so off the beaten path."

"Smart," Jake goes on, "But what if he actually takes the bait? What if he shows up here and we're here with you?"

"You won't be. Look around you—he shows up and I'm guessing you two will find a way to make yourselves scarce."

"Good point," Perry says. "But how will we know someone's coming?"

"Because Dante, who should be here no later than 3:20, will be outside. When he gets here, I'm going to head outside and tell him what to be looking for. And I made it clear in that email the meeting I've set up here is for 4:00 p.m., so we've got some cushion in there."

"Okay," Perry goes on, "so what if he shows and we've made ourselves scarce? Then what? What are you going to tell him then?"

"About what?"

"About who you had to meet, and why?"

I reach under the island, open a cabinet door, take out a stack of eight fabric swatch books, and toss them on the island.

"Isn't it obvious? I needed to meet with the decorator about the fabrics we've finally decided on for the couches in the living room and in our offices."

Perry and Jake look at each other, then back to me.

"Not bad," Perry says. "Sounds like you've covered all the bases. Except you forgot one thing."

"You're going to say my belt," I respond, "or lack of one, and no

I didn't. I said in the email I was first going home to change. We all know he isn't going to say anything about it anyway—that would just give him away. But let's say he finds a clever way to inquire. Running around the way I do, it isn't conceivable someone doing a quick change could forget their belt?"

Perry pauses as she soaks in my words then shrugs.

"Okay. Sounds like you've got this covered. So—it looks like we've got some time."

"We do—which is good because I have some new information to fill you both in on. When I was digging deeper last night, I came across information about thefts of the kinds of precious metals I saw in Cobus' building. Heists that took place at ports. The first one I read about happened in Belgium in 2009, but there were more recent ones—recent, like last year and 2013 recent—from a number of ports including those in Rotterdam and Hamburg. And we're talking big fucking numbers—fifty-five hundred pounds, seventy-five hundred pounds—big fucking numbers. It's all measured in something called troy pounds. I started learning about the difference between troy pounds and regular pounds, and the difference about the ounce component in the different numbers, so—"

I stop and catch myself from veering off track.

"—Anyway, that doesn't matter. What matters is the math. And these were like forty-, fifty-, ninety-million-dollar scores."

"Damn," Jake says.

"Damn is right."

"What could he do with it?" asks Perry. "I mean, it makes perfect sense. Between the ports we're talking about, the cities he's been expanding into—but what could he be looking to *do* with it? And what's to say the companies mining these metals aren't involved?"

"Meaning?" I say.

"Meaning if we play devil's advocate, what if we're looking at this wrong? What if the producers aren't being taken for a ride, but are actually in on it somehow? Maybe even pulling the strings?"

"Good questions," I reply. "And I think I know just who to ask. Someone I've wanted to reach out to since this all started, but have been afraid to. Come 4:01 p.m. today, I'll no longer be afraid to make that call."

"What if four comes and goes, and we're in the clear?" Perry asks.

"I keep wearing my new arsenal of Assiagi belts, we go on about our business as if we're still oblivious, and we work double time to put these deals together."

"Is there a new game plan?" Jake asks.

"If four o'clock comes and goes and we're clear? Hell yeah, there's a new game plan," I say. "And it goes like this."

* * *

I look at my watch.

4:05 p.m.

Nothing.

CHAPTER FORTY-THREE

6:30 P.M.

I'm sitting in the back of The Ship, on Pettit Avenue in Queens, talking on the iPhone with Morante. Head turned right, my eyes survey the identical bayfront row houses lining the street. Then they settle on number 9009. The building is made of light pink brick, with a staircase of darker brick leading up to the door, which has a white canopy above it.

"So what was her answer?" the detective asks after I tell him I let Tiffany know we have her on camera reentering the building.

"She came clean about how it went down. The timing. The prior planning. All of it. She also told me while she knew it was wrong, she had no choice. She was as devoted as, unfortunately, it sounds like she was scared."

"Did you buy it?"

"I did. But I think I'll really understand if she's being honest or if she's really just a damn fine actress after one more conversation with my friend Shand. In the meantime, there's someone I need you to check out. According to Tiffany, this particular individual could be the reason for all this."

I give him the name.

"When will you be speaking with Shand?"

"Tomorrow morning."

"I should come with you," Morante says.

"All due respect, Detective, I think we should wait on that. Esparanza's dead, that isn't going to change. But there may be a way for me to make it all right for Madame Martine, still make Shand feel it, and get everything back in its rightful place."

"How so?"

I explain what I'm thinking.

"Uh-huh—okay. But I'm going to meet you anyway. I'll wait in the car while you speak with Shand, but then after that I need to take an official statement from you regarding Shane's disappearance."

I swallow.

"The team handling it is overwhelmed with people to interview. Based on his history in law enforcement, they're determined to find him. I told them I'd get you out of the way."

After we hang up I find another contact to make one more call.

"Hey, Jonah—what can I do for you?"

"I'm sorry about earlier, Peter. I didn't mean to alarm you. I assure you, everything is okay."

Peter Vitoli, Chief Engineer at Three-Fifty-Nine Park Avenue South.

"Okay. Yeah, I mean, I've definitely been concerned, so—anyway, yeah, I appreciate the call."

"Of course. Again, I apologize for all that. It seemed like a bigger deal than it was. I promise."

"Is there anything else I can help you with?"

"Actually, Peter, there is. There's something I need quickly, and I think you can help me get it."

When our conversation is over, having been holding my phone in my left hand, I switch it over to my right hand to put it into my suit jacket pocket. When I do I drop a collar-stay I don't recall removing from my collar. I look down at my pants. There's a bit of fresh blood on the dark fabric covering my right thigh, fabric that has three small new holes in it.

* * *

I ring the doorbell. Fifteen seconds later a man I haven't seen in ten
years—a man who helped raise me, then helped save me—opens
the door. Without a word we embrace in one of the warmest hugs
I've ever felt.

"My God, Jonah. My God."

Thank you.

For everything.

Thank you.

We hug a few seconds more, then separate. Mattheau, a man of
Haitian descent with a dark, political, violent, Tonton Macoutes
past, was my father's driver after fleeing his homeland from the time
I was just a boy. But Mattheau was not just our driver. He was so
much more than that. He was the gentle side to my father's gruff
side of parenting. He was what my mother—who died when I was
five—was supposed to be to me. Whereas my father constantly gave
me lessons about having balls, determination, fearlessness, and ego,
Mattheau taught me it's okay to be gentle, to let the heart feel, and
to experience regret—regret one should try to avoid by living on a
meaningful path. Unfortunately, like so many kids before me born
to privilege, he may have been trying to teach me but I didn't exactly
listen. I only started to understand the lessons he sought to teach
me ten years ago—when a three-week period that tore my life apart,
and saw me accidentally kill a dirty cop—and every day since.

Mattheau helped me hide the body, which gave me time to flee,
and ultimately get my life back. His past may have given him the
mindset to want to live on a more righteous path, which he did
once he safely made it to the U.S., but his same past allowed him—
without a shred of doubt or fear—to help me deal with a dead body.
Like I said, he has a violent past that has hardened part of his soul to

stone. And like they say, you can take a man out of a war zone, but you can never take the war zone out of the man. Mattheau taught me more about this life than he'll ever know. Because of him, I understand what it means to be loyal to a fault. Because of him, I understand we—as humans—can go to places within ourselves most people wouldn't even want to know exist.

"Look at you," he goes on. "I mean, I've seen you in the magazines and on TV and whatnot, but to see you in person, it's—it's—overwhelming."

Mattheau knows Jonah Gray.

He sees Ivan Janse.

"I only look like this because of you. I only had the chance to go through all of this, to get my life back, to get to this very moment standing here, because of you."

"I was loyal to your father."

"You were loyal to me."

About to say something more, Mattheau stops. Instead he gently reaches out and grabs my arms.

"Come on. Come inside."

Mattheau has definitely aged. Wearing a sky-blue shirt tucked into jeans with no belt and New Balance sneakers, I follow him into his modest home. He's nearly bald, yet his dark-skinned body seems to have remained fit. We walk past the quiet, poorly lit living room and into a small kitchen, where he offers me a seat on a maroon vinyl chair around the yellow Formica table. The appliances all look to be from the '80s, and the white walls are lined with white wooden cabinets. I sit down.

"Can I get you something? Water? Some whiskey?"

"No, thanks. Please," I say, gesturing to the seat across from me, "just sit with me."

Mattheau joins me at the table.

"I knew one day you'd show up at that door."

"I wanted to sooner. Truly. Every day since I returned two years ago. But I couldn't. For you. I—"

"I know, Jonah. I understand."

"You were never tied to the body being hidden. You were never connected to me in any way once I was back. Morante never connected you to any of it. In the chaos of what all of that was—from inception to conclusion—you were just a ghost. I wanted it to stay that way for you. You deserve that; *that's* the life you came here looking for. Being that I became this public figure, I just couldn't take the chance of being connected to you and having to explain who you are. Or worse, putting you in a position where people could ask you questions. I couldn't do it. For you. You made it clear to me the authorities could never know who—"

"Jonah," he cuts me off, "I get it. And I appreciate it."

He reaches toward the middle of the table, his hands waiting for mine. I reach forward and take them. I give his hands a squeeze, and we each sit back again.

"When I saw you for the last time," I say, "you put that Agliani Brothers' business card in my hand, and told me the address on the back—this address—is where I could find you when I returned. Why here?"

"Because once everything happened, to be safe I knew I couldn't go back to my house."

"Well, then, whose house was this?"

"An acquaintance from Haiti. Let's just say, with what I had run away from myself, there was always the chance my past might catch up to me. Contingency plans have always been a part of my life. And always will be."

"I guess it's a good sign you're still here, in this house, after all these years."

"It is."

"So then, if I may ask, what are you doing these days for identification?" I go on.

"I'm still known to the U.S. government—and any other government—as Mattheau Gregoire. The same group in Haiti that helped me and others escape our affiliation with the Tonton Macoutes makes sure I'm always equipped with identification as needed. Same as it has been, same as it will always be."

"In that case, there's something I need from you. I want you to know, with all my heart, if there was any other way—any other person I could come to for this—I would have. But there isn't. So I'm here. And unfortunately I'm under the kind of time crunch that means we'll have to leave the serious catching up with one another for another time."

Mattheau straightens himself in his chair. The look of concern that takes over his face is one I've seen a thousand times from him as a boy and a man. It's an expression of genuine, real, and deep concern. The kind of concern reserved for a parent.

"What is it, Jonah?"

"Get what you need," Pop always said, "clean up the mess later."

Time to clean up the mess.

"I need you to take a little trip for me. And I need you to leave tonight."

CHAPTER FORTY-FOUR

8:04 P.M.

After stopping home for a quick suit change I walk into Red Cat, a sexy yet subdued and charming Chelsea staple serving consistent Med-American fare and top-flight cocktails to the gallery groupies. The tall, beautiful, African American hostess greets me. I tell her my name. She says my guest has already arrived and is waiting for me at our table. Hardwood underfoot, soft, tavern-esque lighting overhead, I follow the hostess through the space, passing the bar on our right into the main dining room.

I see Cass in the rear of the dining room, tucked away in a perfectly romantic corner table with a red, leather L banquette for us to sit next to one another and look out over the restaurant. Upon seeing me she stands up.

"I can take it from here," I say to the hostess.

"Very well then, Mr. Gray. Enjoy your evening."

As I make my way through the dining room, absorbing the usual pairs of eyes that recognize me, my eyes remain solely on my dinner partner. Someone managed to get home after work before coming to dinner. Wearing a short A-line Dress with a painterly feather pattern and lace-up front, and patent leather ankle-strap spiked heels, Cass looks white hot. And the look on her face tells me she knows it.

"How are we tonight?" I say as I reach her.

I give her a gentle kiss on the cheek. As always she smells as good as she looks. I remember running my hands through her long, lush, thick brown hair.

"I'm well, Mr. Gray. And ready to talk business."

I shouldn't be here.

"Dressed like that?" I go on, letting her watch my eyes give her a quick up and down. "I'll bet you are. You look fantastic."

The corner of her glossed lip curls up.

"I had to make an appearance at a cocktail party before meeting you."

Bullshit.

"Good. Then I get to be the beneficiary of you having to make that appearance."

I gesture to the banquette with my hand. We sit.

"So—since the theme of tonight is business, let's get through that before we turn our attention to the menu. Where exactly are we?" I ask.

"You know exactly where we are. We're still in the evaluation stage, probably will remain there for another few days."

"Why?"

"Why what?"

"Why is it taking so long?" I go on. "Your client has the offers. He, via you and Feller, now knows the players and what they bring to the table. We all know that time is money for everyone involved. What's the real holdup as to Landis pulling the trigger?"

A forty-something waiter with perfectly coiffed hair and a five o'clock shadow appears at the table.

"Good evening. I'm Douglas and I'll be your server tonight. May I start you both out with something from the bar?"

I look at Cass.

"I'd love a Belvedere dirty martini, up," she says.

"Absolutely," Douglas says, "and for you, sir?"

Nothing.

Get up, and walk out.

It isn't worth it.

Is it?

"Whatever the bartender says your best tequila is, have him pour me some over a couple of rocks."

"You got it."

"Again, Jonah, this is nothing more than due diligence. This is a big transaction for a guy like Landis. I don't blame him for taking his time."

"So then why didn't you tell him you were meeting with me the other night?"

She thinks for a second.

"I didn't want them thinking I wasn't looking at this objectively, Jonah. You want the truth, that's the truth."

"Why would they presume anything? You discussed our past with them?"

"They're men, Jonah. There's no doubt they were able to read into the way you greeted me in that conference room. Anyway, it doesn't matter. What matters is that if I'm going to give them an ultimate recommendation—whether it be Resurrection, or anyone else—I'd better be damn sure it's the right fit."

My iPhone vibrates in my pocket. I take it out. Cass, like me, sees it's Perry calling. Eyes locked with Cass', I pick up.

"How's the flight?" I ask.

"Fine. A little bumpy, but nothing bad. Where are you, babe?"

"Grabbing a bite with Landis and Feller. Trying to wrestle this building away from them."

"Tell them I say hi. And that if you don't get what you want, they'll have to answer to me."

"I'll be sure to tell them. What's up?"

"Quick question. I know, according to Malkoff, KoolBev has decided they want either of these two spots. But while I can sense they're leaning toward the Southeastern Financial Center, I really think the Wells Fargo Center is the better space for them. Should I plead my case? Or just get this done?"

"Are you seeing Wells Fargo as marginally better, or substantially better?"

"Substantially."

"Then plead the case. They trust you. They'll listen to you."

"Thanks, babe. Good luck. Back tomorrow."

We say good-bye and hang up.

"She was calling from the plane?" Cass asks.

"The beauty of flying private," I say.

"Ah. Right. Private."

"Anyway," I go on, steering us back on course, "you know what I think? About what's going on here?"

"What's that?"

"That you're playing me. And that you have no intention of letting that building fall into my hands."

The waiter places our drinks on the table. I tell him we need more time with the menu.

"Don't be absurd, Jonah. Then why would I be here listening to the rest of your . . . vision?" she asks, sultrily, biting the corner of her lip.

She lifts the napkin in her lap and re-crosses her legs in my direction. I can't help but to look at her magnificent legs. And I'm not shy about staring a bit longer than I should.

"Why would I waste my time then?" she goes on.

"Is that what this would then be?" I answer her question with one of my own, moving my eyes back to hers. "Us wasting time?"

Don't do this.

That one she answers easily. By saying nothing at all. We clink glasses and each throw back a healthy sip.

* * *

9:58 p.m.

Just blocks from Red Cat, after suggesting a post-meal stroll, we stumble into the lobby of the High Line Hotel, a Chelsea seminary-turned-hotel on Tenth Avenue at Twentieth Street.

"What are we doing here?" Cass asks.

"The owner may be interested in selling. I figured, since we're close by, why not have a look. In fact, wait here for a second."

I walk over to the reception desk, converse quickly with the receptionist, and return with a card-key.

"Why not take a look at one of the rooms?"

"Now, now—Mr. Gray. I thought this was supposed to be a business evening."

"It was. But is it just me, or did the business part come to an end before we even ate dinner?"

There it is. The lip-bite again.

"The High Line Suite," I go on, holding up the card-key. "I mean, I refuse to get involved in any hotel that doesn't have pristine suites."

Fuck.

I shouldn't be doing this.

But I can't help myself from doing this.

"Well," she says, after a pause, "I guess it couldn't hurt to have a quick look."

I push open the door to the suite, which is adorned with vintage furniture apropos of the building. Cass enters in front of me. Two steps inside I spin her around and kiss her deeply. She drinks it all in, kissing me back hard.

I stop. I take two steps back. And look her up and down.

"Walk over to the window. I want to see you in the night light."

Slowly, letting me take in her ridiculous form, she moves across the room to the window. Back still to me, she rests her hands on the windowsill and bends slightly forward as she looks over the grounds of the adjacent private park. I take my jacket off, throw it along with my iPad on the oversized king bed, and loosen my tie. I turn the lamp beside the bed on to a soft glow. I walk up behind her, unzip her dress, then return to where I was across the room.

"Turn around," I say.

She does.

"I have one question. Is it just me—or do you want me to see what you have on under that dress even more than I want to see it?"

She gently wriggles the dress off her shoulders, and lets it fall to the ground around her feet. Underneath she's wearing a matching white lace G-string and bra, which stands out beautifully against her deeply bronzed skin. She takes a step forward, over the dress.

"You remember this body?"

"You know I do. Do you remember what I used to do to that body?"

"You know I do."

I shouldn't be doing this.

It's wrong.

Fuck.

It's right.

Isn't it?

"The bra and panties. Still too much clothes for my liking," I say. "Take them off."

She does as I say and tosses them on the floor. I begin unbuttoning my shirt.

"Now lean that perfect little ass against that windowsill."

Again, she does as I say.

"Close your eyes."

She does.

"Now put your hand between your legs."

She does.

"What do you see in that dirty little mind of yours?" I ask.

She licks her lips, and moans softly.

"I see you tearing this body up the way you used to."

"Is that right?"

"Uh-huh," she says, eyes still closed, licking her lips. "It is."

"Open your eyes."

She does.

"Get on all fours. Crawl to me, same as you used to. Show me how much you want this."

Without hesitating she gets down like I tell her, starts crawling toward me. My shirt now unbuttoned, I take off my already loosened tie and toss it on the bed.

"You just need some Jonah tonight, don't you?"

She nods as she keeps coming toward me.

"Then say it. Tell me what you need."

"I need some Jonah tonight. Now."

"What would you do for some Jonah right now?"

This is wrong.

"I'd do anything."

"I'll bet you would. Would you crawl over broken glass for it?"

Stop.

"I would."

"Would you crawl through fire for it?"

"I would."

"Would you get on your knees and beg for it?"

Don't stop.

Keep going.

"I am on my knees begging for it."

"You want me to take that body of yours as my own tonight, don't you?"

"I do."

"Then say it. Tell me what you want."

She stops crawling.

"I want you to fuck me like you used to, Jonah. And I want you to fuck me like you used to . . . now."

"AND—SCENE!" a voice shouts from the bathroom.

"Wait—what?" Cass says, lifting her hands from the ground, now kneeling.

"You weren't kidding, babe," Perry says as she comes storming out of the bathroom, "that is one dirty little girl."

"What the fuck is this?"

Perry ignores her words, smacks me on the ass as she comes around me, and kisses me on the lips.

"I must say, I think you went a little overboard with the 'perfect ass' comment. I mean, hell yeah, the girl's got a nice ass. But perfect? As in more perfect than mine?"

"Was all part of the performance, beautiful. No one could ever have a more perfect ass than you," I say back.

"Oh," Per goes on, touching her hand to my face, "so sweet."

"How's Florida?" I ask.

"Apparently not as interesting as New York tonight."

"Hey, what the *fuck* do you two think you're doing?" Cass, sharply, cuts in. She stands all the way up and folds her arms.

Perry, fire in her eyes, turns to her.

"Look up there," Perry says, pointing to the corner of the room where the dark brown molding joins the wall and ceiling, "and there," she goes on pointing to another spot. "Dropcams. That little scene that just played out between the two of you—it's all in the cloud, baby, from two different angles. Trust me, you'd have missed them even if you weren't trying so hard to get laid."

Cass looks at both locations Perry pointed out. She looks back at me. Then to Perry.

"You mean . . . you two . . ."

Before she can get anything else out, Perry steps to her and smashes her across the face with an open-faced slap.

"That's for going after my man. You do it again, what you just felt becomes a lot worse."

Cass, tears and fear welling in her eyes, hand on her cheek, straightens back up.

"You two are crazy. I mean—why?"

"I don't like being played, Cass," I say. "You understand that as well as anyone. We both know you have control of this situation with Landis and Feller, and we both know that I'm the right buyer for this property. If you were truly on my side, you would have helped make that happen. And fast."

Cass says nothing. She folds her arms again, still naked, and listens.

"I think this is about the fact you hate losing almost as much as I do," I go on. "You lost me. What better way to get back at me than sticking it to the girl I ended up with? While at the same time leading me on to think I really might have a chance at getting this property, when—like I said at dinner—I don't think you're about to let that happen."

"Why not?" Cass asks.

"Because Feller told me—based on your recommendation— they're leaning toward Wiler-Jenks."

Cass holds her position. After five seconds, her arms drop to her sides. She looks from me to Perry, then back to me.

"Jonah, listen. It's not that simple. If—"

"This is how this is going to work," I cut her off, walking toward the closet. "First thing tomorrow morning—like, seven a.m. first thing tomorrow morning—you'll be calling Landis and Feller and letting them know you've done some long, hard thinking on the matter, and when all aspects of a potential buyer are lined up side by side, Jonah, and Resurrection, are really the ones best positioned to make this site's redevelopment happen the right way. From his relationship with Jason Eder to his relationship with Jordan Hecht to the fact he has an anchor tenant in hand ready to go, while Wiler-Jenks may have done more development in this part of the city, the right choice—the wise choice—would be Jonah."

I reach the closet, take one of the two robes hanging inside from its hanger, and start back toward the two girls.

"By ten a.m. the latest," I continue, "Landis and Feller—and you, if you want, doesn't matter to me either way—will be on the phone with me to announce the great news. That I've been awarded the right to give Landis and his family an inordinate amount of cash to buy a two-story, dilapidated, about-to-fall-on-its-ass warehouse. To which I'll respond, in my sheer delight, I have no problem absorbing the cost of drafting up the purchase agreement, which my attorney will have a first draft of to them by the end of the day."

I stop in front of Cass and hold out the robe. Dejectedly, she takes it. I go on.

"That's how it's all about to go down. Otherwise, and I mean if there's one *single* deviation from what I just laid out, that little scene that played out earlier finds its way back down from the cloud. Only with a little editing to disguise my voice and change the name Jonah to another possibly linked to your past. Understood?"

Like a schoolgirl who's been caught cheating, Cass nods.

"Good," I go on, "then everyone goes home happy. Well, I mean, at least almost everyone goes home happy."

CHAPTER FORTY-FIVE

TODAY'S BELT, ALONG with all the other belts, is tucked away five stories above in my closet. I'm sitting at the island in the kitchen. I miss Neo. He's always with me this time of night. The lights are off; the only illumination is from a spotlight above the center of the island and what moonlight is able to sneak in the window behind me. I look at my iPhone. 1:31 a.m.

It's time.

Time to make a call I've wanted to make since this all started, but was afraid to.

I go to P in my contacts, find the name I need, and hit dial. It's ringing. Not how a phone sounds ringing in the States, but those long, more hollow, international rings.

"Hallo?"

Gaston Picard—my father's longtime banking guru, and friend, in Switzerland. Gaston assisted me in transforming myself, Perry, and Max once we were on the run in Europe and helped us settle in Amsterdam, where I was ushered—albeit unbeknownst to me—into Cobus de Bont's protection. Two years ago, my final return home looming, was when I learned from Cobus himself that Gaston was also the financial wizard behind managing his affairs—for both the real estate empire I helped him build, as well as whatever other empire it was he presided over. That's why, once I was back home and had ultimately cleared my name,

I moved any and all financial related-assets out from Gaston Picard's care and into the hands of two other managers—one here in the U.S., and another in Switzerland. Not because I didn't trust him, or wasn't appreciative for what he had done, but because the fewer ties to Cobus de Bont, the better. As, again, I honestly thought—or perhaps tricked myself into thinking—we were truly even.

Little did I know that would never be the case.

"Gaston—it's Jonah."

1:31 a.m. in New York means 7:31 a.m. in Switzerland. There's no response from the other end.

"I'm sorry to call this early. I am. It's just that—"

"No," he cuts me off, "No, Jonah, it's okay. I'm just—I'm, you know, just surprised to hear your voice."

"I know. I can imagine."

"How are you? I mean, I've been following along with all your newfound fame and continued success, so I feel safe in assuming all is well. No?"

"Unfortunately, Gaston, you know what they say about all that glitters . . ."

"All too well, Jonah. What has you calling me this morning?"

"It's Cobus."

Nothing.

"Now I know you probably—"

"I can't discuss this, Jonah," he tries to shut me down.

"Gaston, please. I wouldn't be calling unless I was at a real dead end here."

"Jonah, he's a client. Plain and simple. It would be wrong of me to discuss any of his affairs."

"I understand that. I do. But I need to understand what he's into, Gaston. I *need* to. He's in Manhattan and has me looking to tie him into the commercial real estate community here. I simply have to understand how all the pieces fit."

"Why?"

"Because I need to know exactly what it is I'm protecting everyone from. I need to know what I'm protecting myself—and my profession—from."

Nothing.

"Please, Gaston. I know about the precious metals he stockpiles. I know—"

"Jonah, enough. Please. I have to hang up now."

"No! Gaston, please. I need to know how this works, and why he has these materials. Please."

"Good-bye, Jonah. Please take care of yourself."

"Something! Just give me something! Please!"

Nothing.

He doesn't speak, but I know he hasn't hung up either.

"Someone once told me the best business a man can be in is owning a junkyard," he finally says. "You know why?"

"Why?"

"Because you make money on both sides of the building. You get paid for the things you take in, and make more money for the things you offload."

"A junkyard," I repeat, quietly, processing. "But I don't understand. If he—"

"So long, Jonah. And take care of yourself."

Gaston's gone.

A junkyard.

Huh.

I place the iPhone on the island's marble. I reposition myself on my stool, my arms now folded. I start to play over all the possible scenarios of how Cobus could profit from two different sides of obtaining these materials. Ninety minutes later, no matter what picture I paint, one thought keeps coming to the forefront. These metals are two things—necessary in certain industries, and priced according to their supply, which is finite. These people—the people who own the businesses these metals are necessary for—are the easy target. The goal in business is always to keep costs down as much as possible as the fastest way to increasing revenue and profit lines. So why not buy these materials from someone—Cobus—who put nothing into their production, therefore can sell them for a much lower price and still make off like—well—a criminal?

That would make for a nice, neat fit for one side of the junkyard analogy. The front side of the building. But what about the back of the building? In the junkyard analogy, that would mean someone is paying Cobus to take these materials off their hands—but why would anyone in the chain of supply here do that? From the mining companies to possible distributors, there's simply no way to come out ahead. So—how then? And why?

* * *

5:18 a.m.

I'm still on the same stool at the island. In front of me, next to the iPad, is a small plate with some crumbs from a turkey, tomato and mustard sandwich on rye I made about an hour ago along with the knife I used to cut it in half. Using the iPad I've researched different potential avenues of thought, but nothing has panned out as a meaningful direction. I'm fully stumped.

I feel something wet running down my wrist, into my hand. I look down. The gauze covering the scissor wounds on my left forearm is ripped open, and the knife I used to cut my sandwich—which

I'm holding in my right hand—is cutting into the healing wound, opening it again. I stop cutting, but I don't lift the blade out of my flesh. I stare at it. I press the blade down again. Not in a sawing motion this time—just pressing it down, like that first downward push of a knife into a birthday cake. I watch, mesmerized, as the deep red, in this light almost black, blood comes up the sides of the shiny silver utensil. I can see remnants of the mustard from the knife mixing with the blood. Is that bad for me? If mustard gets into my bloodstream?

I stare, mesmerized, as I press the blade down harder. What is that I feel? Is it simply pain? Maybe. But if it's pain, why don't I want to take the blade away? Why do I crave what it will feel like to press this knife's blade deeper into my flesh?

Suddenly startled by what I'm looking at, I shoot up off the stool. The knife bounces away from me on the island's marble leaving a ragged trail of blood markings before it settles. I look again at my forearm. The blood is now flowing harder, dripping onto the floor. Holding my arms out in front of me, I ball my hands into fists. I close my eyes. And, without letting any noise escape from my mouth, just start screaming this silent scream so hard, so violently, every muscle in my body starts shaking.

And there it is.

Light bulb.

I stop my silent screaming and shaking. My eyes open. I focus on the thought that just entered my brain.

It can't be.

No.

Unless, I mean—no.

It can't be.

Or can it *absolutely* be?

My feet immediately take me over to the sink. I turn on the faucet and rinse my forearm, my wrist, and my hand. I dry myself with paper towels, taking a few extras to press into my bleeding wound for temporary stoppage. There's another call I need to make.

I snap up the iPhone, find the necessary contact, and dial. This is going to be interesting. It's ringing. Again, those long, hollow, international rings. This time I'm calling Amsterdam, where it's now 11:19 a.m.

"*Hallo?*"

Angelique. My former assistant who Cobus has since moved into his own office.

"Hi, Angelique. *Dit erkennen gesproken?*"

That's "Hi Angelique. Recognize this voice?" in Dutch. Upon hearing my voice, she changes to English as most Dutch can easily do.

"Ivan. My God. How are you?"

"I'm okay, Angelique. And it's Jonah. How are you?"

"Right—Jonah. So crazy all of it. I miss you. I loved working for you."

"I miss you too. You were always so loyal and sharp."

"You trained me well, Iv—I mean, Jonah."

"It wasn't difficult, Angelique. Your aptitude is off the charts. It always matched your desire to excel at the things you do. Any new piercings and tattoos?"

"You've been gone almost two years. What do you think? I probably had new ones not even a week later."

"That . . . actually makes a lot of sense," I say.

She giggles.

"So, my former boss, to what do I owe this great pleasure today?"

"Angelique—there's something I need. And I believe you, today, are the only one who can help me get it."

"Shoot."

"I need Cobus' personal, not corporate, brokerage account history for the last three years."

"Sorry, Jonah. I don't have access to anything like that. In fact, I don't think he keeps personal records of any kind in the office."

"Actually, he does. You know the three drawers in the credenza on the rear wall behind his desk? The three drawers with the locks on them?"

"Of course."

"The documents I need are in there."

"How do you know?"

"Because when I was at the height of my time working side by side with Cobus, there were multiple occasions when I just walked right into his office—as you recall I did so often—and he was perusing brokerage and banking records from Bank Mendes Gans. A bank de Bont Beleggings didn't use for any of their corporate banking. Each time this happened, Cobus either thought or hoped I wasn't aware of what he was doing. He'd just casually work the documents back into the drawers as we discussed whatever it was we were dealing with. Angelique, I need you to get into those drawers."

"My God, Iv—damn, sorry, Jonah. I could lose my job for something like this!"

"I know, Angelique. That's why I would never ask something like this of you unless it was absolutely necessary. And today—right now—it's absolutely necessary. Cobus is still here in New York, correct?"

"Yes, he is."

"Then you need to make this happen for me. Please."

"How will I even get into them without keys?"

"That I need you to figure out. I need you to figure out fast."

I hear her sigh.

"Okay, Jonah. Okay. Let me see what I can do."

CHAPTER FORTY-SIX

8:42 A.M.

I'm riding in the back of The Ship. Dressed to the hilt as usual for my day, forearm redressed, my iPhone to my ear.

"Jonah. Good morning," Shand says.

"How are you, Greg?"

"I'm well."

"What's your schedule like this morning?" I ask.

"A bit jammed, as usual. Why do you ask?"

"I've given what you said a lot of thought. I'd like to discuss how we might proceed in person."

"Well, now, that sounds more than important enough to fit into this morning's schedule. What time are you thinking of coming by?"

Just as we end our call, my phone rings.

"How are we today, Minnie?"

"Okay, Jonah. I'm ready for it."

I cringe at the thought of what might next come out of her mouth. But nothing does.

"For . . . what?" I ask, gingerly.

"To sell One Hundred Three Church. I'm ready."

"This is something you've discussed with your whole family?"

"Well, of course it is, Jonah—but who gives a shit about that anyway? The big decisions, as you know, come from me. We may all have to agree on this end, but if I tell this family it's time to sell then they know better then to fuck with that. So that's exactly what I've done. Told them it's time to sell. Because you convinced me it's the right move."

I stare out the window. Midtown Manhattan silently glides by.

"Jonah? Did you hear me?" she goes on.

"I did, Minnie. I did."

"So, then, Mister Secrets-And-Shit, do I get to know who I'm selling this cash cow to now?"

"You'll see the name on the paperwork. Then we can discuss it from there."

We end our call. I go to M in my contacts, and dial Shawn Magnus, my attorney's, cell. He doesn't pick up. It goes straight to voice mail.

"Good morning, Shawn, it's Jonah. I need a purchase agreement drawn up this morning. And I'm sorry to do this, but I need you to make it your top priority. I need this deal to keep moving ahead at full steam."

* * *

I follow Shand into the same conference room at Spectrum's headquarters we spoke in previously.

"Can I have someone bring some coffee? Tea? Water?"

"None for me, thanks," I say. "I'm fine."

He closes the door. We each sit in the same seats we sat in during our last conversation.

"So," I say as his ass hits his chair, "what do you have in mind? You know, about making this Mr. Esparanza situation go away?"

"So, to be clear, you're saying you're on board?" Shand answers my question with one of his own.

"I'm saying that in order to really evaluate this option, I just need to be crystal clear on the matter. According to you, there is—*possibly*—another member of Mr. Esparanza's crew from that night who forget to mention, when originally questioned about that night, the deceased said he wasn't feeling well. And that he was going to look for a quiet place to rest for a little bit."

"Precisely."

"But what about the way he was found?"

"It becomes less of an important question once this statement comes to the surface, Jonah. But for argument's sake, he placed his boots neatly next to where he planned on laying down for just a few minutes. After all, he was fully clothed. So why wouldn't this make sense?"

"Resting on a cold, hard, concrete floor?"

"He was on the verge of a heart attack. It is certainly within the realm of possibility his mind was concerned with more pressing issues than where it was he'd be resting."

"Uh, huh . . . " I agree, nodding. "I see where you're going. But I have some other questions."

"Such as?"

"Such as—how does this all work with the kids and all? You know—once shit goes down?"

"Kids? What kids? What are you talking about?" Shand asks, clearly confused.

"I'm sorry. Let me be clearer. Once Julie—your wife—finds out you've been fucking Madame Martine's assistant Tiffany, how will that work with the kids? Is she the kind of woman that will entertain an amicable split with everything brushed under the rug for the sake of two young children? Or is she the vindictive type that will go for the jugular? Look to ruin you, and in the process—no matter if these kids are young or not—let them know from day one what a lowlife piece of shit Dad is? I only ask because, well, I've seen a number of people go through some pretty wild divorces these last years. Is there any real way to know how these things will go—you know, with kids in the mix and all? I don't have kids. That's why I'm asking. I mean—you must have thought about these things, right?"

All the blood having left Shand's face, he shifts in his seat.

"You've—um—you've spoken with Tiffany?" is all he comes up with as he clumsily tries to figure out what to do with his hands.

"I have. And while I know she loved that the attention surrounding the missing prototype bottle was being drawn right where she would have hoped—to Marilena—it was the lobby cameras that did her in. While it is clear Tiffany left the building at seven twenty on the night in question, it is equally clear she reentered the property at 7:48 p.m., just twenty-eight minutes after leaving."

"H-how could that be? Why?"

"How? Simple. She came back in wearing a different jacket, hood up, and sunglasses thinking 'no problem' in terms of the main camera she walked past on the way out catching her—I'm guessing at your direction. What you *didn't* think about seriously enough, unfortunately—which, surprises me, considering the business you're in—was the range of the other cameras in the lobby. Another one, all the way across the space, is what picked up the front of her turning away from the camera she was trying to avoid. Once we picked up on this and zoomed in—voila! Now, as for the 'why' part of your last question, this is where it gets really interesting. Which we'll get to."

"Jonah, please—" Shand says as he starts to stand up.

"Shut up! And sit your ass back down!" I raise my voice, pointing my index finger at his face as if it's the gun in my waistline.

He does.

"In my house? You want to pull this shit in *my* house?" I go on. "A house I literally invited you into and have been paying for you to patrol? To clean? To look after?"

I stand up, and start slowly walking around the room.

"Tiffany told me this all came from you. And that you promised her, the same way you promised this young, naïve, vulnerable little girl you'd be leaving your wife for her, that this would all be okay. The plan, according to her, went exactly as you had outlined. She would come back into the building, as she did, she would take the prototype, as she did, and she would meet you on the vacant floor of the building once you were able to make it to the property, which she did. But, unfortunately for you, a few things didn't exactly go your way."

I stop, take one of the seats across the conference table from Shand, and sit down again. He swivels and faces me. This time I lean back in my chair and put my feet up. I keep going.

"The other day, when we spoke, I asked if you often visit properties you service the way you did that night. You said no. Then, when I asked if on those unusual nights you *do,* if you visit more than one property, you said yes. This was easy enough to try and corroborate. I checked the entrance logs for all of my properties. Then I had my detective friend—the one downstairs who's been assisting on this— ask for the records for that night for all of your other properties outside my portfolio. This was the only building you entered that night. And you did so to meet Tiffany as per her instructions. Only when you did so—you didn't count on one thing. That Mr. Esparanza would be getting serviced by one of the younger, female, attractive members of that same overnight cleaning crew on the same vacant floor where you and Tiffany were to rendezvous with the stolen goods. Do you know what unfortunately—or, fortunately, depending on who you ask—happened because of this coincidence?"

Shand, downtrodden, beaten, shakes his head "no."

"It *literally* scared the life out of Mr. Esparanza. You and I— we've been speaking about all the different ways the man could have died; what the—*circumstances*—could have been surrounding Esparanza's heart suddenly stopping. What you don't know is that I—we, meaning my detective friend and me—know exactly what happened. When the deceased and that girl heard those elevator doors open—and he thought about all that would come with his being found in this compromising position—he had his fatal heart attack. Did you mean to do that? No, of course not. And did the man go out while he was literally, to the moment, getting a piece of ass behind his wife's back? Yes. But that doesn't change what happened. That man died when he heard the elevator open at the exact time you were apparently meeting Tiffany. The moment actually scared his heart into submission. You can take that little nugget with you."

I stand up and slowly continue around the table.

"Anyway, the lock," I continue. "Again, it was the right idea to have the lock to Madame Martine's office appear to have been manipulated, since Tiffany had the key. But you should have better instructed her on how to do this. She scratched the handle and area around the lock up pretty good, but when the inside of the lock was examined in a forensic manner—one thing was clear as the water in the Galapagos Islands. The inside of the lock was as pristine as the day it was first used, having only ever been opened—or attempted to be opened—by one of the keys that fit inside it. No one tried to get into that door lock. Tiffany, I'm guessing at your direction, just did a shitty job of trying to make it look like someone did. Which brings me, finally, to the why. Do you want to explain this part of it all to me?"

"Jonah, you may think you—"

"Shut up! I wasn't really asking," I cut him off. "For the life of me, I couldn't figure out why a guy like you would get involved with crap like this. So we had to do a little digging. It turns out Spectrum, while still doing decently when all the subsidiaries are taken into account, isn't going quite as strong as it was only three years ago. In fact, your business as a whole is barely breaking even—which makes sense when you take into account all the competition that's popped up in the space over these last few years with a resurgence in the economy. Then, at the suggestion of Tiffany, we decided to look into someone named Suzanne Ornstein. As an acquaintance of my detective friend was easily able to learn, a large chunk of your personal holdings are in the stock of an American company called GMHO Global—one of the largest corporations in the world. A corporation that has a subsidiary called LivLiv Style Center, which is a women's fashion, make-up, perfume, and accessory company. A company where your only sister, Suzanne Ornstein—whose maiden name is Suzanne Shand—is a vice president. A company that, like, Spectrum, has seen better days."

"Jonah, look. If you'll just let me—"

I crack him across the jaw as I've come full circle around the table and reached him. The surprise in his eyes as his hand moves to his cheek makes it clear he realizes it's time to fully succumb.

"Nothing you have to say is worth shit to me, Gregory, and I have a busy morning. We both know that this—getting this coveted new fragrance—into your hands, once your brainwashed little bang doll made it known it was on its way over from Paris, was a much easier opportunity for getting something back on track than turning around your entire business. But as a typical lowlife like yourself often tends to overlook when it comes to their self-interest, people got hurt. Tiffany got hurt. Madame Martine got hurt. Esparanza got hurt. I got hurt. So now, I have one question. And it's one I really want you to answer."

"Okay."

"Can you get the prototype back?"

"I—I don't know."

"Well, that's too bad. Because unless you can, my detective friend downstairs is coming upstairs to arrest you for breaking and entering, conspiracy—he's got a whole laundry list of things you'll be charged with. And then apparently the two of you will be heading over to your sister's company for a little chat. So I'll just—"

I head to the door and put my phone to my ear.

"Wait! Jonah—wait."

I stop and look at him.

"I can probably get it back."

"Then I suggest you do so. And when you do—only if you do—this is what's going to go down. You are going to put out a press release saying that an internal investigation in corroboration with ownership—Resurrection—has resulted in not only sorting out what happened with this missing prototype, you are going to make it explicitly clear it was an inside job within the confines of Spectrum Global. Then, in this same statement, you will make a personal apology to Madame Martine, her firm, myself personally, and my firm. Lastly within this statement, in light of the awful situation that has gone on under your leadership, you will be saying with finality that you will be resigning from Spectrum effective immediately. Am I clear so far?"

Shand nods his head yes.

"Good. After that, you'll be selling your stake in Spectrum Global to me at a steep—and I mean steep—discount. Since I'm a man always interested in expanding my investment portfolio. I mean, doesn't it seem like a company like Spectrum would be a great sister company for a firm like Resurrection?"

"Jonah, don't you think that's—"

"This isn't a negotiation. I would think you'd understand that by now."

Shand opens his mouth to say something. He stops himself.

"Why?" he finally asks.

"Why what?"

"Why not just throw me to the wolves?"

"You know, Gregory, that's a good question. One I thought about long and hard on the way over here. I'll tell you why. A woman named Mrs. Esparanza. A woman that—no matter how her husband went out—doesn't deserve the humiliation that would come with the full story of how these two ridiculous situations were in fact intertwined. I mean—it doesn't bring him back to life, does it? This woman was proud of her hard-working husband, of their marriage, proud of the life they carved out for themselves. Why should she have to endure that shame with her family, her friends, in her community? She shouldn't. Any more than a woman named Mrs. Shand should have to. Besides, when it comes to you and your wife? I'm guessing Tiffany might have more to say about that one."

CHAPTER FORTY-SEVEN

9:37 A.M.

"Jonah," Carolyn's voice says through the phone intercom, "I have Mr. Landis on the phone. Shall I put him through?"

"Please do."

The phone rings in my office. I pick up.

"Good morning, Jerry. How are you?"

"I'm well, Jonah. I'm here with Cass, as well as Norm, and I'm happy to tell you I'm the bearer of good news this morning."

"Good morning Norm, Cass," I go on.

Feller gives me a nice hello. Cass says nothing.

"So may I assume it's the good news I've been hoping for?"

"You may, Jonah. We're going with Resurrection. It was not an easy decision, but in the end, after much deliberation, and after some final points Cass presented this morning on your firm's behalf, we decided it's the right fit."

"That's great news. Really. I know how much this means to you, Jerry—to you on behalf of your family's legacy. I appreciate your having faith in me. And, Cass, whatever it is you may have said, thanks for tipping the scales in our favor."

"When it's meant to be—it's meant to be," Cass says, bitterness in her voice.

"Amen to that, Ms. Lima. Amen to that."

* * *

9:57 a.m.

On my desktop, I send an email to Cobus.

Your first ship has come in. We're drawing up the purchase agreement for One Hundred Three Church Street, which I'll have to Arnon immediately so the language can be hammered out in short order over the course of the day. Shall we say breakfast tomorrow in my office for your first signature?

Arnon is Cobus' in-house counsel.

I fire the email off. Just as I do, Carolyn comes through the intercom again.

"Jonah, I have a Mr. Moishe Greenbaum downstairs at the security desk who says he'd like to speak with you."

Huh.

Fucking Anshel's Fucking Moishe.

"Absolutely, Carolyn. Bring him up."

Five minutes later Carolyn enters my office, Fucking Moishe behind her. I stand up behind my desk. Fucking Moishe, dressed as always in a fine suit topped off with a yamaka, walks toward me.

"May I bring you two gentlemen anything?" Carolyn asks.

We shake hands.

"Coffee? Perhaps some Manischewitz?" I further Carolyn's offer, looking to both keep things light and remind Fucking Moishe when in my house I do, and say, as I please.

"Very funny," Fucking Moishe responds as we shake hands, "and no, thanks, I'm fine."

Carolyn exits, leaving my door open as she knows to do when unfamiliar people show up announced. Without question she's going to get either Perry or Jake. This way they can stand outside my door, and we'll have a second set of ears to corroborate my side of whatever discussion takes place.

I motion with my hand to one of the seats in front of my desk, offering for Fucking Moishe to sit.

"Actually—I was hoping we could speak somewhere private."

"This isn't private?" I say, looking around to emphasize my point.

He looks at the open door, then back to me.

"There's something I want to show you."

"Show me?"

I pause. Then I come around my desk.

"Come on."

He follows me into the adjacent, private conference room. I walk over to the button on the wall that frosts the dividing glass. I press it, and turn back toward my guest. Just as I do, a crushing blow comes clear across my chin.

My knees buckle as I start to fall to my right, but I catch myself. Now in a crouched position I look back up, only to see the tail end of a vicious roundhouse kick that slams into the left side of my head sending me all the way down. My left ear's ringing. And I can feel the wetness of the blood trickling out of it.

"You want to come into our house and try to light us up?"

I start to get up, but receive a tremendous kick to the gut that sends me back down.

"I thought I'd return the favor," Fucking Moishe goes on. "Only I bring along a third degree black belt with me."

I continue to try and get myself back up. I sense him coming again. Now understanding the situation I'm in, I surprise him with speed of my own. Still on my knees, Fucking Moishe not two feet from me, I pull the piece from my waistline. And aim it at his balls. My assailant stops dead in his tracks.

"Take two steps back. Now," I say, calmly.

His arms up off his sides at about a thirty-degree angle, palms out, he does as I say. Simultaneously, my eyes never leaving his eyes, I get to my feet much faster than I'm guessing he'd imagine someone who'd just absorbed those blows could. I move the aim of the gun from his groin to his face.

"That's all nice and well, Fucking Moishe, but didn't anyone ever tell you to bring more than your fists and feet to a gun fight?"

Nothing. He just swallows. With the tips of my left hand's index and middle fingers I dab at the blood on the side of my head. I hold the fingers in front of my face for a quick look.

Nothing like the sight and smell of blood in the morning.

"Get on your knees."

His eyes are now locked on the gun. Whether it's defiance, or simply shock, he doesn't move or say anything.

"Let me make this clear," I continue. "I have no reservations—none, zero—about unloading a round or two into you. The shot is heard, people come running, my case for self-defense is as clear as it gets. And I can tell you with 100 percent certainty, the first bullet that leaves this gun shreds one of your knees. So I'm going to tell you one more time."

Not your day, Fucking Moishe.

I hear Pop's voice in my head.

"Being unprepared is one thing."

"Being unprepared against a stronger foe means you should never have come through the door."

"Get. On. Your. Knees," I continue.

Finally, he does. His eyes move from the gun back to mine. I slowly walk behind him. Our eyes remain locked, his eyeballs moving with my each step, until they can no longer follow me.

"I must say, I somewhat admire the balls on you. Who knows—you just may even be as much of a prick as your father."

I press the tip of the gun to the back of his head.

"I walk into your house, and speak as if I own the place," I go on. "You walk into my house, and try and do the same. I end up with blood coming out of my ear. Which means—"

I put both my hands together around the gun. I wind up and swing the butt of the pistol to the right side of his head as if I'm swinging a baseball bat. His knees are literally lifted off the ground before he drops to his left.

"—You end up with blood coming from your ear."

I stand over him, now straddling him, and put the tip of the gun straight down into his temple.

"You tell Daddy Dearest this deal better close as fast as I dictate. If it doesn't—well—do either of you really want to see what kind of shit storm might come your way? The way I see it you'd get the best of both worlds. My wrath, and the wrath of the DOB, which I've already made clear is just a phone call away. Are we clear?"

Fucking Moishe, on his side, nods meekly.

"Are we *clear?*" I say again.

"Yes—yes, we're clear."

"Good. Don't you get it, Fucking Moishe? We're not really that different."

Out of the corner of his eye, he looks up at me.

"We were both raised by wolves," I add. "Now, time to go forward and prosper."

I stand up and raise my foot over his bloody ear. I drop my heel, hard as I can, into his head.

* * *

1:18 p.m.

I'm standing in one of the examination rooms in Dr. Crowder's office. The door opens. In he walks with Neo in his arms. My little comrade, giddy as me about our being reunited, starts to shake and shimmy so hard he almost falls out of the doctor's arms.

"This adorable little package is for you," he says, handing Neo to me.

I hold Neo up to my chest and give his warm little body a gentle squeeze as I've done what seems like a million times before. I raise him in front of my face. He licks my nose. I kiss him all over his face.

"How's my tough guy doing?" I ask.

"He's doing okay," the doctor answers on his behalf. "I'd like him to be adjusting to the food a little better, which means a bit of an upset stomach is still on the horizon for a few days, but I've seen worse. As you can see his spirits are certainly on the rise, and his energy level seems to be as well."

"Can I bring him home?"

"I want him monitored closely. And if there's a problem, you're to call my cell, day or night. But, yes, you can take him home."

* * *

3:16 p.m.

I'm in Jake's office. We're sitting on opposite ends of the L-shaped black leather Ralph Lauren couch. Jake bites into a fresh jelly doughnut; a bit of the red, gooey center plops out of the pastry onto his white shirt.

"Fuck me," he says looking at the stain, then back to me as he stands and heads to his desk for some tissue. "So what the fuck do I tell him?" he continues.

Before I can answer I hear my iPhone start pinging. It's a text from Angelique, my former assistant.

You owe me . . . it reads.

A second later a photo comes through. Then another. And another. One by one the photos stream in, and one by one I enlarge and examine them. Cobus' personal brokerage statements, going from last month backwards, from Bank Mendes Gans.

"Yes," I say to myself, smiling, "*YES—*"

* * *

4:57 p.m.

"I must say, Joonah, I never doubted you for a moment."

"Is that right?" I respond into my cell. "Then why not give me more than thirty seconds before strategically leaking the situation to the media?"

"I don't know what you're talking about," Madame Martine responds. "But we both know hundred-million-dollar product rollouts wait for no one, Joonah. And whatever it is that took place—well—we all need a little . . . motivation, from time to time."

"I take the security of my tenants extremely seriously, Madame Martine. I'm sorry this happened. But I can assure you, nothing remotely like this will ever take place again."

"I know it won't, Joonah. Not just because you're saying it, because I know you mean it. That's why I moved into your building in the first place. Sure, it would have been so much easier to just stay put. But I believed you were truly going to look out for me. For my employees. For my brand."

"Do you still believe that?"

"I do. Because you said you wouldn't stop until this was made right. And you succeeded. I mean it when I say I never doubted you. I also want you to know how much I truly appreciate your working so diligently to get the matter resolved in short order. I'm not sure avoiding this situation would have been as easy as simply being in another property. What I am sure of is that very few other owners would have taken what happened so personally. And been able to get the results you did. For that, I'm grateful."

CHAPTER FORTY-EIGHT

7:44 P.M.

"The site is perfect for your business."

I'm sitting with Roddy and L at one of the bar booths in Bodega Negra, a swank, trendy Mexican joint in the Meatpacking District's Dream Hotel. Our drinks are placed on the table, along with some pork belly and Peking duck soft tacos to get us started. I lift my neat shot of Clase Azul Ultra Tequila to my lips, throw it back, and ask the waiter to return with another.

"Not only will your current clientele follow you," I continue, "you position yourself in a completely different part of Manhattan that opens you up to a whole new demographic for business. Plus—you are now considerably closer to Queens and Long Island for when that word of mouth keeps ramping up and up. Personally, I think it's a home run."

"Of course you do," Roddy says, "it keeps you on track with your assemblage."

"When it comes to business, Roddy, I don't bullshit. I may play as hard as anyone on the ball field, but I never bullshit—anyone in this city who knows me will tell you that. Does this help me get where I need to go? It does. But do I unequivocally see this as a great move for your business? Absolutely."

"I must say, Gray, you're a hard man to say no to. Especially when what you're saying seems to make a lot of sense."

"Read a paper once in a while, Roddy," L says, "my boy is as legit as they get. And, for what it's worth, I'd lease the space from Jonah with an option to purchase. That's just me. Just sayin.'"

The waiter puts my shot down. I throw it back, order another, as well as one each for Roddy and L.

"I'm a big believer in preparation, Roddy. Nothing more, nothing less."

"So, I think seeing the site would be the next logical step," Roddy says.

"Indeed it would be," I respond. "I'll set it up."

I get an email from Magnus. It reads, *Been back and forth all day with de Bont's counsel, and we're all comfortable with the language. The purchase agreement is attached for you to review, but you're all set to have Mr. de Bont sign tomorrow. Good luck.*

Get where you need to go.

Always.

Clean up the mess later.

* * *

9:52 p.m.

I reach the front door of Silver Rock. I put my key in the door, but immediately realize it is unlocked. I turn the knob and enter.

The entrance, like the rest of what I can see of the first floor from the foyer, is low lit for evening. Everything is quiet, although I believe I hear the faint sound of music coming from the top floor. I walk toward the elevator, step inside, and hit five.

As the cab ascends, the music starts to get louder and louder with each floor. By the time it hits five, I can tell the music is playing extremely loud before the doors even open. When they do, Sia's "Breathe Me" overruns me. Like the ground floor, the top floor of

Silver Rock is dreamily resting in soft, low light. As I slowly walk forward, it's like the song is following me, and swallowing me, at the same time. It pours from every speaker, in every room, of our master bedroom floor.

I see Neo coming down the hall toward me. He's trotting, like a little horse, somewhere between a walk and a run. As he nears me something looks wrong. It looks like something's on his head.

I scoop him up. As he licks my nose, I study his little cranium. In the near darkness, it looks like there are a couple of faint, black streaks in his head's fur. I look closer. As I do, it registers that what I'm looking at appears to be blood.

I drop my briefcase. I reach my free hand around my back, and pull the piece out. I kiss Neo on the nose, lock him in the closest bathroom, and head toward the bedroom.

The music fills the hallway, fills me.

Ouch, I have lost myself again

Lost myself and I am nowhere to be found

I lock my jaw, clench my teeth, and get my chin up. Elbow cocked, gun up next to my face, I gird myself for whatever chaos awaits me. I move forward. I'm ready for anything.

I'm ready for war.

As I near the bedroom, unable to hear anything but the music, I see someone moving toward me. Unfortunately, because of the lighting, I'm mostly getting the figure's shadow. I stop dead, put the gun up, and aim at the head. Surprisingly, the figure's not moving fast. Just the opposite.

It seems to be . . . carelessly.

Is whomever this is dazed from something they just saw?

Dazed from something they just did?

I re-wrap my fingers around the piece's grip panel, making sure it's as sturdy as possible in my hand. As I do, the figure's face comes into my vision for a moment because of the right angle under one of the hallway's sconces. No fucking way.

Natey-Boy Landgraff?

The moment I notice his face, he notices me. As our eyes lock, he stops. His hands, palms out, go up in front of him.

Gun extended, ready to maim, I storm toward him. He doesn't move, or in any way try to flee. Hands still up, he just starts shaking his head, as if saying "no" to whatever questions he thinks must be running through my brain.

He's saying something just as I reach him, but because of the music it's impossible to hear him. In a blink I crush him across the face with the piece, sending him into the wall. Before he can even process or deal with the shot, I lift him with my left hand, by his neck, so hard he's six inches off the ground, and pin him to the wall. With my right hand, I put the tip of the gun under his chin. Blood pours from his nose down, in, and around his mouth, onto his neck and around the tip of the Glock.

"What did you do?" I scream in his face.

Hands still up, as if surrendering, he continues to furiously plea with me. Only I still can't hear a thing.

"What did you do?" I scream louder, yet slower, so he can read my lips if not hear my voice.

"I didn't do anything!" he yells back at me, spittle of his blood and spit hitting me in my face, going into my mouth. "I didn't do anything! I swear!"

I have enough experience with Natey-Boy Landgraff at this point to know the truth behind his eyes, to understand his millionth. I believe him. I ease up just enough for him to get his feet back on the ground, and take the gun away from his chin. But I keep my other hand around his neck for safekeeping.

"What is happening?" I scream directly into his ear.

I turn my head, so my ear is directly in front of his mouth.

"Victoria texted me earlier and said Perry had called her, out of her mind. Whacked, and asked her to come over. I wrote back asking her why, but never heard back. I've been trying her for the last two hours, only to still get nothing. So, worried, I came over here. I rang the bell a bunch, but no one answered. I turned the knob eventually, and the door opened. I heard music playing upstairs, so I came up here."

I turn back to him, and shout again in his ear.

"That still doesn't answer my question! What is happening?"

I look Landgraff in his face again. He doesn't say another word. He just gestures toward the bedroom with his eyes.

I leave him alone. I walk directly to the end of the hallway, to Perry's and my master bedroom. As I approach I can see the doors are open.

Once in the doorway, and able to see what's going on inside, I stop. My jaw drops to my chest. My gun drops to my side. Perry and Victoria are both naked on our satin-sheet covered bed. There are a few thick, black, bloody scratches up and down Victoria's back no doubt from Perry's long nails. I can see some of this blood on her hands. Sia still going strong all around us, I can see streaks of the blood on the sheets.

Be my friend, hold me
Wrap me up, unfold me
I am small, and needy

I put the gun back in the rear of my waistline and place my hands on my hips. Then I just watch, trying to process what is happening.

Trying to understand.

* * *

3:17 a.m.

Perry's been sleeping for hours. Victoria and Landgraff are long gone. I'm standing, naked, in Perry's walk-in closet, in the area where she gets ready with her hair and make-up before she gets dressed. The space is dimly lit. Staring in the mirror, into the eyes of Ivan Janse, who's staring back, I wait.

So many questions.

Where are the answers.

I *need* the answers.

I wait.

Zero hesitation, I thrust myself forward and ram my head straight into the mirror. Instantly pain blasts through every atom of my skull. The skin covering my forehead stings like a thousand hornets just attacked. I look up. The glass is still intact yet uneven, haphazard lines shoot out from the point of impact like an imperfect sunburst.

Stop.

Don't stop.

From the sight of the raging fire still burning behind my eyes, like a reflex, I slam my head into the mirror again. This time glass falls everywhere. My head is throbbing. The bone, the skin—every sensory nerve from my neck up is begging for mercy. In the reflection where mirror still remains, I see a gash has opened up at my hairline. Blood spreads down my face like a sped-up video of a spider web being spun.

Stop.

More.

Sleep?

More?

I look down. From the mess on the vanity I pick up a giant, triangular shard of glass. I look at the gauze covering my forearm.

Don't do this.

Do this.

Underneath, where I know the scabbing wound resides, I slice into myself. My arm starts shaking. Fresh blood begins to flow, soaking the cotton.

My heart's racing.

My pounded brain's spinning.

I'm exhausted.

Arms slack at my sides, I fall backwards onto the floor.

"What's going on?" I hear Perry's tired voice ask.

I look up behind me. I see Perry's naked body, upside down, standing in her closet's entryway. I start laughing as uncontrollably, and as hard, as I've ever laughed before.

CHAPTER FORTY-NINE

9:04 A.M.

Cobus steps into my office.

"My God, Jonah. What happened to you?"

As always, Cobus is in his black suit from head to toe. I, too, am dressed in my usual uniform, minus the jacket, which Carolyn hung for me. I stand up, come around my desk, and walk toward him.

"Looks worse than it is. The elevator in the house isn't working properly, so I decided to use the stairs for a late-night snack. Took a little spill."

I reach him and we shake hands.

"A *little* spill?"

"Come on," I say, changing direction, "the documents are ready to be signed."

Cobus follows me into my conference room. The necessary signature pages of the purchase agreement are on the table, front and center.

"Arnon was quite pleased with your attorney's work, Jonah. As they say, one down, two to go—no?"

"Something like that," I respond, handing Cobus a Montblanc pen, and gesturing with my other hand for him to have a seat.

"Carolyn!" I yell. "Can you come in here?"

Cobus sits down and signs the documents. Once he's done, I take back my pen. I hand the documents to Carolyn.

"Please have these scanned and emailed immediately to Shawn, and to Cobus' in-house counsel, Arnon."

"Of course," Carolyn says, immediately setting off.

"Ah—Jonah. I knew you'd come around. Won't you now join me?"

Cobus now gestures to the seats around the table. Slowly, I walk to the side of the table from where he's sitting. I pull out one of the chairs. I sit down.

"You and I were meant to work together, Jonah," he continues, "because I need people around me who get things done. And you, my friend, know how to get things done. That's why, when this is all said and done, we'll be that much closer to our firms one day joining forces in some capacity."

He holds his hands up in front of him, and interlocks his fingers.

"I mean, the more . . . *intertwined* . . . our businesses get," he continues, "the more it will make sense for them to move forward as one. Wouldn't you agree?"

I don't respond. I just stare back at him.

"How about at least congratulating me, Jonah? After all, I did just make my first New York City purchase."

"Congratulations, Cobus."

"See? Was that so hard?"

"You just bought Eleven Ninth Avenue," I go on, "the most desired redevelopment site in the Meatpacking District, if not in all of Manhattan."

Cobus pauses. He processes my words.

"Excuse me? I just bought One Hundred Three Church Street."

"No you didn't," I shoot back quickly. "That's the building you *thought* you were buying. But I got in here at six a.m. this morning and changed the language in this document to reflect the purchase of Eleven Ninth Avenue. And—as you will see in the contingency language—if, and only if, I first receive the property free and clear from the current owners as I'm in the process of doing. At that time, and only at that time, will it be turned over from me, to you. Don't worry, the language is very clear about how this will all work. As is the language in the appendix stating Resurrection will be the sole fee-based consultant to oversee the redevelopment of the site, and exclusive agent for filling the space—both roles I need to fill in order to keep the promises I've made to the current seller. If you have any questions, Arnon will easily be able to clarify for you. Anyway— you know why? You know why it needs to be from me directly? Your purchase of this property you had zero intention of buying?"

Seething, he says nothing.

"Because I won't let you touch the good people of this city—the good owners of this city. Those who are part of the commercial real estate industry in this city. New York City. New Deal City. My city. Me? You put me out there to bring you real estate gold, and that's exactly what I did. Trust me—I thought about making you sign a document that simply said you're my silent, 49 percent partner of the site, but I wouldn't be able to ever sleep again knowing you and I owned anything together. Not with what I know about you. What I gave you is in the true spirit of what real estate is all about. You want to absorb buildings for your other dealings? You want to align your criminal self with unknowing participants in this city? That's up to you. I just refuse to lead you to them, or be involved in any way. I know you wanted the other buildings. Instead of giving you those, I could have given you nothing. Instead, I gave you something in the middle—a site that everyone wants for the true spirit of what commercial real estate in this city is all about. That needs to be enough. Enough for us to finally, once and for all, be even."

"You'd better be fucking with me," Cobus says through clenched teeth.

"Oh you're being fucked with, all right," I respond. "In fact, with regard to the level with just how much you've been fucked with— we're just getting warm."

Cobus, still trying to make sense of what is happening, starts to speak, but stops himself.

"What's on your mind?" I ask.

I stand up.

"Don't worry. As you can see," I continue, "I seem to have forgotten my belt today."

I sit back down.

"I'll tell you what's on my mind, Jonah. You must have a death wish."

"I don't. In fact, it's quite the opposite. I'm so fascinated by trying to figure out how to best feel what this life is all about, that I've gone to great lengths to ensure my safety going forward from the thug, piece-of-shit, deranged-animal fuck that you are."

"Oh, is that right?" Cobus asks, smirking. He leans forward and puts his elbows on the table, resting his chin in his hands. "And how is that?"

"We'll get to that. But first, I must say, I was pretty baffled by what exactly it is that you do with your—*other*—business. I mean, once I saw the rhodium and iridium stockpiles in your basement in Rotterdam, and started to learn about the thefts of these types of precious metals that have gone on at the ports in the cities you just happen to be expanding into. From there, one side of the equation made sense in terms of how you make money. By stealing these metals, then selling them to those in need at a steep discount, you still make out hand over fist, and everyone wins. But knowing you, and, well, to be honest, how well you understand the financial world, I just knew in my gut there had to be more. You know, Cobus, many say the junkyard business is the best business of all to be in. You know why?"

"Enlighten me," he responds, chin still in his hands, smiling, thinking he's taunting me.

"Because a junkyard owner makes money on both sides of the house—what he brings in, and what he ultimately sells. While I was able to, as I just explained, figure out how you were making money selling the booty, I couldn't figure out how you were making money on the risky side of bringing the goods in. And then—wham!"

I slam my hand down on the table. Cobus doesn't flinch.

"That's when it hit me!" I go on. "I remembered those times back when we worked together, and I'd come into your office while you were reviewing your personal brokerage account statements. You do remember what I'm talking about—right? When you'd try to casually put them away, as if I didn't notice what it is you were reviewing?"

No answer. And his smile seems to have gotten a little smaller.

"Anyway, I remembered that these statements were from Bank Mendes Gans. Now, I need to digress here. I think, Cobus, in all this—in all your subtle chest pounding and territory marking—you've forgotten something very important. I have some pretty serious fucking connections in this world too. All it took was my reaching out to one of those connections, a very high-up individual in the Bank Mendes Gans universe, and cashing in on a long over-due favor."

I reach for the iPad on the table. With a tap of the screen, the sixty-inch flat-screen on the wall comes to life. Cobus turns to have a look. The picture on the TV is of one of his recent Bank Mendes Gans statements.

"Just like that—voila!" I exclaim. "I have in my possession your statements from the last three years! Isn't that cool?"

I start tapping the iPad. With each tap, the image on the screen slides to the previous month's statement's first page.

"How the—" Cobus says.

"Once I had these, and was able to look through them, I easily confirmed what I thought. That you were trading the stocks of the mining companies in the aftermath of these reported thefts. That's how you made money on the bring-the-goods-in side of the operation. It's all there in those statements clear as day. Because these rare metals are mined in relatively small amounts globally as opposed to the likes of gold and silver and platinum, and they are priced accordingly, these thefts were, and are, in the mining world, a big deal. It was without question these firms who lost this inventory would be affected—as even though you were, and are, selling the goods at a discount, technically they had been removed from the global inventory because they couldn't be accounted for. You knew this, as you orchestrated the heists. Therefore you were in the perfect position to take huge positions in these stocks, as you did, enter at precisely the right time, as you did, and exit with the same impeccable timing, as you did. Money on both sides of the junkyard."

Cobus looks back to me, smiling again.

"Do you have any idea who you're playing with?"

"The crazy thing is," I keep going, dismissing his last comment, "I only got a glimpse into this side of your other business with regard to precious metals. I'm guessing you execute the same tactics with other commodities, like coffee or crude oil."

"You forgot animal products and plastics," Cobus says.

"Right! Plastics!" I reply, matching his sarcasm with some of my own.

Cobus straightens himself back up in his chair. His face, in a blink, goes from smiling to serious.

"Today's a sad day for you, Jonah. Want to know why?"

"Enlighten me."

"Because you're a dead man."

"No, I'm not."

"No, you're not?"

"Correct. And I'll tell you why."

I tap the iPad. A new image appears on the flat screen. Cobus looks.

"No," he growls under his breath.

"Oh, yes." I respond.

Up on the screen is a live image of Cobus' wife, and two children, having a late lunch in a restaurant in Amsterdam.

In the game of life, I've been cast in a lead role.

Unbeknownst to Cobus, I'm also the head writer.

Unbeknownst to Cobus, I'm also the director.

"Do I want it to have to be like this? No. But with a guy like you, I don't have a choice but to get damn serious in terms of the lengths I'll go to in making myself clear, and keeping you at bay. I remember what you told me on that flight we took to Moscow—the one where you made it clear to me you were not who I thought, and in fact someone who is watched so closely when he travels that if you don't come off your plane first, everyone on that plane is immediately killed without a question asked. You're the one who made the rules to this game."

And as my father always told me, in life, no matter what game it is you find yourself in, you play to fucking win.

"I swear, Jonah. If anyone touches—"

"Save it," I cut him off, standing up. "What you're seeing on that screen, that is by no means the only way your family will be watched. This was just an easy way of showing you that the surveillance of them will be thorough, and it will be constant. You say even the possibility of your having been harmed gets those around you killed, without a question. I'm saying, today, right now, if anything happens to me—or those on my list, and, yes, there's a list—your wife gets gutted in front of your children. Without a question. Something I might have felt worse about if you hadn't cut the head off an innocent man simply to make a point to me. On that same day I, or anyone on my list, is harmed, all the mining companies you ripped off will be supplied details of your scheme, as well as copies of your personal brokerage statements. I, like you, Cobus, have people in my life who have seen themselves go in their own histories to places few men ever learn they can. Thankfully, those people remain more loyal to me than I ever could have hoped for."

I toss the iPad on the table. I start for the door. Midstride, I stop.

"The man you killed, an ex-cop turned personal security guard, was a man named Shane Concord. I need his body delivered to the police, to the morgue—wherever—and without any ties obviously to me, simply because his family deserves better. They deserve to bury him with respect. Understood?"

Cobus, motionless, looks at me.

"Oh, one more thing," I go on, "tell Pirro, or whomever it is at Assiagi you deal with, Resurrection is ready to handle the retail boutiques assignment. I think we're the perfect firm to handle this. Don't you?

I continue on toward the door. Cobus remains in his seat. Once I reach the doorway, I stop again, and turn back toward him.

"Shit, look at that," I say.

Cobus swivels his chair around to face me. I untuck my shirt. Underneath it, just above my waistline and directly on my skin, is an Assiagi belt.

"I guess I wore a belt after all," I go on. "You know, funny thing. That little black voice transmitter, recorder gadget? Turns out someone I know has a family member who used one recently. And, lucky for me, they were willing to let me borrow it. Which means this conversation we just had—all of it, from the moment you came into my office this morning—is now in the cloud. And, along with everything else that goes on if something happens to me, will also be turned over to the authorities by my guardian angel."

"Tell me something, Jonah. Do you really believe you can just turn around, walk out of here, and go forward in life not looking over your shoulder?"

"I do. Because I know if something happens to me, somewhere in the world your wife's insides will be spilled all over the floor. Whether or not you really want to chance if I can make good on that—that's up to you."

"You are either a very brave man, Jonah, or a very stupid man. Time will tell."

"Indeed it will. But make no mistake about one thing, Cobus. In the Netherlands, in Germany, in Brazil—wherever—you may be running some kind of show. But when you come to *this* house, Manhattan, The Deal House, *my* house—you'd be foolish to ever make the mistake again of who's in charge. I don't give a fuck who or what you are anywhere else in this world. When you're in my house, I think we're all clear now on the matter of who you call Master."

I turn and finally head out.

"Carolyn will show you out," I hurl back over my shoulder. "Good luck with the new restaurant business."

CHAPTER FIFTY

Sitting on the couch in her office, I watch Perry work Sturner on speakerphone.

"I know it, Bobby, but what can I tell you? The buyer backed out because apparently you're about to enter some serious litigation over a certain portion of a landmarked lobby you decided to do some renovations on. Can you blame them?"

"We weren't aware of the landmark designation, Perry. I have no doubt we'll be able to prove that should the issue make it as far as actual litigation."

"Then why didn't you disclose this little situation to us at the outset?"

"Because we've only been speaking preliminarily, and I'm sure the issue will be handled in short order."

"Actually, Bobby, after speaking with our attorneys on the matter, I'm not so sure. I think you have a real problem on your hands, which is why you were so willing—whether you want to own up to it or not—to unload the property. In fact, knowing what I now know, I think the value of the building has dropped considerably. But I'll tell you what. I had a conversation with Jonah. And if you really *are* looking to unload the property, so you can unload all the legal headaches coming down the pike, Resurrection may just be willing to absorb said headaches. So long as the building comes at a steeply discounted price."

"I can't believe what you did to that pretty face," Perry mouths to me.

Just as she does, my iPhone gets a call. I hold it up so Perry can see. Minnie. I step out into the hallway and walk toward my office.

"Thanks for getting back to me, Minnie," I answer.

"Fuck you, Jonah. I got your damn message. What do you mean the buyer isn't interested anymore?"

"You know this industry as well as anyone, Minnie. Things can turn on a dime. You understand that. The buyer decided to go in another direction."

Before reaching my office, about thirty feet down the hall, I can see Jake inside his office. His door is open, and he's standing behind his desk on the phone explaining to Gary Albert our buyer for Eight Twelve Seventh Avenue has unexpectedly decided to move on. I keep walking.

"And you, of all people, couldn't sway them back?"

"I couldn't. But I'll tell you what. If you truly are ready to sell, Resurrection will step up and buy it from you. But—and I mean, *but*—in no way do I want you to think this was ever some backdoor kind of strategy to insert myself as the buyer at the last second when I was the real buyer all along. Seriously. I'm willing to take the building, but only if you feel like you are really ready to part with it because of all the things we discussed. If the buyer bailing means you want to hold on, then by all means, you should 100 percent, absolutely do so. And you won't hear another word about it from me."

I close my eyes, and force myself to push the words out.

"Other than, I promise you a night out for dinner for putting you through this."

"Jesus, Jonah. This is a boatload to process."

"I get it, Minnie. I do. But the building—"

"Fuck the building, Jonah. I need to figure out where we can go for dinner that's dark enough I can trick you into a little game of Grab Ass. Will Perry be coming?"

* * *

Standing in my office, behind my desk chair, I look out over the Manhattan skyline toward downtown. I close my eyes, turn my head right about ten degrees, and open them again. My eyes settle far south on the recently completed Four World Trade Center.

Four World Trade Center. Owned by The Port Authority of New York and New Jersey. The site of the original nine-story Four World Trade Center destroyed in 9/11, the new and improved version was completed in 2013. Seventy-two stories. Designed by award-winning architect Fumihiko Maki. The building is primarily occupied by the Port Authority itself, but also includes tenants such as . . .

I turn back to my desk, reach down, and bring Google up on my computer. "Sun Tzu," I type into the search box, "*The Art of War.*"

A few minutes later I pick my iPhone up off my desk, walk over to the couch, and sit down. I look through my contacts. When I find who I'm looking for, I place the call.

"Hello?"

"Hi, Liz. It's Jonah."

"Hey Jonah. Look, I've told you this before. I can't discuss Perry with you."

"Actually—I'm not calling about Perry. I never imagined having to do this. But I'm calling about me."